"YOU'RE TALKING ABOUT the alien rock?"

"The rock that changed the world," Shade confirmed. "The rock that rewrote the laws of physics. The rock that turned random teen sociopaths into superpowered killers. *That* rock."

"And you're . . . you're saying there are more coming."

"According to my father's calculations, and he is very good at his job. He's tracking the rocks. One lands today off the coast of Scotland. That's ASO-Two. Another, ASO-Three, hits in just a few days."

Cruz shifted uncomfortably, obviously realizing that Shade was no longer making idle chitchat. A message was being delivered. A question hung in the air.

It was a clear test, a clear challenge, and Cruz passed, saying, "You're going to try to take that rock."

"No," Shade said. "I won't *try*. I'll succeed." Then, after a beat, added, "Especially if you help me."

MONSTER

MICHAEL GRANT

KATHERINE TEGEN BOOKS
An Imprint of HarperCollins Publishers

Katherine Tegen Books is an imprint of HarperCollins Publishers.

Monster
Copyright © 2017 by Michael Grant
All rights reserved. Printed in the United States of America.
No part of this book may be used or reproduced in any manner whatsoever without
written permission except in the case of brief quotations embodied in critical articles
and reviews. For information address HarperCollins Children's Books, a division of
HarperCollins Publishers, 195 Broadway, New York, NY 10007.
www.epicreads.com

Library of Congress Control Number: 2017932879
ISBN 978-0-06-246785-0

Typography by Joel Tippie
18 19 20 21 22   PC/LSCH   10 9 8 7 6 5 4 3 2 1

First paperback edition, 2018

To the GONE fans,
best fandom ever, with my gratitude.

The author wishes to acknowledge two technical advisers,
Rebecca and Jake.

PART ONE: ORIGIN STORIES

Shade Darby, Four Years Earlier

"IT'S THE MONSTER!" Shade Darby cried out, speaking to no one in particular.

The monster was a girl who appeared to be in her teens but was in reality mere days old. She was known the world over from her first recorded appearance, during which she had torn off a man's arm and eaten it. While the man watched in shock and agony.

The girl, the creature, the *monster*, now covered from head to toe in blood, stood in the middle of the highway.

There was no traffic on the highway. There hadn't been in a year. That was how long the dome had sat astride the 101 at Perdido Beach, creating the world's longest detour.

One day the dome had simply appeared, a perfect sphere twenty miles in diameter that extended down beneath the ground as far as it rose into the sky. That dome was centered on a nuclear power plant but encompassed vast tracts of forest, hills, farmland, and ocean and almost all the town of

Perdido Beach, California, which lay at the extreme southern end.

The instant the dome appeared (impenetrable, opaque, and utterly impervious to drills, lasers, and shaped explosive charges), every single person fifteen years of age and older had been ejected.

Ejected.

They had popped up on the beach, in the road, on lawns, in homes, in people's swimming pools. Some had been injured or killed, suddenly materializing in front of speeding trucks. Some had drowned, finding themselves without warning a mile out to sea. A few had materialized in solid objects, with one man skewered by a lamppost, like a human shish kebab. And some had been turned inside out, for reasons that no one had understood then or later.

One of the first scientists to be called to the scene to explain this incredible, impossible, and yet terrifyingly real phenomenon was Dr. Heather Darby of Northwestern University, in Evanston, a suburb of Chicago. She had soon realized that this would be no overnight jaunt and that the study of the dome would take months, if not years.

So Dr. Heather Darby had flown her daughter out to stay with her in the temporary housing complex hastily erected by the military.

For Shade Darby, thirteen years old, it had been wonderful. First and foremost, there was the beach. Evanston had a beach but it did not compare to the long stretches of golden sand south of Perdido Beach. Then there was the excitement of being in a sprawling, makeshift compound teeming with soldiers and police and scientists and media and, of course, the Families of the captives in the dome.

The Families. People capitalized it, because everyone knew what that meant. They'd been all over TV, the Families. Hysterical at first, then angry, and finally depressed and resigned and hopeless.

But most of all for Shade, there was the awe-inspiring, overwhelming presence of the dome itself. It was a mystery so profound that no human had yet come close to understanding it, not even her mother.

Finally, after many months, a decision had been reached in secret to explode a small nuclear device—that was the official term; normal people called it a bomb—at the desert-fronting eastern edge of the dome. It was the very first thing to have any impact whatsoever on the dome. And the effect it had was . . . well, the greatest show the world had ever seen, because suddenly the dome had gone . . . transparent.

When the dome first appeared and ejected everyone fifteen and over, it was speculated that all those under that age were still inside the dome, but no one knew for sure. Many thought the dome might be a solid, a massive ball, like the world's biggest ball bearing, just sitting there. But most believed that approximately 332 children, aged fourteen down to newborn, were trapped inside.

Oh, the theories!

The theory Shade Darby liked best was that they were all inside, all those children. She wanted to believe that some benign power had taken care of them. Shade, like most people, hoped that they were all somehow okay.

Then the dome had become transparent, and the world seemed to freeze in place as every television and news website on earth stared through cameras mounted on TV trucks, drones, helicopters, and satellites—not to mention millions of individual smartphones—at what lay revealed.

The children definitely were inside. They were not okay. They were not at all okay. They were filthy, starved, scarred in body and mind, armed with everything from spiked baseball bats, lead pipes, and kitchen knives to homemade flamethrowers, shotguns, and automatic weapons.

And there were far fewer than 332 still alive.

They stared out through the dome, those wild children, and the world had stared back.

A savage, descent-of-man, dystopian madness.

And of course an instantly trending Twitter and Instagram meme. #Dome #PerdidoBeach #LOTF #BubbleKids. And then, when those inside had managed to communicate through scribbled notes held up for the cameras, the world learned what those on the inside called it, and a new hashtag was born: #FAYZ.

The mordant acronym FAYZ: Fallout Alley Youth Zone.

But the dome was not the only warping of reality, for it soon became clear that some of those inside, not all, but some, had acquired fantastic powers. Supernatural powers. Comic book powers. Powers they did not always use for good.

Shade had been there every day since the dome had gone

transparent, watching rapt and often appalled. Her mother had standing orders for Shade to stay away from the dome, but Shade was the daughter of two scientists, and curiosity ran very deep in her genetic makeup. So each day, as soon as she was sure her mother was occupied, Shade would wrap her too-noticeable auburn hair into a bun and cover it with a cap, then sneak from the grim barracks down to the dome, joining the throng of families.

It was the Families who kept it all from being mere spectacle. The Families would hold up signs. *Do you know Monica Cowell? Is James Tipton safe?* Please tell me if my son, my daughter, my sister, my grandchild is alive and safe.

#NameTheDead.

Many of the parents and grandparents learned that the one they had been praying for had been dead for months. Dead from starvation. Dead from animal attack. Dead from suicide.

Dead from murder.

A girl who called herself the Breeze, a skinny, puckish girl who could move at impossible speeds, wrote signs and held them up to be seen and photographed.

Sorry, your son Hunter is dead.

Sorry, your daughter Carla died eight months ago.

Sorry. Sorry. Sorry.

Life had not been peaceful inside what the media and the authorities and even the president of the United States called the Perdido Beach Anomaly. PBA. PBA lacked the bitterly dry humor of FAYZ, which solemn adults thought too glib.

Anomaly: something that deviates from what is standard, normal, or expected. Synonyms: oddity, peculiarity, abnormality, irregularity, inconsistency, incongruity, aberration, quirk, rarity. "PBA" was safe and bloodless and sounded scientific, but Shade knew that all it signified was "We don't know."

Theories? Lots of theories. But understanding? There was none of that.

Shade had watched it all, heard the cries of grief, seen the tear-streaked faces. It was sickening but fascinating, and impossible to look away from.

Inside the dome, frightened children huddled close to their side of the transparent force field. Two very different worlds stared at each other, like monkeys in a cage, though which side were the monkeys was not at all clear.

Outside the dome, parents held up signs to be read by six-year-olds armed with butcher's cleavers and gnawing on raw fish. Ten-year-olds sat sullen and listless, drinking from whiskey bottles. And nothing could be done. The atmosphere outside was thick with sadness and despair. But beneath all that sadness and despair, at a discreet distance where it could be hypocritically denied, were excitement and anticipation.

It was the greatest show on earth.

Shade sat cross-legged on the folded blanket she'd brought, arm's length from the dome wall. Just beyond, right where she could have shook their hands if the barrier were gone, sat half a dozen kids, ranging from toddler to teen. More behind them, and more still, stretching north and south. Refugees unable to cross the invisible border. Dying while the world watched with morbid fascination.

It was strange and disturbing, being so near, seeing everything yet hearing nothing. A few days earlier, Shade had been in this same spot eating a cereal bar, and the kids on the other side had watched her every bite with a predatory intensity. They had salivated like dogs. Shade had not made that mistake again.

Then had come rumors of a terror to dwarf all others in the dome. A terror called Gaia, though the signs held up inside the dome used half a dozen different spellings. Guyuh. Gayu. #Gaia.

Dozens of fake Gaia Twitter and Facebook and Instagram accounts under that name, all finding the notion terribly amusing. Until the tape.

Not long after the moment the nuke had detonated, the dome's force field had failed for just a split second; for reasons no one understood then or later, a young man named Alex, an adult of sorts, had been attempting to climb the dome. The dome had flickered for just a split second and he had fallen through, becoming the only adult inside. His bad luck.

It had been his arm that Gaia had torn from his body. She had then cooked the flesh with a blast of searing light from her hands and ripped the medium-rare flesh, chewing and swallowing as the man named Alex lay traumatized and weeping at her feet. This event had been caught on video. The video practically burned down the internet, as everyone on planet Earth not living in a cave or a coma watched it in appalled fascination.

That had taken a lot of the fun out of #GaiaForPresident.

It was that girl, that monster Gaia, who now appeared at the south end of the dome, covered in blood and burns, her clothing rags.

Shade Darby's phone rang, making her jump. Her mother, of course. She knew why her mother was calling. Dr. Heather Darby was making sure her daughter was safe in the barracks, because Heather Darby, at that moment just a hundred feet away in a tent crammed with scientific equipment, knew her daughter did not always listen to her.

Shade let the call go to voice mail. No way was she leaving. No way was she going to miss this. The show was approaching its climax; Shade could sense it. Something big was coming.

There came the chime of a text. Shade did not even look at it.

And then, as Gaia stared balefully down at the huddled mass of frightened children pressed against the dome wall, she raised her bloody hands.

"Shade! Shade Darby!" Her mother's voice was barely audible above the rising swell of voices as people cried out and pointed.

Gaia raised her hands, and beams of light so bright that Shade could scarcely look at them stabbed from Gaia's upraised palms into the crowd of children pressed desperately, hopelessly inside the dome.

For what felt like slow-ticking minutes, Shade stared in

disbelief. Children were sliced through by the beam of light. Children burned. A boy no more than seven years old melted like a candle in a microwave, burned and melted, and from Shade's throat came a rising wail, a scream, and all around her screams and bellows of horror, and then it had all risen in pitch, because sound did not escape the dome . . . but light did!

"Shade!"

Gaia's killing beams scythed through the children in the dome but stabbed as well through the transparent barrier. Laser light burned cops, tourists, and media. It burned the Families. It burned the tacky souvenir stands with their plastic dome key chains.

People became herd animals, a mass of wildebeest spotting a lioness springing from the tall grass. People recoiled, backed away, saw the person standing beside them decapitated, and ran in sheer panic, all reason gone, shoving and climbing over one another as those deadly beams swept left and right, and people were cut down as they ran. Arms and heads dropped away like macabre litter, torsos ran two steps before toppling over. Seared human meat smoked and sent up a nauseating barbecue smell.

Shade felt her body tingling, felt her heart seem to stop then speed up, felt the echo of her own screams inside her head as she lay facedown, hugging the ground, but never looking away. She never once looked away as trapped children, their mouths open in unheard cries of despair, died before her eyes, died so close she would have felt their last breath.

Then behind Gaia came a creature that seemed almost to be made of gravel. It barreled down the hill, heavy and awkward, a boulder with thick legs and windmilling arms. It slammed into Gaia and sent the blood-drenched monster-child flying. There came a ragged cheer from the onlookers crawling on the ground like Shade, or cowering at what they hoped was a safe distance behind emergency vehicles and National Guard Humvees.

Inside the dome a handsome boy with dark hair and a commanding air appeared. He was improbably armed with a shoulder-held missile, like something from a news report of distant war. He leveled the missile and fired it at Gaia. The missile flew leaving a trail of smoke and sparks, traveling a short distance, and missing its intended target. It exploded silently against the inside of the barrier, a dozen feet above Shade's head. She recoiled in reaction, pressing her face into the dirt, hands over her ears though there was no shock wave.

The explosion inside the dome shattered the stone creature, stripped the outer covering away, leaving, for just a moment, an almost-human shape. A boy. But a dead boy. He fell alongside dozens of others, and bloody Gaia howled silent rage and brutish laughter.

She was, Shade thought, the most amazing creature she had ever seen or imagined: fearless, insane, evil, and powerful. A demented young goddess. Fascinating.

Beyond Gaia, the boy who fired the missile seemed to shrug. They were speaking, Gaia and the dark-haired boy, an almost normal-seeming conversation. Others on the inside looked on, tense, but keeping their distance. The boy was a teenager not that much older than Shade herself, but he did not have youthful eyes.

Then came a blast of light so intense it burned Shade's retinas, blinding her temporarily. She rubbed her eyes and blinked, and when she could see again, both the dark-haired boy and bloody Gaia were ashes.

And suddenly Shade heard new sounds, from a new direction, from *inside*! Screams. Cries. Moans of pain and the gibbering of pure terror. She smelled the smoke of the burning forest at the far end of the FAYZ. She smelled the final, sickening excretions of the dead so near at hand. She smelled the brackish odor of freshly spilled blood.

A dead child sagged forward and lay across the line of the dome wall, hand outstretched, almost touching Shade.

The dome was . . . *gone*!

A panicked mob of the starved, filthy, ragged, scabbed, heavily armed inhabitants of the Perdido Beach Anomaly rushed heedlessly out into the world. Dozens of them clambered madly over their own dead and wounded friends. One, in her panic, kicked Shade's head, stunning her. Shade tried to rise to avoid being trampled, and a girl, no more than ten or eleven years old, raced screaming by, swinging a machete at imaginary pursuers. The blade caught the side of Shade's throat.

No pain, not at first, just shock as Shade pressed her hand to the wound and gaped as it came away red to the wrist.

She sank back onto the ground, wanting to cry for help,

wanting to call to her mother now, her mother who no longer cried her name.

Shade felt suddenly dizzy, woozy, feet and hands not working quite . . . She rolled onto her back and looked up at the cloudless sky. Strange. The sky. Blue. She felt the rhythmic pulsing of her lifeblood escaping the confines of her arteries.

She blinked. She thought the word "Mom," and fell swirling down into unconsciousness.

Ten minutes later, Shade woke to find herself lying on a gurney, flashing lights everywhere, her vision blurred, head pounding, needles in her elbow, a blood pressure cuff around her wrist, thick bandages around her throat. An EMT squeezed a bag of plasma to force the lifesaving fluid into Shade's collapsing arteries. Shade, barely clinging to paralyzed, nightmarish consciousness, blinked furiously to clear her vision, and focused at last on a black plastic body bag. And on the gloved hand of the fireman pulling the zipper up.

Up and over her mother's face.

CHAPTER 1

The Meet Cute

"THE FIRST SUPERHERO was not Superman," Malik Tenerife said to Shade Darby. "It was Gilgamesh. Like, four thousand years ago. Superstrong, supersmart, unstoppable in battle." He raised a finger for each point.

"First name Gil, last name Gamesh?"

"That's very cute, Shade. Pretty sure they were making that same joke four thousand years ago. Gilgamesh, baby: the first superhero."

"Not going with Jehovah?"

"I don't think gods count as superheroes," Malik said.

"Mmmm. They do if they aren't real gods," Shade countered. "I mean, Wonder Woman is an Amazon, Thor is one of the gods of Asgard, and wasn't Storm from *X-Men* some sort of African deity?"

Malik sat back, shaking his head. "You know, I kinda hate when you do that."

"Do what?" Her innocent expression was not convincing,

and she didn't really intend it to be.

"When you pretend not to know something and then kneecap me." For a boy who supposedly hated it, he was smiling pretty broadly.

Shade laughed delightedly, something she rarely did. "But it's so fun."

His face grew serious and he leaned forward across the tiny table. "Are you really going to do this, Shade? You know it's a felony, right? A federal crime? Worse, this is national security we're talking about."

Shade shrugged. They were at the Starbucks on Dempster Avenue, in Evanston, Illinois. It was busy, jammed with the usual early morning crowd—college kids, ponytail moms, two women in the fluorescent vests of road workers, high school kids like Shade, college kids like Malik, all breathing steam and tracking wet in on their shoes, all stoking the caffeine furnace.

It was noisy enough that they could talk without too much concern for being overheard, but Shade wished Malik had not used the word "felony," because that was exactly the kind of word people had a tendency to overhear.

They sipped their drinks—Grande Latte for Malik, Tall Americano with a little half-and-half for Shade—checked the time, and left. Malik was a tall, lithe black boy, seventeen, with hair in loose ringlets that had a tendency to fall into his eyes, the endearing effect of which he was quite well aware. Those occasionally ringleted eyes were perpetually at half-mast as if to conceal the penetrating intelligence behind them. His expression at rest was benign skepticism, as if he was not likely to believe you but would keep an open mind.

Shade was a seventeen-year-old white girl with auburn hair cut to give her the look of someone who might be inclined to curse, smoke weed, and just generally be trouble. Only two of those things were true.

She had brown eyes that could range from amused and affectionate to chilly and unsettling—effects she deployed quite consciously. She was tall, five foot eight, and had the sort of bone structure that would have caused people to say, "Hey, you should be a model," but for the impressive scar that ran just beneath her jaw on the right side and behind her ear and gave her a swashbuckling air. If there were ever a movie role for Blackbeard's pirate niece, Shade would have been a natural for the part.

Shade was effortlessly charismatic, with a hint of something regal about her. But despite the charm and the cheekbones, Shade was not a popular kid at school. She was too bookish, too aware, too impatient, too ready to let people know she was smarter than they were. And beyond that, there was something about Shade that felt too old, too serious, too dark; maybe even something a bit dangerous.

Malik knew where that feeling of danger came from: Shade was obsessed. She was like some online game addict, but her obsession was with a very real event, with fear and death and guilt. And it was no game.

It was chilly out on the street, not real Chicago cold— that was coming—just chilly enough to turn exhalations to

steam and make noses run. The little business section of
Dempster—Starbucks, pizza restaurant, optometrist, seafood
market, and the venerable Blind Faith Café—was just west
of the corner at Hinman Avenue. Hinman—where Shade
lived—was a street of well-tended Victorian homes behind
deep, unfenced front lawns. Trees—mature elms and oaks—
had already dropped many of their leaves, gold with green
accents, on lawns, sidewalks, the street, and on parked cars,
plastering windshields with nature's art.

Shade and Malik walked together down to Hinman where
the bus stop was. There were six kids already milling around.

"Well, I'll see you, Shade," Malik said. There was something off in the way he said it, a tension, a worry.

Shade heard that note and said, "Stop worrying about me,
Malik. I can take care of myself."

He laughed. He had an unusual laugh that sounded like
the noise a hungry seal made. Shade had always liked that
about him: the idiot laugh from such a smart person. Also,
the smile.

And also the feel of his arms and his chest and his lips
and . . . But that was all past tense now. That was all over and
done with, though the friendship remained.

"It probably won't work," Malik said.

"Are you rooting against me?" Shade asked archly.

"Never." The smile. And a sort of salute, fist over heart,
like something he'd probably seen on *Game of Thrones*. But it
worked. Whatever Malik did, it generally somehow worked.

"I'm going to do it, Malik. I have to."

Malik sighed. "Yeah, Shade, I know. It's called obsession."

"I thought that was the name of a perfume," she joked, not expecting a laugh and getting only a very serious look from Malik.

"You know you can always call me, right?"

Shade lifted her cup to tap his and they had a cardboard toast. "You should not be hitting on high school girls," she said.

"What choice do I have? Northwestern girls aren't dumb enough to buy my line of bullshit," he said, and started to go, walking backward away from her, toward the Northwestern campus just a few blocks north. "Anyway, you'll be a college girl next year."

He was six months older than her, always a year ahead.

"Also, wasn't the Sandman basically a god . . . ," Shade called after him.

"I'm going to class now," Malik said, and covered his ears. "I can't hear you. Lalalalala."

But Shade's focus had already shifted to the new kid at the bus stop. A Latino boy, she guessed. Tall, six-two, quite a good-looking kid.

Wait. Nope. Maybe not a boy, exactly.

Interesting.

He or possibly she looked nervous, the new kid. His dark eyes were wary and alert. And made up, with just a little eyebrow pencil and a delicate touch of mascara.

The others at the stop were a pair of freshmen boys who looked like they should still be in middle school; a black kid named Charles or Chuck or something—she couldn't recall—who had never yet been seen without earbuds; and two massive, muscular members of the football team, one white, one black, neither in possession of a definable neck.

"That is going to be trouble," Shade muttered under her breath. Both of the Muscle Twins were eyeballing the new kid with a bored, predatory air.

No one spoke to Shade as she positioned herself a little apart, on the sidewalk, where she could watch. She sipped her coffee and waited, watching the football guys, noting the nudges and the winks. She could smell violence in the air, a whiff of testosterone, sweat, and pure animal aggression.

She noticed as well that the new kid was quite aware of potential trouble. His eyes darted to the football players, and when they moved behind him, Shade could practically see the hairs on the back of his neck stand up.

Evanston had always been the very epitome of enlightened tolerance, but a perhaps gay, perhaps trans kid and bored football players with their systems pumped full of steroids did not always make for a good mix. And lately Evanston had begun to change, to fray somehow, to fade a little as if it were a movie being shown on a projector with a dimming bulb.

"Hey, answer a question for us," the white player said to the new kid. Shade saw the newbie flinch, saw him withdraw fractionally, but then, with a will, recover his position and face up to the player who was an inch shorter but heavier by probably a hundred pounds of muscle.

"Okay." It was a distinctly feminine voice. Shade cocked her head and listened.

"*What* are you?"

There was a split second when the new kid thought about evading. There was even a quick glance to plan an escape route. But he didn't back down.

"My name is Cruz," the kid said. He wore his black hair long and loose, almost to his shoulders, swept to one side. Shade shook her head imperceptibly, watching, analyzing.

"Didn't ask your name, asked what you *are*." This from the black player. "See, I heard you're crazy. I heard you think you're a girl."

Shade nodded. Ah, so that was it. Shade was gratified to have an answer. She had never really talked to a trans person before, maybe she should make an effort to meet this new kid—assuming he survived the next few minutes.

Mental check: *he* or *she*? Shade made a note to ask Cruz which worked best for him. Or her. And decided in the meantime to insert female pronouns into her own internal monologue. Not that her internal monologue—or her pronoun choices—would matter to the kid who, from all indications, was seconds away from serious trouble.

Cruz licked her lips, glanced up the street, and sighed in obvious relief: the school bus was wheezing and rattling its way up the street. Thirty seconds, Shade figured. Cruz thought she was safe, but Shade was not so sure.

"I don't *think* I'm a girl, and I don't *think* I'm a boy, I just am what I am," Cruz said. There was some defiance there.

Some courage. Cruz wasn't small or weak, but she was both when compared to the football players.

"You either got a dick or you don't got a dick." The white one again. Obviously a philosopher. Shade had the vague sense that his name might be Gary. Gary? Greg? Something with a "G."

"You seem way too interested in what I have in my pants," Cruz said.

Shade winced. "Mmmm, and there we go," she said under her breath.

The bus rolled up, wheels sheeting standing water from the gutter. It was the black one (who Shade believed was named Griffin . . . or was she confusing her "G" names?) who shoved Cruz into the side of the still-moving bus.

Cruz lost her footing, staggered forward, and threw up her hands too late to entirely soften the impact of her face on yellow-painted aluminum. There was a definite thump of flesh-padded bone against aluminum, and the rolling bus spun Cruz violently, twisted her legs out from under her, and she fell to her knees in the gutter.

The bus stopped, the door opened, and the gnome of a driver, oblivious, said, "Let's move it, people."

Earbud boy and the two frightened freshmen, as well as the two lumbering thugs, all piled aboard.

"There's a kid hurt out here," Shade told the driver.

"Well, tell him to get on board, he can see the nurse when we get to school."

"I don't think she can do that," Shade said.

Cruz sat on the curb. Blood poured from her nose, and hot tears cut channels in the red, all in all a rather gruesome sight.

Don't think about a face covered in blood. Don't go back to that place.

Shade made a quick decision, an instinctive decision. "Go ahead, I'm taking a sick day," Shade told the driver. The bus pulled away, trailing vapor and fumes.

"Hey," Shade said. "Kid. You need me to call 911?"

Cruz shook her head. Her breath came in gasps that threatened to become sobs.

"Come with me, I'll get you a Band-Aid."

Cruz stood and made it most of the way up before yelping in pain as she tried her left ankle. "Go ahead, I'll be fine," Cruz said. "Not my first beating."

Shade made a soundless laugh. "Yeah, you *look* fine. Come on. Throw an arm over my shoulders, I'm stronger than I look." For the first time the two of them made eye contact, Cruz's tear-filled, furious, hurt, expressive brown eyes and Shade's more curious look. "I live just down the block. You can't walk and you've got blood all down your face. So either let me call 911, or come with me."

It was all said in a friendly, easygoing tone of voice, but much of what Shade said tended to have a *command* in it, like she was talking to a child, or a dog. Lack of self-confidence had never been an issue for her.

They nearly tripped and fell a few times—Cruz had to lean heavily on Shade—but in the end they made their way down the sidewalk and turned left onto the walkway that led through a gate, beneath the tendrils of an overgrown and fading panicle hydrangea bush, to Shade's back door.

They entered through a kitchen much like every other kitchen in this well-heeled neighborhood: granite counters, a restaurant-quality six-burner stove, and the inevitable double-wide Sub-Zero refrigerator. Shade fetched a baggie, filled it with ice, and handed it to Cruz.

"Come on." They headed upstairs, Cruz holding the carved-wood railing and hopping, with Shade behind her ready to catch her if she fell backward.

Shade's room was on the second floor, walls a cheerful yellow, a gray marble bathroom visible through a narrow door. There was a queen-size bed topped by a white comforter. A desk was against one wall. A dormer window framed a padded window seat.

And there were books. Books in neat shelves on both sides of the desk, between the dormer and the southwest corner, piled around the window seat, piled on an easy chair, piled on Shade's bedside table.

Shade swept a pile of books from the easy chair and Cruz sat. Shade stepped into her bathroom and came back with a bottle of rubbing alcohol, tissues, a yellow tube of Neosporin, a box of bandages, and a glass of water.

"Put your leg up on the corner of the bed," Shade instructed. Cruz complied and Shade laid the ice bag over the twisted ankle. "Take these. Ibuprofen; it will hold the swelling down and dull the pain."

"You're being too nice," Cruz said. "You don't even know me."

"Mmmm, yes, that's what everyone says about me," Shade said with a droll, self-aware smile. "That I'm just too darn nice."

Cruz carefully wiped blood away, using her phone as a mirror. Then, suddenly remembering, she pulled a small, purple Moleskine notebook from her back pocket. It was swollen from curb water in one corner, but otherwise unharmed. Cruz stuck it into a dry jacket pocket with a sigh of relief as Shade fetched a trash can for the bloody Kleenex.

"Shade Darby, by the way. That's my name."

"Cool name."

"It's something to do with the moment of my conception. I gather there were trees. Not the kind of thing I ask too many questions about, if you know what I mean. And you're Cruz."

Cruz nodded. "In case you're wondering, I have a dick."

That earned a sudden, single bark of laughter from Shade, which in turn raised a disturbing red-and-white smile from Cruz.

"Is that a permanent condition?" Shade asked.

Cruz shrugged. "I don't have a short answer."

"Give me the long one. I'll tell you if I get bored." She flopped onto her bed.

"Okay. Well . . . you know it's all on a spectrum, right? I mean, there are people—most people—who are born either M or F and are perfectly fine with that. And some people are born with one body but a completely different mind, you know? They know from, like, toddler age that they are in the wrong body. Me, I'm . . . more kind of neither. Or both. Or something."

"You're e), all of the above. You're multiple choice, but on a true-false test."

That earned another blood-smeared grin from Cruz. "Can I use that line?"

"I understand spectra, and I even get that sexuality and gender are different things," Shade said, sitting up. "This is not Alabama, after all. Or it didn't used to be. Our sex ed does not end with Adam and Eve."

"You're . . . unusual," Cruz said.

"Mmmm," Shade said.

"I like boys, mostly," Cruz said with a shrug. "If that clears anything up."

"Me too," Shade said. Then, with a small skeptical sound, she added, "In theory. Not always in reality."

Cruz gave her a sidelong glance. "I saw you with that boy, the tall, dark, and crazy-good-looking one?"

"Malik?" Shade was momentarily thrown off stride. She was not used to people as observant as herself.

"He likes you."

"Liked, past tense. We're just friends now."

Cruz shook her head slowly, side to side. "He looked back at you, like, three times."

"So, you're a straight girl trapped in the body of a gay boy? Walk me through it." Shade deliberately shifted the conversation back to Cruz, and she was amused and gratified to see that Cruz knew exactly what she was doing.

Smart, Shade thought. *Too smart? Just smart enough?*

"I am e), all of the above, trapped in a true-false quiz," Cruz said. "You can quote me on that."

"Pronouns?"

Cruz shrugged. "More 'she' than 'he.' I don't get bitchy about it, but, you know, if you can . . ." Now it was Cruz's turn to shift the topic. "You read a lot."

"Yes, but I only do it to make myself popular." The line was delivered flat, and Shade could see that Cruz was momentarily at a loss, not sure if this was the truth, before realizing it was just a wry joke.

It took Cruz maybe a second, a second and a half, to process, Shade noted. Slower than Shade would have been, slower than Malik, but not stupid slow, not at all. Just not genius quick.

"I'll call us in sick," Shade said, and pressed her thumb to her phone.

"I don't think you can do that."

"Please." Shade dialed, waited, said, "Hello, this is Shade Darby, senior. I'm feeling a little off today, and I'm also calling in sick for—" She covered the phone and asked, "What's your legal name?"

"Hugo Cruz Martinez Rojas."

"Hugo Rojas. Yeah, she's hurt. A couple of our star football players roughed her up. Yes. No. Uh-huh." Shade hung up. "See? No problem. The school is already dealing with the swastika incident. They don't want any more bad publicity."

"Swastika incident?"

"Spray paint on the side of the temporary building, the one they use for music. A swastika and the usual hate stuff, half of it misspelled. It's two 'g's,' not one. One 'g' and it's a country in Africa. Sad times when someone does that, sadder still when they can't even spell it."

Cruz had removed most of the blood from her face and neck, but Shade went to her, took a tissue, and leaned in to wipe a fugitive blood smear from the corner of her mouth.

The gesture embarrassed Cruz, who turned her attention again to the bookshelf beside her. "Veronica Rossi. Andrew Smith. Lindsay Cummings. Dashner. Marie Lu. Daniel Kraus." Reading the authors' names from the spines. "And Dostoyevsky? Faulkner? Gertrude Stein? David Foster Wallace? Virginia Woolf?"

"I have eclectic tastes," Shade said. She waited to see what Cruz made of the rest of her collection.

"*The Science of the Perdido Beach Anomaly.*" Cruz frowned. "*Powers and Possibilities: The Meaning of the Perdido Beach Anomaly.* That sounds dramatic. *The Physics of the Perdido Beach Anomaly.* Way too math-y for me. *Our Story: Surviving the FAYZ.* I read that one myself—I guess everyone did. I didn't like the movie, though—they obviously toned it way down."

"Mmmm."

"You're very into the Perdido Beach thing."

Shade nodded. "Some would say obsessed."

Some. Like Malik.

"And you like science."

"My father is a professor at Northwestern, head of astrophysics. It runs in the family."

"And your mom?"

"She's dead." Shade cursed herself silently. Four years of saying those words and she still couldn't get them out without a catch in her voice.

"I'm sorry," Cruz said, her brow wrinkling in a frown.

"Thank you," Shade said levelly. She had the ability to place a big, giant "full stop" on the end of subjects she did not want to pursue, and Cruz got the hint.

"My father is a plumbing contractor," Cruz said. "We used to live in Skokie but, well, I had problems at the school. It was a Catholic school and I guess they like their students to be either male or female but not all-of-the-above, or neither, or, you know, multiple-choice. I started out wearing the boys' uniform, and they didn't like it when I switched to a skirt."

"No?"

"It *was* a bit short," Cruz admitted slyly, "but they don't make a lot of plaid skirts in my size."

"What do you do when you're not provoking violence at bus stops?"

Cruz had a silent laugh, an internal one that expressed itself in quiet snorts, wheezes, and wide grins, sort of the diametric opposite of Malik. "Are you asking what I want to be when I grow up? That's my other secret. I've gotten to the point where I can mostly deal with the gender stuff, but writing . . . I mean, you tell people you want to write and they roll their eyes."

"I'll be sure to look away when I roll my eyes," Shade promised.

"Yes, I want to be Veronica Roth when I grow up. You know she's from here, right? She went to Northwestern."

"What do you write about?"

Cruz shrugged uncomfortably. "I don't know. It's probably just therapy, you know? Working out my own issues, but using fictional characters."

"Isn't that what all fiction writers do?"

Cruz did a short version of her internalized laugh.

Shade nodded, head at a tilt, eyeing Cruz closely. "You . . . are interesting." Something in the way she said it made it a benediction, a pronouncement, and a small, gratified smile momentarily appeared on Cruz's lips.

After that they chatted about books, ate chips and salsa, and drank orange juice; they watched a little TV, with Shade leaving the choice of shows to Cruz because, of course, Shade was testing her, or at least studying her.

Cruz actually is interesting. And . . . useful?

The day wore on, and the swelling in Cruz's ankle worsened until it was twice its normal size but then began slowly to deflate like a balloon with a slow leak. The pain receded as well, beaten back by ibuprofen, ice, and the recuperative powers of youth.

All the while Shade considered. She liked this odd person, this e) in a true-or-false world, this person who tried to wear a skirt to Catholic school, this smart but not too smart, funny, self-deprecating, seemingly aimless creature who wanted to be a writer.

Person, Shade chided herself. Not creature, *person*. She was aware that she had a tendency to analyze people with the intensity and the emotional distance of a scientist counting bacteria on a slide.

Blame DNA.

Shade needed help, backup, support, she knew that, and her only currently available choice was Malik, who would resist and delay and generally try to get in her way. Malik was a chronic rescuer, one of those boys—young men, actually, in Malik's case—who thought it was their duty in life to get between every bully and their victim and every fool and their fate. Had he been at the bus stop, he would have launched himself in between the two football players and gotten a beat-down, and it would be his blood she was wiping away, and him she was making ice packs for, and him here in her bedroom . . .

And that is not a helpful place to go, Shade.

They had been drawn to each other from the start, four years ago when Shade had returned to live with her father after the life-changing disaster at Perdido Beach. At first they'd been friends. He had visited her in the hospital after her second surgery, the one to repair the nerves on the right side of her face—she had not been able to feel her cheek. In later years they had become a great deal more, each the other's first.

The breakup had been Shade's decision, not Malik's. He had wanted more of her, more commitment, more openness. But Shade liked her secrets. She liked her privacy, her control over her life.

Her obsession.

Now Shade reached a conclusion: time to pull the pin on the hand grenade, or light the fuse, or some such simile.

Fortune favors the bold, and all that.

"My father is actually doing some work for the government," Shade said.

"Like for NASA?"

"Mmmm, well, not exactly. How are you at keeping secrets, Cruz?"

Cruz waved a languid hand down her body. "I'm a gender-fluid kid who had been passing as *muy macho* until, like, six months ago. I can keep a secret."

"Yeah." Shade nodded, tilted her head, considered, careful to keep a gently amused expression on her face to conceal the cold appraisal in her eyes.

She owes me. I rescued her. She has no friends.

She'll do it.

"My dad's, um, tracking the path of what they're calling an ASO—Anomalous Space Object. Several, actually. Seven, to be precise, ASO-Two through ASO-Eight."

Cruz lifted a plucked eyebrow. "What happened to ASO-One?"

"Oh, ASO-One already landed on Earth years ago. They think all eight ASOs are pieces from the same source, an asteroid or planetoid that blew up, sending some interstellar shrapnel our way. One of the pieces—ASO-One—managed to catch a ride on Jupiter's gravity well and got here ahead of the rest. Just about nineteen years ahead. The other fragments took a longer route. But ASO-Two through -Eight are scheduled to intercept Earth over the next few weeks."

Shade saw that Cruz had not made the connection, not figured it out, and that was a little disappointing. But then, a flicker and a frown, and Cruz made direct eye contact and asked, "Nineteen years ago? Wasn't that . . ."

Shade nodded slowly. "Mmmm. Nineteen years ago ASO-One entered Earth's orbit and slammed into a nuclear power plant just north of the town of Perdido Beach, California."

That froze Cruz solid for a long minute. Her eyes searched Shade's face, trying to see whether Shade was just kidding. Because this wasn't some little secret, like "I've got a crush on . . ." This was a secret two high school kids who barely knew each other should not possess.

Cruz swallowed a lump. "You're talking about the alien rock?"

"The rock that changed the world," Shade confirmed. "The rock that rewrote the laws of physics. The rock that turned random teen sociopaths into superpowered killers. *That* rock."

"And you're . . . you're saying there are more coming?"

"According to my father's calculations, and he is very good at his job. He's tracking the rocks. One lands today off the coast of Scotland. That's ASO-Two. Another, ASO-Three, hits in just a few days."

Cruz shifted uncomfortably, obviously realizing that

Shade was no longer making idle chitchat. A message was being delivered. A question hung in the air.

"It's supposed to land in Iowa. Or it was," Shade said. "Now, with some updated numbers, they think it will land in Nebraska. There'll be a whole government task force there to grab it: HSTF-Sixty-Six: Homeland Security Task Force Sixty-Six. Yes, they'll be there with helicopters and police escort and various scientists. In Nebraska."

The air between them seemed to vibrate.

"Nebraska," Cruz said.

Shade nodded. "Uh-huh." Time to go all-in, to trust her instincts. "But the truth is it will land in Iowa, as originally calculated."

"So, um . . ."

"So . . . someone changed the inputs," Shade said, her voice low and silky. "Someone with access to my father's computer. My dad is a genius, but his memory for little things isn't great, so he sticks a Post-it to the bottom of his keyboard. You know, for his password."

The play of emotion across Cruz's face was fascinating to Shade. First Cruz thought she was hearing wrong. Then she thought Shade was teasing. And then, finally, even before she asked, she knew Shade was telling the truth.

Cruz, Shade thought, should never play poker: her face revealed all. She could practically see the shiver go up Cruz's spine.

Cruz said, "You." It was not a question.

"I'm pretty good at math," Shade said. "And Wolfram Alpha helps."

"You changed your dad's calculations?"

Shade nodded and tilted her head to the "quizzical" position. "The question is, Cruz, *why* did I change the numbers?"

It was a clear test, a clear challenge, and Cruz passed, saying, "You're going to try to take the rock."

"No," Shade said. "I won't *try*. I'll succeed." Then, after a beat, added, "Especially if you help me."

CHAPTER 2
Dropping the Name Tag

"YOU KNOW . . . YOU look familiar," the woman said, narrowing her eyes. She was a mother with a two-year-old in her shopping basket and a five-year-old tagging along and playing with the candy in the checkout rack.

"I get that a lot," the cashier said.

"You're one of those Perdido Beach people! The black one. The lesbian! That's you! Oh, my God, that's you!"

Dekka Talent shook her head, putting on her tolerant smile, not easy in the face of being identified as "the black one" and "the lesbian." She tapped the Safeway name tag on her chest and said, "I'm Jean. But, like I said, I get that a lot."

"I can't believe you're working as a cashier! You don't really look like the actress who played you in the movie."

"Ma'am, did you find everything you wanted?"

"What? Oh, yes, except for the brand of orange juice my son . . . Wait, can I get a selfie with you?"

"Ma'am, if you'll just push the green button there on the credit card machine . . ."

It had been a week since the last "recognition moment," as Dekka Talent thought of it. Progress. If you graphed it out over the last four years since the end of the FAYZ—what most of the world still called the Perdido Beach Anomaly—the number of recognition moments had definitely declined. Declined, but hadn't stopped entirely.

Dekka's work shift ended without any selfies. She punched out, changed out of her faded blue smock into motorcycle leathers in the locker room, and exchanged a few pleasantries with other employees either coming on shift or going off. She politely refused an invitation to after-work drinks—she was still just nineteen years old, though people assumed she was older. And she was broke besides—she'd had to buy new tires.

There was a seriousness about Dekka, a metaphorical weight that people could feel, and that, along with her dark skin and dreads and general air of don't-give-a-damn, left people seeing her as older. Older and tougher because, with some nonmetaphorical weight, with her powerful legs and shoulders, you might pick a fight with Dekka, but only if you were drunk or very stupid.

Dekka walked outside to the artificially bright, slightly chilly parking lot. Dekka's pride and joy, her candy fire red and black Kawasaki Ninja 1000 waited under its transparent plastic rain cover. Dekka hated her job, but in decent weather the ride from the Strawberry Safeway, up the 101, and across the San Rafael Bridge to the apartment she rented in Pinole was the best part of her day. Unless it was raining, which was seldom in the San Francisco Bay Area.

Dekka folded the rain cover and thrust it into one side of

the hard plastic saddlebag, and a few groceries she'd picked up into the other side. She settled her helmet over her dreads, relaxed in the reassuring anonymity from the black visor, and was just about to fire up the engine when two very large black SUVs pulled into the mostly empty lot.

The SUVs came to a stop, forming a sort of loose V directly in front of her.

Dekka started the engine, feeling the familiar reassuring throb that vibrated all through her body, glanced left to make sure she could turn away, and the passenger window of the second SUV rolled down to reveal an identity card deliberately illuminated by a cell phone light.

"No, no, no, no," Dekka said, but in a tone of resignation, not fear. She sighed, killed the engine, and pulled her helmet off. "Really? After an eight-hour shift on my feet?"

Two men and a woman climbed from the second SUV, each showing ID. They were all dressed in Official Civilian Outfits: dark blue or black suits, ties for the men, an open collar for the woman. They might as well have had the word "Government" tattooed on their foreheads.

"Ms. Talent?" the woman asked. "Dekka Jean Talent?" She was middle-aged, stocky, with a wide, flat face that suggested Slavic roots.

"What's this about?" Dekka asked, guessing at least part of the answer. They weren't there about the damaged canned goods she may have taken on occasion without exactly getting specific approval. Nor were they there to collect for the speeding ticket she got rocketing down the PCH north of

Bodega Bay the week before.

"I'm Natalie Green," the woman said, producing a brief spasm that might be a type of smile. "I'm with Homeland Security. This is Special Agent Carlson, FBI, and Tom Peaks."

Dekka did not miss the fact that Tom Peaks was not identified by his affiliation, or that his identity card had been very quickly folded away before she could really see it.

"What?" Dekka asked.

"We would like a few moments of your time."

"Why?" She was not yet worried—this was not her first encounter with authority. From time to time some branch of government would decide to question her, usually about one of the other Perdido Beach survivors. She had steadfastly refused to give any information at all—there were still those who wanted to prosecute some of the survivors, and Dekka would do nothing to help make that happen.

What happened in Perdido Beach stayed in Perdido Beach.

Well, aside from about two dozen survivor books, a movie, and a TV series "inspired by" what everyone else called the PBA, the Perdido Beach Anomaly, but what Dekka, like all who were *there*, would always and forever call the FAYZ.

Natalie Green shrugged, tried out her scary millisecond smile again, and said, "Maybe not out in the open in a parking lot? If you would come with us . . ." She gestured toward the second SUV.

"Really?" Dekka asked again, sounding irritated—which was hardly unusual for her. Patience had never been one of her virtues.

"Ten minutes. Fifteen, tops," Natalie Green said. "We won't leave the lot."

Dekka cursed, not quite inaudibly, and said, "Whatever."

The driver of the second SUV got out and came around like a well-trained chauffeur to hold a door open for her, and then remained outside as Green and Peaks sandwiched Dekka into the middle of the backseat and Agent Carlson took shotgun.

"Nice," Dekka said, looking around at the posh leather interior. The dashboard glowed blue and red. The heater streamed air onto the windshield, holding a line of condensation at bay.

"Ms. Talent, first of all, it's an honor to meet you," Green said. "I've read most of the literature that came out of the PBA, and it's clear that you were very important to the survival of those people, very central to stopping the worst excesses."

"Uh-huh," Dekka said, slow and guarded. "Don't tell me you want a selfie."

Blank stare.

"Okay," Dekka said with mounting impatience. "Can you just tell me what this is about?"

"It's been four years—well, a little more than four years." It was the first thing Tom Peaks had said. He had an odd voice, too high to match the serious face. "You're, what, eighteen years old now, a legal adult?"

That voice could get grating pretty quickly.

"Nineteen, and who are you, again?"

"Tom Peaks."

"Yeah, I heard your name, but *who* are you?"

He was in his late thirties, wore moderately fashionable glasses, and parted his sandy hair on one side with military precision. His blue eyes were overlarge behind the glasses, intelligent, alert, and almost rude in the directness with which he stared at her. "I'm with DARPA. That's the Defense Advanced Research Projects Agency."

"Okay."

"Are you happy working at Safeway?" Green asked. She was annoyed by Peaks, thought he was pushing himself into what she, Green, should be managing.

Dekka gave Green an incredulous look. "No one is happy working at Safeway. It's a minimum-wage job. Half my income goes for rent."

"You never went back to school? No plans for college?"

"I'm not very smart."

Now it was the FBI agent's turn, talking over his shoulder and watching her in the rearview mirror, which he had tilted for that purpose. "All due respect, Ms. Talent, we have a pretty good idea of your IQ. You're certainly bright enough to be doing something other than cashiering. You could take the GED."

"Maybe I just love touching vegetables."

"Or maybe you already got your GED, passed it in the seventy-fifth percentile, and were offered a full scholarship to Cal State San Fran and decided to turn it down and do various dead-end jobs: you delivered flowers, you worked at Toys 'R' Us during Christmas, you temped . . ."

"And again: Why are we talking? Why am I not on my way home to feed my cat?" Dekka was beginning to feel trapped. She glanced at the door handle and saw that it was not locked.

"We've done studies of the PBA survivors, especially the ones who acquired . . . *powers*, for lack of a better word," Green said as Peaks and the FBI man watched. "Of the three hundred thirty-two kids initially trapped in the PBA dome—"

"We called it the FAYZ," Dekka interrupted.

"Of those three hundred thirty-two kids, fifty-one developed one supernatural power or another. Most were relatively weak powers. Only nineteen of you developed major powers and survived. You were one. And of those nineteen, seven have since developed serious psychological disorders."

"It was kind of stressful, what with the starvation and the violence and the forty percent death rate." Dekka made no effort to tone down the sarcasm.

Peaks said, "Yes, there's that, but we suspect there's more to it. Some of you adjusted well to life outside the PBA . . . the FAYZ. You among them, even though your parents were not exactly enthusiastic about you rejoining the family. And yet, you were among the most traumatized. Honestly, when I read about some of what you endured . . ." He shook his head in sincere wonderment. "And still, despite having a power, a *significant* power, and despite suffering terribly, and forming part of the leadership with all the additional stress of that, you seem to be well-adjusted."

Emphasis on seem, Dekka thought. *You're not there when I wake up at three in the morning screaming with my bed damp from terror sweat, mister.*

Or maybe they are, Dekka added, mentally scrolling through her memories, looking for any sign that the privacy of her little apartment had been violated. Not that the FBI would leave traces.

"Yes, I am a great big bundle of happiness and adjustment," Dekka said. "Are we done?"

"Ms. Talent," Peaks said, "may I call you Dekka?"

"Sure, Tom."

"I would imagine you've tried to put all that behind you. You're looking to get back to normal. Four years on, and you're still trying to *find* normal."

That was too close to the bone for a smart-ass response, so Dekka stayed mum, watching those intelligent, slightly lens-distorted eyes as they stared frankly at her.

"You are, in fact, among the least affected. Lana Lazar spent time in a mental health facility."

"I know, she's a friend of mine," Dekka snapped. "She's fine, now."

"Others, like Sam Temple, the supposed hero of the FAYZ, have had—"

"Hey!" Dekka's finger was instantly in Peaks's face. "'Supposed hero'? Screw you. You don't disrespect Sam Temple where I can hear it."

She reached across Green for the door handle and popped the latch.

"I apologize," Peaks said quickly.

Shaking her head, as if disagreeing with her own choice,

Dekka closed the door again and rounded on Peaks. "If you'd lived through one-tenth of what Sam Temple lived through, you might start drinking, too, if you ever nerved yourself up to crawl out from under the bed to start with." Then, in a calmer tone, "Anyway, he's on the wagon. Sober for sixteen months."

"Fifteen months, twelve days," the FBI agent said from the front seat. Then, in an actual moment of humanity, he added, "I've got nine years, four months, and nineteen days, myself." He superstitiously rapped his knuckle on a piece of wood trim.

"So you people do still keep an eye on us," Dekka accused.

The FBI's Agent Carlson and Homeland Security's Green both nodded. Peaks said, "Of course the government keeps track of you. At one time you possessed extraordinary powers. You, Ms. Talent, were able—by a simple act of will—to cancel the effects of gravity. Incredible! Sam Temple could fire killing energy beams from his hands. There was a girl who had the power to move at speeds just short of breaking the sound barrier. And—"

"Brianna," Dekka said softly. Then, with a wistful smile, "The Breeze."

"You were friends," Green said, not quite a question.

But Dekka was no longer listening. She was seeing Brianna's wild, reckless grin; hearing her fearlessly proclaim that she was off to this fight or that; feeling a sudden gust of wind and catching just a glimpse of ponytail standing straight back as Brianna blew past.

Other memories were there, too, dark and awful images, but Dekka brushed those aside. Four years and she still could not think about Brianna without crying. It was an unrequited love, maybe a ridiculous love, but love just the same, and it still warmed Dekka. And sometimes it burned her.

Dekka took several deep breaths and cursed herself for the need to wipe at tears.

You were brave one too many times, Breeze.

"Our point is," Peaks persisted, "you are almost uniquely normal, stable. No alcohol or drug issues, aside from the occasional joint or beer. No psychological breakdown. No wild or reckless behavior—other than speeding violations on your motorcycle. Of all the people who gained—and then lost—these supernatural powers and endured the PBA, the FAYZ, you, almost alone, seem to have avoided going . . . becoming . . ." He searched for the right word, so Dekka supplied it.

"Crazy. That's the scientific term: crazy." Dekka felt a sudden longing for her dinky apartment and especially its tiny shower. Four years on, the FAYZ had left its marks: she ate too much, a common problem for people who've been close to starvation; she still had nightmares, though less frequently; and she took two long, hot showers—drought be damned—every single day, reveling even now in the luxury she'd been denied for that one-year lifetime in the FAYZ.

Peaks nodded, accepting the word. "You didn't go crazy. There's something about you, maybe genetic, maybe psychological, that made you particularly resistant to whatever the powers do to those who possess them."

"It's not about the powers," Dekka said, "it's all of us who were there. It was a whole lot of bad things we had to do to survive."

"No," Peaks said flatly. He shook his head by millimeters so that it was more a vibration than a back-and-forth. "The numbers don't lie. Among survivors of the Perdido Beach Anomaly who did *not* have any mutations, thirty-six percent have had serious psychological or behavioral problems. Among those with major powers? The number is closer to ninety percent."

Dekka stared at him. Then at Green. And at the eyes of the FBI man watching her in the rearview mirror. "What is this? What is this about, what do you people want?"

"We will be happy to tell you." Green again. She pulled out her phone and tapped the screen a few times. "There's a document on this screen. Read it, sign it—thumbprint will do—and we can tell you everything."

Dekka took the phone and read, flicking down the page. "This swears me to secrecy."

"Under penalty of law, and we are very serious about prosecuting unauthorized statements," the FBI agent said without turning around.

"Yeah?" Dekka said with a short laugh. "Well, it's been fun, folks, but I'm sweaty and I smell like the vanilla almond milk some brat spilled on me. So, good night."

Again Dekka reached for the door, and when Green didn't move aside a hard look came over Dekka's face.

Peaks leaned into her, to an intimate distance, an

uncomfortable distance that conveyed just the hint of threat. "We need one of you, preferably you. But if you refuse, our next stop is Sam Temple. And I think we both know he'll agree to help us."

"Hey, Sam's sober, and Astrid's got her head screwed on straight, so leave them the hell out of this. Leave them both alone." Peaks met her gaze, unflinching, and Dekka sighed. "Ah. So it's like that." She shook her head, realizing she was trapped. "You have any idea how many times that boy, that *man*, saved my life?"

"Many times." Peaks again, and now the pitch was lower, lending an almost compassionate tone. "I've read all the published stories, Ms. Talent, and many unpublished statements. So I know as well that you saved him. Many times. I know that you were his strong right arm whenever things turned dangerous."

Then Green spoke up, sounding disapproving. "You're a lesbian, and black, and yet you're inevitably referred to as the 'strong right arm' to a white male. Doesn't that grate on your nerves? Aren't we supposed to be past that—"

Dekka let go a snort and sat all the way back in her seat, willing herself to remain calm. "A white male?" she echoed, her voice vibrating with suppressed anger. "He's not *a white male*, he's Sam freaking Temple. You can read all the accounts you want, but you don't know what he did, and how . . ." Tears threatened to well again. Dekka stabbed a finger at Green. "Every single person . . . every single one . . . who came out of that hellhole alive is alive because of him. Sam Temple's strong right arm? You can chisel those words on my tombstone, lady, and I'll be a proud and happy corpse."

"We'd rather have you," Peaks said, and took Green's phone and held it out for Dekka. The document glowed up at her. "Press your thumb on the button."

Dekka did it, because if she didn't, Sam would. He would of course be furious if he found out she was protecting him. The thought brought a small smile to Dekka's lips. Sam and Astrid didn't need more of the FAYZ; they needed college and work and lives and hopefully, someday, a bouncing little baby that they'd name Dekka if she was a girl.

That was Dekka's fantasy for them, anyway.

"Am I going back to work tomorrow?" she asked.

Tom Peaks shook his head.

Dekka unclipped the name tag with her cover name—Jean, her middle name—reached across, rolled down the window, and tossed the tag out to clatter on the blacktop.

"Wherever you're taking me, my bike had better get there, too, and without a scratch. Oh, and fill the tank."

ASO-2

ANOMALOUS SPACE OBJECT-2 struck planet Earth after its million-year trip, landing precisely where it was expected to land—in a section of the North Sea just off the coast of Scotland that had been surrounded by NATO ships—American, British, and Dutch. Below the water one British and one US submarine were holding the perimeter around a French deep-sea exploration submersible. Ships from the Russian navy and the Chinese navy looked on from a barely discreet distance, their surveillance equipment all atingle.

But the meteorite played a trick on all of them. The seventeen-pound object hit perfectly in the target zone moving at about ninety thousand miles an hour, but like a rock slung sidearm toward a pond, it skipped.

The first skip carried it six miles.

The second skip carried it just two miles, but that two miles took it to the Isle of Islay, where it struck a rock outcropping—still moving at fantastic speed—and broke apart.

Homeland Security Task Force 66 immediately diverted every resource at its disposal—the international naval force and their marines, land-based police and military forces—and turned the sleepy Isle of Islay—pronounced "eye-la" and best known for sheep and Scotch whisky—into something between a war zone and a bad action comedy. Within an hour, the coast of Islay was beset by dangerous-looking ships, while helicopters buzzed around like bees who thought Islay was their hive.

All the activity brought the islanders out of their homes and fields and businesses to see what was going on. Once they had deduced that the military and police of several nations were all searching for a meteorite, out came the metal detectors and the sifters and the shovels. The locals might not know what the rock was, but they knew it had value.

Yet it was not greed that caused the biggest problem; rather it was kindness. It was young Delia Macbeth, fourteen, who saw her little brother, Sean, just four years old, playing with a chip of dark rock. The chip was oddly shaped; in that if you held it a certain way it looked a bit like Mickey Mouse. Sean was sucking on the rock, and at first Delia did the proper big-sister thing and took it from him. Then Sean started bawling, so Delia did the easy thing and gave it back.

After all, it was just a rock, and if Sean wanted it that badly . . .

Search teams swept the lower half of the island and

eventually recovered 60 percent of ASO-2.

Sixty percent.

The other 40 percent was scattered across fields and woods. And about three ounces of it was in the greedy fist and slavering mouth of a four-year-old with a notoriously bad temper.

CHAPTER 3
The Committing of Crimes

DAYS PASSED. HOMEWORK was done. School was attended. But school had ceased to be the center of Cruz's life.

They had dinner once with Shade's father, Professor Martin Darby, just back from Scotland. He was a good-looking man, a silver fox type, formal by nature but trying to be accessible. "Please, call me Darby, everyone does."

He tried to play the cool dad, but his interest and attention were elsewhere. He seemed overly formal with Shade, and she returned it in kind. Not that there was any hostility; on the contrary, the affection and mutual respect were clear, and something Cruz envied terribly. But Professor Darby's mind was not on his daughter, let alone his daughter's new friend who—even a distracted astrophysicist had figured out—was not a *boy*friend.

Above all, Shade and Cruz planned. Which was to say, Shade planned with ferocious efficiency and relentless logic, as it began to dawn on Cruz that while the scheme might seem wildly improbable, even impossible, it was no such thing for her impressive new friend.

Cruz had never met anyone like Shade. Not even a little like Shade. It was as if there were two people living in that pretty, scarred body: a high school science nerd and a shark. Sometimes Cruz played a little game with herself, seeing Shade's unblemished left side as representing an interesting but essentially normal high school girl; and the right side, the side with the scar, as the shark. The girl Shade Darby was funny and relaxed and even moderately empathetic; the predatory fish? Well, as the famous movie line went, the shark had "lifeless eyes, black eyes, like a doll's eyes."

Yes, there were times when Shade frightened Cruz a little. But that frisson, that sense that she was dealing with a person far larger than could possibly fit within this girl, just added to Cruz's growing infatuation. Writers—even unpublished ones—loved characters, and Shade Darby was definitely a character.

Was it the shark that kept Cruz from asking Shade why she was doing this? Was it the invisible but very real barrier that Shade erected around that question and around her past?

At the very least, Cruz wanted to ask about the scar. It was not subtle, it was like something out of an old Frankenstein movie, a good six inches long and cross-hatched. Shade could have worn her hair in such a way as to hide it, but she didn't. She could have worn turtlenecks, but she didn't. She wore the scar proudly, it seemed to Cruz. Or was the right word "defiantly"? It had the odd effect of accentuating her prettiness, but at the same time it gave her an aura of toughness and mystery.

I don't want to push her. I don't want to lose her.

Cruz had thus far in her writing life stuck to short stories and the occasional bit of not-great poetry. But she had enough of the instincts of a writer to recognize that here was a *story.* Maybe a cautionary tale of obsession. Maybe a weepy rise-above-it tale in which Shade coped with the death of one parent and the emotional absence of the other. But that was certainly not how Shade saw herself, and when Cruz was with Shade she could not help being swept up in Shade's determination. Shade was like an ebb tide sweeping Cruz out to sea, out to danger, and yet . . .

And yet, you are willing to be swept, Cruz. Aimless and friendless, you are just so much flotsam on the river of life.

One thing had become clear: there was no more harassment from anyone at school, and somehow this was Shade's doing, though Cruz had no notion of how her friend managed it. The student body simply seemed to have figured out that Cruz was under Shade's protection, and that was all it took. Cruz did not become popular overnight. In fact, if anything she felt people avoiding her, but they did not hassle her, and for now that was enough.

Cruz sometimes wondered what Shade was like before losing her mother. Had she always had this split personality? Had she always had a gift for ruthlessness and the iron will to go with it? Had she ever just been a normal high school girl? Did whatever it was that took her mother's life harden her?

And was it the kind of hard that was only on the outside, or did it go all the way down?

Cruz had covered pages of her purple Moleskine with notes about her new friend. Her *only* friend. She had started by thinking Shade's plan to steal the rock was fantasy, the kind of desperate nonsense a girl with delusions of grandeur or a simple hunger for adventure might come up with. That mistaken belief lasted only a very short while, for it was clear, absolutely, unmistakably *clear*, that Shade Darby meant to steal the rock.

That she meant to experiment with the rock.

And though Shade never quite said it, Cruz knew it was all connected to the absent, never-mentioned but always somehow present Dr. Heather Darby, PhD.

Then, too suddenly, the date came. ASO-3 was on its long glide path to Earth, orbiting once before it would begin its tumble into the atmosphere. And by then whatever doubts Cruz had became irrelevant.

Because the line was before them—and both girls knew they were going to cross it.

Shade drove a dull but sensible Subaru, a few years old, clean inside and out, in a color that could best be described as Forgettable Beige. It was so at odds with Shade's personality that Cruz guessed it had been Shade's mother's car.

Cruz herself did not drive. She could have, she could easily pass the test, but she was not yet ready to face the trauma of something that was simple for everyone else: answering the question "Male or female?"

Yes or no, up or down, in or out, male or female, and no, there could be nothing that did not fit into a binary. Either/or, not some of this and some of that.

"Where's my phone?" Cruz asked in sudden consternation, patting various areas of her body before vaguely remembering she'd left it in Shade's room.

"I took it," Shade said. "Look in that bag by your feet. There are two burner phones in there."

Cruz looked as Shade pulled out of the driveway and turned in the direction of the freeway.

"These are crap. These aren't even smartphones."

"Cell phones—especially smartphones—are tracking devices," Shade said, distracted by traffic. "They leave a record of your movements. First thing Sixty-Six will do when they see they've been robbed is look for cell phone signatures at the crash site. It wouldn't be hard to connect my cell phone to my father, and burners are not exactly iPhones. We did discuss this, Cruz."

"I just . . ." A heavy sigh. "I just didn't think you meant it. We're practically cave people now. I'm going to go into withdrawal." Cruz pulled out her Moleskine and a pen.

"What are you writing?"

"I'm writing that a monster has kidnapped me and plunged me back into the twentieth century."

"I thought writers enjoyed the chance to write, free of distractions." A car sliced too close to their front bumper and Shade leaned on the horn. "Hey, asshole!"

Cruz did her silent laugh and for a while was lost to conversation, bent over her notebook, pen held in her left hand in an awkward-looking position.

"You stick your tongue out when you write," Shade observed.

"I do not!"

"You get the tip between your teeth and it sticks out between your lips."

Cruz made a rumbling sound of irritation, added a sentence to the Moleskine that ended with an unnecessarily emphatic exclamation point, and put her notebook away.

"You're sure your folks won't send cops to look for you?" Shade asked.

"I'm totally, absolutely, a hundred percent sure," Cruz said grimly, then chided herself. *No, no, don't go to the bitter place, we're having an adventure. We're committing a federal crime.*

Yay?

"You wouldn't believe how little interest they have in where I am," Cruz said, trying to inject some lightness into her tone. "And your dad?"

"I checked. He's in Nebraska." Cool, calm, unruffled.

She must know this will put her father in a bad spot, Cruz thought. *But she won't stop.*

Won't? Or can't? Obsession? And why am I going along? Am I really this desperate for a friend?

But of course Cruz knew the answer to that question. Yes, she was desperate for a friend. Yes, she enjoyed the odd status that came from being associated with Shade at school. But mostly, Cruz admitted, she herself had no goal, no plan, no clear idea of what she wanted to do. And Shade did.

I'm a puppy who hopes Shade will throw a stick I can fetch.

Traffic was awful as usual in Chicagoland, but in time they emerged from beneath low rain clouds to a sunnier suburbia west of the city and soon were moving along open interstate, penetrating the vast spaces of the American agricultural heartland.

It was autumn, and the corn that extended for hundreds of miles around was being harvested. Giant, insect-like machines painted red or green powered slowly but relentlessly, stripping off the ears and leaving forlorn pale yellow stalks and mulch behind.

"How long is this drive to hell without apps?" Cruz asked.

"Four and a half hours. You know, Cruz, the human race survived for a million years before the first phone, let alone the first app."

"Survived," Cruz said, raising a finger. "Survived. But it wasn't really *living*."

"We have music."

Cruz turned on the stereo and punched buttons until she came to the loaded files. She scrolled through Shade's music, thinking it an opportunity to get some insight into her new friend's soul. She found a number of things she didn't recognize, experimental music, but also more familiar reggae, blues, pop, rock, punk, even classical. If there was a coded message in Shade's playlists, the message was that she sampled widely and committed to no particular genre or artist.

But there were a few things more accessible.

"Seriously?" Cruz asked. "Beyoncé? What else, Taylor Swift?"

"I suppose you'd like something more cutting edge?"

"Not really," Cruz admitted. "Luis Malaga? Cantea?" Cruz peered at Shade, waiting for signs of recognition. "Nothing? OV7? Come on, Shade, they've been around forever." She sighed. "What can I say, I move to the beat from south of the border."

"Isn't that all, like, accordions?"

"I am going to pretend you didn't say that."

"Mmmm. To cover the awkwardness you could put on some of *my* music," Shade said, batting her eyes.

Cruz had found the right song, the one with the most plays. "Yes, yes, this is definitely Shade Darby," Cruz said, and hit play. The guitar was twangy, and the voice was thin but strong.

You can stand me up at the gates of Hell,
But I won't back down.

Cruz sang the refrain with a small adjustment.

Hey, Shade will stand her ground.
And she won't back down.

It was the shark who cast her a chilly, sidelong glance. Shade had a great sense of humor about lots of things, but not as much about references to her . . . her interest . . . to use a kinder word than obsession.

They listened to music for a while until something ska came on, which they both liked, and Cruz began to dance in place.

"You're bouncing the whole car," Shade said, sounding like someone's mother.

"I know. Help me!"

Soon the Subaru was bouncing happily as they both danced in place, arms flailing, heads bobbing, shoulders twisting, Shade inevitably more controlled, more contained, less committed to the music than Cruz. But after three hours of corn, corn, the occasional freeway off-ramp, and still more unstoppable corn, they were both sick of music, hungry, and needing to pee fairly desperately. They pulled off into a Wendy's.

They peed, then ate: a salad and fries for Cruz, who was toying with vegetarianism without quite committing, and a burger for Shade, who had no reluctance to eat animal flesh.

"You know, you attack your food," Cruz observed. "You cut it in half like you're the perfect little miss, then you go all Hungry Hungry Hippo on it."

"Did you just call me a hippo?"

Bellies full, they set off again, racing now toward the setting sun.

"We're getting close." Cruz indicated the GPS with her chin.

"Mmmm. We're there, basically." Shade switched to her instructional voice. "A degree of latitude is about seventy miles, a minute is a little over a mile, and a second of latitude is, give or take, a hundred feet. It works a bit differently with longitude, but if the calculations are correct, we're looking for a rectangle about a hundred feet by eighty feet."

"Ladies and gentlemen: the human Wikipedia. Wiki-Shade."

Shade pulled over onto the shoulder of the road, corn to their right, a fallow field of rich, black Iowa topsoil across the road to their left. Shade pulled a smaller, portable GPS unit from her bag. "This will get us down to the seconds."

She booted up the portable GPS device, and while she waited for it she deleted their destination from the car's GPS.

"You're kind of getting into this whole spy, cloak-and-dagger stuff, aren't you?" Cruz teased.

"I kind of am," Shade admitted, allowing herself a rare grin at her own expense.

The handheld GPS booted up, and after a moment's peering and muttering Shade said, "Okay, we go down that dirt road, go a half mile, and it shouldn't be far."

The sun was setting as they parked beside a wooden gate wide enough to admit trucks and harvesting combines. In fact there was a green John Deere combine parked maybe two hundred yards away, looking like some fantastic alien monster turned in for the night.

"Lucky timing," Shade said. "Late enough the farmers won't be working out here, and just an hour and a half to go."

"An hour and a half?" Cruz whined. "People could be talking about me online and I wouldn't even know."

"Mmmm. And somehow you actually think that's a bad thing."

As early autumn darkness fell, they sat staring at the impact site—what Shade hoped and Cruz feared was the impact site—just an abstract rectangle within the larger rectangle of the unharvested cornfield. Cruz still harbored the secret hope that this was a wild-goose chase, that Shade had made an error and the rock was going to land safely in Nebraska. Or somewhere.

But at the same time, despite her greater caution, Cruz had a second level of thought that whispered, *It would be interesting, though, wouldn't it?*

As if sensing Cruz's ambivalence, Shade reached across to squeeze Cruz's hand, something she had never done before. It was a little awkward, and at first it seemed forced or calculated—and with Shade you could never be sure—but Cruz squeezed back and they held that pose for a minute.

We are about to commit a felony, Cruz reflected, *and all I'm thinking about is how that gesture is a girl-girl thing. How needy am I?*

They sat in companionable silence as the sun disappeared and navy-blue darkness stole over the field. The windows were down, it was not quite warm but not cold, either, and they heard a whole world of insect life, buzzing, droning, rising and falling like a stadium full of bugs doing the wave. High above a jet drew a coral line across the sky, picking up the sun's dying brilliance.

"I hate to say it, but this is more fun than I've had in years," Cruz said.

"I hate to say it, but me too."

"If we don't get arrested," Cruz added.

"Ten minutes."

"What if the calculations are off?"

"Then it won't hit here. It will smash into some other field, maybe even a town. Could be miles away, could be on another continent."

Shade touched the scar on her neck, drawing a finger along it, feeling the raised flesh, feeling the cross-hatching of the stitches. Cruz had noticed the gesture before, as she had noticed the faraway look that came with it.

They tried to stay cool and nonchalant, but the tension rose minute by minute. They made small talk, but it was pitiful, distracted stuff. They would start in on some teacher and lose the thread. They would start again on some fashion or celebrity, and again lose the thread.

Cruz asked her to dish on Malik: nope. Still, she did not ask the question her mind was screaming at her: *Why are you doing this, Shade? What is the connection to the scar?*

"This probably won't work, not without the dome," Shade said. It was the first negative thing she'd said, the first expression of doubt, and that tiny admission of worry, of fear, of vulnerability added new layers to Cruz's affection.

Shade might be tough, determined, and at times perfectly ruthless, but there was a human in there.

"Or it *will* work," Cruz said. "In fact, I bet it does."

"Hope is the best form of torture," Shade said dryly.

There was a persistent lump in Cruz's throat that she could not swallow away.

"Three minutes," Shade said, and there again Cruz saw the predator: the focus, the fearlessness, the hunger. No more stroking of scars, no more dreamy, faraway look.

Cruz felt herself teetering on the edge between hope and fear. That nervousness finally gave her the courage to ask. In a rush she blurted, "Shade, why are we doing this?"

Shade sighed and looked out through the windshield, more profile than detail in the gathering gloom. Finally, she said, "Like the man said who climbed Mount Everest, Cruz: because it's there."

"What's there?"

Shade turned to look at her friend. The shark looked, too. "Okay, you have a right to know. I was there the day the PBA barrier came down. I was right there, inches away. I saw that creature, the one they called Gaia. I saw what she did. It was . . . awful. The worst thing I've ever seen. You have no idea. People, little kids, cut up like pigs at a butcher's shop. But the power . . . It was like watching a god, Cruz." Then, after a beat, she pointed at the scar. "It's where I got this. A scared little girl with a great big knife."

Cruz, confused and alarmed, said, "Wait, Gaia was evil, not a god."

"Mmmm. They won't be able to capture all the ASOs, Cruz. And if the rock has the same effects outside the dome . . . well, the world may be about to become a very strange place. A very, very strange place. And what I saw that day . . . well, no one could stop that monster. No one could stop her but someone with an even greater power. Gods aren't always good or kind. Some are monsters."

"I'm not—"

"If it works, there will be other monsters, Cruz. Other Gaias. And more people will be hurt. More people . . ." And for a moment Shade seemed unable to go on. Then, her voice abruptly steely, she said, "Thirty seconds."

No, Cruz thought, that wasn't quite the whole truth. It was related to the truth, but it was just the story Shade told herself.

"Time," Shade announced, tension almost choking the word off. "Ten . . . nine . . . eight . . ."

"I hope this works for you, Shade."

"I know, Cruz. Four . . . three . . ."

And there it was in the night sky to their left, a spark, not very bright, like someone tracing a laser pointer across the sky. It was a tiny missile—the estimate was four kilos, just under ten pounds—moving at thousands of miles an hour, a shooting star come to bring them hope. Or to dash that hope.

"Two . . ."

For the first time since Cruz was a very little child, she wished upon a shooting star.

"One," Shade whispered, and the meteorite hit the ground. There was no explosion, just a dull, flat sound, like someone dropping a big sandbag. A puff of gray dust rose, barely visible in the darkness, but just exactly where Shade expected it to land.

"Wow," Cruz said.

"Mmmm," Shade agreed. Her casual act was not even slightly believable.

They took a breath, then all at once piled out of the car. Cruz pulled a shovel from the back and raced to catch up to Shade, who was galloping ahead.

The ground was plowed into furrows that tripped Cruz repeatedly. And, too, there were the six-foot-tall stalks that snatched at her with Velcro talons and slapped her with heavy ears of corn. They came to a halt when they reached the first charred and broken cornstalks and advanced more slowly after that, as if sneaking up on someone. And suddenly, there it was, looking for all the world as if a rogue tractor had come through dragging a narrow plow. The rich, black earth was gouged, with a mound of ejected clods marking the spot where the rock went subterranean.

"There! Dig there!" Shade ordered.

Cruz dug. And dug. She uncovered a narrow tunnel like something a hefty gopher might have made. "Go that direction another ten feet," Shade instructed, her voice ragged, in tenuous control of her emotions.

And then, as Cruz slammed the blade into the ground, they heard the metallic impact of steel shovel on rock.

They looked at each other, Shade and Cruz, and time seemed to stop.

"Okay," Shade said at last, voice quavering. "Dig it up."

It was gray, the color of pencil lead, not much bigger than a softball, but more oval than round, with a pitted surface. To every appearance a regular unimportant meteorite, like thousands that impact the Earth every day. Shade flicked the flashlight off, and they were rewarded by a faint but vaguely sinister glow, slightly green. Shade reached for it.

"Don't touch it!" Cruz cried. "It's probably hot!"

"Actually, it's more likely to be cold. It was a long, long time in absolute zero, and it spent just seconds in the atmosphere."

Cruz shook her head in rueful amusement: Of course Shade would have thought of that. Of course.

Shade touched the rock—touched it with the solemnity of a medieval Christian pilgrim touching a piece of the true cross. Shade ran her fingers over it, feeling its contours, gently exploring the pits and cracks, brushing dirt away almost tenderly.

"This is it," she said. "I can't believe . . ."

"We should probably get out of here," Cruz said nervously. She carried the rock on the shovel blade back to the Subaru while Shade used cornstalks to obscure their tracks.

Cruz set the rock in the back of the car. Then, feeling transgressive, feeling that it wasn't her right somehow, Cruz touched it, touched an object that had traveled an unimaginable distance. It was just a rock, really, just a faintly glowing rock. But it had a power Cruz could feel, an attraction.

Frodo and the Ring, Cruz thought, and laughed nervously at the comparison, because the thought came with an extra question: *Is Shade Frodo? Or is she Gollum?*

"It won't take Sixty-Six long to get here," Shade said, brushing dirt from the knees of her jeans and kicking the clods from her shoes. "We can't hide the fact we beat them to it, but we can confuse the scene a little, at least."

"Not much we can do about the tire tracks, I guess."

"No," Shade agreed. "But as soon as we get back to the interstate, we're going to cut a divot into one of the tires. Just enough that if anyone ever checks, it won't be a perfect match."

"Have you been watching *CSI* reruns?"

"I may be a criminal mastermind."

Cruz said nothing.

Shade started the engine. And then they stopped for just a moment, staring at each other with solemn expressions.

"Wow. We did it," Cruz said.

"Well," Shade said, "we did the first part of it."

CHAPTER 4
Bad Start, Worse Finish

THE SUBARU DRIVEN by Shade and Cruz pulled away and the young man climbed from the cabin of the parked green John Deere combine where he'd been waiting and watching.

Justin DeVeere turned to his girlfriend, Erin O'Day, and as he gave her his hand to help her climb down—not easy in the entirely inappropriate, skintight dress she was wearing—he said, "I wonder if I should have killed them and taken it."

Justin DeVeere was nineteen but already in his junior year at Columbia, where he studied art, but was not much of a student. He could paint or sculpt or assemble whatever he liked and so overawe his professors that they would hand him As merely for showing up. He was, people said, a prodigy. He was, people said, a young Picasso or Rothko. He was on the verge of becoming the Next Big Thing in the art world.

Justin DeVeere was brilliant and utterly devoid of a moral center. Extremely talented, sociopathic, and maladjusted. A loner, an outsider, a predator awaiting the right prey.

Those were not the things Justin's *enemies* said, it was what he knew about himself. Justin had taken IQ tests—152, which made him smarter than 99.9 percent of humanity. He had also taken the so-called psychopath test and was unmistakably a member of that manipulative, ruthless, often charming tribe. A brilliant psychopath. A talented psychopath. A young monster.

That was how Justin DeVeere saw himself, how he knew himself to be: a brilliant, talented monster.

But he was no monster to look at, and he was quite aware of that as well. Justin always managed to look the part of the young artist, dressing in skintight black jeans and a series of T-shirts on which he silk-screened bits of text in cuneiform or Sanskrit alphabets. Only he knew that the messages were either some version of "F— You" or a sexual reference.

He was not big, not as big as he'd have liked anyway, just five-nine, white with straight black hair worn loose, down to his shoulders, pale gray eyes, and, as another artist had once said while attempting unsuccessfully to seduce Justin, the face of God's cruelest angel.

Justin's partner-for-now, Erin O'Day, was twenty-eight, mother of a nine-year-old she had shipped off to the very best schools in Switzerland at age five and had not seen since. Justin was not supposed to know this about her, but he did—Justin was not a respecter of privacy. Erin was beautiful, sophisticated, fashionable, and sexy, but Justin had never had a problem attracting beautiful women and girls. What made Erin O'Day special was that she was the heir to a fortune estimated by Forbes magazine at three hundred million dollars.

Sexy women, Justin could find any day. Three hundred million dollars? That was quite rare.

Erin was part of New York society, moving effortlessly through glittering events, including the endless charity balls where she promoted young Justin. It was at one of these balls that she met Professor Martin Darby, who had been drinking and talking more than he should have. He had told her about tracking the Anomalous Space Objects and hinted that his work was top secret.

It never ceased to amaze Justin just what Erin could get away with merely by being blond, beautiful, and poured into a dress with a plunging neckline, all of course enhanced by the kind of jewelry and fashion that screamed "money." According to Erin, the professor had lost his wife and was clearly lonely for female companionship. And—again according to Erin—he didn't get anything beyond some drinks and a dance or two.

Erin had had no real notion of what to do with the information, but Justin did. Justin had a friend who had a friend who was a serious hacker, and for just five hundred dollars of Erin's money, Justin gained access to Martin Darby's computer and learned the secrets of the Anomalous Space Objects.

Justin stood now gazing thoughtfully at the field, tilting his head, making slight adjusting motions with his hands, imagining a murder scene. Playing the part, pretending to actually think he should have killed the two because he knew full well it would turn Erin on. Erin had never known a person who could say *I wonder if I should have killed them* and mean it. It was viscerally exciting to her. It made her heart run mad, and sent chills of fear tingling up her spine.

Yes, Justin knew Erin O'Day and how to play her. And he remained faithful to her because while there were plenty of beautiful women in the art world, and fewer who were both beautiful and rich, he had met only one who was also excited by the darkness Justin knew lay at his core.

"We're in the middle of nowhere," Erin said. She was irritable, not being a fan of cramped, chilly tractor cabins. "Our names are on flights from New York to Des Moines. We've left a trail."

"Speaking of trails," Justin said, "you wrote down their license plate number?"

Erin opened her phone, swiped a few times, and held up a dark photo of an Illinois plate, fuzzy from a distance but readable.

Justin stirred restlessly, stamping his feet to warm himself while still self-consciously gazing at the dark cornfield. "I was just picturing how it would look, you know, when the sun came up, when they were found: blood splatters all over the cornstalks. I'd arrange the bodies so that . . ." He paused to consider, eyes narrow, hand drawing shapes in the air. "I'd make them strip naked first, just leave on one or two random bits—a sock, a scarf, something enigmatic that made it appear to be a clue, then bang, bang—" He mimed firing a handgun.

"No one would ever be able to make sense of it, but there'd be fifty conspiracy theories online in a week," Erin said.

Then, adopting a more mature tone, she added, "But that's not why we're here."

"Anywhere I am, I'm there for art," Justin said, smirking to take the edge off his pomposity, and inwardly rolling his eyes at his own BS. "Come on, let's see if they left us anything. Can you go get me the black light from my bag?"

"In these shoes?"

With a sigh, Justin fetched the bag, unzipped it, pointed his phone light into the bag, and withdrew a battery-powered wand that shone black (more purple than black) light into the hole he'd widened.

"Hah! Here's a chip right here." He held up a thin, sharp-edged fragment no more than an inch and a half long and a quarter of an inch thick.

"Is that enough?"

"Who knows?" Justin asked. "I guess we'll find out. If it isn't, we'll track the license plates."

"What do we do with it? Crush it and snort it?"

"In the PBA they were just exposed to the radiation. But I think that's the slow and inefficient way," Justin said. He frowned. "The bigger question is, where is the team of scientists who were supposed to be here? I was expecting heli-copters and big trucks. So, who were those two, how did they get here, what did they take away, and what do they intend to do with it?"

"That's four questions."

Justin checked an app. "There's an early flight to LaGuar-dia, tomorrow morning. We can make it, easy."

"Or we can make it right here," Erin said with a leer.

"What, here?" he asked, faux innocent.

"I thought we were clear on who's the boss . . ."

Justin grinned up at her and said, "Yes, ma'am."

He was not in the mood, not really, much more interested in the Anomalous Space Object than the Predictable Female Object, but her desire for him, and his ability to feed that desire, were vital parts of moving large chunks of money from her hands to his.

And there were worse ways to pass the time in an Iowa cornfield.

Afterward, they walked back to the rental car concealed off the main road in a little stand of trees. They drove to Des Moines, stopped at a Walmart en route, and checked into the DoubleTree hotel near the airport. Justin set up the mortar and pestle he'd purchased at the Walmart and ground the rock fragment to a powder.

Then he dumped it out onto the nightstand and used a credit card to form the powder into a line about six inches long.

"Want some?" he asked, holding out a straw he'd pocketed from the bar downstairs.

Erin considered, eyeing the gray line dubiously. But Justin knew she'd refuse. Erin liked others to take risks for her amusement; she didn't take many risks with herself. "That's all for you, baby."

Justin shrugged and snorted half the line. The rest he scooped up with the credit card and stirred into his vodka and orange juice.

"Feel anything?" Erin asked.

"It stings, that's for sure." He sneezed and wiped his nose, then drank the laced beverage in one long swig. "Well, I guess we'll see. It may not work. You know, it only worked for some of the kids in Perdido Beach. There may be a genetic factor or something. And then there's the question of the dome."

"It'll work for you," Erin said with quiet complacency. Of course Justin knew she was pandering to him, flattering him. But he also knew she was conflicted, had been all along, wanting to hold on to Justin's talent, wanting to maintain at least some control over him, enjoying the dangerous rush of his company, and even (probably) enjoying his lovemaking. But at the same time she was fascinated by the idea of her young prodigy acquiring *powers*. She wanted to see that, to be part of that.

The artist unbound.

At which point, Justin suspected, he might no longer need her money. Or her. The possibilities were endless.

They had a bare three hours of sleep before their respective phone alarms rang. They showered together, with predictable results, and took the shuttle to the airport. They caught the ten a.m. Delta flight and settled wearily into first-class seats, reclined their chairs, and picked unenthusiastically at an early lunch of swordfish with crayfish garnish, before falling asleep.

Justin slept like only a nineteen-year-old can—deeply, totally, effortlessly, waking only in time to hear the captain on the intercom warning of strong crosswinds at LaGuardia that "might make for a bit of a bumpy landing, folks."

As if on cue, the plane bucked, rising on a gust and then falling too fast with the sickening sensation of a roller coaster hurtling down from the first big drop. Then, just a few thousand yards from the runway, wheels already down, there came a powerful gust that shoved the plane sideways, knocking Justin's head forward.

A startled cry that some might interpret as fear came from Justin's lips, which he then twisted into an ironic smile in hopes that his nervousness would seem to be a joke.

It wasn't a joke. The next swerve was positively terrifying, wild enough to cause the drinks cart to break free and slam into a bulkhead. A flight attendant seated in the rear-facing jump seat grabbed it and pinioned it with her feet.

Justin had no special fear of flying, but he had a very healthy fear of death, and a deep dislike bordering on phobia about being out of control. Adrenaline flooded his arteries. His muscles tensed. He gripped the armrests, as if twisting the leather would let him steer the plane.

And then . . .

Suddenly Justin's roomy first-class seat wasn't so roomy. It was odd, he thought at first, an illusion, a psychological effect of nervousness. But yes, it was as if the seat was narrowing. Justin's shoulders felt too large, and when he turned his head his chin actually scraped against a bulbous, massive swelling that rightly belonged on a whole different person, a much larger, much more muscular person.

"What the . . ." Justin blurted. He was blowing up like an inflatable bed, muscles bulging at shoulders, thighs, arms, all of him growing. His seat belt stretched and then snapped!

"What's happening?" he cried, snatching at the broken seat belt with fingers that were not right, not right at all.

He screamed.

The pilot fought the crosswind, and the plane rocked from side to side as they skimmed above Brooklyn. The engines surged and faded, surged and faded. Justin caught a glimpse of a cemetery just below them.

"Justin!" Erin cried suddenly, staring at him, mouth open, shying away from him as far as her own seat belt would allow. "You're . . . you're . . ."

"What? What?" he cried, and now it was his voice that was not right, not his voice at all! His voice had become this huge thing, deeper, more masculine, gravelly. He sounded like some weird cross between Vin Diesel and Darth Vader.

"Look at your face! Look at your face!" Erin practically screamed. But of course he couldn't, he couldn't look at his own face, but he could see that the rest of him was becoming something very different. It was almost impossible to believe that it was him.

Madness to look down at your own body, hands, feet, and not recognize them!

"My God, it's happening!" he said in that voice like truck wheels going over wet gravel. "It's happening!"

"D-d-does it hurt, baby, does it hurt?" Erin squeaked. She looked ten years older with her face distorted by fear.

"Just so . . . Just . . . weird. I . . ." Justin said.

And still he grew, swelled, thickened, his legs masses of

bunched muscle. His black jeans tore, *rrrriiiiip*, and exposed limbs that looked like armor, like naked bone, like . . . no, like *shell*, like the hard chitin that formed a lobster's shell. Tiny pricks, wicked little rose thorns rose from the armor that covered his legs and, now, arms.

Snap! The armrest broke off.

Erin screamed, words all gone, in full panic now, and she yanked off her own seat belt and fell on her rear end in the aisle, legs pistoning, trying to escape being crushed. The flight attendant seated in the rear-facing jump seat said, "Ma'am, return to your—" before she froze mid-word, eyes bulging in horror, jaw trembling as she saw Justin.

They were seconds from touching down when the fingers of Justin's still-human right hand melted together and he cried out in gibbering terror. His right hand no longer had fingers, no longer had a wrist. It was a spear, a sword, dirty blue and coral in color . . . and it was *growing*!

This is not what I wanted! I wanted to shoot light beams!

Even his terrified mind was ashamed of that juvenile complaint. It was working, he was morphing into something very different. He was becoming . . . *art*!

As the sword arm grew, his left hand thickened, and it split in half, split bloodlessly wide open between middle and ring finger, forming a hideous lobster-like pincer that swelled until it must have weighed fifty pounds all by itself. Justin whinnied in terror.

It ought to hurt, some small, still-aware part of his mind knew, *it ought to be agony.*

But it was not painful, not really, just mind-bending, insane, impossible.

Impossible!

But all the while his right hand, the sword, kept growing, growing, the melted fingers flattening first into something like a boat's paddle that thinned at the edges and glittered as it became, unmistakably, a blade. Now, with startling speed, Justin's blade hand grew outward, longer and longer till the blade tip sliced straight through the side of the cabin, ripping the aluminum flesh of the plane just below the window as if it were no more substantial than a paper bag.

"Aaahh!" Justin's bladder emptied into his ripped jeans, but that was the least of his concerns.

The window cracked and blew out. A hurricane of cold wind rushed in, grabbing inflight magazines and menus and whirling them around the cabin. And now came more screams, screams of disbelieving panic as everyone in the first-class compartment saw, and lurched up from their seats and backed away, toward the cockpit or down the aisle into coach, piling over one another while the jet shuddered and rocked violently. Everyone was in a panic, rushing to get away, staggering, slipping, shouting, everyone but the elderly couple seated just ahead of Justin and Erin who were either asleep or amazingly oblivious.

Justin tried to draw his sword hand back, but it was too long (*not my fault!*), too long to fit inside the plane, and instead of retracting, that blue and coral blade sliced upward (*not my fault!*), ripped effortlessly through the molded plastic and the aluminum outer skin of the plane, ripped up through the overhead luggage compartment, bisecting carry-on bags, and the plane lurched more wildly than ever and an appalled Justin (*not my fault!*) saw that the cut he'd made was widening. An inch. Two inches. Three! The plane was breaking apart, and in a few more seconds the rear 70 percent of the plane would break off and they would all die in a fiery crash.

And people will say it's my fault, but it's not—I didn't ask for this!

The wheels touched tarmac with a rubber squeal, the plane bounded, slewed sideways, bounced again, screams and screams and screams all the while, and Justin screaming, too, and Erin knocked into the now-empty seats across the aisle, staring at him with eyes so wide her pupils were just dots surrounded by white.

And then, miraculously, the plane was rolling on all three wheels, rolling down the tarmac, but the screaming did not stop because now they all knew that a monster was among them, a nightmare creature who rose from his seat, head scraping the ceiling. He turned heedlessly to look back at the passengers and swept his blade hand forward, slicing through the seat ahead and the elderly couple occupying those seats (*not my fault!*). The blade cut through their chests and the tops of their bodies, from mid-chest upward, toppled off, landing with a wet and heavy impact, like cattle in a slaughterhouse, nothing but slabs of meat. Blood and gore bubbled up from their torsos, and in pure panic now, seeing what he had done (*not my fault!*), not knowing what else to do, Justin surged toward the exit door, but his blade swept on, slicing through the galley, through the bathroom, and through the back of the cockpit, and suddenly there were no controls, and quite likely (though Justin could not see for sure), no pilots, either.

The plane was rolling too fast, the reverse thrusters had not been engaged, and with no one steering, the jet veered wildly off the runway, careening with unstoppable momentum toward the terminal building and fiery destruction.

It was then that Justin's mind cleared enough to see what he must do.

He swept his blade upward, cutting through the ceiling, and continued on, cutting a jagged path around the circumference of the fuselage until, with a deafening screech of tortured metal, the front of the plane fell away. Justin saw the terrified eyes of the flight attendant still buckled into her jump seat as she was carried off with the cockpit section.

The cockpit section slewed right, tumbled madly, turned again and again, sparks everywhere, and was struck by the right wing, which sheared off from the impact, spraying jet fuel over the runway. The right-side jet engine snapped off the broken wing and cartwheeled fantastically, bounding away like a living thing, still running on the last of its fuel.

The main body of the plane slumped hard to its right, as the wheel on that side had been carried away with the wing. Erin tumbled into Justin, and her wrist was stabbed by one of his thorns, but he caught her in the crook of his arm. The fuselage, now skidding on its side, bucked and vibrated with an end-of-the-world sound of ripping aluminum and carbon fiber, the lower edge chewing and sparking along the tarmac. The forward momentum that would have slammed them into the terminal at a deadly speed bled off, and the fuselage stopped suddenly, sending loose luggage and unbelted passengers flying forward.

Just above them, not fifty feet away, faces pressed to the glass of the terminal windows stared down with mouths open.

And then: silence. Silence as everything, including the remaining engine, stopped. Dust and smoke filled the air. The fuselage was cantilevered, the broken front down, the bent and twisted tail up, the entirety lying half on its right side, with the remaining left wing soaring up and away at an angle.

Justin stood at the front of the plane, his now-massive shape filling the open circle where once the plane had had a front. His feet were the claws of a T. rex. His shoulders were chitin-armored boulders. His head was five times its normal size. His flesh was hard and shining dully. His hands—a massive pincer and an unwieldy blade—were blue and coral. His body, where exposed, was the sickly white of a trout's belly.

"We have to get out of here!" Erin cried. She'd lost both her shoes, her hair was a mess, and her face was smeared with tears and the blood and gore of the elderly couple. "Listen to me: we can't stay here!" Erin screeched. "We have to get away! You've killed people!" Her hand gripped his thick, inhuman forearm, then recoiled from touching him.

Justin could feel that his face—the face he had not yet seen—was not good at expressing emotion. He did not seem to have lips quite where they should be, and his tongue was like something you might cut out of an ox. He was scared, stunned, overwhelmed, but even in the midst of that flood of emotion, he sensed something . . . something dark and distant yet right there inside his brain, something that was . . .

. . . *watching* him.

He shook off that thought and forced himself to recognize and accept what Erin was saying. He had probably killed the pilots and the flight attendant. He had certainly killed the old couple. He hadn't meant to (*not my fault!*), but they were dead just the same and he was looking at their torsos, sagging ovals of exposed organs and hanging viscera, still buckled in.

Even now, even amid the rising chorus of screams joined by cries of pain, even in the swirling midst of his own impossible nightmare, some part of Justin wished he had a camera: there was a terrible, gruesome beauty to all of it. The bodies. The gore. The impossible angles. The swirling dust. Shirts and underwear, the contents of carry-on bags, draped over seat backs like some demented granny's idea of doilies.

A beautiful annihilation.

A new note could be heard in the screams, the beginnings of rage to join the horror. Justin saw staring eyes, animal fear in bulging eyes, pointing fingers, mouths open in shock and disgust, and all of it turning to fury against him.

And there were cell phone cameras.

Justin grabbed Erin around her waist—careful, so careful with the pincer hand that looked as if it could snap her in two. He lifted her insignificant weight and hopped down to the tarmac. *Effortless!* His claw feet gripped the tarmac, sinking into it like bare toes in mud.

The smell of jet fuel was all around. The emergency slide unfolded from a rear door, and in seconds the people on the plane would get free of the wreck. The people . . . and their cell phones.

"Lighter," Justin said in that harsh, deep, reverberating voice.

"What?"

"Give me your lighter. Now!"

Erin fumbled in her clutch purse, spilled out a bottle of pills, a pack of foreign cigarettes, a tampon, and came up with the lighter, holding it out for him, and he cursed. "My hand is . . . ! You have to do it!"

"Do what?" she demanded, desperate just to get away, to run, to hide, to find a place that would serve her enough alcohol to somehow wipe the nightmare from her mind.

"Witnesses," Justin said coldly.

And in his mind he felt an unsettling pleasure, because now was *his* time. Now the clear, direct, emotionless reptile that had always been a part of him saw clearly what Erin could not. Or would not.

The first of the passengers were sliding down the inflated ramp. The ramp was at a too-steep angle and a woman fell off halfway down, landing bruised but alive on the runway.

It took Erin a few seconds to understand what Justin was saying, what he was demanding. "No, no, no, I . . . I can't . . ."

Justin's massive claw now closed again around her midriff, and the message was clear. "Do it! *Do it!*"

With trembling fingers, Erin flicked the lighter, a spark, a flame.

Justin used his massive claw to rip her dress, tearing off a long shred, which hung like a limp flag from his pincer. "Light it!"

Shaking so violently she nearly dropped the lighter, Erin set fire to the swatch of fabric.

A passenger saw and shouted, "No, you idiot, there's jet fuel everywhere!"

"Yeah," Justin rumbled. "I noticed."

He tossed the flaming fabric into the shallow pool of fuel that edged toward his claw feet.

Jet fuel is kerosene, and kerosene does not catch fire as quickly as gasoline. The fabric burned blue as Justin threw Erin over one massive shoulder and turned to run, run, run, and behind them came the screams and shouts of "Fire! Fire!"

Justin ran, great bounding leaps, twenty feet with each step, each impact ripping the concrete, ran away from the terminal and across the runway, kicking heedlessly through landing lights, passing beneath the nose of a taxiing FedEx plane, racing in panic toward the fenced perimeter of the airport as the flame spread and the smoke billowed and the screams of the doomed chased him.

And the dark watchers laughed silently.

CHAPTER 5
A Perfect Specimen

ARMO (A NAME formed by rearranging his true name, Aristotle Adamo) was a white male, seventeen, six foot five inches tall, muscular, blond, blue-eyed, with a jawline Michelangelo would have wished he could sculpt. By his own admission, Armo was not what you would call an academic sort (1.7 GPA). But neither was he a jock, despite being heavily recruited by his high school's basketball team, football team, and even water polo team.

He was also not a gamer, a surfer, a geek, a nerd, or member of any other sort of group. Chess club? No. Math club? Hah! Armo's math skills ended at long division and fractions. Cheese-tasting club? Definitely not.

Armo was not part of any clique because there was one, only one Armo at Malibu High School. MHS was neck-deep in the beautiful children of Hollywood, but still there was only one Armo. There was not a straight girl or gay boy at MHS who had not looked longingly after him. He was gorgeous, and worse than that, charismatic, and worst of all, he knew it, accepted it as natural, and didn't care. His self-confidence went deep, down to the bone.

"ODD," the counselor read from the sheet of paper on his desk.

"Odd?" Armo asked.

"Oppositional Defiant Disorder. That's what the shrink, the um, sorry, the psych eval said. You're smart enough to manage at least a C-plus average without trying and a B if you worked at it. Maybe you won't be going to Harvard, but you could go to a decent state school, make something of your-self."

"I'm already something," Armo said complacently.

The counselor, a sad, brown mouse of a man, could not, despite his best efforts, avoid feeling himself to be something out of DNA's recycling bin by comparison with the young god lounging in the too-small chair. The counselor sighed and thought, *You may be a pain in the ass, but at least you'll never lack for female and/or male companionship.*

"Why don't you take Spanish? You know you need a lan-guage credit to graduate."

"I don't want to take Spanish, I want to take Danish. My family is Danish."

"We do not offer Danish as a language option."

Armo shrugged.

The counselor said, "You understand that everyone in Denmark speaks English, right? Usually better than most Americans?"

A faint smile twisted the corner of Armo's lips. "This is why it's important to keep Danish alive. It's my heritage."

"Oooookay." The counselor laid his hands palms down on his desk in a gesture that signaled surrender. "Okay, Armo. But you won't graduate. And if you don't graduate, you won't go to college."

"Yeah."

"And that will make it very difficult for you to get a decent job."

"Like school counselor?"

Armo's face was blank, but there was a spark in his blue eyes, and despite the implied insult, despite the brick-wall refusal to go along with, well, anything, the counselor found himself smiling.

That shut him up, Armo thought.

"Can I take off now?" Armo asked, and thirty seconds later he was back out on campus, striding to the parking lot as the churning mass of students rushing between classes parted before him like the Red Sea before Moses.

The parking lot was a sea of BMWs, Mercedes, and Teslas. There were also, at the other end of the spectrum, numerous Priuses and Leafs. But there was only one beat-up, orange and white, 2003 Dodge Viper. Many of the cars of the rich kids at Malibu High were fast, but only one did zero to sixty in 3.8 seconds, with a top speed of 189.5 miles per hour, and made the earth shake from the throaty rumble of the Viper's enormous engine.

No one but an idiot gave a seventeen-year-old a car that

fast, but fortunately for Armo, his father was a former stunt man who had managed to become an action movie star. His father figured if fast-and-furious was good for him, it would surely be good for his son as well.

The Viper's cloth top was down, and Armo hopped smoothly over the door and dropped onto the cracked leather seat. This, this right here, this moment, when he was in his car, when he was done with school for the day, with the sun shining and the ocean sparkling, this was his favorite part of the day. He loved this moment. He looked forward all through the tedious day to this moment. The moment of escape.

Of *freedom*.

He keyed the accelerator and felt the 8.3-liter, 500-horsepower engine come to life, startling a pair of seagulls into dropping the French fry they'd been fighting over.

Armo roared down Morning View Drive, pulled onto the Pacific Coast Highway, and was hit so hard by a gasoline tanker truck that the Viper went airborne for fifty feet, spinning in midair as Armo thought, *Uh-oh: that was a mistake.*

The Viper landed on the far side of the PCH, bounced over the low metal railing that fronted the beach, and came to rest upside down on the sand, knocking a three-inch crack into Armo's thick skull.

For a long time, a very long time, Armo saw, smelled, tasted, and heard nothing.

Nothing. A very long nothing.

And then . . . a sound! Meaningless, but something rather than the nothing.

Two days after that single sound, Armo opened his eyes and saw blurry figures.

The next day he opened his eyes again and saw a man's face. There was something familiar about the face, but he couldn't place it, just vague, distorted memories of previous brief emergences into consciousness. His grip on awareness was still extremely weak, in and out, with no way to know how much time passed between each brief contact with reality.

The next day he opened his eyes again and said, "Water."

"Your fluids are in your IV," a male voice said. "You are in a medical facility. Your injuries are healing nicely."

"Whuh?"

"I'm Dr. Park. You are safe, you are in a medical facility," that blandly comforting voice said. Armo squinted and sort of saw the doctor, a plain-looking, middle-aged Asian man with graying hair. "You're going to be all right."

"A damn sight better than all right," a female voice with a hint of the Old South said, but he'd have to turn his head to see her and found he couldn't quite do that.

"Tomorrow we'll get that neck brace off you and try some liquids," Dr. Park said. And Armo went back to sleep.

The woman's voice said, "One more day, Park. Then he's mine."

The next day Armo was feeling much better. He could see clearly, though the dull beige hospital room was nothing much to look at. He saw himself, most of himself, stretched out under a white sheet. He tried to move a leg and it moved. Tried to move the other leg, and it ached, but it, too, was still attached. Hands? There they were, right in front of his face, and he could count to ten on his fingers.

"So, how are we today?" Dr. Park bustled into the room.

"Water?"

The doctor poured some from a plastic jug into a paper cup and held it to Armo's parched lips. The pleasure was exquisite.

"What happened to me?" Armo asked.

"Well, you had a disagreement with a tanker truck. Broken leg, broken collarbone, multiple contusions and abrasions, the most serious matter being a cracked skull."

"Is my . . ." Armo pointed with awkward fingers at his crotch.

"Yes, your penis and testicles are undamaged." Dr. Park rolled his eyes.

Armo sighed relief. "My car?"

"Totaled, I'm afraid."

Armo fought back tears. "Is my mom or dad here?"

"We'll talk about all that later," Dr. Park said. He did something with a small toggle on the clear plastic line that ran into the veins of Armo's wrist and a wave of weariness flooded him. Armo closed his eyes, but he did not lose consciousness—Dr. Park was not an anesthesiologist and gave him a dose that would put a normal-size person under, but Armo was not a normal-size person.

Armo listened as a second person walked in. He'd heard this voice before, the tense female voice out of the South. The last time it had said, *A damn sight better than all right.*

"How's our patient?"

"Much better. The leg fracture is almost completely healed. The skull fracture is knitting up well. His vitals are steady, in fact—"

"So he'll recover completely?"

"He'll likely have some memory loss," Dr. Park said.

"So much the better."

"I don't think we—" Dr. Park began in a chiding tone, but the woman cut him off.

"It may well make him more manageable. Anyway, we'll give him enough to fill whatever hole is in his memory."

Armo heard the woman walk slowly around, from his right side to his left, then back. "You must admit, he's a nearly perfect specimen. Big, strong, and not overly bright."

Armo frowned at that but quickly resumed a blank, unconscious expression.

"I don't know about that, Colonel," Dr. Park said. "According to his school record, he's a rather difficult character."

Colonel Gwendolyn DiMarco, US Army, laughed. "Then I suppose it's a good thing he soon won't be quite human."

CHAPTER 6
Hanging with Dead People

SHADE KNEW SHE was being watched.

She opened her eyes slowly, peeking at first, and seeing just what she expected: Gaia sat in the easy chair.

Shade's heart pounded slow and heavy, a bass drum playing a dirge. *Booom . . . Booom.* She did not move her arms or head, perhaps could not move them with dread running through her veins and arteries like a drug, like a poison. Only her eyes were hers to command, and she looked only at the girl.

Gaia sat silent and still. The only movement was the slow dripping of blood that ran down her forehead to encircle her eyes before pooling and then spilling down her cheeks. Blood tears.

But then Gaia's mouth began to move. It was as if she was chewing something too big to fit in her mouth. Her teeth bit and then ripped at something Shade could not—

—and then she saw!

It was the arm she had ripped from the first and only adult to enter the FAYZ. It was the arm and Shade could see it, could see Gaia's teeth stripping blackened, crispy skin. The arm did not bleed, but blood drops fell from Gaia's face and she grinned as she chewed, and grinned as she looked directly at Shade.

And the arm . . . the arm was growing in length even as Gaia tore the wriggling veins from the flesh, it grew and changed and now there was a shoulder, a white, feminine shoulder, not a man's shoulder—a woman's shoulder—and now a neck. Chills raised goose bumps all over Shade's body and a low moan formed in her throat, a moan she could not quite force out, a sound that wanted to escape but couldn't.

No. No. Noooo. Nooooo! NOOOOO!

The arm had made a shoulder, the shoulder a neck, and now the hair, now the auburn hair and an ear and in that ear the earring Shade had bought her mother on Mother's Day and—

"NO!" The sound came this time, a muffled cry, as if she were forcing it up through mud.

Shade's whole body tingled, but it was no longer chills but something strange and new and . . .

Gaia grinned and turned the partial carcass in her hand to face Shade, turned it slowly, slowly, an ear, a cheek . . .

"NO!"

Suddenly Shade slammed into something hard. A second impact a second later as she fell onto her hip.

She was awake. Gaia no longer sat in the easy chair.

Awake.

Shade breathed a shaky sigh of relief. It had been a nightmare.

Then she saw her legs and screamed.

As had become Cruz's habit, she headed to Shade's house. It was a stunning day, one of those days you got in autumn in Chicagoland, when the sky was a perfect robin's egg blue, and the air was as crisp and clean as a hotel sheet, and the leaves were a carpet of gold and red beneath trees that would soon be outlined by snow or glistening with ice.

Cruz paused once to write that down in her Moleskine. Then she ran up the back stairs and knocked at Shade's kitchen door, which Shade opened instantly, as if she'd been lurking.

"What's up?" Cruz said, and Shade held up a notebook. On the page in black block letters: *House Is Bugged*.

At the same time Shade said, "Hi, Cruz, come on in, girl, we have homework to get done."

"Yes," Cruz said stiffly. "Yes, we do."

Shade led the way to the living room. She picked up a lamp and tilted it so Cruz could see the bottom of its weighted base, and there, where Shade had peeled back the felt, was something that looked a bit like a component stripped off a circuit board.

Shade replaced the lamp and led the way to her father's study, a small, book-crammed space between the main stairwell and the seldom-used parlor. She held up a hand, stopping Cruz. Then she pointed at a corner of the crown molding where there was what looked like a nail hole. She pointed at her eye, then up at the nail hole, and down at the direct line of sight to Professor Darby's computer.

They backed out silently and tramped upstairs to the bedroom. And there was the next shock: someone or something had beaten deep indentations into the top of the wall facing Shade's bed. And Shade's usually neat bed was tilted at an angle, with the front legs snapped in two. And her comforter had been ripped in half, so that the inner stuffing extruded.

Yes, something . . . odd . . . had clearly happened.

Cruz turned concerned, baffled eyes to Shade and saw on her friend's face a look of triumph.

Shade jerked her head toward the bathroom, where she turned on the water and let it run loudly.

"I doubt they'll have put cameras or mikes in my bathroom, or even my bedroom, but I don't want to take any chances."

"What happened?" Cruz asked in a terse whisper.

"I did it!"

"You did what?"

"I ground up an ounce of the rock, made powder out of it, mixed it with peanut butter, and gagged it down."

"Oh, my God! I thought you were waiting!"

"You may not have noticed this about me," Shade said with unmistakable glee, "but I am not patient. I took it, and nothing, nothing for hours. I was depressed. I couldn't believe it was all for nothing." Her words tumbled out in an excited rush, very unlike the Shade who Cruz had never seen overly excited or emotional.

"And . . . ," Cruz prompted.

"And I went to sleep. I had a nightmare, a bad one, and when I woke up I was on the floor."

"The floor?"

"Clear across the room," Shade said. She made a hand gesture representation of a person flying across the room and smashing into the wall. "And . . ." She held her fingernails up for inspection. They looked as if she'd been digging in chalk. Or a plaster wall. Chills ran up Cruz's spine.

"In my nightmare, I leaped," Shade went on. "I leaped! Practically flew! And in reality, in *reality*, I leaped. Sixteen and a half feet, I measured it! I leaped out of bed so fast, so hard, I ripped right through my comforter. The impact woke me up, Cruz, and I . . . I was on the floor!"

"Jesus Christ," Cruz whispered. Half her mind was gibbering, *Oh, my God, she did it!* in a giddy, triumphant way, and the other half was thinking, *Oh, my God, she did it*, but in a very different tone.

"Cruz. I did it. It works! I have . . . a power."

"What . . . but, wait, what power?"

"That we have to discover, Cruz. I can't believe it. I hoped, I wanted . . . It worked, Cruz, it worked!"

"Congratulations?" There was enough doubt in her voice to earn a sharp look from Shade, but Shade was not going to be put off.

"Do you know what this means?" Shade asked, practically jumping in place.

"Not really," Cruz admitted.

"It means the ASO works even without the dome. And that fact means that I was right: if bits of the ASOs are out in the world—and they almost certainly are—I won't be the only one. There will be other people with powers, Cruz, some good, some not, but I will not be one of the random bystanders getting burned, I will—" Shade stopped, and for a moment looked guilty, as though she'd said something she did not intend. "I'll be able to do something," she finished lamely.

"About what?" Cruz asked.

"I won't be one of the helpless bystanders, that's all," Shade said. She sat on the closed toilet as if exhausted. For a while she said nothing. Then, with eyes cast down as if she were inspecting the floor tile, she began to speak in a rushed, low voice, as if every word was distasteful. She was performing a duty, not unburdening herself. She shook her head slightly as if denying what she was saying. "You've seen the videos, Cruz, but I was there. People, kids, just this far away . . ." Shade stretched her arm out and seemed to touch something in the air. "And I heard her call me. Call my name . . ."

Cruz knew then. She knew as certainly as if Shade had told her.

Cruz crossed herself slowly, not warding off evil, but invoking God's attention to her damaged friend.

"Your mother," Cruz said.

The muscles of Shade's jaw twitched. Her scar stood out white against reddening skin. "A lot of people died there that day. Helpless. Just innocent bystanders." She repeated the word, and raised a finger as if she was a teacher making an important point. "Helpless," Shade repeated, and the word was not self-pitying, it was not a plea, it was an angry accusation. And the accused was Shade herself.

Cruz watched as Shade raised her hand to her scar, as she had done in the cornfield. Shade seemed self-conscious, knowing Cruz was watching, but was unable to stop herself from touching the tactile proof of her own weakness.

Cruz wanted to ask, *Who was helpless?* but the answer was obvious. Shade was helpless. Little thirteen-year-old Shade Darby had been helpless.

"It was madness," Shade said. "The dome came down and the kids from inside were just running in panic, climbing over dead bodies, just . . . I told you that's how I got this." She pointed at the scar. "Machete. I came close to dying." She sighed heavily, then tried to soften the tragic tone with a wry smile. "I nearly died. And my mom did."

Cruz wanted to take Shade's hand. Wanted to hug her. But now the shark was back, and the human girl who had been helpless four years ago to stop the slaughter, to save her mother, had been pushed down and away. There was a distance to Shade now, a disconnect from her own emotions, and Cruz withdrew her tentative hand.

It's not just powers she wants, Cruz realized. *It's revenge. Revenge against a creature long dead.*

"There's a strange mental side effect, though, probably some reaction to the change—"

"Wait, what change?"

Shade winced. "It's weird, Cruz, but it did something to me physically. It was dark, so . . . but my legs . . . Fortunately, changing back is easy enough. Just form the picture of your real body in your mind and . . ."

"So, what was the side effect?" Cruz asked.

"There was . . . well, it was weird, like a delayed nightmare after the main nightmare. It's hard to explain." Shade concentrated, eyes drifting up and away as people's eyes do when they're trying to recall something intangible. "It was like . . . remember that scene in *Lord of the Rings* when Gollum looked into the swamp and saw dead faces under the water staring up at him?"

"You saw dead people?"

"No, they weren't dead, and I don't think they were people." Shade avoided eye contact, glancing sideways suspiciously, over her shoulder, as if she was anticipating someone sneaking up behind her. "Just an extra nightmare, Cruz, like I said, a holdover, I mean I was asleep when the change started. But the important thing is, Cruz: it worked," Shade said. The normal Shade, Cruz's friend, reemerged, as if from a dark vision, and in a more enthusiastic voice said, "I need to test it, work with it. Somewhere private where I won't be exposed or accidentally hurt anyone."

"How could you hurt anyone?"

Shade held up her palms for inspection. Then she pulled up her sweatpants, pulling them up to over her knees. "I hit that wall hard enough to knock divots into it, Cruz, then fell eight feet onto hardwood, and do you see a bruise or a scrape?"

Cruz did not.

"It's not just the ability to leap out of bed," Shade said. "I must also be very strong, and very, um, I don't know . . ."

"Invulnerable?"

"Yes! Maybe," Shade said, and bit at her thumbnail, dislodging some of the packed gypsum from the impact with wallboard. And then, as if drawn by magnetism, her finger touched her scar again.

"This is incredible, Shade. And scary as hell. But what's all this about bugs and cameras?"

Cruz whispered the words "bugs" and "cameras."

"Ah, that." Shade dropped her hand to her side. "After Iowa, the government team, you know, HSTF-Sixty-Six, must have started to suspect my father. I'm not surprised—in fact, I expected it. When I came home from school I searched. There are probably other bugs I haven't found, but unless the task force wants to risk taking video of a minor girl in her bedroom or bathroom, I doubt there's a problem in either room."

"But how long have they been there? They could have heard everything!"

Shade shook her head. "No. If they'd had surveillance on us earlier, they'd have stopped us before we went to Iowa. No, this is recent, this came *after* Iowa."

What kind of person actually expects their house to be bugged? Cruz wondered, but said nothing. The answer was obvious: *a person like the obsessed person in front of me.*

"What do we do?" Cruz asked. She was buying in, accepting the knowledge that Shade was not merely exploring possibilities or having a little adventure but that Shade wanted power. And she wanted it for a revenge she could never hope to get.

And yet, I'm going along.

"We do homework, Cruz. Down in the living room in plain view of any cameras. Then you go home. Tonight, I hop in the car and drive to Jewell-Osco, where I pick you up and we go test this out."

It was a bizarre day, to say the very least. The two girls hunched over books and laptops, scribbled and typed, doing work that no longer mattered to either of them if it ever had, making stilted conversation for the benefit of listeners.

"Where's your dad?" Cruz asked at one point.

"Kazakhstan, believe it or not."

Cruz believed it: according to Shade, the next chunk of rock, ASO-4, was scheduled to land in a very inconvenient part of the world. Professor Darby was presumably there.

Shade slid her a note, facedown. Cruz palmed it and read it under the table they were using as a desk. *I've got workmen coming to fix the wall before my dad gets back.*

Cruz made a wry expression that meant, *Of course you do, because: you.*

Cruz left with a promise to be at Jewell-Osco at ten o'clock, after Shade had done the obligatory Skype with her grandmother—one of Martin Darby's attempts to provide adult supervision when he was away.

Rain had come and gone while Cruz was in Shade's house, and as she set out for home the trees dripped so energetically it might as well have been raining. A left turn onto Dempster brought Cruz to the Starbucks above which her family lived in a two-bedroom apartment.

As Cruz neared home she began to alter her appearance, taking off a silver chain, sliding rings into pockets, turning her collar down, scuffing at the legs of her jeans until the cuffs lay flat.

She was not denying who she was, not really, she told herself, just reducing the visible triggers that might cause a paternal eruption. It was an everyday decision for Cruz: how much to be herself, how much to risk, when to be bold, when to run scared. It was both automatic and exhausting.

How am I "presenting"? How are people seeing me?

She would say it didn't matter, but it was not so easy to take that whole *don't give a damn* attitude when there were people out there who would tease, bully, beat, even kill her for the crime of being . . . *interesting*.

"And now I'm interesting but with a friend who has super-powers," she muttered. She asked the sidewalk, "What have I gotten myself into?" She knew in her heart that no good would come from this. She knew deep down that she should flee, put miles between herself and Shade Darby.

I should call the FBI . . .

The thought percolated through her mind, enticing, oddly empowering. She *could* end this, end it now before worse things happened. But not before tonight, for sure, not before she'd actually seen it with her own eyes.

And then? Then was then. She would decide *then*.

She ran the mental checklist, wondering just what would set her father off this time. Her father was not a violent man, she had no fear of his fists; his aggression took the form of sarcasm, slights, sneering looks he didn't bother to hide. It wasn't that his teasing or bullying was terribly clever or original—that would have at least showed some effort on his part. No, it was not that he was particularly good at being cruel, it was simply the fact that he was her father being cruel.

My father.

She could pretend that she didn't care what her father thought of her, but she could never really *mean* it. She would never stop caring. It would never not hurt.

From that thought, of course, it was down and down in the spiral of shame, blaming herself, hating herself, hating the world for having done this to her. What kind of God would play this game? What kind of sick divinity would sit up in heaven and say, *This one shalt be all of the above . . . LOL!*

Cruz pictured God throwing back his great, bearded, cis-male God head and guffawing, haw, haw, haw, and the angels snickering behind their hands.

Cruz paused, pulled out her Moleskine, and wrote, *God as bro. Bro-god. Angels try to expand his consciousness?* It was maybe not a great premise for a short story or novel, but Cruz had learned to write down even the ideas that seemed dumb. Dumb now might trigger smart later.

As she climbed the interior stairs that always smelled of coffee from the Starbucks, she heard an insistent, aggressive, whining voice and instantly knew her father had started drinking early. Five twenty in the evening, when he usually didn't get home until six—or eight if he stopped at a bar on his way. She took a deep breath, hesitating with her hand on the doorknob. She heard the first sound of an argument breaking out: a dish clattering in the sink, and then her mother's voice, pleading, weak, and self-pitying.

Every night.

Cruz hoped she could get past them to her room, her sanctuary, while they were distracted, so she pushed in, welcomed by the rich, earthy smell of mole warming on the stove. Her father was still in his work clothes, black work pants with muddy knees, a denim shirt with his name, *Manny*, in red on a white oval patch. He was not a big man, maybe four inches shorter than Cruz, with curling black hair and a brush mustache.

". . . no overtime means you cut back, Maria, not tomorrow, not some other day, right the hell now! How stupid are you not to get that?" Manuel "Manny" Rojas said.

Maria Rojas was first-generation Mexican, having crossed the Rio Grande on her father's back when she was eight. Manny Rojas was US-born, second generation, with parents from Chile. Cruz did not think her father ever spoke Spanish, and her mother rarely did, answering instead in heavily accented English.

"I can no take the steaks back," Maria muttered under her breath.

"I can no take the steaks back, I can't, I can't, because I'm helpless!" Manny mocked her. Then he spotted Cruz. "Oh, good, now this."

Cruz nodded at them both, tried to plaster on a bland

smile, and kept moving, longing for the relative peace of her room. But her father followed, mincing behind her.

Cruz felt her heart beating hard, a beat heavy with dread and sadness. She knew the next move, and sure enough as she reached the door to her room, her father leaped ahead and ostentatiously opened her door, saying, "I'll get that door for you, *miss*."

Cruz stepped back and waited as he pushed the door open. She said not a word. Sometimes that worked; sometimes not. This was a "not" day.

"You know, *Hugo*, if you really want to cut your dick off, I've got a pair of wire cutters that should do the trick."

He often said cruel things to her, laughing as if to say, *It's just a joke, lighten up*, but this was a new low. Cruz knew she shouldn't let it get to her, but it did. Of course it did. Her father, her *father*, despised her.

"Why not just use a knife?" Cruz asked, wishing she sounded nonchalant and defiant, but knowing she sounded pathetic and weak and everything the man before her despised. "I could kill myself with a knife, which is what you want."

Shock registered on Manny's face at that, though whether it was shock that she had spoken back, or shock at the realization that she was talking about suicide, she could not guess.

"Excuse me," Cruz said, and closed the door on him.

She waited there, her room dark, hearing his breathing on the other side, half expecting him to push his way in and heap more abuse on her. Hoping that he would knock and say he was sorry. Fat chance. After a while he stomped off and she sagged in relief, tears filling her eyes, feeling the wave of shame that came from knowing that he would now be just that much harder on her mother.

It was in that moment of exquisite emotional agony, that moment of turmoil, that moment of slight and ineffectual resistance, that moment when the chasm of self-loathing once again opened beneath her, that it first occurred to Cruz:

If it worked for Shade . . .

Out came the notebook. Cruz wrote: *If it works for Shade, why not me?*

Until that moment that insidious thought had never, not even once, not even briefly, occurred to her. The rock—ASO whatever—was all about Shade, about her curiosity, her arrogant belief in herself, her desire to be more than she had been four years before, more than the thirteen-year-old girl blaming herself for her mother's death.

So, does that make Shade the only person in the world who should have a power?

If it made sense for Shade to roll the dice without knowing what might come up, didn't it make equal sense for Cruz? She flopped onto her bed and grabbed the stuffed elephant she'd had since childhood and hugged it to her chest.

I could have powers. And then let that bastard bully me. Let him try.

But that fantasy was short-lived. Cruz had never wanted to hurt anyone, not even people who hurt her. She wanted just one thing in life: to be left alone to ask herself questions about who and what she was, to be able to carry out the experimental, delicate, personal work inside her own mind without the world demanding concrete answers and condemning whatever answer she came up with.

It wasn't that she hated her male body, but it had never felt entirely like it belonged to her. She was sure that she wanted to try hormone treatments, but was not at all sure about surgery, not sure if that was the final answer. She wanted to explore the idea. Why should that be hard? Why should that be a problem for other people? How was it even any of their business?

She pushed her stuffed animal aside and blocked out the sounds of the escalating parental argument by checking out new music on Reddit, thinking she'd find some things Shade might like.

When she tired of that, she went back to work on the story she'd been writing for months off and on, typing away on her laptop in fits and starts. The story was already too long and involved to be a short story, but she felt ridiculous thinking of herself writing a full-length novel. Anyway, the character she had created, the one who bore an almost embarrassing resemblance to herself, seemed dull compared to Shade.

Her still-new friendship with Shade Darby had warped her worldview. Shade's determination was more interesting than Cruz's ambivalence. Cruz admired Shade's self-control, her ability to step back and look at the world through coldly analytical eyes. She knew that she herself should do just that: take a big step back and think through what she was getting herself into. But it was hard, Cruz reflected, to concentrate when you could almost feel the pillars of normalcy crumbling beneath you. It was very hard to put words on paper when your imagination was busy picturing an entirely different reality.

What powers had the kids inside the PBA acquired? She opened Wikipedia and found the list: killing light, telekinesis, teleportation, the power to heal with a touch, to move at speeds that would amaze a cheetah . . . and a body made of rock, an arm like a boa constrictor, the power to make others see your own nightmare visions. Powers for good, powers for evil.

Power corrupts, and absolute power corrupts absolutely. The old quote floated through her mind, trailing the counterpoint behind it: *Yes, but if power corrupts evil people, then surely good people must have power, too?*

When the alarm clock on her phone went off, she grabbed her bag and set out to meet Shade, tiptoeing past her father, who was finally asleep in his chair with a football game on. Her mother asked in a weary voice where she was going and didn't bother to pay attention to Cruz's answering lie.

Cruz walked around the corner onto Chicago Avenue, and down the dark, cold street past the indifferent rushing cars of commuters to the bright lights of the Jewell-Osco. Cruz waited by the parked grocery carts, ignoring the sneering looks of a couple ushering their little girl past as if Cruz was a disease carrier. The Subaru pulled in, right on time.

"You finish your paper?" Shade asked as Cruz hopped in.

"Um . . . I'll take an incomplete."

Shade sighed like a disapproving parent, shook her head, and said, "Well, who knows? Maybe the world we'll grow up in will be very different than we expect and all that education will be useless."

"Yeah. I was thinking that, too."

"Maybe we'll be the ones to make the world different," Shade said with a significant glance.

That glance made Cruz queasy. "Look out, light's changing."

Shade stepped on the gas and accelerated through the yellow light as an old bald man in a Mercedes leaned on his horn and showed them his middle finger.

"Where are we going?" Cruz asked.

"To a very quiet place," Shade muttered.

I borrow your confidence, Cruz thought. *Do you know that, Shade Darby? Do you know that you're the shark and I'm just the remora fish attached to you?*

Do you secretly despise me?

They passed a gloomy, Gothic stone arch that marked the gate of the cemetery that divided Evanston and Chicago. They drove slowly down a side street into a quiet neighborhood of stone and brick Victorians that had mostly been converted to apartments or condos. The street ended in a cul-de-sac, where Shade parked.

"Seriously?" Cruz asked.

"More than serious: grave," Shade joked.

They climbed out and pushed through an unlocked iron side gate. They walked silently down a path that brought them to the cemetery's perimeter, marked by a low brick wall topped by a three-foot-high chain-link fence. There was a hole in the wire and they squeezed through.

"How come you know about this hole in the fence?" Cruz asked suspiciously.

"My mother is here," Shade said in a flat tone that discouraged further questions. But still, Cruz saw her look away toward the east end of the cemetery, and saw, too, the look of sadness that crossed her face like a shadow and then was duly suppressed.

My father, her mother, Cruz thought. *Do we ever escape our parents?*

There was no denying that the cemetery was a strange and spine-tingling place, quiet but for traffic sounds and the whine of a plane passing overhead on its approach to O'Hare. There were tombstones, mismatched, some humble, some quite grand with impressive plinths supporting plaster angels and blank-eyed saints, crosses, and the occasional Star of David or Muslim crescent.

The cemetery formed a rectangle with rounded edges, one side facing Lake Shore Drive and Lake Michigan beyond. A main pathway bisected the cemetery lengthwise like a spine, with smaller paths extending like ribs. Trees that offered welcome shade on hot days were now sinister, looming creatures, bare branches silhouetted against the orange glow of the city lights to the south. The pitying faces of chipped and pitted stone Madonnas seemed to disapprove of both of them.

Cruz crossed herself and intercepted an eye roll from Shade.

"Hey," Cruz said, "a graveyard at night is no place to go all atheist."

"There's a quiet little area up here," Shade said.

It was a spot where trees blocked most of the artificial light, a space with very old-looking tombstones, and when Cruz bent down to peer closely she saw that at least one dated from the nineteenth century.

"Okay," Shade announced, apparently unfazed by the gloom, and perhaps, unlike her friend, not tortured by memories of a dozen horror movies set in graveyards. "If a groundskeeper comes, I'll tell him we got lost looking for my mom's grave."

"Yeah, and if the ground opens up and you see zombies, run! Now, how do we do this?"

"I reread the Ellison book, the part about Sam Temple when he first exhibited signs of developing a power. Her theory is that it was strong emotion—anger, whatever—that put him in touch with his power."

"Okay, strong emotion," Cruz said. Then, with deliberate drollery, "Strong emotion. In *you*."

"I have emotions," Shade protested weakly. "I just . . . I don't . . . I guess I don't like them."

"Is it because they make you feel vulnerable?"

"Of course," Shade agreed readily. "You know why men have all the power in this world, Cruz? I'll tell you. Because *Homo sapiens* is about 200,000 years old, as a species. All of human *civilization* from, like, Ur of the Chaldees—"

"—there's a blast from history lectures past," Cruz interrupted, vaguely hoping to head off another round of WikiShade. But it was too late.

"—to the present day is not even ten thousand years, just five percent of that 200,000 years. Ninety-five percent of human history was small bands, tribes living hand to mouth, hunting, picking berries, eating bugs. Longer, really, since earlier hominids . . . But, anyway, little-known fact: in primitive societies women actually provided most of the food. But they also got pregnant, and it's hard to chase wildebeest when you're pregnant, or nursing. It's hard to fight off the hyenas when you've got a baby in your arms. So that's what the men did: they had the larger muscles and they kept the predators at bay and killed the occasional wildebeest for protein."

"That's why I was probably never going to be a very good boy," Cruz said, teeth chattering from a combination of cold and nerves. "I never wanted to kill wildebeest."

"Might be very tasty," Shade suggested. "Anyway, hunting and fighting are what the men did, and they learned that they had to suppress their emotions, especially fear, in order to do it."

"So . . . you're trying to be male?" This was said with a tone of irony, though Shade must have missed it.

"No. I'm just trying to . . . to . . ."

"Win?"

"Slap me. Hard."

"What? No! What are you talking about?"

"Pain," Shade said. "It creates emotion."

"You can't come up with a better way?"

"Slap me. Do it!"

"I do not want to—"

"Oh, stop being such a wimp!" Shade snarled. "Pretend I'm one of those football players."

Cruz realized Shade was provoking her, but even knowing that, her blood started to boil, just a little. The rage at her father that she had suppressed, but that did not wish to stay suppressed, was too raw, too recent, too near the surface.

"Come on, you wimpy, weak—"

Whap!

Shade's head snapped sideways. She gasped in pain and surprise; Cruz gasped in horror at what she'd done.

Part of me meant that slap, Cruz thought.

"Ow-uh!" Shade said, holding a palm to her face.

"You made me!"

Shade held up her hand, calling for silence. She was trying to channel the pain of the slap into . . . well, into doing whatever it was her sleeping mind had done the night before.

For the next ten minutes they tried everything. Cruz twisted Shade's ear painfully. There was more slapping. There were hurled insults, which had the frustrating effect of giving them both the giggles. Cruz even launched into a sort of improvised ghost story. Anything to push Shade's emotional buttons, to cause a purely emotional reaction and hopefully get her to act without thinking, to access the power the way— according to Astrid Ellison's book—Sam Temple, the original PBA *power*, had done.

But Shade was simply not a person out of control. Shade was the living avatar of self-control.

"It's me," Shade said after endless attempts that had left her a bit bruised and very frustrated. "I don't . . ." She formed her hands into claws that seemed to scratch at the air, as if she was reaching for something, like she was trying to grab hold of something: human feelings? "I don't get emotional easily," she concluded lamely.

"You think?" But Cruz was thinking that she knew how to evoke a reaction from Shade. But would it be too cruel? "You blame yourself for your mother's death," Cruz blurted.

Shade's eyes glittered in the dark.

"That's it, right?" Cruz demanded. "That's what this is all about?"

Shade had gone very still.

The shark has doll's eyes.

"That won't work," Shade said at last, and her voice surprised Cruz. It was low and not at all angry. It was, to Cruz's amazement, a sad, defeated voice. "She was looking for me, calling me. I didn't answer because I wanted to watch. It was exciting. I'd never imagined anything like it, so I didn't answer and she was looking for me."

Cruz immediately switched directions. "Sweetie, you were a kid acting like a kid. You can't blame yourself for her death."

"Sure I can," Shade said flatly. She turned toward her mother's grave. "Not a hundred percent, maybe not even fifty percent, but some percent. Some percent greater than zero. I never lie to myself, Cruz. I don't mind lying to other people, but I don't lie to myself. I know why I'm doing this.

I know it's guilt and revenge. But it's also curiosity, same as it was then. I want to *know*, Cruz. I want to know what it's like to have power. Real power. So you can stop trying to psychoanalyze me."

"I'm not psychoanalyzing you," Cruz said. "I'm . . . I'm kind of writing about you, I guess, at least in my head. So I'm trying to understand."

Shade turned to her, head tilted skeptically, almost mocking. "I'm not hard to figure out. *You're* hard to figure out. You haven't figured yourself out yet, Cruz."

Cruz took Shade's hand, and to her surprise, Shade squeezed her hand back.

"Hello, ladies."

The voice sent adrenaline flooding into Cruz's veins. Shade and Cruz turned and saw two guys. Two guys who were clearly not there for innocent reasons. Cruz's hand drifted to her phone. Could she call 911 before the guys started in? Or would an attempt at a phone call just be the signal to start the beating Cruz knew must be coming?

Shade, too, felt the rush of adrenaline, but her mind was crystal clear. She saw two white men in their late teens or early twenties. Neither was in a uniform, therefore they were not cops. They were also not random street people: no overloaded shopping carts or dirty overcoats.

The one on the right had a club of some sort stuck in the back of his pants, but the one on the left was dominant—their stances revealed this—so if the one on the right had a club, the dominant one likely had something worse. Maybe a gun.

The balance of power was impossible: two strong, young, likely armed men versus Cruz and Shade.

Not a winning formula. At least not to Cruz, whose heart sank into her stomach. But a quick glance at Shade revealed a small, tight smile.

"Good evening," Shade said.

"Good evening to you, milady," the one on the left said. He had sunglasses perched atop his head, despite it being night, so they were not a mere possession, they were either a fashion statement or perhaps booty from some earlier robbery. "Kind of late for a lovely lady and a big old homo to be hanging around a graveyard."

"We came to visit a grave," Shade said calmly.

"Yeah? This grave?" Sunglasses pointed to the nearest headstone with his toe.

The headstone read, "Joseph Crouch, beloved husband." And below that, the date: "July 18, 1902."

"Yes," Shade said. Her chin was thrust forward, defiant. Cruz, however, was measuring distances, wondering how fast she could run and whether Shade could—or would—keep up.

Sunglasses raised one booted foot, rested it against the headstone, and pushed. It did not fall over. "Jenks, give me that crowbar."

So the club they could not see earlier was a crowbar. To Cruz, this meant that they were indeed thieves, maybe even grave robbers. Her fear deepened: she had been beaten before, and she knew the damage cold steel could do. Her fear was visceral, very real, and it chilled her to the marrow.

"I got it!" Jenks said, digging the sharper end of the steel bar into the grass at the base of the headstone.

"You boys must be new to the whole vandalism thing," Shade said.

Cruz gasped, mouth open in astonishment. Cool and calm was great, but now Shade was provoking them.

Sunglasses dropped the phony smile and his face became a mask of malevolence. "Now give me the damn crowbar, Jenks." With the steel in his hand he said, "I'll tell you what I can vandalize pretty well."

"Man with weapon versus unarmed girl," Shade taunted. "That's about what a guy like you is capable of. Let me guess— no job, no girlfriend, no clue, no plan, so you're down to: beat on people."

"Well, I'll start with a beating and we'll see where it goes." He stepped in and swung the crowbar sideways into Shade's arm. It should have broken the bone. It should have evoked a cry of pain. Instead, the steel bar bounced back, as if it had been struck against a spring.

Cruz frowned at Shade's arm. Then her gaze was drawn to Shade's face. Shade Darby's head was changing shape, narrowing, like her features were being squeezed into an invisible mold. Her eyes grew within a narrower visage, large, glittering, slanted, focused. Her lips thinned and her mouth was smaller. Her hair—the hair Cruz had so admired—was wrong, all wrong, not hair at all, really. It was drawn back into something like a series of spikes, drawn back sharply, as if lacquered, like some fantastic punk style, forming points and edges so sharp they might cut flesh.

Shade blinked and Cruz practically screamed, because for a moment a translucent membrane had come down over Shade's eyes. Snake's eyes.

There came a low grinding sound, a wet fleshy squishing, and Cruz stared in mounting horror as Shade's legs extended, grew, lengthened, until what stuck out from the cuff of her jeans was nothing even remotely human. The legs were long and brown and seemed to be made of rusted steel, and they ended in feet like no foot Cruz had ever seen.

Shade's legs suddenly bent backward, the knees reversing direction. Her thighs swelled with muscle clad in dull armor the color of dried blood.

In seconds Shade was a terrifying hybrid creature, human mostly from the waist up, though a sleek, streamlined version of herself. From the waist down she might have been some terrifying insect or great bird. Shade stood balanced easily on narrow, spiky claws. Altogether she was several inches taller than normal, with her weight forward like a speed skater in motion, her face and hair looking as if they had been smeared back by a hurricane wind, her hair backswept into reddish spikes.

Cruz gibbered in incoherent terror, nonsense sounds, the urgent need to flee all but irresistible. And suddenly Shade was gone! There was a sudden sharp gust of wind and a loud *crack!* Cruz heard the heavy sound of bodies falling on grass, and to her amazement, the two punks were on their backs.

The Shade-not-Shade creature stood vibrating between

Cruz and the fallen men, vibrating like she'd grabbed a power line. A buzzing sound came from her, like a large mosquito.

"Sorry. Need. To. Talk. MoreslowlyIguess," Shade said in a voice that sounded syrupy, like someone slowing the replay on an audio file. "I. Did it!"

Cruz nodded, struck dumb, able to do nothing but stare.

Shade had something in her hand—her relatively normal hand. It was the gun, the one Sunglasses had in his waistband. Cruz was about to tell her to throw it away when Shade did just that. She threw the gun in the direction of the lake. The gun should have flown twenty or thirty feet and landed on the grass between tombstones. Instead there was a *crack!* and the gun, breaking the sound barrier, sailed over the tallest headstones, over the length of the graveyard, over Lake Shore Drive, and splashed in the water of Lake Michigan, a quarter mile away.

The two vandals crawled off, yammering to each other in scared voices about "crazy bitches!"

Shade, still vibrating said, "I think. I have. Super-speed."

"Yeah," Cruz said.

Shade jumped, straight up. She flew up and out of sight, a darkness against stars, then fell more slowly at gravity-normal speed and landed hard, buckling her back-turned knees.

She recovered quickly and said, "Jump. Good. Landing. Notsomuch."

Then Shade's new and unutterably disturbing form began to fade to normal. Cruz stared in fascination at the legs reversing direction again, at the feet becoming human feet once more. It was not as simple or as easy as a dissolve between two images; there was more movement, more twisting and shrinking and fleshing out. But finally she was Shade again, a girl standing in ripped jeans. Shade retrieved her shoes, took a knee, and laced them up.

"Good," Shade said. "I was worried I couldn't change back despite last night. That's a relief."

"Okay, that . . . ," Cruz began before realizing she had no descriptors big enough to cope with what she'd seen.

"It's amazing, Cruz," Shade said. But her tone did not mirror the words. She sounded wary, worried. Which, Cruz thought, was the very mildest possible reaction to having your entire body transform.

They got back to the fence and found it quite a bit harder to squeeze through with the jagged wire pointing at them rather than away, but when they finally pushed through, cursing small wounds, they saw that they were not alone.

Shade sighed, shook her head ruefully, and said, "Malik?"

"Yeah." He was leaning against his car, a little two-seat BMW. "I sort of, um . . . followed you," he said.

"You saw?" she asked.

"I saw *something*," he said. "Something that should not be possible. Not even in a graveyard at night. What the hell have you done, Shade? What the hell have you done?"

ASO-4

ASO-4 WAS SCHEDULED to land in the mountains on the border between Pakistan and Afghanistan. An American SEAL team, launched secretly from a base in Kazakhstan, where Professor Martin Darby and a dozen others watched helmet-cam feeds on monitors, raced to the impact site, hoping to get in, seize the meteorite, and get away before hostile tribesmen knew they were there.

It was night, and the night belonged to the SEALs with their owl-eyed night-vision equipment.

Two helicopters landed while one stayed aloft, turning circles, its guns and missiles on a hair trigger, sensors scanning. Farther aloft floated a drone flown by a pilot sitting seven thousand miles away at a console at CIA headquarters in Langley, Virginia. Farther up still, two USAF F-16 jets bristling with smart missiles zoomed back and forth at near Mach 1 speeds. Some distance away flew the USAF airborne refueling tanker and the USAF E-3G, which watched everything with its array of electronics. And finally, three hundred miles up and well outside the atmosphere, a French satellite trained its cameras down and relayed its pictures to Paris, Langley, and the Pentagon.

But all that technology was of no use in the end. A Kazakh interpreter had earned two hundred dollars (and his life) by giving advance warning to members of the Haqqani Network, among the world's best-trained, best-disciplined terrorists. The Haqqanis had no notion of what was happening, just that a SEAL team was landing two miles away from a nameless village of six families, all devoted to raising goats and transporting opium.

The Haqqanis had long since learned to be wary of American technology. They knew about the eyes in the sky. They knew that their heat signatures would be picked up, so they had arrived early and nestled deep in rock crevices, piling brush above themselves and driving a small flock of sheep and goats into the area to add to the signal confusion.

The SEALs landed, leaped out, and formed a perimeter. They were the best-trained soldiers in any army and the Haqqanis had a cautious respect for them, so they waited to see just what all this hubbub was about before starting a fight.

From the second helicopter came different soldiers. These moved with far less liquid grace, and instead of automatic weapons they carried instruments.

The Haqqanis watched, puzzled, as these new arrivals walked back and forth in a grid pattern, before finally circling around a small patch of what, to the Haqqanis' eyes, looked a bit like a bomb crater.

Then out came a metal chest carried by two soldiers, and the rest of the technicians busied themselves wrapping plastic around a particular rock about the size of a car tire.

The Haqqani mission leader had seen enough: whatever this rock was, it was worth a very big commitment of American and allied resources. If the Americans wanted this particular rock that badly, then it must be worth something to a tribe that made its living off extortion, terror, opium, and hostage-taking.

Rifle and machine-gun fire opened up in the night, arcing toward the SEALs, killing one instantly and wounding another.

Rocket-propelled grenades flew, trailing sparks and smoke, and slammed into one of the two parked helicopters.

The SEALs began an orderly, disciplined withdrawal, but the technicians either dropped to the ground or fled for the helicopter.

Now it was a melee, a firefight, with Haqqanis shooting down and SEALs shooting at targets they couldn't really see. It was quickly clear that the SEALs could not hope to hold on, and they withdrew by stages to the surviving helicopter, two of their number struggling to drag the heavy chest and its rock cargo.

The drone found a target and sent a rocket into the dark rocks, blowing one of the Haqqanis apart and injuring another.

The helicopter was hovering now, just a foot off the

ground as the men with the chest covered the last, desperate few yards. And then a sharpshooter's bullet took off the side of one man's face. He fell, and a fellow SEAL jumped down from the helicopter, threw the wounded man over his shoulder, and slung him into the helicopter door as an RPG round barely missed, pelting the beating rotors with noisy shrapnel, sending sparks flying.

The SEALs' helicopter rose, turned, and roared away.

The chest, and the rock it contained, remained behind.

The Haqqani leader knew he had minutes, maybe just seconds, before the jets blasted the area and annihilated every living thing. He sent three of his best men at a run to seize the chest.

Sure enough, the F-16s fired their missiles and the little dell exploded in fire and smoke.

But by then the chest was in the entrance to a shallow cave, and the Haqqani battle chief was frowning down at what looked like nothing but a rock.

He had lost three men, leaving three widows and five orphans. And it began to occur to him that if this really was just a rock, he was going to have some explaining to do.

CHAPTER 7
An Unhappy Guinea Pig

THERE WAS A quick stop at Dekka's apartment to grab a few things and her black-and-white cat, Edith Windsor ("E" for short). With the FBI man Carlson watching, Dekka threw a few shirts, some underwear, and socks into a duffel bag. The cat went into a plastic cat carrier.

"Anything else?" Carlson asked.

Dekka stood in the center of her living room. The tiny kitchen was separated only by a counter. The bedroom door stood open and Dekka wondered if she should make the bed before leaving. There was a sense of permanence about this departure, not necessarily as if she'd never see the apartment again, but rather as if this were the closing scene of the last four years of her life.

Only now did Dekka see that those last four years had been a dream, unreal, somehow. The FAYZ was *real*. This life, this depressing apartment, her crappy job, the stack of unpayable bills on the coffee table, her barely there social life with her dull friends, her nearly nonexistent love life, all of it a gray, badly lit, poorly photographed home movie that no one wanted to watch, least of all her.

And what was next for her?

"Back to the FAYZ," she muttered.

"Didn't hear you, what?" Agent Carlson asked.

Dekka shook her head. "One more thing." She took her framed picture of Brianna, the one Brianna's parents had given her, wrapped it in T-shirts, and packed it away in her bag.

Dekka and her cat were sent off in a convoy of black SUVs to the south, down the 101 through the brightly lit streets of San Francisco, down the Pacific Coast Highway, past Monterey and Carmel. They left the PCH and headed east along ever-narrower roads into rugged, wooded hills, with night closing in all around. They reached a high chain-link gate with a guardhouse and three uniformed security types with machine pistols slung. Their IDs were checked, flashlights blinding Dekka as she produced her driver's license.

Once they were through the gate, the road paving was dramatically better, smooth as butter. It curved up and east, up and east until they crested a hill and Dekka saw what might have been an isolated high school or a minimum-security prison: half a dozen two-story buildings painted tan and marked with stenciled numbers. Stadium lights turned the whole place eerily bright.

"It's a Defense Department facility," Tom Peaks narrated. "They used to do research on radiation back in the fifties when it was built. It has an official designation, but everyone calls it Hidden Valley Ranch, you know, like the salad dressing. Or just the Ranch."

"It's not Defense Department anymore," Dekka said. "Those weren't military police, they were private security."

Peaks nodded and smiled, as if he was the proud teacher of a student who'd said something clever in class. "Very good. Yes, it is no longer technically DoD. It's now run by Homeland Security, specifically HSTF-Sixty-Six, a designation you may hear from time to time. But don't worry, it is all very secure and very well guarded—fences, electronic sensors, cameras. And those guards may be contract help, but they're all former MPs or other ex-military. You'll be quite safe."

And quite trapped, Dekka thought, *which was probably your point.*

The convoy parked and Peaks showed Dekka into one of the buildings, a charmless, two-story elongated rectangle that must once have been an army barracks. Building 104, according to the stenciled number.

They climbed stairs, Dekka banging her cat carrier while Peaks helpfully shouldered her bag, to reach a doorway half-way down a gloomy hallway. Inside was a small one-bedroom apartment, with a kitchenette and, oddly, a grand piano that filled a third of the main room.

"I don't play," Dekka said.

"Oh, that. Yes, we had a Romanian gentleman staying here, a concert pianist. You're welcome to tinkle away, you have no immediate neighbors."

"Swell." Dekka set Edith Windsor down and turned to Peaks, anxious to get rid of him and use the bathroom. "Food?"

"You'll find everything you need," Peaks said. "Get a good night's sleep. I'll send someone for you at seven a.m."

"The hell you will. I'll go at nine a.m., and that's my best offer."

Peaks smiled and nodded. "Fair enough." He left, pulling the door behind him.

Dekka stood in the silent room, so like a bargain hotel, she thought, one of those places with the word "suites" in the name. She tested the door: it was not locked, which was reassuring. She raised the blinds and looked out on a view of bulky air-conditioning units and a bit of parking lot, which frankly was no worse than her own apartment's view of a Dumpster and part of a smaller, dimmer parking lot.

In the cupboards they'd stocked E's favorite cat food, along with snack foods that were suspiciously familiar. They were making no effort to hide the fact that they had spied on her and entered her apartment to gather information. They even had the Peet's Sumatra coffee Dekka liked but usually could not afford.

There was a small but new refrigerator with milk, sliced honeydew melon, sliced cheddar cheese, Genoa salami, Sierra Nevada Pale Ale . . . *My God*, Dekka thought, *they've even stocked the freezer with Ben and Jerry's Half Baked.* It was as if they'd moved her own refrigerator to this new place, minus the spilled maraschino cherry juice and the withered carrots.

Dekka fed E, who stared balefully at the food, then stalked off to find . . . yes, there was a cat box with fresh litter. Of course there was—Peaks and his people had thought of everything.

Dekka unpacked her duffel bag and regretted that she forgot to pack her favorite ratty chenille robe, but in the closet there was a brand-new version of it hanging.

"Okay, then," Dekka said. She popped open a beer and drank half of it in one long swig.

"Wi-fi?" She opened her laptop and waited while it searched for a wi-fi signal. It found one labeled "Guest—DT," which was not password-protected. She signed on with no trouble, checked a few favorite sites, and then opened her email and typed:

I am being held prisoner by DARPA.

She typed her own email address as the destination, then hit send.

She was not surprised when the email sat spinning in her "out" tray for a long while before the system gave up and suggested she try again later.

"Uh-huh. Later. Right."

She had internet access but could not email, and was fairly certain that she could not text, DM, or even leave a blog comment. She was connected but cut off, able to see but not speak. She tested her Netflix and iTunes accounts; both worked fine. Then she tested her ability to upvote a post on Reddit, and once again: nope.

Download yes, upload no.

She considered looking for the cameras they had no doubt installed in the little apartment, but this was a DARPA facility, and this apartment was obviously built to hold people under observation, so Dekka accepted the reality that she would likely never find their surveillance equipment.

Instead she pushed back from her laptop, stood in the center of the room, and said, "Fine for now. But where's the thermostat? It's hot in here. And I need to know my bike is safe."

There was no answer for a long minute. Then a voice that came from . . . well, everywhere . . . said, "Climate control is on the wall to the left of the closet. Your motorcycle is safe in the main lot with the cover on."

"Thanks, fairy godfather," Dekka said.

She showered—they had her favorite brand of shampoo, not the cheap stuff she usually bought but the nice stuff she occasionally got discounted or damaged from work. She dried with very nice towels, put on the robe—it was identical to hers except for the lack of chocolate stains and the hole she'd burned with a dropped joint.

She had another beer and considered. Normally she might talk to the cat, but not with people listening.

Not the worst situation I've ever been in. Not by a long shot.

And that thought called up a wave of memories, some still so raw after four years that she had to squeeze her eyes shut and search for safer territory.

Free rent, free beer, Netflix works . . .

But of course she knew this was not the whole of it. She

was a lab rat, she supposed, some kind of experiment. After all, DARPA was all about research, wasn't it? Supersmart scientists all beavering away looking for new and exciting ways to kill America's enemies?

I'm a lab rat. But I'm a lab rat with two pints of Half Baked.

Ten minutes later there was only one pint of Half Baked, and between the hot shower and the long drive and the stress of uncertainty—along with a degree of excitement, she had to admit—Dekka got sleepy. She took from her bag the one personal item she'd brought, propped her picture of Brianna on the nightstand, and fell asleep.

The next morning the fun began.

Dekka endured hours of psychological tests, followed by part of an afternoon of physical tests, with mounting impatience—patience had never been Dekka's thing—before finally calling an irritated stop.

"We're done," Dekka said.

"Actually," the medical tech said, "we still have—"

"And yet: we are done."

"But we—"

"Hey. Listen to me. Listen to the words coming out of my mouth." There was a voice that Dekka could access when necessary: it was her *don't screw with me* voice. It was not the voice of a nineteen-year-old young woman, it was the voice of a person who had survived hell and was impressed by absolutely no one. "We. Are. Done. So pull the damn needle out of my arm."

The tech pulled the needle out and slapped on a bandage.

"Thanks."

Tom Peaks appeared, as she suspected he would. "So, are you all finished up here?" he asked brightly.

"Can we not waste time pretending that you don't have me under surveillance every minute of the day?"

Peaks emitted a snort that might have been a laugh. "All right, let's do that."

"Good. What happens next is that you tell me what all this is about." It was not a question or a suggestion, it was her precondition for going forward.

Peaks jerked his head toward the door. "Join me for a cup of coffee?"

He led her down the stairs, down below ground level, to a long hallway that led to another long hallway—it was a corridor kind of place, the Ranch: more of it underground than above. Finally they arrived at a set of stairs that they climbed to reach a mostly depopulated cafeteria. Peaks fetched coffee and they sat at a table beside a window that opened onto an interior courtyard. There was a small knot of people in the courtyard smoking, and Dekka felt the inner tug of the reformed ex-smoker. She had smoked for almost two years after escaping the FAYZ, and quitting had not been easy. Not even a little bit.

Peaks laid his briefcase on the table, slid his laptop out, and opened it so she could see the screen. Peaks then came around the table to sit beside her. He tapped keys and a YouTube video opened.

Dekka instantly recognized the freeze-frame. "I've seen it."

"Let's watch it again." The video was poor quality, a fixed camera, obviously a surveillance camera showing the bright interior of a 7-Eleven, and they were looking down at rows of food and a cold case beyond, stocked with beer and bottled water.

And suddenly there was what looked like a girl. The girl just appeared, considering the potato chips. She was unusual in the extreme: her skin appeared to be gold, like the doomed woman in the old James Bond movie *Goldfinger.* Her hair was black, but looked less like thousands of small strands and more like a sort of flexible plastic.

The girl moved in the blink of an eye to the magazine section. She grabbed three celebrity gossip magazines and was suddenly, simply . . . gone.

"Like I said: I've seen it."

"You know who it is."

Dekka shrugged. "It looks like Taylor."

"Who is . . ."

"One of the kids from the FAYZ. She could teleport."

"And she was unaccounted for after the barrier came down," Peaks said.

He was sitting beside her, so that she had to turn to meet his steady gaze with her own. "Taylor was a malicious little gossip and troublemaker."

"Taylor *was*? Past tense?"

Dekka said, "She used to be a girl—a normal-looking girl, kind of pretty, really. She had the power of teleportation, and sometimes she was actually helpful. But toward the end, something happened that turned her into . . . into, I don't even know. Some kind of weird gold Play-Doh creature."

"Who had powers. Still has powers. Even now, even long *after* the dome came down. That video is just six months old."

"Looks like," Dekka drawled, refusing to speculate further. She'd always assumed the tape was a clever fake.

"Any idea why she didn't take food but did take magazines?"

Dekka shrugged. "She doesn't eat. Didn't eat, not after she, you know, became *that*. And she always was a superficial little ninny, so gossip rags would be about right."

To Dekka's relief, Peaks didn't press it further: she'd been avoiding thinking about it, preferring to believe it was all some fake. Her relief was short-lived.

"Now," Peaks said, "I want to show you something you have not seen on YouTube, because we've got the only copy." He tapped the keyboard and a window with the logo of the NSA—the National Security Agency—came up. More tapping, a password. And then, a view window.

It was an aerial shot and looked like it had been taken from hundreds of feet above. "Drone?" Dekka asked. Peaks did not answer. And then something came into view. A person. Dekka saw the top of his head, his shoulders, the tips of his toes as he walked. Then . . .

"Jesus!" Dekka was on her feet, her chair knocked over, her whole body electric, tingling.

"It's a bit hard to make out," Peaks said laconically, playing it cool. "You can see much better in slow motion." He pointed the mouse and the video advanced more slowly.

And there it was.

There it was: the ten-foot-long tentacle that snapped like a bullwhip, and snatched up what may have been a rat or a frog.

Dekka stared and breathed hard. Speech was impossible. Her attitude of cool indifference was gone. Her eyes blazed.

"I think we both know who that is," Peaks said with sincere sympathy.

"Drake." Dekka's voice was flat. She could barely breathe.

"Drake Merwin." Peaks nodded. "A violent, sadistic psychopath. A rapist. A torturer. A murderer."

"All that," Dekka snarled, transfixed by the freeze-frame Peaks had left on-screen.

Drake!

Brianna had chopped him into bits, and yet he lived.

Sam Temple had watched him burn to ashes, and yet he lived.

Peaks closed the laptop. "More coffee?"

"You have beer?" Dekka rasped, and her trembling hand twitched toward the cigarettes she no longer carried.

An aide appeared out of nowhere and Peaks sent him off to return moments later with two bottles of Sierra Nevada—apparently the official beer of the Ranch—and two glasses.

"I'm sure you can see why we are concerned," Peaks said, pouring the foamy liquid for both of them.

"He's a monster. I mean that." She stabbed a finger down on the tabletop for emphasis. "A monster in body and mind."

"Yes," Peaks agreed. "But that's not why we are worried.

The problem both Taylor and Drake represent is this: they have somehow retained the powers they had in the PBA, the FAYZ if you prefer, while people like you have not. We think we know why."

"Okay. Why?"

"Both of them not only acquired powers, but somehow they've kept them. Kept them four years after the PBA came down."

"Looks like," Dekka said, clipped, tense, waiting.

"They, unlike you, Dekka, were *physically altered*. They were *physically* changed. Only Drake, Taylor, and Charles Merriman—Orc—were altered physically. Orc died, and we've seen no sign of him. But something about that difference, the physical change, means Drake and Taylor still have their powers outside the PBA."

"You need to find him, then dig a deep hole and throw him in. Throw a nuke in after him. You don't know what you're dealing with."

"Actually, we do. That video was taken quite by accident from a military drone on a training run in the Joshua Tree National Park. Out in the desert. And when we ran a search we turned up eighteen instances of rape, mutilation, and murder in the area over the last four years. It's all being blamed on illegals coming up from the border, of course, the convenient scapegoats, but it was him. People coming across the border don't carry bullwhips. They don't spend hours flaying victims alive, then leaving them to burn in the hot sun."

Dekka felt her stomach turn, felt her heart pounding,

felt . . . *fear*. Fear like she had not felt in years. "You have to warn Astrid. He hated—*hates*—her."

"Ms. Ellison is watched twenty-four hours a day. We have armed personnel—"

"You don't know what he is," Dekka said, her voice rising. "You don't know. You do not *know*!"

"Please, sit down," Peaks urged.

Dekka sat and swallowed her beer in a single, long gulp.

"Here's the thing, Dekka. It's been kept very secret, but pieces of the same space body that created the PBA, the same mutagenic asteroid, are arriving on Earth. The first three pieces, ASO-Two, -Three, and -Four, have already come down. Now, we are doing all we can to retrieve all of that . . . object . . . but it is entirely possible that some will escape, may even fall into the worst possible hands. We could have more Drakes. We could have a lot of Drakes. Dekka, we are looking at the possibility of a world inhabited by dozens, or hundreds, or thousands of people with extraordinary powers."

"What the hell am I supposed to do about it?" Dekka demanded. "I'm a cashier, you're the government!"

Peaks looked at her, patient, waiting for her to calm down. Dekka saw that he was waiting for her to calm down, and really wished she *could* calm down, but every hair on her body was tingling, her palms were sweating, and she was nowhere close to calm.

Drake!

But Dekka knew how to *look* calm.

She licked her lips, exhaled a long, slow breath through her barely open mouth, and said, "You need to just tell me."

"All right." Peaks leaned back, satisfied that she was listening. "You are an extraordinary person, Dekka Talent. Slightly above-average IQ, a little hot-tempered, loyal. Brave?" He made a little admiring snort. "Your record is *quite* clear on that. But the thing that we like best about you is that you are, for lack of a better, more scientific word, strong. Mentally strong. Emotionally strong." He smiled and shook his head in sincere appreciation. "Some combination of DNA and life experience . . . you are really quite extraordinary."

"Thanks. But you told me all that and it's flattering and all, but let's cut the bullshit, okay? What do you *want*?"

"Well, it's like this. We have some of the rock—what we're calling the ASO, the Anomalous Space Object. You have direct experience of possessing and using the power the ASO can convey. You are therefore very unlikely to suddenly turn into a . . . a *Drake*. So we want to test it on you."

"Test what?"

"We want to expose you to the rock. We want to see if these fragments are still capable of causing mutation. We want to see, Dekka, whether you can once again acquire *powers*."

"Can't be done, not outside the FAYZ, that's what everyone said."

"Yes, well, we suspect that everyone is wrong. I have another bit of tape to show you. Did you happen to see anything about the plane accident at LaGuardia?"

"Yeah, the one that broke up on landing?"

"The video I have isn't very good; the person shooting it

on their phone was terrified." He tapped his laptop and up came yet another video. It was narrow, with the phone held vertically. At first she could make nothing out, just what looked like airplane seats and wildly gyrating lights and arms and heads. The soundtrack was screams, cries, shouts, loud prayers: terrified humans begging for mercy.

Then the picture steadied for just a few seconds and Dekka saw a monster, a coral-tinged, huge, hulking creature with what looked like a long blade where the right hand should be and something like a lobster's claw for the left hand.

The picture slipped, more wild gesticulations, more screams, and the sound of metal screeching and jet engines suddenly louder.

The video stopped.

Dekka waited.

Peaks said, "The plane did not simply break up. It was sliced open, opened up on one end by someone armed with a blade capable of cutting through aluminum like a can opener on a can of cat food."

"That's no one I ever saw or heard about in the FAYZ," Dekka said.

"No. It's a young art student, believe it or not. We are almost certain that he traveled to Iowa and managed to take what we were calling ASO-Three. But we don't believe he was the only one. There are four distinct sets of footprints, though an effort was made to obscure them. So someone else, right here in America, may also have pieces of the meteorite. And that's not even getting into foreign locations."

Dekka had nothing to say. Her mouth was dry. Her heart felt as if it was trying to pump molasses through her veins.

"And worse, far worse is to come. Most of the ASOs are small, like the one that's been stolen but that we will soon recover. But there's one rock coming—we call it the Mother Rock—which, if it were captured by some enemy force, might be enough to build a massive mutant army. We need to understand this phenomenon, Dekka. We need to know how this happens, how it can be controlled. Sixty-one people died on that flight. Most were burned to death, which is a very bad way to die. We've done the best we can to cover up the cause, spreading all kinds of wild rumors to discredit the truthful accounts, but it's only a matter of time before people see the truth."

"So you want to test the rock, the ASO rock, on me, see if I develop powers."

Peaks leaned forward, eyes burning behind his spectacles. "In this world there are very, very few people who can be trusted with that kind of power, Dekka. Power corrupts. Power distorts. It can bring out the best in people, but it is much more likely to bring out the worst. If this rock, this ASO can create that"—he pointed at the freeze-frame of the bladed monster—"we could be on the verge of a massive change that would upset every institution of government, business, society in general. Drake. Taylor. This art student. It is our duty to stop these people."

"You want me to turn into *that*? No thanks!"

"Ah, but our young art student was able to revert, to turn

back into himself. It seems as if the power and the morph are inextricably linked. This makes it worse, you see, because people with powers can change back, disappear into the population. Dekka: they must be stopped."

"*You* stop them," Dekka said. "I've had my war."

"I know that," Peaks said. "We aren't looking for that. We aren't looking for soldiers, Dekka, we need to understand the effects of the ASO. We need to test it on you, see whether you—uniquely qualified *you*—regain your power. And then, Dekka?"

"Yeah?"

"Then we need to find a way to take that power away. Because only then can society be safe from the Drakes and the Justins."

He was very convincing, and Dekka knew she had no choice but to help. But at the same time, there was a lie buried in that nice speech. Dekka sensed it, but couldn't quite put her finger on it.

"All right," Dekka said. "You can stick more needles in me."

CHAPTER 8
Daddy Issues

"I WANT SOME."

They were in Malik's room, the day after the cemetery.
Cruz had thought Shade's house was posh, the very symbol
of upper-middle-class Evanston. But Malik's home made
Shade's look like a shack. His mother was something important at a bank in Chicago, and his father was an author of
best-selling mystery novels. (A fact that Cruz filed away for
future use: a published author might be very helpful someday
to an aspiring young writer like herself.) Their house fronted
Lake Michigan and was filled with abstract art on the walls
and African sculpture resting in lit alcoves or atop marble
stands in the spacious formal rooms.

Malik's own room was nearly the size of Cruz's entire
apartment. Cruz knew there were people who lived like this,
but she'd always somehow assumed those were TV people,
celebrities, not regular humans.

Malik had a small collection of classic electric guitars

hanging on one wall, framed posters of Jimi Hendrix, Chuck Berry, Slash, Prince, and various other presumably great guitar players who Cruz did not recognize.

They sat, the three of them, Shade in an easy chair, Cruz in a cool, hanging swing chair that made her desperately jealous, and Malik on his bed.

"Want some what?" Malik asked.

"Rock," Cruz said. "I want some of the rock."

"You know the Law of Holes, Cruz?" Malik asked. "It goes like this: when you're in a hole, stop digging."

"Mmmm," Shade said, "and why are you so sure we're in a hole?"

"Really?" Malik asked with a skeptical tone. "You think, what, you're good? All set? Shade, you committed a federal crime; you acquired a power. You think the whole government of the United States of America is just going to let that happen? Some girl can turn into some creepy, plasticky, half-flea-looking thing and outrun the speed of sound, and the government is just going to shrug and say, *Whatever*? Have you thought through what this power means, Shade?"

Shade didn't answer, just gave a little hand flourish and eye roll that meant, *You're going to tell me anyway, so go for it.*

"A person with super-speed," Malik said, reminding Cruz of WikiShade, "can go anywhere, steal literally anything: money, secrets. You could zoom into a bank and clean them out. You could go to the Louvre and take the Mona Lisa. You could run into an investment bank, harvest every password. You could do the same at the CIA or the NSA. And not to get too grim about it, but you could run right past the Secret Service and kill the president of the United States. It's better than super strength, or firing energy beams, or telekinesis, or invisibility; it's better than just about anything but teleportation or mind control."

"Teleportation," Cruz mused under her breath. She thought, but did not say, *That would be a cool power for a writer: observe anyone, anywhere, anytime.*

"The government has to stop you, Shade, they have no choice," Malik said.

"Thank God we have the brilliant Malik to tell us the obvious." It was a bit snide, even for Shade, but Malik was used to her.

"You say your house is bugged, which means they suspect you, or at least your dad, so it's only a matter of time," Malik said.

Shade shifted uncomfortably and, looking more defensive than Cruz had ever seen her, said, "It's a fait accompli."

Cruz raised her hand like she was in school. "What is 'fate accomplee'?"

"It's French," Shade and Malik said at the same time.

"It means, accomplished fact, something that's done and can't be undone," Shade said. "Like stealing ASO-Three. Like eating it. Like becoming"—she waved a hand—"whatever it is I've become. Fait accompli."

"I helped steal the rock," Cruz said. "So I'm in trouble, too. So I think I have a right to, you know . . ."

Shade shared a glance with Malik, who shook his head.

"Don't look at me, I am not interested. So far I'm just an accessory *after* the fact. And I am not interested in becoming *super* anything."

"You already have super-condescension," Shade said.

"Yeah, totally unlike you, Shade."

"That YouTube of the plane crash? That creature?" Shade said, almost plaintive. "Come on, we all know it's the ASO, that flight was coming from Iowa. Someone else already got hold of some of the rock."

"Proving what?" Malik demanded. Then he crinkled his nose. "This shirt smells. Sorry, I haven't changed since my run." He rolled off his bed, went to his closet, chose a T-shirt from among about a million, and stripped off his sweat-stained shirt with no sign of modesty.

Cruz turned a disbelieving look to Shade as if to say, *You broke up with that? Beautiful, smart, and rich is not good enough for you?*

Shade's look was a mix of amusement and perhaps a little regret, an acknowledgment that yes, Malik was a very fine specimen indeed, a sculpture to rival any in his parents' house, and smart to boot.

Cruz silently mouthed, *You are a moron.*

Shade smiled and gave Cruz the finger in a subtle, under-hand way.

"Proving," Shade said belatedly, "that there may be more out there, more like him. Like me. The government can try to put the toothpaste back in the tube, but I don't think it'll work."

Malik sighed. "Maybe. Maybe we are on the verge of a total rearranging of life, maybe Chicago is about to become Gotham and New York is going to be Metropolis. There are three types of supers, Shade: Hero, Villain, and Monster. Superman is a hero and Batman is an antihero, which is a subset of hero. Magneto or Lex Luthor are villains. Hulk and, say, the Punisher are monsters, people dangerously out of control."

"Yeah, and who stands up to Magneto?" Shade demanded. "Heroes, that's who. This character who killed the people on that plane is a bad guy. There will be others. Who stops them?"

"The government, if they aren't busy chasing you," Malik said, exasperated. "Why are you doing this, Shade?"

Shade stood up suddenly, nervous energy getting the better of her. "And what if the government becomes the villain?"

Malik leaned back and frowned.

Shade, sensing an opening, paced back and forth, glancing now at Malik, now at Cruz, like a TV lawyer making her case to the jury. "You don't think the government is going to use the rock for their own purposes? You don't think someone at the Pentagon is thinking, 'Oh, cool: Super soldiers? Super cops? Super spies'?"

Malik's silence was acknowledgment. But he rallied. "Now you're like a gun nut arguing we need guns to overthrow the government."

Shade shook her head, thinking out loud, on a roll, looking at the floor. "This is the same government that set off a nuke next to the dome, the PBA, because it was blocking the highway. I'm not saying they're evil, just saying that the temptation is there and—"

"The temptation is there partly because they need to find ways to stop people like you!" Malik insisted.

Shade talked right over him. "—I guarantee you they're looking for ways to use the ASOs. So are other governments. The ASO is one big, unpredictable weapon. We're going to have government supers and individuals like the plane guy. The world is changing, Malik. I didn't make it happen, I'm just saying since it is happening I don't want to be standing there doing nothing while . . ." She stopped suddenly, knowing she'd said too much. She switched gears. "What if there had been no Sam Temple or Dekka or Brianna to fight back against Caine and Drake and Penny? Not to mention that . . . that *creature* . . . Gaia?" Shade demanded.

Cruz did not immediately recognize the names, but she understood what Shade meant. What if only the bad people had powers?

Shade grabbed her phone and tapped something in. Waited. Then read aloud:

> "*Things fall apart; the centre cannot hold;*
> *Mere anarchy is loosed upon the world,*
> *The blood-dimmed tide is loosed, and everywhere*
> *The ceremony of innocence is drowned;*
> *The best lack all conviction, while the worst*
> *Are full of passionate intensity.*"

Malik groaned. "Yeah, I know the poem, we read it in AP English Comp."

Cruz again raised her hand, still feeling like she was in school. "I don't." Shade handed her her phone.

"The best lack all conviction," Shade said to Malik. "It's the worst who are full of passionate intensity."

Cruz read aloud the final lines:

"And what rough beast, its hour come round at last,
Slouches towards Bethlehem to be born?

"Well, that's cheerful," Cruz said.

"I saw one rough beast," Shade said. "Its name was Gaia. Now we've seen another. More are coming. The center isn't holding. Maybe I'm not the best, but I'm not the worst, either."

Malik's stony expression softened. "Of course you're not, babe. You're totally obsessed, a bit ruthless, and God knows you're manipulative, but you're also decent and basically kind. If you weren't, I wouldn't . . ."

They exchanged a look full of history, a look Cruz envied. Shade and Malik might not be dating, might argue constantly when they were together, but the first time Cruz saw Malik she had known he was still in love with Shade. And if Shade didn't quite mirror that emotion, she was at the very least fond of Malik.

"I am what I am," Shade said to him. "There's no way to change what's happened. Anyway, we were talking about Cruz." She pulled a baggie from her purse and held it up. It contained a small amount of gray powder. "I ground some more."

"You're like a drug dealer offering free samples," Malik said, but Cruz saw that his eyes followed the baggie with glittering interest.

"Cruz was there with me in Iowa," Shade said. "She has a right, if that's what she wants."

"I don't really want powers," Cruz said. "I just want . . . You know what I want." The last part came out in a low, embarrassed mutter.

"We both had bad luck in life, Cruz, me the day the dome came down, you with, well, parents who don't appreciate God's little joke."

"They have an operation that can solve that problem," Malik said. "I get that it's expensive—"

"My parents won't consent," Cruz said bitterly. "Even if I suddenly had the money. It's a whole long process, not just some quick operation. And that's if I even get to the point of being sure, which would be way easier if the whole world wasn't yelling at me. Aaarrrgh!"

"Cruz is somewhat conflicted," Shade said dryly. "Multiple-choice in a true-false world. You wouldn't understand."

"Of course I understand," Malik snapped. "It's an obvious metaphor."

"There you go, Cruz, now you see the condescending Malik. He always has to think he's the smartest person in the room."

"Riiight. Unlike you," Cruz said, but she whispered it.

Malik shook his head, but he was already accepting defeat.

"Whatever. You've got your shovel, and I know you, Shade, you'll keep digging."

"Might dig straight through to China," Shade said, trying to lighten the mood.

"The antipode of Chicago is not China, it's the Indian Ocean, about twenty-five hundred miles south of Sri Lanka." Malik, naturally, to which Shade responded with a little flourish of *ta-da* hands, inviting Cruz to witness Malik's obnoxiousness.

Cruz ignored Shade and contemplated Malik, who, sadly, was now wearing a shirt. She'd been describing herself as "gender fluid," and she was most comfortable with female pronouns, but she had resisted defining herself as the clichéd girl-trapped-in-a-boy's-body. How much of that was her own reluctance to commit, to define herself, and maybe to suffer the consequences?

Was Malik right? Or was Shade?

Or was this Cruz looking for another multiple choice in a binary world?

"Cruz?" Shade asked, sounding concerned, but Cruz did not answer. Cruz sat looking at the baggie, looking at the dust that might give her power after a life of powerlessness.

What if it makes me a monster?

It won't, she told herself. There was no monster inside her just itching to get out. She would never hurt anyone.

"Got any peanut butter?" Cruz asked abruptly. "That's how Shade took it."

"You two are crazy," Malik said. Then, with a sigh, "Is chunky okay? My little sister likes chunky, so we get chunky."

After a while Shade and Cruz left, Shade having a gyne-cologist's appointment, and Cruz now having decided to actually finish the paper she had so studiously avoided writing. She walked to the city library and studied there, eyes swimming with boredom, mind not even slightly engaged with the books before her.

Is it working?

Finally, reluctantly, she headed home, performing the ritual of defeminization as she went, torn between relief and resentment that the rock had apparently done nothing to her.

It had long bothered her, this need to disguise herself, to try to minimize the triggers that would set her father off. But now it was more than annoying, it was infuriating. Shade accepted her. Malik accepted her. Much of the world, not all, but much of it accepted her. Why couldn't her parents accept her? She was still the person she'd always been, the exact same child they loved.

Why did it matter so much? Why did people get angry at her for the crime of dressing and acting and talking the way she wished? And like a taunt of her own devising, a voice in her head repeated, like a refrain:

Shade would never be afraid.

She was halfway up the stairwell to her apartment—the stairwell reeking of pumpkin spice since the seasonal latte was back at Starbucks—when she realized she'd been stomping rather than creeping up the stairs. Cruz slowed her pace, tried to slow her breathing, pushed down on the anger that wanted so badly to explode.

She opened the door. Normal sounds—the TV, the dishwasher. She crept in, practically tiptoeing now, feeling the flicker of a simple hope that she could reach her bedroom without hassle.

But there was her father, coming straight toward her, heading for the bathroom. He did not speak, just looked at her. Cruz stepped aside.

She was hungry and wondered if this was a good opportunity to grab a snack to take to her room. The kitchen was empty, and she was just about to snag a box of Wheat Thins when her mother came in.

Her mother, too, did not look at her. In fact, it was as if Maria Rojas hadn't noticed her six-foot-two child at all. Cruz shrugged. If that's the game they wanted to play, fine. She opened the refrigerator door, looking for cream cheese, and her mother yelped.

"Aaahh!"

Maria was staring at the refrigerator, frowning, her face suspicious and wary. Maria pushed the refrigerator door shut and turned away, muttering in Spanish.

Cruz opened the refrigerator door again and this time Maria screamed. Manny Rojas came at a run, three feet of toilet paper stuck to his shoe.

"What?" he demanded.

"The door," Maria said in a gulping panic. "It open all by itself."

"What the hell are you talking about, woman?"

Something electric was climbing up Cruz's spine.

No, impossible!

She had left the box of Wheat Thins on the counter. She lifted it, making a rustling noise that instantly drew her parents' attention.

"What was that?" Manny, Cruz's father, this time.

Cruz, feeling as if she was in a dream, held the Wheat Thins directly in her father's line of sight. Nothing. No reaction.

Cruz waved her free hand before his face, peering intently at his eyes. Not a flicker. Not a movement of his iris.

He can't see me!

What had been a tingle was now a rush, a thrill that raised goose bumps on Cruz's arm. She could see the bumps, she could see her arm, she could see the Wheat Thins, she could see everything.

And they did not see her. Or anything she held.

She set the box on the counter and stepped back.

"Whee Tins!" her mother shrieked. "Look, Manny, look!"

"Okay, Wheat Thins, so what?" he demanded, getting angry at all the strangeness.

"They were no there and then they there!"

"You're crazy, woman, have you been drinking?" But he looked around himself, suspicious, worried.

Cruz retreated to the hallway. Retreated all the way to the front door. She leaned back against the wall, trying not to gulp air, trying to control the hammering in her chest.

I'm invisible!

Bugs or no bugs, she had to see Shade like *right now*. She bolted, clattering down the stairs, stopped on the street outside, wanting further proof. There was a ponytailed mom leaning over her baby in a stroller. Cruz put her hand directly between mother and child and . . . nothing!

Oh. My. God!

She ran toward Shade's house, just a block away, but as she ran she had the unsettling sensation of being observed. She glanced around: no one. She peered at the nearest windows: no one was staring at her.

But still she felt it, the feeling of being watched. And more than just watched. There was a feeling of malice, a feeling that someone was not only watching her but secretly laughing at her.

She shook it off, knocked on Shade's door, and, when it opened, pulled Shade out onto the rear deck and whispered, "Can you see me?"

"I haven't gone blind, Cruz."

"I was invisible! I guess I stopped being, um . . . but I was absolutely invisible!"

"Are we talking metaphorically?"

Cruz shook her head. Then she focused the swirl of wild emotion inside her and . . .

"Whoa!" Shade said.

"You can't see me now, can you?"

"Okay, that is amazing. Get inside! Now, before someone sees . . . or doesn't see you."

They moved immediately to Shade's bathroom and turned on the water for the benefit of any microphones.

Cruz flickered back into view.

"How did it feel?" Shade asked, and Cruz knew there was something specific behind that bland question.

"Fine. Normal," Cruz said. "Except . . ."

"Except?"

"I had this feeling . . . Probably just paranoid."

Shade drew breath and exhaled slowly. "Like something was watching you?"

Cruz nodded slowly.

"Something you can't see, something you can only feel. Something dark and . . . and, well, not necessarily nice?"

"Yes," Cruz said. It came out in a low hiss.

"Right," Shade said, as if she was ticking off a checklist. She shook her head, silently arguing with herself. "It's probably just paranoia caused by the weirdness of the morph."

Cruz was willing to accept that. Wanted to accept it. It made logical sense. But did it feel true?

No.

But Cruz told herself she'd worry about that another time, because really what was exploding inside her mind was the fact that she had . . . *the power of invisibility.*

"Let's go somewhere and test this out," Shade said. "Come on, I have to tell my dad we're going out. He's home, so wipe the insane grin off your face."

They headed downstairs and into the living room to say a quick, polite hello to Martin Darby.

And that was when the front-facing windows of the house lit up in flashing blue and red.

CHAPTER 9
On the Run

BLUE AND RED lights flashed against the curtains and the frosted glass of the front door, and instantly Shade *knew*. She knew what this was, knew what it meant, and knew that a huge gaping pit had opened up beneath her. Her stomach churned, her jaw clenched, her heart beat heavy and slow.

There was the sound of *people* knocking on a door, and then there was the sound of *police* knocking on a door. The one said, "Are you home?" The other said, "Open the door! *NOW!*"

Shade and Cruz rushed to the door and arrived in time to see Martin Darby turn the doorknob. He opened the door and all hell broke loose.

"Back, back, back away!"

"You, against the wall!"

Half a dozen men in helmets and black tactical gear, each armed with an automatic weapon, rushed in. One threw Shade's father to the ground, and another shoved the muzzle of his gun in Cruz's face and backed her against the wall, then roughly grabbed Shade's shoulder and slung her beside Cruz.

There was a great deal of yelling.

"Do not move!"

"Who else is in the house?"

A bespectacled man who looked like he should be working at the DMV squatted beside Martin and shoved a piece of paper in his face. "Homeland Security. We are serving a search warrant."

"What the hell?" Martin yelled into his own Oriental rug.

Through the open door Shade saw a veritable Christmas tree of police lights, a big black SWAT van, black SUVs, regular Evanston cops, even an ambulance. More men and women poured into the house; they were in white coveralls, crime scene people, technicians.

Shade sent Cruz a significant look: yes, this is about the rock. And yes, professional searchers would absolutely find it in the heat register where Shade had stashed it.

"Get him up," the bespectacled man said, indicating Professor Darby.

Two SWAT guys grabbed Martin's arms and stood him up, keeping their hands on him like he was some kind of criminal. Anger and guilt competed within Shade's mind. There was something simply infuriating in seeing her father treated this way.

My fault.

"My name is Tom Peaks, I'm with Homeland Security and DARPA. Let's get right to it, Professor Darby: turn over the rock. Do it now, do it painlessly, and maybe we can—"

"What the hell are you talking about?" Martin tried to shake off the SWAT guys, but it was like trying to shake off a pair of pit bulls.

"Professor, this can be easy and quickly over, or it can be traumatic as we tear your house apart," Peaks said. "I just flew in from the West Coast and I'm tired, so let's go down the easy path, what do you say?"

"What I say is I don't have the first clue where the ASO is. As I've been telling my direct supervisor at the task force, Dr. Redeagle—"

"Yes, I know what you've been telling HSTF-Sixty-Six, I read all the reports. I *run* HSTF-Sixty-Six, Professor Darby, and whether you know it or not, you work for me." Peaks let that sink in, then motioned to the SWAT guys to release their grip on Martin.

Martin climbed to his feet. "Leave my daughter and her friend alone," he demanded with all his professorial authority.

"No one is bothering them," Peaks said, and then, noticing that there was still a gun in Cruz's face, said, "I don't think we need that." He put a hand on the gun barrel and pushed it away. "Listen to me, Professor Darby, it is unarguable that you altered your calculations so as to mislead the search team. No one else could have done it."

Shade's face was carefully blank. Cruz took her cue from Shade and stared at the air.

"Anyone might have hacked our network. It's not my fault

if your security is inadequate." After the initial shock, Martin had accessed his inner professor and was now bristling with offended dignity.

From the rest of the house came shouts of "Clear!" as SWAT members moved from room to room on the ground floor and upstairs. The search for the rock would begin in minutes and with experienced searchers it wouldn't take long.

"Oh, man," Shade said in a long, unhappy exhalation. "I am so sorry, Dad. So, so, so very sorry."

Peaks ignored her. Cruz did not. Her eyes went wide.

"Leave him alone. It wasn't my father who changed the numbers," Shade said in an abashed but not exactly humble tone. "It was me."

Peaks's head jerked. His eyes widened in amazement because now he was seeing Shade change . . . change . . . *changed*, all in a matter of seconds. He started to yell but Shade was no longer there. She raced into the kitchen, yanked a twelve-inch chef's knife from the block, zoomed through the front door and out to the street, slashed like a crazed killer, and returned, vibrating to a stop.

The sight of her caused a nearly comic recoil from everyone, including Martin.

"Listen. I'm sorry." She had to drawl at what to her was a comically slow speed, but still she suspected she was hard to understand. "But I. Just cut. The tires. On all. Your vehicles."

"You? You . . . what?" Peaks sputtered. He reached for his phone, fumbled, frowned, and slowly realized Shade was holding it.

"Here! On me!" Peaks roared, and instantly came the rushing tramp of feet. Two more SWAT members came pelting down the stairs, their weapons leveled.

And then their weapons were no longer in their hands and Shade had both guns slung over her shoulder.

It really was absurdly easy. She could have done far more, far worse.

Power!

"Shoot her! Take her out!" Peaks yelled, and more SWAT members converged, all yelling, "Down down down!" at Martin and Cruz, trying to get a clear shot, and Martin yelling, "No!"

But again, Shade was no longer there, and their weapons were no longer in their hands, but lay in a heap on the parlor couch.

"That's. Not. Going. To work. Mr. Peaks," Shade said, coming to a stop.

Martin was staring at his daughter dumbfounded— staring at a version of his daughter at least. To a father's eyes she would have been at least somewhat recognizable, but he must have had doubts.

"Sorry. Dad," Shade said. "Cruz? Go to. The car."

Shade knew this was a moment of truth for Cruz. Cruz had just achieved at least some of what she had hoped for, maybe, and now Shade would have them on the run—on the run from the United States government, no less.

Shade had plenty of time to contemplate the fact that she would have to admit to Malik that he was right. At least somewhat right. But maybe not all the way right, because right now, if Peaks or his gunmen made a move against her father, she could stop them. She was the power here, not Gaia.

Not *Peaks*, she corrected herself.

It could all end . . . might well end . . . in prison bars or gunfire, Shade knew. Cruz knew that, too. The emotions played across Cruz's face in slow motion. It was suddenly becoming shatteringly clear to Cruz that her life was no longer her own: she was with Shade, bound to her, unable to escape the results of what they had done. She was a criminal, just as much as Shade. And Shade could see the realization dawn on her friend's face, the fear, the excitement . . . and the resentment that Shade expected would grow over time.

They could put her in prison, in a box, treat her like . . .

No time for regrets, no time for guilt, Shade told herself sternly. That was all just emotion, feeling; what mattered now, *right now*, was winning this confrontation. Later she'd find a way to . . .

. . . to what, Shade? To what? Undo the damage? How are you going to do that, Shade Darby?

"Cruz," Shade said with steely insistence, out of sync, not really sure if it was taking Cruz forever to move or if that was just the way the world was when you were hyper-accelerated. "Go!"

Cruz spun on her heel and ran for the car. It was a madhouse on Hinman Avenue, flashing lights and rushing cops, all staring and pointing at the slashed tires of their vehicles, all with guns drawn now.

Half a dozen of them spotted Cruz, leveled weapons, and

shouted, "Freeze! Freeze!" Cruz froze and then the guns and the eyes behind them wavered, perplexed.

Cruz had become invisible.

Good girl, Shade thought.

Cruz ran on, around the side of the house, slipping on wet leaves, and tumbled into the minivan's passenger seat.

Shade was already there, waiting.

"Oh, my God, Shade! Oh, my God!"

Shade made a buzzing sound, then carefully slowed her speech and said, "What. Took you. So long?"

Shade drove, not as Shade, but as this new creature, this sleek, plasticine avatar of Shade, with her creepy insectoid legs bent awkwardly sideways to fit beneath the wheel. The minivan speedometer passed sixty before they'd blown past Starbucks. It hit eighty within a block, ninety, then a hundred miles an hour, with the Subaru careening through traffic that looked to Shade as if it had come to a stop.

It was all scarier for Cruz, who saw cars weaving and heard the horns blowing and noted the occasional one-finger salute being raised by outraged commuters.

"It. Will. Be okay," Shade lied in slow motion.

Right side of the road, left side of the road, the sidewalk, Shade sent the Subaru screaming west down Dempster. Cruz took a dream-slow look in the rearview mirror and in a syrupy slo-mo voice said, "N-n-o-o-o-o-o c-o-o-o-p-s."

But it was not the police that Shade felt watching her, following her. Eyeless eyes and soundless laughter, enjoyment, malice, dark and greedy obsession, the things she had dismissed as "paranoia," were back.

Far away and yet right here, right inside my skull.

"Text Malik," Shade said, and now both her voice and the car were slowing down. She was de-morphing, becoming fully human. She could not bear that vile, insinuating scrutiny for long.

"What do I say?"

"Text him to meet us at the mall. Tell him to hurry and bring tools and wire."

"Tools and wire?"

"They'll put out a BOLO for us," Shade said.

"A what?"

"Be on the lookout. BOLO. We need a different car."

Cruz did not look happy. Shade turned her gaze away. Later she could deal with what she'd done to Cruz. Later she could deal with what she'd done to her father.

The Westfield Mall was just a few miles to their north and they drove there, carefully obeying the speed limits, and at last, trembling, pulled into a parking spot.

"Jesus, Shade," Cruz said. She sounded awed, and not in a good way. But Shade did not want to talk, not now, not yet. The dark watchers were gone but the memory of them persisted. It was a dirty feeling, a feeling of being used, like she'd just found a Peeping Tom watching her undress. It was too intimate, that strange attention, too sure of itself.

Malik pulled up in his little BMW two-seater. They rolled windows down and talked across the few feet separating them.

"What is it?" Malik asked.

"All hell just broke loose!" Cruz said.

"Which kind of hell?" Malik asked, as calmly as if he were asking their favorite type of pie.

"The FBI-kicking-in-the-doors kind of hell," Shade said tersely.

"Gee, Shade," Malik said, "I don't think your clever plan is working out real well."

"You going to snark or help, Malik?" Shade snapped.

Malik cursed under his breath and pulled his car into an open spot. He climbed in behind Cruz and said, "We need something no one will notice, something common. Cruz? Find something on YouTube on hot-wiring cars."

The simple act of finding the right vehicle proved ridiculously hard to do, because the YouTube video explained that new cars were a whole lot harder to hot-wire, so they narrowed the search to old cars, the Subaru prowling up and down the aisles.

"Wait a minute," Malik said, snapping his fingers. "We don't need to hot-wire, not with your *ability*, Shade."

They saw a Mercedes SUV just pulling into a spot.

"Excuse me," Shade said, and began the swift transformation—swifter, easier each time—and then was gone in a blast of wind and a door slammed way too hard. Cruz and Malik caught a brief glimpse of her as she raced up behind the woman driver, who was extricating a toddler from a car seat. Shade dipped into the woman's purse and took her key chain in less time than it took the woman to blink.

Malik hopped into the driver's seat. "I got this, switch the plates."

The Mercedes plates came off and were swapped for the

plates of an Acura three rows over. Cruz got in the back, Shade climbed awkwardly into the front passenger seat, in the middle of resuming her normal appearance, and they drove off.

"We just stole a car," Cruz said. Her normally olive face was unnaturally white, tinged with green.

"The least of our problems," Shade said.

"Yeah," Malik said, "this will go really well when I explain to some cop that it wasn't the fault of the young black male, it's the fault of the white girl. She's the car thief, Officer, why are you pointing a gun at me?"

"Oh, my God, where do we go?" Cruz wondered.

Malik said, "I have a place we can go. At least for as long as it takes the cops to connect me to all this. My cousin has a place."

Shade leaned forward and put a hand on his shoulder. "Sorry, Malik."

"Right," he said.

"Pop the SIM card out of your phone, Cruz," Shade instructed, as she did the same. "Throw it out of the window."

"The rock!" Cruz said. "We left the rock!"

"Nah," Shade said, and produced the object from her bag. "I had plenty of time to grab it."

CHAPTER 10
Turning White to Red

HE WAS HAVING the most lovely dreams.

Armo lay in a drug-induced dream state. He was, despite being in a dream, aware that he was bound at wrists and ankles and lying on a steel gurney. He was aware, in that vague, amused sort of way that the drugs allowed, that he was a prisoner. That he was being used. That he was surrounded by machines with bright LED lights and various people in white smocks with masks over their mouths.

It was an odd thing about Armo: ever since he was very young he'd had the ability to lucid dream. A former girlfriend had been the first to explain that this wasn't normal, and so he had looked it up, and sure enough most people lucid dreamed only on rare occasions. It seemed that back in ancient times it was more common, and part of what made some people think they had the gift of prophecy.

But Armo was pretty sure this dream wasn't the sort of thing prophets saw, because this dream was, to put it bluntly, the sexiest dream he'd ever had.

Armo was a D-plus student, but he was not an idiot. He knew the dream wasn't his—that it was coming from elsewhere.

In the dream there was a Yoda-like figure—not in the sense of being a small green troll, but rather someone meant to seem wise. Someone you definitely wanted to obey. And that person and the person who sometimes stroked his face as he dreamed were almost certainly the same person. The same woman. The woman in green with a heavy brass ring with raised letters around a red stone.

The woman with the steely southern accent.

The dream version of the person kept whispering that if he obeyed her in all things, he would have all his heart's desires. It was she, the dream woman, who sent him out to battle demons and trolls and mutants, all to save gorgeous women and be rewarded with the most astonishing sexual favors.

This, the dream woman said, this is your future when you obey me. You will be a hero! A warrior! And you will have many, many women!

When you *obey*!

It certainly sounded good to Armo's hallucinating consciousness. All except one part: that whole "obey" thing.

Even lucid-dreaming Armo didn't like that word. It was instinctive, automatic. Since childhood, when Armo heard the word "obey" or a phrase like "just do what you're told," these things happened: his lips would thin into a horizontal line that curled just slightly up on the right side; his jaw muscles would flex and his nostrils flare; he would fill his lungs; his heart would slow; and there would come slight, almost unnoticeable movements of shoulders and hands, a shifting of weight, and his gaze would narrow to a tunnel.

Like the school counselor and two psychologists had said: Oppositional Defiant Disorder. Armo knew the term, and he had never disputed it. Armo didn't see himself as a bad person, not even a rude or unkind person. He didn't use his size to beat people up or bully anyone. He loved dogs and anything with fur. He was, in his own estimation, a decent dude.

He just didn't like doing what he was told. In fact, anytime Armo did something bad, it was almost always because someone had ordered him *not* to.

Of course, none of the physical manifestations of Armo's disorder occurred at this moment, because Armo was drugged out of his mind and practically paralyzed. And yet the woman, the real-world woman, evidently sensed something . . . off . . . about him. He could tell.

From a million miles away, Armo heard her say, "Doctor, are you sure the conditioning is effective?"

Armo did not hear the answer, just the unease in the woman's voice.

Yeah, dream lady, you feel it, don't you?

He slept for a while then, probably a long while, deep, deep sleep, and this time with no dreams, lucid or otherwise.

When he woke again, he was alone on a cot. He blinked. He took silent inventory: hands, legs, shoulders, all seemed to be working. Eyes left: a steel wall. Eyes right: a small cell with a desk bolted to the floor, and a steel toilet and sink combo thing.

Am I in jail?

He sat up and had to fight the urge to throw up as a wave of drug after-effect nausea passed through him, followed swiftly by a crashing headache.

He now saw that he was naked, and he felt a bit chilly, not to mention a bit exposed. He sat there a while, blinking uncomprehendingly at a transparent wall, at what appeared to be a single sheet of obviously very thick glass. He had the impression of large, open spaces beyond, but it was gloomily lit and the glass distorted everything. Had to be a distortion, because otherwise he was looking out at a sort of prison, or zoo, with murky figures in similar cells.

And that couldn't possibly be real. Could it?

There was an itch on the back of his neck. He reached to scratch it, and his fingers touched something small, cool, and metallic. The flesh around it was puffy and swollen, tender to the touch. Despite the headache, despite the nausea, despite his utter bewilderment at his location or condition, where he was, why he was there, what was going on . . . he was sure the cold object on the back of his neck was some type of control device.

His mouth pressed into a flat line, slightly curled up on the right; his nose flared; his—

And then, there she was, again: the woman. The one who stroked his face when she thought he was unconscious and called him her "perfect warrior." She tapped a keypad beside his cell door and he heard her speak in the voice of the woman from the dream.

"Good morning, Armo. I'm Colonel DiMarco. I am your direct superior. From this point forward you will obey me, and follow my orders to the letter."

"Cold in here," he said.

"It won't be for long." A slight smile there. A confident, even cocky smirk.

There's ODD, and then there's stupid—Armo tried not be stupid, so he said, "Yes, ma'am," and looked down for a moment, signaling submission and concealing from her the defiance in his eyes.

"Good. Now, we're going to do a small experiment. You will feel some . . . what do they say? Discomfort? But through it all you will obey the sound of my voice."

There was a second person, a man, standing a little back, his face hard to see through the thick glass. And farther back still, ghostly figures in white lab coats.

"Yes, ma'am," he said.

The dream/real woman smiled and said, "Let's go with 'Colonel,' shall we? Say 'Yes, Colonel.'"

Armo thought, *You are piling up trouble for yourself, lady.* But he said, "Yes, Colonel."

Colonel DiMarco said over her shoulder, "Proceed."

And half a second later Armo's head exploded. The pain was staggering, literally staggering, and he dropped to his knees and tried to claw at the device on his neck. But his fingers had gone strange and clumsy.

Pain off.

He gasped. Sucked air. The pain was gone but still echoed through him.

But something else was happening, something very, very odd. He held his hand in front of his face. It was his hand, but bigger, with short, stubby fingers now ending in wickedly curved claws that even as he watched seemed to change from something brown and biological to something artificial and metallic.

Impossible!

He watched transfixed, horrified, trying to tell himself it was all just some kind of weird nightmare, but if it was a dream it was very convincing—as convincing as the translucent white hairs that suddenly sprouted from the back of his hands and ran like a tsunami up his arms.

"The polar bear DNA infusion is working," DiMarco said excitedly. "Controlled mutation! I told you it could be done!"

"But to what end?" the barely visible male asked, sounding skeptical and a bit defensive. "He has impressive claws and musculature, but does he have any powers? The kind of powers we can use effectively and control?"

"We shall see," DiMarco said, sounding smug to Armo, though he was rather distracted by the changes in his body, the claws, the muscles, perhaps a slight increase in height, and a definite increase in weight.

They're doing this to me!

It was no longer cold in his cell. He glanced at the toilet on the wall: there was a thin coat of ice on the water in the bowl, and steam came with each exhalation, and yet he did not feel cold.

DiMarco's distorted voice came through the speaker. "Now we're going to see what you can do."

He rumbled an answer. The rumble surprised him, like a dangerous purr down deep in his throat.

"Armo: you will raise your left hand."

A pause. A long pause.

And up went his right hand, claws and fur and all. Then he lowered it.

"No, your left hand. The other one."

Armo slowly raised his right hand.

"No," DiMarco snapped. "The other hand. Your left hand! Jesus, is he dyslexic?"

Armo lowered his hand and stuck out one foot. Balance was hard, but he had extraordinarily strong muscles in his legs and maintained the pose for several seconds.

"There appears to be a problem with his conditioning," the male voice said nervously.

"Just . . . it's his first morphing, he'll get it. Armo! Listen to me!"

Armo's lips were somewhat hampered by teeth that were far larger than he was used to, so he could not press his lips into a line. And his eyesight was blurrier than usual. But he could still flare his nostrils and begin the minute adjustments that prepared his body—well, *this* body—for action.

"You will sit on the cot. That is an order and you must obey me!" She held up her hand, pressed the red-stoned ring close to the glass, and he felt a strange yearning to listen, to do what she wanted him to do, because if he did he'd be a hero, and he'd have many women, and be loved and admired and . . .

. . . *and no longer be Aristotle Adamo who calls himself Armo.*

"Do it!"

That yearning to obey, to get his reward, was strong, but it was nothing next to his instinctive, compulsive, irrational need to say . . .

"NO!"

It came out as a strangled, half-coherent roar, and Armo the defiant was suddenly filled with more blind rage than he had ever known before.

He hurled himself at the glass.

Wham!

Again.

Wham!

Again.

Wham!

And then whatever slight self-control Armo had was swept away on a torrent of madness. Rage filled him. He could feel it, he could feel the adrenaline, he could feel an animal fury that took control of him. Armo became almost a bystander, as if watching from a distance as the body that was not quite his went completely, utterly, *berserk.*

For a full three minutes Armo ripped and tore and pummeled everything around him. He shredded the cot. He beat the toilet and sink away from the wall, water spraying in a jet. He lifted the twisted steel toilet and bashed it against the glass again and again and again with a violence unlike anything he'd ever imagined, wilder than anything from the DiMarco-induced dreams.

DiMarco backed away from the glass, her face a snarl to match his own, but she was small and weak and he . . . he was power and violence made flesh. He was insanity! He was all the manic fury in the world distilled down into one white-furred, two-legged, canine teeth–baring, roaring, mindless engine of destruction.

The control device, still in his neck, stabbed him deep, like needles in his brain, but the pain was just gasoline sprayed on an open flame. He reached clumsy paws around, dug one great claw into his own flesh, and with a beastly roar ripped the module out and threw the bloody thing at the glass.

"Gas! Gas!" DiMarco's voice cried.

Armo heard the hiss of the gas and even in some distant way knew what it was. But the beast he'd become was all out of damns to give. He raged and hammered and roared, but slowly, slowly he weakened, limbs growing heavy, already-dim eyesight dimming further. But by then his fur was no longer white but red with his own blood. His blood smeared the walls and the glass, which was cracked and starred though unbroken.

"I'll kill you! I'll kill you! I'll . . . kill . . ."

He weakened . . . settled onto his rear end . . . felt a very different gaze on him, watchers without eyes, laughers without mouths, many and one, and somehow both far away and right here.

His last roar was for them, for those silent voices. "And I'll . . . I'll . . . kill you, too."

ASO-5

THE *OKEANOS EXPLORER* had begun its life as a US Navy surveillance ship by the name of *Capable*. It was now a National Oceanic and Atmospheric Administration research vessel, 224 feet long, 43 feet wide, with a complement of forty-six crew, officers, and scientists.

It was overly full at the moment because in addition to the crew and the scientists, a detail of six contractors had been added for security. These were ex-Delta and ex-Marines whose job was to keep an eye on the crew and the scientists as they retrieved ASO-5: the Mother Rock.

The *Okeanos* also had one supernumerary with no assigned duties: the chief engineer's fifteen-year-old son, Vincent Vu.

Vincent was third-generation Vietnamese-American, born in San Jose, California, raised by both parents in a stable, kind, pleasant home. Vincent was a good student. Vincent was a good big brother to his two little sisters. But Vincent had been trouble since he hit puberty, and his teachers and, later, his family recognized that something had gone wrong with him.

The doctors said it was bipolar disorder. They were correct, but their diagnosis had been incomplete because Vincent had not told them everything. He had not told them, for instance, about the voices. The voices had warned him not to divulge their presence, because then the doctors would say that Vincent was schizophrenic.

Vincent had access to Wikipedia and WebMD and all the rest, so he knew what schizophrenia meant. Bipolar was a serious stuff, a major mood disorder. Schizophrenia, well, that was to bipolar disorder what pancreatic cancer was to high blood pressure: orders of magnitude worse.

Or *better*, the voices suggested. Without us, the voices whispered, you'd never even know that your mother was only a hologram. And you might not know that you are destined for greatness, that you are not a normal human, that you are born of the pit.

That your true name is *Abaddon*.

He had Googled that name, Abaddon. It seemed he was one of Satan's angels, said to sit upon a throne of maggots.

The doctors had meds for his bipolar disorder, which Vincent hated taking because they left him feeling logey, droopy, fuzzy. And frankly, he enjoyed the manic periods and had no desire to give them up. It was during the manias that he set out with a camera bag over his shoulder and obsessively photographed shapes and juxtapositions, unfinished high-rise construction, crushed vehicles at a junkyard, abandoned factories, outdated computers—anything that was hard angles and devoid of humans.

Unfortunately, Vincent didn't always avoid human subjects. A camera traced back to Vincent had been found in the girls' locker room at school, and Vincent had been expelled.

As was so often the case, Vincent's timing was bad. His father was a career diplomat on a mission to Hanoi. His mother was chief engineer on the *Okeanos* and had been told the ship would be setting out immediately on a secret mission. No one thought Vincent's only surviving grandmother could handle him.

The *Okeanos* had been in such a hurry that its chief engineer, Vincent's mother, had to join the ship by helicopter when it was already twenty miles out to sea. Janet Vu, having no other choice, had brought Vincent along, thinking that maybe a sea voyage would do him good, clear his mind. It wasn't exactly normal to bring family members, but still, the unexpected arrival of the slight young man with the overly focused gaze and the odd habit of laughing at jokes no one else heard would have excited no great concern had this been an ordinary scientific mission. But Vincent—and only Vincent—had not been screened by security.

Still, what could be done? The ship needed Janet Vu and she came with Vincent. Anyway, in his more normal periods Vincent was a smart, curious, pleasant kid. He was a little guy, so thin you could hardly see him in profile. And within a couple of days at sea no one really noticed him rushing around with his cameras, clicking away at coils of rope and masts and the big radar "golf ball" above and behind the bridge. He was especially fascinated by the deep-sea submersibles, and the mantis-like crane and the very large lead-lined shipping container, the mysterious box, that had been chained to the deck just behind the mainmast. The box was interesting to Vincent only in that no one aboard was supposed to know its purpose.

Naturally within hours of sailing, everyone knew the box's purpose, or at least its purported purpose. Vincent knew from the schizophrenic voices in his head that it was all a lie and that the box was there to contain mermaids who were to be captured and taken to SeaWorld.

ASO-5 came down in the Pacific hundreds miles from shore. It created a terrific splash and rocked the *Okeanos* on the ripples. The ROVs—Remotely Operated Vehicles—aided by powerful underwater search radars on a Navy antisubmarine ship, tracked its long, long tumble to the ocean floor. And even as the dust cloud was settling, they located the Mother Rock.

Getting it aboard was a whole different problem involving both of the ROVs, a steel mesh net, and, as it rose to tolerable depths, divers with underwater drills and cables.

The rock was carefully, slowly, painstakingly brought aboard, straining the crane, smashing one man's foot, and finally shut into the box. The hinged top was locked down with six high-strength padlocks, and the access door was secured by a combination lock known to no one but the captain and the chief of the security detail.

And Vincent Vu, who had unobtrusively shot video of the captain tapping in the combination.

Meanwhile, in Scotland

SEAN MACBETH, FOUR years old, was hungry, and he was teething.

Sean had a method of dealing with the teething—he sucked on a chip of ASO-2. It was not soft and gummy like his binky—which in any event he'd dropped behind the sofa—or his favorite board book, which he chewed more often than he read—but it was still strangely satisfying. When your gums ached and itched, it was nice to have something hard to bite down on.

Sean's hunger was a consequence of his big sister, Delia, having been caught up in some texting drama involving Mary and Dougal and Iain. (Mary liked Dougal but Dougal liked Fiona, even though everyone knew Fiona was only toying with him. Iain was such a nice boy, but maybe too immature for Mary.)

Anyway, Delia had forgotten her mother's careful instructions about feeding Sean, and now Sean was hungry, teething and . . . oops, he had just pooped himself, which was satisfying at first, but began to irritate Sean after a while.

Sean got angry.

He got very angry.

His face turned red. Tears started from his eyes. He drew a deep breath and let loose with a screech that could wake the dead, but that did not distract his sister from her texting.

Having literally no idea where food came from—except that the kitchen was involved—Sean got angrier and angrier.

And then, Sean began to change.

His pudgy pink body grew larger, as large as the family's retired sheepdog, Gromit, who watched, puzzled, barked once, and ran for the door.

Sean grew larger and longer, especially longer. Twenty feet long. Twenty feet long and consisting of a series of translucent green segments. Tiny triangular feet sprouted from beneath the segments, half a dozen at first, then more as he needed to bear the weight of the middle of his long, green body.

And Sean's face was no longer at all what it had been. His head looked like a misshapen red apple. His eyes were blank green pupils in yellow ovals. And from the top of his head grew two fuzzy purple antennae.

Sean, four years old, was a very hungry caterpillar.

A twenty-foot-long, green and red, very hungry caterpillar . . . with no mouth.

But then a mouth appeared, a terrifying hole rimmed with needle-sharp teeth. Sean tried to move, but his legs were not very useful, so his legs changed, becoming more insect-like, propagating in pairs the length of his brightly colored caterpillar body. Now he could move. Now he could slither into the kitchen.

It was a homey, pleasant, rustic kitchen with a small stove and ancient refrigerator. Food, Sean had observed, came from the refrigerator, but, lacking hands, he couldn't open the door.

So Sean bit into the refrigerator, his needle teeth chewing right through the aluminum to reach the tasty goodies within, though it seemed the aluminum was also perfectly edible, despite making an awful noise as it was chewed.

As he ate the refrigerator and the cabinets, Sean the caterpillar grew larger still. Twenty-two feet. Twenty-five. He was so long that part of him extended into the hallway, where Delia saw it, tore the earbuds from her ears, and screamed.

She screamed and, having no other way out, climbed out her first-floor window and went running down the road toward the village of Portnahaven. Portnahaven was a fishing village built around a tiny inlet where fishing boats lay in the mud at low tide. Delia ran screaming past whitewashed stone and stucco homes, past the modest church, and burst through the door of An Tigh Seinnse, a tiny pub where her mother worked the afternoon shift, and to the amusement of a handful of afternoon drinkers shouted, "There's a monster caterpillar eating our house!"

Sean, for his part, found that no amount of eating seemed to quell his hunger. In fact, his hunger was now out of control;

it filled his entire toddler's brain. Something dark and far, far away was watching him and, Sean was sure, smiled, though the dark thing had no mouth.

Eat, the dark thing whispered soundlessly. *Eat*.

Sean ate.

CHAPTER 11
A Really Bad Commute

QUICK ACTION BY Erin allowed them to grab a taxi from LaGuardia to JFK and grab two seats on Virgin America to Seattle. The thinking—if that panicky, jittery, shell-shocked state of mind after the annihilation of the plane at LaGuardia could be called thinking—was simply to put miles between themselves and the scene of the crime. Three thousand miles on the first available flight.

It will take the cops a while to identify us, Justin thought, *hopefully long enough.*

They stayed overnight at Erin's sister's home in Lynnwood, south of Seattle, a depressingly average family home where Justin had to sleep on the couch. Then they borrowed/took the sister's car and drove south to San Francisco, muddying the trail for pursuers.

Justin and Erin were at a roadside scenic pullout in the Marin Headlands, the great hills that anchored the northern end of the Golden Gate Bridge, sitting in that borrowed Volvo

SUV, looking through bleary eyes at the bridge and the bay beyond.

It was autumn and a workday and gloomy besides, so they were nearly alone. A camper van was a half-dozen spaces away; a determined cyclist powered his way up the hill, bearded face earnest and focused; a massive crow perched on the back of a wooden bench, preening and staring at them.

"Good omen or bad omen?" Justin wondered aloud, eyeing the crow sourly. He was in a foul mood, exhausted, frightened, and depressed. So was Erin, he knew, though the way she looked at him (and sometimes refused to look at him) created a sour realization that she was having a very different sort of reaction from his. Erin's depression and avoidance were undoubtedly caused by the memory of the aftermath of the crash—when Justin had tossed that lit swatch of fabric and the whole thing stopped being an accident and became deliberate murder. He knew that act—that "necessary" act, he still insisted—had not sat well with Erin.

They had both heard the stories on the radio. Justin DeVeere was a mass murderer. Of course, he reminded himself, she was in this, too. Her swatch of fabric, her lighter.

Stuck with me now, he thought. *And I'm stuck with her.*

Justin's state of mind was perfectly rational to his way of thinking. He'd done only what he had to do to survive. It wasn't malice, just calculation. By destroying the aircraft and the people on it, he had hoped to erase any evidence, and yes, twelve people had survived and were talking to the FBI and, worse still, the media. But that didn't mean the initial decision was wrong.

No, there was only one true priority: survival. And anyone or anything that reduced his chance of survival had to be dealt with in the most effective way. That wasn't him being some kind of bad guy, it was simple evolution, survival of the most fit.

And who was more fit than the dagger-handed monster who now lived within him?

A blue containership with the letters *MAERSK* painted along the side slipped under the bridge, heading toward Oakland to unload electronic goods from China. It swept through light fog gathered beneath the center span.

"Picturesque," Erin said bleakly.

"Clichéd," Justin sneered. "It's just a picture postcard, basically, a shot you can find in a thousand versions online."

"Whatever."

Silence fell. There had been a lot of silence between them. A lot of silence and a lot of sidelong looks.

"We need a plan," Erin said. She had a tooth that was bothering her, and she poked at it with her tongue, which garbled her consonants. Her hair was a mess, her makeup was nothing like the neat perfection Justin had come to expect, and she was dressed in her sister's "mom" clothes.

This was not art, Justin thought, any more than the too-pretty view was art. Art was struggle and shock and the bleeding edge of the new and the never-before-seen. Like the . . . event . . . at LaGuardia. He closed his eyes and saw the blue flame racing across the spreading pool of jet fuel. He saw the way the escape chute crumpled like a leaf in the fire and spilled its absurd occupants into the flames.

A little girl in profile, back turned to him, stark against the rising flame, *that* was art, *that* shocked and challenged.

"Golden Gate Bridge," Erin muttered. "Everyone's favorite suicide spot."

Was Erin considering it? he wondered. Did he mind?

With an inner sigh he realized he would. She was someone to talk to, after all, someone to enjoy in bed, someone to do useful things like flick a lighter when his hands were no longer hands.

"I can't survive prison," Erin said, biting her tense fist. "I can't! This is unfair, all of it. If they had just left us alone. If they would . . ."

"You happen to have a plan?" Justin asked.

"No, Justin, no, I don't have a plan!" she shouted, turning her face and her somewhat asymmetrically penciled eyebrows on him.

Justin shook his head slowly, thinking, not interested in her impotent anger. "They never really deal with this in the movies. In the movies Tony Stark has his mansion, and Spider-Man has his aunt May and his secret identity. The closest to this is probably Hulk, he's always on the run—"

"Jesus Christ, Justin!" Erin snapped. "Are you aware that this is not a comic book? This is real life. The real FBI is after us! They have our names, for God's sake, they know who we are! Every credit card, any access to a bank, any time we have to go through the TSA . . . hell, any random cop who pulls us over for a busted taillight!"

"What are they gonna do?" Justin asked with weary

irritation. "They can't stop me. At least not with bullets, I'm pretty sure. I mean, if I can cut through metal . . ."

"It's all some big male fantasy for you, isn't it?"

Justin laughed derisively. "You know, Erin, you talk tough about being on the edge, but really you're just a little rich bitch playacting."

"Yeah, you got me, Justin." She held up her hands in mock surrender. "I confess: I don't like being a hunted animal. I don't . . ." She tensed and fell silent. In the rearview mirror she spotted a park ranger's white-and-green SUV driving slowly past, going up the hill.

"They don't have the prison that can hold me," Justin boasted.

"Well, they have one that'll hold me. And I am not bullet-proof."

"I can protect you," Justin said gruffly, trying to sound older than he was, wishing he could access his morphed voice, that ground-vibrating growl.

"Uh-huh. Sure you can."

"Gotta go balls out," Justin said.

"Here we go," Erin said with vicious sarcasm. "Balls out. The whole array of male fantasy, here it comes, 'balls out.' What does that even mean, 'balls out'?"

"It means I am what I am," Justin said, pouting in the face of her withering sarcasm. "It means things are what they are, what's done is done."

"Any more clichés you'd like to spout? You know, a penny saved is a penny earned? A stitch in time saves nine?"

"Too late for a secret identity," Justin said, more to him-self than to her. "The whole world is out to get me. Us. What choice do I have but to go balls . . . to just stick it in their faces, you know? Be the monster. Play the role to the hilt."

"Meaning what, exactly? I mean, setting aside your 'stick it in their faces,' 'balls out' crap, what do we *do*?" She glared at him, like it was all his fault.

"It's not me," Justin said, a crafty smile taking shape.

"Don't be cryptic, okay? Not in the mood."

"The thing I become, the monster—it's not me. Hulk and Bruce Banner."

"I swear to God I will drive this mommy wagon right over this cliff!" A few feet of gravel and a symbolic but useless cable fence were all that separated them from a long plunge down the nearly vertical cliff face to the rocks and the waters below.

"Bruce Banner becomes Hulk, but Hulk is not Bruce Ban-ner. Legally. Listen to me, Erin: it wasn't me, it was *him*. *He* cut up the plane. Him. My alter ego. Legally, I'm not responsi-ble, so how are they going to arrest me and try me and throw me in prison?"

He saw her processing this, saw anger and fear soften, just a little. Her eyes were shrewd now, calculating. "What about me? I don't have that excuse."

Justin shrugged. "The monster kidnapped you."

Erin nodded, but the nod of assent became a shake of negation. "You don't think the FBI has thought about that? They'll shoot on sight and claim we were attacking them. Problem solved." But then, another reversal. She snapped her fingers. "We need to make our case. We need to make this very public."

"I'm listening."

"Twitter, Instagram, Facebook, all of it. We put it out there. Pictures, videos . . . we put you *and* the monster out there. It'll trend like crazy. If we do a video, it'll be viral in ten seconds." In her mounting excitement she twisted to face him. "Your Lump thing, what was it? The comic book thing?"

"Hulk?"

"Hulk, yeah. People know that, right? I mean, normal people, not just nerds? If we use that as our example, people have to get it."

"People will get it," Justin assured her. "Maybe not your snotty art gallery crowd, but regular people."

The part of Erin O'Day that was all about publicity and fashion and the latest thing was thinking out loud now and Justin nodded along, feeling the possibilities. "We say we just want to be left alone. We'll get away, you know, stay away from people, from civilization, find a place in the mountains . . . tell people we just want to keep the monster from hurting anyone."

"It's the closest thing we have to a plan," Justin said. Then, slyly again, "We'll need a name for it. Him. My monster."

Erin was about to snarl at him again, but checked herself because he was right and she knew it. The creature needed a name to separate it from Justin. Still, she couldn't quite suppress her snark, so she said, "Lobster Boy?"

"Funny. How about the 'Dark Artist'?"

"No, that's still all about you. The creature is not you, remember?" She had one finger in her mouth, poking the painful tooth, so the next part came out garbled. "Sword Master?"

He considered. "That's not bad, but it sounds like some fencing expert in tights. It should be something scary. The Dagger. The Blade . . . no, that's been used."

"Colossus?"

"He's a Marvel superhero," Justin said.

"Does it matter?"

"I don't want every comix nerd on earth calling me out for plagiarism," Justin mumbled. "Wait, I have—"

And then the park ranger's SUV came creeping down the hill and pulled in behind them, not hostile exactly, but partially blocking their escape.

Erin's face went gray.

"Be cool, Erin, and maybe we can bluff our way out of this," Justin said.

Erin rolled down her window as the ranger came up, wary but not jumpy.

"Ma'am. How's your day going?"

"Fine," Erin lied. She turned on the charm. "Now, I know I wasn't speeding, Officer, because we're parked."

"Yes, ma'am, but we're checking . . ." A definite hesitation as the ranger saw Justin, and then his tone shifted dramatically. The ranger's hand went to his pistol, resting there, very far now from relaxed. "I'm going to need you both to step out of the vehicle and show me some ID." He keyed the microphone clipped to his uniform. "This is Franklin, I could use some backup." Not signaling panic, but trying to contain the situation until backup could arrive.

Justin opened his door.

"Keep your hands where I can see them."

Justin raised his hands in a parody of surrender and Erin saw what was needed: a distraction. She pushed her door out, fast, causing the officer to take a step back and yell, "Ma'am, I need to see your hands."

"Sure you wouldn't rather see these?" Erin asked coyly, and pulled the top of her sweater down.

"Whoa! Ma'am, that's not necessary, just—"

"Don't you like girls?"

At this point the ranger realized she was distracting him, stepped back, and drew his weapon. Justin's blade arm stabbed straight through the Volvo, pierced the front passenger door, the seat, the farside rear door, and with a downward twitch sliced effortlessly through the ranger's arm.

The gun—and the hand holding it—fell to the ground.

"Aaaahhh!" the ranger shouted, staring at his blood-spurting stump in disbelief.

A second park ranger's vehicle was rushing up the hill, and in his crack-of-doom voice Justin said, "We have to go!"

The injured cop was on his knees, his stump under his opposite armpit as he scrabbled awkwardly for the gun, yelling in pain and fear.

Erin jumped into the Volvo and started the engine, but now Justin was nearly twice the height and four times the bulk of a normal human, far too big for a car seat. So he used his massive left-hand claw to rip the seats from the back row, tossing them wildly over the side of the cliff. He squeezed through the door but could only lie down, his huge T. rex feet pressed against the windshield and his terrible blade sticking through the back window.

"Go, go, go!"

Erin drove up onto the gravel walkway, sideswiped a handicapped parking sign, bounced back onto the pavement, and flew down the hill. They passed the second ranger vehicle, the driver eyeballing Erin suspiciously. Down the winding road, faster and faster, the heavy vehicle—heavier by far with the morphed Justin—reached the bottom, narrowly avoided a cyclist, and fishtailed toward the Golden Gate Bridge.

Now the question was one of time. Could they get across the bridge and through the tollbooth into the city, where they could at least hope to get lost? Or would the park rangers have time to alert the California Highway Patrol down on the bridge?

They zoomed onto the bridge. Midday traffic was light, but a wall of fog was rolling in from the ocean, so that the massive red cables were half hidden, swooping up in graceful arcs only to disappear in pearly, translucent mist.

The bridge was 1.7 miles long—they crossed it in two minutes, but as they neared the automated tollbooths on the San Francisco side, Erin spotted the CHP car on duty there turning on its light bar and gliding swiftly to cut them off.

Erin cursed, and Justin, unable to see in his awkward position, rumbled, "What?"

"Cops!"

A second car was racing from the city to join the first, and these were not park rangers, these were California Highway Patrol, and the CHP were far more accustomed to violent, high-speed confrontations on open roads than park rangers.

Traffic slowed at the tollbooth, with cars rolling straight through, but at no more than thirty miles an hour, and as the Volvo neared the toll sensors the first CHP was directly in front of them. Erin swerved to go around, but the second CHP, closely followed now by a San Francisco Police Department car, swooped in to block traffic beyond the toll kiosks.

"We're blocked!"

Erin turned a dramatic, tire-squealing left, bounced crazily over a concrete rise, sideswiped a white van, and plowed into a Prius. She aimed the Volvo back toward the bridge and floored it, and angry horns blew.

"What are you doing?" Justin demanded, seeing things at a tilted angle as his huge head crammed up against the back lift gate.

The CHP on the San Francisco side were momentarily blocked by their own traffic jam, but now, ahead, there were more red and blue flashing lights and sirens were everywhere.

A CHP SUV directly ahead drove straight at them on the wrong side of the road, swerving back and forth as it came, a rolling roadblock. It was impossible for her to get around, and in any case there were still more cops coming from the Marin County side: park rangers, CHP, local cops from Sausalito.

"Go at 'em, straight at 'em!" Justin bellowed.

Erin floored it and hit the left side of the swerving CHP SUV, spinning it, exploding the airbags in the Volvo, momentarily stunning Erin, and knocking her hands from the wheel.

She wrestled the steering wheel, but the Volvo was on just two wheels, cantilevered crazily, and for a heartstopping moment Justin was sure the Volvo would topple over on its side, but the Volvo did not topple and instead dropped back to all four wheels with a spine-rattling impact. Steam billowed from under the hood and the engine made a hard metallic sound that could not possibly be normal.

"Go! Go!" Justin ordered.

Erin floored it again, but the Volvo was barely moving, jerking, rattling, and then, finally, it stopped with a final cough and rattle.

Justin roared, a sound of pure frustration, and kicked and punched the side of the Volvo until the metal tore, and with that he ripped and punched and kicked the rest of the steel and plastic out of the way, then rolled out onto the bridge's concrete road surface.

The cops on the San Francisco side had broken free of the stalled cars and were coming on at speed. Those on the Marin County side were advancing more cautiously, but the bottom line was that Justin and Erin were blocked, and on foot, with very angry CHP, SFPD, park rangers, and Sausalito cops closing in from both sides.

Justin tore the dangling side panel from the Volvo and hurled it at the nearest CHP, who skidded to a stop and popped out with pistol leveled behind the inadequate cover of his car door.

The Marin-side cops took the cue and halted their vehicles, too, and jumped out to level their own weapons.

A voice on a loudspeaker said, "Down on the ground, both of you. *NOW!*"

"Don't shoot!" Erin screamed. "He can't help it!"

Now Justin rose to his full ten feet and spread his arms wide. From the tip of his blade to the tip of his claw, he was twice as wide as he was tall. He held high the blade and the claw and, in a voice that made the vertical cables quiver, roared, "Behold! I am Knightmare!"

The Golden Gate was a suspension bridge with the two massive vertical towers carrying the weight of the two swooping, three-foot-in-diameter main cables. At fifty-foot intervals so-called suspender ropes, actually groups of four three-inch-thick cables, hung taut from the cable. It was these suspender ropes that attached to the road supports and carried the road suspended from the main cables, which in their turn hung from the two great towers.

Justin swung his sword arm and sliced through the nearest set of four suspender ropes. The steel ropes twanged and whipped wildly like electrified snakes.

"Let us pass!" Justin demanded.

"Get down, down, on your face!"

Justin sliced through a second set of cables, and beneath his claw feet he felt the roadway shudder and sag just the slightest bit.

"You'll kill us all!" Erin cried, but her words were lost when . . .

Bam! Bam! Bam! Bam! Bam! Bam! Bam! Bam! Bam!

Suddenly every gun—and there were now at least a dozen—opened fire.

Justin pushed Erin to the ground as bullets struck him again and again, round after round, all pinging and screeching away, deflected by his armored flesh. He barely felt them, they might as well have been Ping-Pong balls. But the noise was deafening, far louder in real life than movies or TV could convey.

"Can you swim?" Justin asked Erin.

"What?" She was on the tarmac, facedown, hands over her ears.

Justin sliced a third set of suspender ropes, then leaped forty feet in the air, rising to the graceful arc of the main cable.

The power!

The main cables were made of 27,572 wires, woven together and covered in cladding. Each main cable supported tens of thousands of tons of steel and concrete, cars and trucks and pedestrians.

"No!" Erin screamed. "Noooo!"

Justin heard her, but her screams were irrelevant. A part of him noted that it was itself a cliché, an outdated one: the screaming, helpless pretty girl and the superhero. Superman and Lois Lane.

At the top of his rising arc, as gravity seized him and again asserted control, he swung his sword arm down and chopped through the main cable in a shower of sparks.

The effect was immediate and drastic. The massive cable whipped back in both directions, yanking Justin with it, spinning him like a wobbly Frisbee. The support ropes snapped or twisted; the road surface sagged sharply to the right and stalled cars slid toward the rail, as frantic drivers gunned their engines and tires spun and burned rubber.

The cop cars slid as well, and the firing stopped instantly as officers and rangers scrabbled to hold on, to save their vehicles and themselves. Everywhere there were cries of panic from terrified pedestrians. A troop of Girl Scouts on a ritual bridge walk screamed in thin soprano as their troop leader fell away from them, pinwheeling toward the churning gray water 220 feet below. And then one by one they slid, helpless, shrieking as they grabbed frantically at any handhold, fingernails torn from their hands as they lost their desperate grips and fell away.

Justin crashed down to the concrete roadway, slid on the precarious slope, dug his claw feet into the ground, and in a transport of mad glee bellowed, "I am Knightmare! Ah hah-hah-hah!"

A taxi tried to run for it, accelerated, fishtailing toward the city, veered down the slope of the tilting roadway, smashed into the railing, and stopped there for a moment held in place, until the road jerked violently and sent the taxi over the side as well.

Justin saw the cabbie's face looking up at him, his mouth a

big O. Justin noticed and filed away the detail of an In-N-Out burger flying from the open window and remaining intact for a hundred feet before the buns separated and the meat and cheese twirled away toward the gray water.

The movable barrier, a string of connected gray blocks used to add or subtract lanes during commute times, slithered like a sidewinder, and temporarily stopped only when it encountered cars that were themselves sliding. Drivers threw their cars into reverse, and tires burned as they fought the inexorable pull of gravity. From the corner of his eye Justin saw a father leap from his sliding car and scramble away as his wife and two children slipped into oblivion.

Hah! There's a detail to remember!

The concrete of the road surface cracked like a dry riverbed, great chunks of blacktop falling down through the structure or upending like impromptu Stonehenges.

Justin found a terrified Erin, holding on for dear life to a twitching cable end.

"My God, Justin, my God!"

"Isn't it awesome?" he rumbled. "Come on!"

Justin swept Erin into the crook of his left arm, nearly crushing the air from her lungs, and leaped out into the void.

They fell at the same time as a CHP SUV, the black-and-white vehicle tumbling beside them through the air, lights still flashing, the driver clawing madly at his door handle, as if getting out would help. Car, cop, monster, and screaming socialite fell in a hail of concrete chunks and flailing bodies, accompanied by a soundtrack of howls and screams, racing engines that turned wheels in the air, and twanging cables that cracked like bullwhips.

Justin saw the water rushing up at them. This fall—this identical fall—killed about forty suicides in any given year, but he knew it wouldn't kill him; he was Knightmare, and Erin was in the crook of his mighty arm, where she would be protected by the chitinous armor.

Even for Knightmare the impact was shocking, a sudden, massive deceleration that tore Erin from his grip and the air from his lungs. Down, down he went. Down and now swept away by the current went Erin. Down through gray water, down and down, impossibly down, and all around Justin like depth charges the police and civilian vehicles, the pedestrians, and the debris plunged, tearing bubble columns in the water. A massive slab of something hit Justin in the back, bounced away, and caught Erin in a glancing blow that expelled the last of the air from her lungs.

Justin sank downward, eyes raised to the horror show. A boy, no more than ten, hit the water directly above him, facedown, a disastrous belly flop that sprayed blood from his ears and mouth and rammed his eyes into his brain.

Justin tried now to swim upward but his sword was less than useless, and he was not quite buoyant. He fell past Erin, past all the bodies that now hung suspended, down to where the trailing end of the great cable sank like a vast orange snake.

Finally, he saw the murk of sand and seaweed and bunched his legs up, timing it with precision. He kicked with all his might, feet slamming mud, and shot upward through the water like a breaching whale. Up right beneath Erin. He reached for her, snagged her ankle with what gentleness he could manage, and dragged her with him to the surface.

"Aaaah! Aaaah!" Erin cried as she gulped air.

Justin had no words. The scale, the amazing, appalling scale of it all, overwhelmed him. He had done all this! He, Justin DeVeere, art student. He . . . *Knightmare!*

Justin kicked his legs, used an awkward stroke of his sword, swung back and forth like a ship's propeller, and tilted his head back to look up. That glance was not reassuring—the bulk of the roadway, thousands of tons of steel and concrete, had not yet come down, and if it did while they were still beneath the bridge, they would very likely die.

But escape was at hand, as it so often was for superheroes, Justin thought. A ship piled high with faded containers and with too much momentum to stop was racing to clear the bridge and reach the safety of the open sea, but it would pass them a hundred yards off.

Justin yelled, "Grab my neck!" He seized a length of cable with his claw and pulled hard, and they shot through the water. Another cable end, another pull, like some aquatic Tarzan swinging from vines, and they were at the ship, the tall steel wall rushing past. The ship's hull rang like a bell as the flailing main cable slapped it, leaving a dent a foot deep, scarred with rust-red paint.

At the last possible moment, Justin stuck his sword into the side of the ship and felt the sudden jerk and then the steady drag as the ship's momentum carried them out from beneath the bridge.

Justin dug his claw hand into the steel as if it was no more than cardboard and climbed the side, stabbing with his sword, biting into steel with his pincer, Erin O'Day clinging to him like that blond girl in the King Kong movie. They spilled, wet, freezing, numb, and stunned, onto the deck of the ship between two stacks of containers. A black Prius lay upside down, its windshield shattered, the small Uber sign still in place.

Erin, on hands and knees, vomited seawater and stomach contents, retching until there was nothing left.

Justin stood unharmed, looking back at the Golden Gate Bridge twisting and tearing itself apart in spectacular death throes. The center section of roadway fell at last, more than a mile of roadway, and hit with the impact of a bomb, sending up a geyser of green water as high as the still-standing towers.

"Wow," Justin said in his huge rumble. "Cool."

And far away, or perhaps very near, the dark watchers silently applauded.

CHAPTER 12
Being Used

"ARE YOU READY?" Peaks asked.

"Beyond ready. Are we finally doing this?" Dekka asked.

"We are," Peaks confirmed. "I apologize for the delay, I had to go to Chicago for . . . for an event."

Dekka felt the return of an old, old friend: fear. It was not a panic fear, not a horror movie fear, more a nervous uncertainty, a combination of hope and worry, anticipation mixed with a dread of disappointment mixed with a countervailing hope that nothing at all would happen.

And I can go back to being Jean from Safeway.

Funny, Dekka thought, how much she had come to accept that life. Fifteen dollars an hour, thirty hours a week. Plus ten long hours at the customer desk of an auto body shop every other Saturday.

When she had a little money to spend, she sometimes drove her motorcycle down to Oakland to Club BnB, had drinks, danced, and occasionally hooked up—not that this ever resulted in a real relationship. In the four years since the end of the FAYZ, Dekka had dated half a dozen women once or twice, and for two months lived with a very nice young woman whose only real failure was that she was not Brianna.

Brianna: Dekka's crush, her love, her obsession. As a legal adult now, she was well aware that it was bizarre, even a little creepy, to still be hung up on a straight twelve-year-old girl. But her love for Brianna had never been physical. It had never been Brianna's body that drew Dekka, not even when she was just fourteen or fifteen herself; it was the fact that Brianna, the Breeze, had been the funniest, most reckless, and bravest person Dekka had ever met.

Brianna had set an impossibly high standard for any normal woman to meet. Unrealistic? Yes, Dekka knew that, just as she knew her obsession was dooming her to a life of disappointment and loneliness.

All that time with Brianna, that whole mad world of the FAYZ, was a million years ago. Sometimes. Other times it was like it was all still happening. Dekka had thought it was all in her past—not just Brianna, but love itself. Where would she ever find the friendship she had known? She was like a combat veteran who welcomed peace but knew that his wartime experiences would make the rest of life dim by contrast.

But now . . .

She'd been five days at the facility, playing along with the tedious physical and psychological tests, playing along though it galled her, remaining compliant, biddable, and in every way not like herself.

Why?

Because I hate being Jean from Safeway. Because I miss . . .
I miss . . .

. . . the power!

Now, as Peaks, a doctor named Amanta Malireddi, a nurse, Jane Prettyman, and two blank-faced, unobtrusive security people accompanied her down a long hallway, Dekka knew where she was going: the Secure Lab, shortened, in the argot of the facility, to the Slab.

At first glance, the Slab was an effort to disguise an austere laboratory as something more humane. There was no strange machinery, just the usual computers, nothing at all that suggested ray guns or lasers or interdimensional portals, or any of the things a Hollywood set designer might have included. The center of the Slab was a simple room, about the size of a suburban living room, with three gurneys, each covered in crisp white sheets. There were the usual small, wheeled, stainless-steel tables holding medical instruments, a cabinet with a multitude of small drawers, and a steel desk.

It was all fairly innocuous. Except. Except that the walls were formed of sections, like panels, which suggested there might be things behind those panels. And there was a bank vault feel to the air, an undefinable sense of massive strength to walls and ceiling and floor, which itself was stainless steel.

The whole place just felt . . . wrong.

As much a prison cell as a lab.

Nurse Prettyman indicated the nearest table, and Dekka hopped up onto it, feeling the fifteen pounds she'd put on since the FAYZ.

I've gotta stay off the Ben and Jerry's.

The nurse attached EEG lines to Dekka's head, so that she looked like a disgruntled but colorful porcupine, black dreads sprouting multicolored wires. A blood oxygen monitor clamped Dekka's right index finger and a blood pressure cuff went around her wrist. Finally the nurse inserted an IV line and hung a small, clear plastic pouch full of what looked like nothing more than distilled water.

"Nine oh three a.m.," Dr. Malireddi said. Then, to Dekka, "I want at this time to reiterate that your participation is wholly voluntary and that you have been informed of the risks."

"Yep."

"All right then, nurse," the doctor said, and the nurse turned the little plastic toggle on the line and the liquid began to flow into Dekka's arm.

"Let us know if you feel any discomfort," Dr. Malireddi said calmly, like a dentist about to start drilling. Peaks was leaning against a far wall, arms crossed over his chest. He was doing his best to seem nonchalant, but Dekka was not buying it. What was happening was a long, long way from nonchalant-land, and Peaks looked tense, unsettled. Worried?

"I feel a little cold," Dekka said. Then, when Prettyman bustled away to grab a blanket, she amended, "No, I mean the . . . the stuff . . . whatever you call it, going in my arm."

"That's normal."

"Glad something is," Dekka said under her breath.

It took five minutes for the liquid carrying the powdered rock to enter her system. Prettyman pulled the needle, made a gauze square, and asked Dekka to hold it in place with a finger as she wrapped a pressure bandage around her arm.

The doctor stared at the EEG readout. "Nominal."

Peaks said, "Nothing?"

"Well, we didn't expect it to be instantaneous," Malireddi said a little defensively. "Nurse, let's put the mobile monitor on her."

This turned out to be a piece of machinery about the size of a compact hard drive that rested in a belt that Dekka buckled around her waist. Wireless electrodes were pressed into the bare flesh at the back of her neck.

"Don't shower with those on," the nurse said in her professional nurse voice. "Call us and we'll send a tech to remove them and replace them when you're done."

"What fun."

It was a complete anticlimax. Peaks and his silent guards walked her back to her quarters.

"You'll let us know if anything happens," Peaks said as they paused at her door.

"Well, me plus the electrodes, plus the cameras you've got watching me, plus, I would guess, various other sensors and monitors you've got built into my room."

Peaks's smile was equal parts rueful and annoyed, but he knew better than to deny it. "Just so you know, we do not surveil the bathroom."

The day passed with unusual leisure for Dekka. There were no more tests, no more probes, no more anything, just a tense air of expectation.

Dekka binge watched *Vikings*.

She interrupted this important work to eat lunch in the cafeteria—lasagna, a green salad, and chocolate pudding—which she finished more quickly than usual, since she could feel dozens of sets of eyes on her.

Back in her room she watched more sword fighting, sailing, and Danish sex, then switched to YouTube for a random wander through cat videos, Amy Schumer stand-up, music videos from promising but definitely not famous bands, news bloopers, Russian dash-cam videos, a cop beating up a student, and more cat videos.

At six thirty came dinner, which she had delivered to her room. General Tso's chicken, dan-dan noodles, and a fortune cookie. The fortune read: *Great changes are coming your way.* That seemed a bit too spot-on, and she grinned at the image of Peaks or his people carefully culling fortune cookies, checking to make sure there were none reading, *Run! Get the hell out of there!*

At eight o'clock she pulled a beer from her mini-fridge and drank it slowly while listening with eyes closed to Brody Dalle, whose husky voice Dekka found wonderfully sexy.

Inspired, she tinkled away at the grand piano in the living room but discovered no hidden talent for music in herself and gave up, acutely aware that her pitiful efforts were stored on some hard drive somewhere.

At ten she turned out the lights and lay with eyes open, staring at the ceiling, her emotions in turmoil. She'd done her best to self-medicate her anxiety with TV, music, and beer, but with the TV off she was left alone with reality, a reality that could be changing drastically.

Or not.

And which was more frightening? she asked herself. The outcome that had her once again in possession of powers? Or the outcome that had her wandering around the Safeway parking lot looking for her discarded name tag?

Which life do I want?

She drifted off with that thought running around and around in circles in her head.

She woke at seven thirty a.m. She made coffee, toasted an English muffin, and spread butter and orange marmalade on it.

She took a deep breath, felt the caffeine kicking her nervous system awake, and tried to cancel gravity and make the coffee machine float through the air.

Nothing.

She tried to cancel gravity beneath herself, something that four years earlier she'd have done with almost no effort. But she remained resolutely seated.

"Okay then," she said aloud, and considered calling to have her electrodes removed so she could shower. But now she heard a sound, a noise, a metallic sort of shriek that grew louder like some poorly wired speaker system blasting feedback and coming down the hall outside.

Screeeeeeeeeeeeeeee!

"What the hell?" Dekka asked, talking to the unseen microphones.

The noise grew louder and she covered her ears; not that

this helped much, as the sound penetrated, rising, falling, picking up harsh percussives.

Screeeee-clang! Screeee-Rrr-Rrr-Rrr-Screeee-thump!

"Hey, are you people hearing this?" she shouted. "Peaks! What the hell?"

There was no answer, and if anything that awful, brain-ripping noise just redoubled in volume. Dekka went to the door and hesitated, with one hand covering an ear and the other hand on the knob. Should she open it and see? Or should she do the sensible thing and—

Wham!

Something massive slammed the door with such force that it bruised her hand on the knob.

"Hey!" Dekka yelled, though her cry was inaudible in the metallic howl of noise that jacked her pulse and blood pressure up through the roof.

Wham!

Dekka backed away from the door fast, looking around for a weapon, any kind of weapon, but she couldn't focus, couldn't think, rage and fear and the pain of the noise and . . .

Wham!

Hardest yet. The jamb splintered! The brass strike plate stuck out. One more hit and it would fly open and . . .

And what? What was happening? What kind of—

Wham!

The door burst inward, revealing three people in steel-gray jumpsuits bulging with body armor. Three faces were concealed behind helmets with black plastic visors.

And there were three automatic weapons, leveled at Dekka.

Dekka yelled a curse word, backed away, stumbled over the piano stool, and—

Bap-bap-bap-bap-bap-bap-bap-bap-bap!

The three automatic weapons erupted as one, little starbursts flashing from the muzzles.

Dekka's body was spasming, seeming to twist from the inside, but she had no time to observe, no time to think, no time to feel. There was only time to react, and she raised both her hands defensively and opened her mouth to scream, an inhuman scream.

MmmmrrrrRRRROOOOOWWWW!

There was a flash of light like the sun itself and a vast shrieking of timbers and wallboard.

And the guns no longer fired.

The three masked intruders were no longer in the doorway, or in the hallway beyond. In fact there was no hallway beyond, nor any walls to left or right. Nor was there a ceiling—a patch of cloud-edged blue was visible above. A crow flew past, unconcerned. A semicircle of utter destruction fanned out ahead of Dekka, thirty or forty feet, so that part of what had been the far wall of the building was open to daylight.

Everything that had seconds before filled the semicircular blast radius had been reduced to shreds: walls, ceiling, wires, pipes, furniture, the piano, everything—reduced to shattered bits, bite-size chunks, and blasted up the hallway in both directions. It was as if everything around her had been run through a blender set on chop: wallboard in pieces the size of a packet of gum; copper pipe ripped into segments no longer than an inch, edges sharply torn; wood studs reduced to the sweepings of a carpenter's wood shop; black keys and piano wire; and here and there, like decorative sugar confetti sprinkled on a cake, the bright bits of lacquered black piano cabinetry.

Dust filled the air. Water poured from a ruptured pipe in the ceiling. A tangle of fiber-optic cable glowed electric blue.

At first she did not see the three gunmen. And when she did, her mind at first refused to accept it. It couldn't be real. Nothing in her experience had prepared her to see this.

"No," Dekka whispered, knowing the answer was yes.

The three body-armored gunmen were shredded. They had gone through the same blender as the walls and ceiling, been torn into the same bite-size chunks, and those bloody bits, those fragments of bone and muscle and organ and brain, and above all blood, blood, blood . . . were everywhere.

Stunned, shocked, paralyzed, Dekka saw a bit of gore hanging from the end of a shattered wooden beam. An eye.

An eye.

It fell to the floor with a soft *plop*, and Dekka found her voice and cried out in horror. She roared like a wounded beast. Her eyes dropped to something shiny at her feet: a brass bullet. She'd seen bullets before, all too often, and there was something wrong with this one. Where the lead slug would normally have been, the brass was crimped.

A blank!

The truth hit her like a hammer blow. *A test!* It was suddenly clear to Dekka: the infuriating metallic shriek to get her adrenaline pumping, the banging on the door, the "gun-fire" with blanks.

Dekka stared at her hands, which had gone up in an automatic defensive gesture when the gunmen burst in. What she saw sent her reeling backward: they were not her hands! They were the hands of a beast, impossible hands, with just three fingers and a thumb, all covered in glossy black fur.

But worse, worse by far, was the crawling feel, the rustling sound of her head. She raised a trembling alien hand and touched not dreads, but what felt like fat writhing worms, or . . .

Snakes!

"No," she whimpered. No, no, it was some distortion from the concussion that . . . the concussion that *she had not felt*.

One of her dreads curved around and the serpentine head at the end looked at her, stared at her with tiny yellow eyes, its fanged mouth open, forked tongue slithering out and back, out and back.

Dekka screamed, screamed and backpedaled, swiping at the snake, hearing it hiss and withdraw.

Impossible!

She closed her eyes, willing the image to be gone, praying to the God she only half believed in to end this hideous too-real hallucination. But behind her eyes she saw a dark place, shapes moving, things that might almost have been human, but that surged through a pool of blue-black, liquid latex.

What?

The black shapes turned eyeless heads to her, black tar forming a parody of her own nightmarish Medusa head.

The dark, inchoate things turned as if she was an interloper at their party, then moved toward her with sudden excitement . . .

"Stop!" she cried, and opened her eyes. She stared at her hands again, at the fur-covered flesh twice the size of her own hands. But now they were changing. A fourth finger, the little finger, was sprouting like a weed in a time-lapse video. The black fur was being sucked back into her flesh.

She raised a trembling hand to feel the writhing, questing snakes on her head grow limp, hang, dry now to the touch. Just dreads once again.

Dekka wanted to scream. Wanted to roar in rage. Wanted to run and keep running.

Taylor. Drake. The ones who were physically altered by the power of the rock kept their powers. A physical change preserved the powers within the world outside the FAYZ.

"My God," Dekka whispered, gazing in fascination at the impossible reality that she had been physically transformed, altered in ways she had not yet fully seen, and might not wish to see. Ever.

What have they done to me?

My God, what have they done to me?

Then, a terrible thought.

"E! E! Where are you?" She searched frantically through the shredded wreckage, calling her cat's name.

She stopped when she found a small rectangle of fur and flesh.

It took ten minutes for the emergency team to dig through the rubble and reach the still-dusty, slightly flooded open space. Two EMTs pushed past her with the calm, efficient hurry of professionals.

"Anyone hurt?" one asked Dekka.

I must be back to normal, Dekka thought, and when she looked at her hands they were once more *her* hands.

Not just transform, but transform back.

She didn't answer, couldn't answer. She let them look, let them figure it out for themselves. Watched them recoil. Watched one of the EMTs vomit in his mouth and then force it down.

Peaks came picking his way through the rubble. He stopped, took in the open sky above, the shredded mass, the blood, and finally turned triumphant eyes on Dekka, stared at her and then around at the devastation. "It works!"

Dekka was on him in a flash. She grabbed his collar with both hands and pulled his smug face close. "I just killed those people! I just killed my cat!"

"I . . . we . . . we assumed you'd regain your *old* power. We didn't think—"

"Yeah, you got that right," Dekka snarled. "This is your idea of a test? Jesus Christ! I killed people!"

"Yes, the test did get away from us a bit."

Dekka stared at him in slack-jawed disbelief. "A bit? A bit? I just killed three human beings and my pet. I just killed them! You have no right! You've made me a killer!"

"You need to calm down, Dekka," Peaks said. He pried her hands from his collar. "I'm sorry about those men, I really am. But they were soldiers. Soldiers sometimes die—"

"This isn't a damn war!"

"Oh, but it is," he said flatly. "It is absolutely a war." And then, his voice low and urgent, he said, "Have you . . . Did you happen to look at yourself, your hands perhaps?"

Dekka's lie came easily. "I was a bit busy being terrified."

"Mmm," Peaks said, eyeing her skeptically. "Yes. Well, whatever you did blew out all the cameras. But in the seconds just before . . ." He let it trail off.

She had no choice but to ask. "What?"

Peaks shrugged. "It looked as if you had been transformed. *Physically* transformed."

"I don't know anything about that," Dekka lied again.

"Of course." Peaks looked around at the wreckage. "You'll need a new room. We can arrange to get you a new cat."

Dekka closed her eyes, wanting to weep for her unintended victims.

She wanted to feel nothing but rage at what had been done to her, at what it had cost in innocent lives.

But beneath the anger, beneath the guilt, beneath the sheer terror, beneath the skin-crawling realization that she could become a monster of cat fur and snakes, beneath the evil imagery of dark forces turning their malevolent and greedy gaze upon her, was a small, not very admirable or moral voice that whispered . . .

Power, Dekka.

You have power.

CHAPTER 13
All Done Being Used

"NOW THAT WE'VE seen that you have acquired extraordinary power—far greater than what you had in the PBA, I think you'll agree—we need to find out how to refine, hone, and direct that power," Tom Peaks said to Dekka.

"No," Dekka said, and there was heat behind that no.

"You seem upset," Peaks said.

"*Upset?*" Dekka laughed mirthlessly.

They were in Peaks's office, a top-floor space that afforded a commanding view of the facility. Dekka had seen the view and was not impressed. The Ranch from any angle still had the dull look of an industrial park, or one of the less whimsical tech company campuses: brick or cinder-block buildings, parked cars, neatly trimmed grass, everything squared away in perfect right angles. Pine forests surrounded the facility, the trees gray, cringing at the approach of winter.

"The scientists want—"

"I don't care what they want," Dekka said dully. Then she

frowned. "Wait a minute, what are you talking about, honing and refining? I thought you wanted to find a way to erase the powers."

Peaks made a face, a pursing of lips, accompanied by a shrug. "In time."

Dekka sat with hands gripping her armrests, her own hands, thankfully, human hands.

My God: the power!

"Seriously," Dekka said. "Cut the crap, or I walk. I won't be your tool. I won't be a puppet. You tell me what's what, or we're done."

"What is it you want to know, Dekka?"

"This is not about learning how to turn off powers."

Peaks was quite still, watching her. "Oh?"

"You want to use me. You want to use me as a weapon."

Peaks tried out a smile meant to be self-deprecating, but that ended up looking ghoulish. "Well, Dekka, I am a humble employee of DARPA, and that is what—"

Dekka was on her feet. "Like hell," she snapped. "I fought my war, I did that already. I don't need a new set of nightmares to wake me up at three a.m.!"

"Dekka, sit. Please." He let the silence stretch until she reluctantly resumed her seat. "Okay then. Everything I'm about to tell you is secret. Top-secret."

"Uh-huh."

"Have you been back to Perdido Beach?"

Dekka frowned, caught off guard by a surprising feeling of guilt. "No. Why would I? It's not exactly a place full of fond memories."

"People have moved back to Perdido Beach," he said. "But most of them leave within a year. The population today is a third of what it was before the anomaly. Houses are cheap, the town is mostly rebuilt, and yet the crime rate is nine times higher than it used to be. Assaults, rapes, murders. Motorcycle gangs and white supremacists and registered sex offenders, that's who dominates Perdido Beach today."

Dekka nodded, wondering why she didn't know this. Had she ever made any effort to find out about Perdido Beach today? No. She had never even Googled it.

"We had a team go into the mine, down to the depths where ASO-One penetrated. Down to where the creature lived."

"The gaiaphage," Dekka said, and swallowed hard after the word. The gaiaphage, that seething, inhuman evil that caused so much fear, so much pain, resulting finally in the birth of the monstrous child Gaia.

"Yes, the gaiaphage," Peaks said. "The unholy mix of alien meteorite, uranium, and human DNA. We sent a team of six. One of the women on that team went mad and attacked her fellow team members with a pickax. She killed two, injured two more. They had to beat her down with sticks and stones. She's a patient here, as a matter of fact, raving mad. A complete psychotic break."

Dekka sat, silent.

"So we sent a second team, this time with two armed Marines. The Marines killed the team, and then themselves."

"Jesus."

"So we sent robots, modified bomb-disposal robots, and we

were able to retrieve samples of what had been the gaiaphage. Just rock now, or so we thought. Dead. Inert. Then we tried a sample on test animals, chimpanzees. One of the chimps tore the face off her handler. And one of the chimps . . . Wait, I have the video."

He tapped his keyboard and turned his monitor for Dekka to see. There was no sound, just video, showing a chimpanzee in a cage, and suddenly . . . the chimp was *outside* the cage.

"Teleportation. Taylor's power," Dekka said.

"We had to kill the chimps."

Dekka snorted. "So you went looking for a better test subject, a better chimp: me."

"We need to understand what we are dealing with," Peaks said. "Whatever is down in that mine shaft still wields some kind of power. Decent people flee Perdido Beach. Criminals and lowlifes are drawn to it. The robots found beer bottles and cigarette butts in that cave. People have been in there, people we don't know, people who were drawn there."

"Why don't you seal off the town?" Dekka demanded.

"And let the whole world know we have a malicious alien presence sitting out in the desert a few miles from the 101? People are still coming to terms with the fact that someone is out there, light-years away in space. People aren't even close to accepting the fact that our entire world, the very laws of physics, are really no more secure than computer software."

"People live their lives," Dekka said with a shrug. "They come to my register at Safeway and buy their milk and their lettuce and go home to their spouses and kids and jobs."

"Several fragments we know of have landed," Peaks said. "You want to know where? ASO-Two came down in the Atlantic off the coast of Scotland and broke apart, spraying bits and pieces all over the Isle of Islay. ASO-Three landed in Iowa and someone stole it—a teenaged girl got most of it, as it happens. ASO-Four landed in the mountains of Afghanistan and fell into the hands of some very bad people." He leaned into her, intensity like steam coming from his eyes. This was not calm, soothing Peaks, this was a scared, angry, determined, even fanatical Peaks. "So we sent a larger Special Forces team in to take back the rock, but there was a delay and our guys got there too late: they were annihilated to the last man. Not shot, though. See, we recovered the bodies. They had been turned inside out. You know how you pull off a glove and sometimes it turns inside out? Like that. Organs and bone on the outside. I've seen some terrible things . . ."

His eyes glittered at that, and some instinct of Dekka's warned that there was more to the gloating tone of his voice. More secrets. More lies.

"The rock is out there, Dekka. Fragments of it are already out there, and more is coming."

Dekka saw sweat shining on his forehead. His hands twined together, fingers twisting, before he caught himself and with an effort resumed his usual impassive expression. "We've got a monster out of some kids' book terrorizing a Scottish island, a terrorist who can turn people inside out, a girl so fast she makes your old friend Brianna look like she's standing still, and some unstable psycho art student calling himself Knightmare who so far has caused something like two billion dollars in damage and killed a hundred and nine people. That's just for starters. We have possession of the Mother Rock, thank God; it's on a ship surrounded by more firepower and surveillance than you could imagine, so it's safe, but ASO-Six and ASO-Seven are yet to land."

Dekka felt herself sinking into her chair and almost wishing Peaks had not told her. The meteorite, identical to the alien rock that caused the Perdido Beach Anomaly, was spreading out across the globe.

Peaks said, "The physicists at CERN and MIT are trying to make sense of, well, the physics. They're scared. They're scared in ways that I lack the education and the IQ to even understand. But I'm not required to understand that, I'm only required to find a way to . . . to counter . . . the likely immediate results."

"Which are?"

He leaned across his desk and lowered his voice, his trick for conveying sincerity.

"Did you see the dark watchers?"

Dekka froze. She immediately knew what he was referring to.

He allowed her silence to stand, taking it as acknowledgment. "We used to think the ASOs were part of a benign alien effort to sow life across the galaxy. We believed the gaiaphage had attained consciousness solely because of a twist of fate—the impact with uranium and human DNA. But we're not so sure of that anymore, Dekka. We are beginning to suspect that the ASO virus is itself intelligent. And that its intentions are not in any way benign. We think it is capable of using any DNA at hand—Justin DeVeere had swordfish and lobster and appears to have a chitin armor, like lobster shell. And you saw the blade arm. But we also think it has the ability to exploit thought patterns. Needless to say, this is decades, centuries, beyond our abilities."

Dekka said nothing.

"Do you understand what that means, Dekka? If true, it means that Earth has already been invaded by hostile aliens. And that means Perdido Beach writ large," Peaks said. "Your gaiaphage metastasized. A new world, Dekka, a world where individuals, some friendly, some not, some good, some not, may acquire powers so great that our police forces and our intelligence assets and even our armies may be unable to cope. And even the best of the people who develop powers, even the heroes, will be watched and, we have to assume, be influenced, by the consciousness that is in those Anomalous Space Objects. Do you understand what I'm saying?"

"It sounds bad," Dekka said, unable to conjure up a better word.

"Bad? *Bad?* Dekka, the world we've known may be coming to an end."

"It's like some kind of comic book movie," Dekka said.

Peaks laughed and sat back. "Believe it or not, we've got a team at work analyzing Marvel and DC comics, trying to work out a scenario, trying to work through the implications of a world where—"

"Is it really that bad? I mean, so we'll have a bunch of Spider-Men running around grabbing criminals."

"Yes, well, unfortunately comic book writers tend not to work through the negatives. There are core human beliefs being subverted here." He tapped his keyboard again and a graph appeared. "See this line?" He traced it with his finger. "That's the number of millennialist cults here in the US. We had seventeen we were tracking before the PBA. We now have eight hundred and nine at last count. Cults, fanatics, lunatics, psychopaths, ambitious dictators, terrorists . . . how do you think they'll all react when they realize that the PBA wasn't just a one-time, one-location thing? How well do you think they'll resist whatever the ASO has in mind for us?"

"I don't have to imagine," Dekka said flatly. "I was there for Round One."

Peaks nodded. "Exactly. Three hundred and thirty-two kids were in the PBA. Forty percent died before the barrier came down. Another twenty percent have died since, mostly from suicide or drug overdoses. Others are in prison for various crimes. And others still are in mental institutions. Far too many to explain just from posttraumatic stress."

"Why hasn't that been in the news?"

"Because we've been covering it up as well as we can, but it's all over social media, all over the conspiracy websites. Dekka, human civilization is on the brink. World War Three is coming . . . unless we can find a way to neutralize the effect of the rock. Unless we can stop the most dangerous of those who acquire powers. Unless," he said with an intense stare that chilled Dekka to the marrow, "we can create a loyal army able to take on and defeat those who handcuffs and prison bars cannot hold. Those who bullets cannot stop."

"That's what I'm supposed to be? Part of your army?"

He said nothing, just waited.

"What if I refuse?"

Peaks shrugged. "Then we will ask you to remain here at the Ranch."

"A prisoner?"

He shrugged again, but added a regretful face, tacked on like an emoji.

"This is nuts."

"The times we live in."

"No," Dekka said. "Like I said: I did this once. I was Sam's soldier, I did this. I did it and I am not going to do it again."

"Dekka, we need you. Your country needs you. The human race needs you."

Dekka looked at the carpet for a long time but saw only memories. And with those memories came pain: the visceral memory of physical agony; the memory of grim decisions that cost lives; the memory of Brianna. And poor Edith Windsor, not a very sweet-tempered cat, but the closest thing to a friend Dekka had.

Had.

"I'm not your girl," she said at last. "Call me a coward, but no, Peaks, I am not signing up for another tour of hell."

"I'm sorry to hear that," he said. He tapped his keyboard and six thousand volts blasted from Dekka's chair. She was unconscious within a second.

Dekka woke hours later. She was on her back, on cold steel. She raised her head but found that a steel band was around her neck so that she could rise no more than an inch, barely enough to let her see what she felt: great, cold weights on her hands.

She saw a cubic foot of concrete, rough rectangular blocks imprisoning her hands, resting on purpose-built additions to the gurney. A jolt of terror went through her.

Cementing!

It was the crude countermeasure Caine and Drake had devised in the FAYZ, once they discovered that most (though not all) powers tended to be focused through the hands.

She had been *cemented*.

Peaks was there beside her now. "I'm sorry to have had to resort to this, Dekka," he said. "But you were given a choice between lab rat and soldier. Now you're a lab rat."

An IV line was in her left arm at the elbow. Sensors festooned her head. Wires rose from her chest.

"I like you, Dekka. I admire you. But one way or the other, you will help us." Then he snapped his fingers, remembering. "But I brought you something." He reached into his briefcase and drew out Dekka's framed photograph of Brianna. He propped it on a table and turned it so Dekka could see. It was not her original frame, and the picture itself had been damaged, looking as if a rat had chewed the edges. "It mostly survived the shredding. I had what's left reframed. So, there you go: just like home."

And then he turned and walked from the room as techs in white jumpsuits closed in around her and she roared curses at his back in helpless rage.

Unlike Drake, who had cemented his early victims with no thought for the putrefaction of flesh that would result, Peaks's people had molded the cement into halves held together by steel bands and fastened with massive locks.

Dekka reached into her mind for the transformation that would unleash her new and terrible power. She was not about to accept this fate. She was not about to be reduced to life as an experimental subject or wired with control devices.

No!

She felt the change begin, a stomach-turning nausea, a creeping of the flesh. Her hands swelled within the cement blocks. She felt pressure, felt pressure become pain, but she glanced at the picture of Brianna for strength and gritted her teeth, bearing the pain.

But then the transformation stopped.

The cementing had worked. She was helpless, her power blocked.

Hours and then days passed, time evident to Dekka only because of the changing of the staff who poked and prodded and stabbed needles into her veins. What they were pushing into her bloodstream she did not know. Her questions were ignored; her threats were ignored; her demands, her recitation of her constitutional rights as an American citizen, all ignored, ignored as if they were all deaf, as if no sound was emerging from Dekka's throat. All communication was one-way: they would speak to her as if she was a child, and her every response was ignored.

"We're going to take the blocks off and give you a bath," a technician said on what Dekka believed was her third day. "Don't worry, though, it will be all female staff."

Dekka rolled her eyes to see him. Youngish with a silly ginger beard.

"What I'm pushing into your veins right now is propofol," the tech explained. "It will put you into a trance state. You will be unable to resist. You will be barely able to move, let alone focus enough to morph."

It was Dekka's first time really hearing, internalizing that word, "morph." But that was not what caught her attention. Rather, it was the careful way the tech explained how she would feel. Because the thing was, she did not feel fuzzy or unfocused or sedated. The propofol was flowing, she could see it drip, drip, dripping in the plastic bag hung just over her head.

Nothing. In fact, if anything she felt energized, clear, aware to a degree she had not since waking to find herself cemented.

She met the tech's gaze. He had eyes of an uncertain color, maybe green, though in this light it was hard to pin down. She shot a questioning look at him. After a furtive look around the room, he leaned close, stretching over her to unlatch her left hand. And in the barest whisper he said, "Remember me, goddess. Remember my service to you."

Goddess?

Dekka said nothing. She gave the most minimal nod, then stared blankly at the ceiling, faking the drug-induced coma she knew all too well.

Female techs maneuvered her into a wheelchair. She sagged convincingly, like a big sack of potatoes. They pushed her down the hall to a room with a deep claw-foot tub, like something from Restoration Hardware.

They began stripping off her flimsy hospital gown and socks, chatting among themselves as if she wasn't even there. They hauled her by main force to the tub and settled her into warm water.

It was delicious on her skin, so sensual that for a moment she hesitated to disrupt the animal pleasure of warm water. But only for a moment.

She'd had no time to experiment with her new power, but she'd had long experience of reaching that part of her mind.

She hoped she wouldn't kill anyone this time. She reminded herself to take care, to *try* not to kill anyone. They were just government employees, after all, just techs and nurses, no different really from the three she'd accidentally slain during her first display of power.

She pictured the power, imagined it, tried to define it, to find a way to focus it. Where to strike? How?

The room had tile walls and no window. No way to know for sure which direction to take. So Dekka picked the largest expanse of wall. And she let her mind go where it had rarely gone since the days of the FAYZ.

The change began.

Dekka felt her skin crawling, sliding over her bones, fur sprouting from flesh, hair moving of its own accord. It was eerie, not painful but deeply disturbing. She looked at her hands as five black fingers melted together to make four. This time she forced herself to pay attention, to observe. Not four fingers, really, four full length and one that shrank and rotated toward her palm.

Cat paws, that's what they reminded her of, these hands, though with longer fingers and no . . . But wait? Did she have claws?

"What the . . . ?" one of the techs yelled suddenly.

The others turned to the tub, gaped, then retreated in a hurry. There was a red panic button on the wall, and one of the techs reached for it.

"Stand back," Dekka said in a voice that was not her own.

She sat up in the tub, drew her legs back, and saw that they, too, were changed, fur-covered but still otherwise human, down to the human-shaped feet. No time to freak out, no time to stare or to run searching for a mirror. Dekka rose in a single effortless motion, held up her freed hands, furry palms out toward the wall, opened her mouth, and screamed.

MmmmmrowwwRRRRRR!

Then a second sound, less biological, as the world around her passed through that invisible blender.

Grrrraaaaaccckkk!

It was a noise like a hundred chain saws biting into a hundred trees all at once.

The wall exploded outward in a storm of shredded tile, wallboard, wood, steel, pipe, and wire. And suddenly she was looking at a large room full of office cubicles. A dozen faces covered in dust and debris stared openmouthed at the space where a wall had once been and where now stood a naked, damp, furry, snake-haired . . . monster.

"Run!" Dekka yelled. "Run away!"

They did.

Something tugged at her, a hand on her shoulder. She spun, ready to do whatever she had to do, and found herself face-to-face with Ginger Green Eyes.

"I thought you might want this." He handed her something rectangular wrapped hastily in a plastic bag. Dekka knew what it was.

"Remember," he said.

Dekka nodded. "I owe you one. Maybe even two."

Dekka raised her free hand, shrieked, and blew out the next wall. Now she was looking at a debris-strewn cafeteria and, finally, through the cafeteria windows: sunlight!

She exploded that final, exterior wall and ran toward daylight. She stopped on seeing a large, portly man lying quivering on the floor. "You," she snapped. "Give me your clothes. Now!"

By the time he had stripped off a dress shirt and slacks and Dekka had put them on, the guards came rushing, weapons leveled.

Dekka aimed at the scattered chairs and tables, exploded them into shreds, and without thinking hurled the debris tornado at the guards. That last move was almost a flourish, a twist of her hands and a directed gaze.

Oh, there are tricks still to be discovered in this body, in this power!

Dekka gazed with intense, almost physical longing at the outside, the weak sunlight, the wedge of blue sky. But the courtyard was filling with armed men and Dekka did not want to hurt them, so she spun around and ran up the corridor, moving now beyond any place she'd explored. Behind her came armed men and women, boots clattering on floor tile, and now there were sirens everywhere and a loudspeaker announcing, *Condition Yellow, Condition Yellow, this is not a drill* in a flat computer voice.

Some part of Dekka vaguely resented the idea that she was only a Condition Yellow. Surely there was a Condition Red, and surely she deserved that designation.

Suddenly, she ran out of corridor, which was just as well since she was terribly out of shape and feeling it—a reality not helped by days locked down and cemented.

"Not as young as I used to be," she panted, hands on knees, doubled over with a stitch in her side. Or else, she thought darkly, this body, this . . . this *morph* . . . this bizarre, terrifying body that seemed to incorporate elements of cat and Medusa wasn't big on endurance. Behind her the guards yelled, "Freeze! Freeze!" and rushed. Ahead the corridor ended in what looked a lot like a bank safe's vault door. There was a control pad, but she didn't exactly have time to play around with guessing passwords.

Time to test the limits of her powers.

She shoved the precious wrapped rectangle into the back of her borrowed pants, raised her quasi-feline paws, and with a roar the massive steel door began to peel apart, layer after layer of steel shreds, revealing more steel just behind, and the guards were yelling, "Halt or we open fire!" in voices barely audible against Dekka's howl.

Dekka tried what she had not yet attempted: as the steel shards come loose, she formed a cup with one of her hands, and the shards of steel formed obediently into a swirling ball two or three feet across and growing by the second. The swirling ball of steel shrapnel spun, and Dekka focused her thoughts on a simple thought: *Hard but not too hard.*

She sent the spinning shrapnel ball flying. It whirled away down the corridor, straight at the guards, who fired futilely into it and turned too late to flee. The steel shredded uniforms, gouged eye covers, cut exposed skin, lacerated exposed jaws and hands. Guards screamed and Dekka, feeling sick at the pain she had caused, turned back to ripping open the steel door. The last layer was coming apart and a familiar male voice yelled, "I don't give a goddamn how hurt you are, shoot! Shoot! Kill her! Take her down!"

Bullets flew, but Dekka had raised her left hand and as the bullets neared they fell, torn into smaller bits.

The steel vault door collapsed, a hole big enough to step through formed, and Dekka wasted zero time doing just that. She leaped through into a very, very different place. The familiar, prosaic corridors of the Ranch—corridors that might as easily have belonged in any government office building—were not part of this vista. She stood now at the rail of a steel platform high above a vast open space carved from living rock. Parts of the dirt and rock walls were held in place by orange plastic webbing. At the corners of the cavern stood three-story steel towers, four of them, each a fortress, with weapons—recognizable things like machine guns, and less recognizable things that still, by their positioning, by the number of uniforms on or near them, and merely by their dangerous look, could only be weapons as well.

The towers were pierced by windows with glass so thick the men behind them were distorted and the light within shone a sickly green. There could be no question that these were guard towers, more massive and sophisticated versions of the guard towers at any maximum-security prison.

And there were prisoners.

Two tall cell blocks were cut into the rock walls, ziggurats of steel and bulletproof glass, five levels in some places, four in others. Each level was a tier of cells, their doors made of glass that in some places was further strengthened by lattices of thick titanium straps.

The facility was obviously still under construction. At the far end of the yawning cavern, cranes and scaffolds festooned a third cell block. Sparks flew from welders' torches, the engines of huge earthmovers roared, low-built trucks slowly hauled great loads of steel, while an overhead conveyor belt trailed cables carrying funnels full of wet concrete.

Dekka did not want to go down there. She did not want to go down there at all. But when she looked back she saw a startling sight: guards dressed head to toe in bulky flame-retardant suits were advancing, spraying liquid fire ahead of them.

Kill or run? And part of her mind thought, *How many times have I faced that choice?*

How many lives had she already taken, in the before and in the now? How many was the right number to die for Dekka's freedom?

She ran down the stairs, her feet slippery on the steps so that she clattered, half sliding, down to the next landing. But her strange morphed body felt pain only distantly, and while this body might be low on endurance it was strong as hell and quick, and Dekka rose instantly. Guards from below rushed up the stairs toward her.

Flamethrowers behind, automatic weapons ahead.

Just how much punishment will this body take?

Dekka gathered herself up, sucked in a deep breath, muttered something that was either a prayer or a curse, and leaped over the railing into the void, fifty feet above the unforgiving packed-earth ground below. As she jumped she spun in mid-air, raised her hands, howled, and shredded the levels of stairs and catwalks and platforms as she fell, destroying everything below the flamers and everything above the gunmen, cutting each off. The shrapnel fell in a rain of steel, and it would cut and it would bruise, but—Dekka hoped—it would not kill.

She hit the ground. Her legs buckled, her spine was a single long, stabbing pain—yes, it seemed there were limits to her body's pain tolerance—but she rolled with the impact and lay winded, facedown. She inventoried her body: Her legs could move. Her arms could move. And to her amazement, when she stood up her muscles lifted her effortlessly.

Okay then, that's great. Now how the hell do I get outta here?

There was an exit door directly below the now-shaky platform, but if she shredded her way through that door she'd likely bring the rest of the catwalk down on her head and kill the men still clinging precariously above. She turned the other direction and ran, ran past parked earthmovers, threaded her way through piled construction supplies, and dodged a truck whose driver saw her and promptly ran his vehicle into the base of the nearest guard tower. Dekka emerged from the construction mess face-to-face with the lowest tier of cells.

She stopped, staring in disbelief. On the other side of the glass was not the narrow jail cell she expected to see, but a room the size of a double-wide trailer. The sides of the room opened onto still more glass-and-steel barred cells. This facility was far larger than she'd imagined.

How many prisoners is Peaks holding?

But that question was quickly replaced by another one.

What in God's name is he doing?

The room beyond the glass was dominated by a stainless-steel table bolted to a stainless-steel floor. Beneath that table hung a thicket of wires, blue, green, yellow, and red, and threaded through those wires was a maze of clear plastic tubes pulsing with fluids.

Atop the table were four glass bell jars.

And within each of the bell jars, a head. A human head.

B-r-r-r-r-r-t!

The bulletproof glass of the nearest cells starred from the rapid-fire machine gun coming from behind Dekka.

Dekka dropped, turned, and saw a drone flying on four horizontal propellers, zooming toward her, gun blazing.

She turned it to scrap metal in midair, but she could see the guns of the two nearest towers now pivoting toward her.

"Condition Red, Condition Red, this is not a drill," the loudspeakers blasted.

Red. That's more like it.

Dekka had begun to learn a valuable lesson: regular people thought of walls as walls, but to Dekka they could be doorways. So could bulletproof glass.

She raised her hands and shredded the glass that came flying off in a shower of crystal shards, whirling around to form a tornado of random-shaped diamonds behind her. She leaped through the hole she'd made and into the chamber beyond, meaning to cut her way right through the far wall and the earth beyond and up into the sunlight.

And then, one of the heads opened its eyes.

"Aaaah!" Dekka yelped.

She stared in shock so profound, it paralyzed. What she'd imagined was some bizarre morgue with decapitated heads mounted for study was quite a bit worse than that. The four heads, the heads without bodies, were *alive*! Alive and watching her, their eyes wide, their mouths moving soundlessly.

But maybe not really soundlessly.

Dekka spotted a handle in the side of the nearest bell jar, lifted the glass, and hurled it aside. And now the mouth was no longer silent. In a wheezing but unmistakably human voice, the head said, "Don't hurt us!"

"Wha . . . what . . ." No more eloquent words came.

"Don't hurt us!" the voice repeated, and it was a child's voice, a child's voice and, Dekka saw, a child's face, a child's head.

All four heads belonged to young people, the youngest maybe ten, the oldest perhaps sixteen, three yelling soundlessly beneath bell jars, the fourth crying, "I want to go home, I want to go home, don't hurt us, I want to go home!"

"What are you? Who are you?"

"I'm Lashawn Wilkins," the near head responded, voice tearful and terrified.

"What are you doing here?" Dekka demanded, but before she could get an answer a second drone came whizzing through the hole she'd made in the outer glass. It zoomed in, hesitated as its controller searched for the target, and then leveled its machine gun right at Dekka's head.

The drone spoke with the mechanically distorted voice of Tom Peaks. "Dekka, stand down, I don't want to hurt you."

"What in God's name are you doing here?" Dekka cried.

"Surviving," the drone with Peaks's voice said. "These four will form the vanguard of a cyborg force capable of taking on people like . . ."

"Like me," Dekka supplied.

"Simple choice, Dekka: You serve your country, or you are an enemy. Join us, or die."

Why was he explaining? Then Dekka saw his problem: the drone couldn't fire at her without hitting some of the decapitated heads. Yes, she thought, but it could still maneuver to get a different angle.

He's stalling!

There was a *shwoop* from a steel door opening quickly at the far end of the room, a door large enough to drive a car through. And indeed, through the door came a vehicle unlike anything Dekka had ever seen. It had rubber tank treads rather than wheels and lay wide and low to the ground, rising no more than three feet. A blank steel box with treads, but even as it pelted toward her the front panel dimpled and a cannon barrel protruded.

And yet it, too, did not fire. It might not need to, for from one side of the robot vehicle now grew an articulated mechanical arm, and at the end of that arm was a whirling blade, like a table saw.

Someone's been watching robot wars on YouTube.

Dekka dropped to her knees, aimed her hands, and shredded the drone, which came apart as if it were made of confetti.

The tracked vehicle zoomed to its left, trying to come around the table. Dekka crawled and then jumped up and dodged left, keeping the four heads between her and the tank.

Now a voice came booming through the public address system: Tom Peaks sounding like Jehovah in a bad mood. "Carl! Kill her and I will free you!"

There was a *shwoop* sound once again, but smaller, nearer, and from the corner of her eye Dekka saw that one of the massive glass cell doors was sliding open.

From that cell emerged a nightmare creature. It had four legs, legs as thick as tree trunks. Its torso was vaguely human, as if the four legs had been grafted onto a white, hairless body that bulged with coiled muscle. The thing had two arms, each maybe eight feet long, so long they would trail on the ground if the creature dropped them. The arms ended in claws that glittered with the dangerous hardness of titanium.

The head was twice normal human size, slung forward on an elongated neck that seemed barely able to carry the weight. The creature's face . . . ah, that's what stopped Dekka from instantly shredding it, for the face was undeniably human—twisted by a mouth bulging with dagger teeth, and with small eyes that blazed red, but that were still unmistakably human.

"Take her, Carl! Now!" Peaks shouted from everywhere at once.

The monster with the prosaic name of Carl rushed with supernatural speed. In half the blink of an eye it was on her, its massive arms coiled around her waist, pinning her arms to her side, and though this strange body of hers was strong, it was like a child in the grip of the creature.

Its huge head, its glittering, mesmerizing mouth, was inches from her face. And it spoke.

"Kill me," it rasped.

"I-I-can't breathe," she managed.

"I will help you, but you must promise to end this. End *me*!"

"But I—"

"Swear! Swear by whatever is holy to you!"

Dekka's head was swimming, her vision reddened, and she felt vast strength in the monster's arms, strength great enough to crush her right here, right now, to end her life in a second's time.

"I swear," she managed through a strangled throat.

The creature released its grip. "Tear those glass doors apart, free those prisoners, and follow me!"

Dekka looked back at the glass walls forming cages. The nearest glass was starred, as if it had been battered from the inside. She couldn't see well through the glass—it was too thick—but she made out one person clearly enough, a very tall white boy.

Dekka made a pushing motion with her hands. "Stand back! Stand back!" The tall white kid backed away and she hoped the others she could not see had done the same. Then she howled and the thousands of pounds of hardened glass disintegrated into a bee swarm of fragments. Glass shards fell and piled up.

"This way!" Carl yelled, and bounded toward the door the tank had come through, the tank that had now circum-navigated the table of heads and was sighting its weapon on Dekka.

The monster shoved her ahead, and the tank opened a deafening cannon fire, 20 mm shells exploding, but all strik-ing the back of the creature named Carl. Smoke rose from behind him, shrapnel cascaded and clattered everywhere, and Carl's body shook with the impact.

Dekka ran for the door, into a tunnel carved into the rock with only the floor paved smooth for the tank.

"Keep going," Carl cried. "It comes up through Tower Two. Go to the top, there's an emergency escape pod there!"

"Show me!"

Carl gripped her arm with one irresistibly powerful claw, the titanium nails stopping just short of cutting her flesh. "My name is Carl Pullings. I'm from El Segundo. Find my mother, tell her . . . *not this*. Tell her . . . tell her Carl loves her."

"Come with me!"

The massive head shook slowly. "You don't understand: they see me. The dark ones, the eyeless watchers, they're in my head. They hurt me! They hurt me! It's pain!" Carl screamed the last word. "Kill me! Kill me now or I swear I'll kill you!"

He released her arm and pushed her away. He was blocking the door, cannon fire apparently having no effect as the tank emptied its magazine in futility.

"I'll find your folks," Dekka said. She squeezed his arm. "Thank you."

Dekka raised her hands, opened her mouth, and Carl flew apart into pieces of gore. Dekka fled, fled in panic and an agony of the spirit, racing down the dimly lit tunnel with tears blurring her vision.

Side tunnels opened to left and right, but she kept straight ahead, her mind shattered by what she had seen, what she had done. Straight and straight and there, yes, the position was probably about right. A circular staircase rose, but it was too narrow, the steps too shallow for the creature she now was.

They see me! They're in my head!

And Dekka, too, saw them, sensed them, felt their amused gaze, felt the brutal minds that seemed to reach into hers with tendrils like black smoke.

"Back to normal, back to normal," Dekka ordered herself, and looked down to see her hands resuming their usual shape. Human once more and free of the watchers, she propelled herself up the stairs, two steps at a time, stumbling, hauling herself up, running, gasping, reaching a door that was blessedly unlocked, and through onto an open platform. She was atop one of the towers in the vast cavern. All around her, robotically controlled machine guns were trained on the main floor below, and something that looked way too much like a massive ray gun. No guards.

And there, on the edge of the platform, hanging over the side, rested three pods the size of subway cars. They were helpfully stenciled Escape Vehicle 2-1 through 2-3, and beside the front hatch was a big red button shaped like a mushroom. She slammed her hand down on the button, and the nearest hatch opened. She spilled inside, gaping at what might as well be a passenger jet, with five rows of seats, four to a row. She had entered from the side and rushed to the front, pushed her way into an unoccupied cockpit with front-facing window and three more buttons, labeled from left to right one, two, and three.

She hit them in sequence—one, two, three—and a canned

voice said, "Please clear the doorways. Please clear the doorways."

Then, with a soft shush, the doors closed.

The mechanical voice helpfully warned, "Please buckle in and prepare for launch."

Launch?

With unsettling speed the escape pod tilted back, bringing the cockpit to face skyward, or at least toward the stalactite-festooned ceiling of the cave.

"Launch in three seconds, two, one . . ."

Dekka fought gravity and exhaustion and hauled herself into the sole seat in the cockpit just in time to be slammed down by a sudden acceleration. The vehicle shot straight up, straight toward the ceiling, straight toward what must at the very least be several feet of rock, but at the last second the rock ceiling shimmered and disappeared.

A hologram!

The escape pod flew up, up though the hologram, up through a short tunnel, burst through a glass dome like Willy Wonka's elevator, and flew on another hundred feet straight up, up into blue sky, up toward towering cumulus clouds, and then came the roar and shudder of rocket engines catching fire. The pod leveled with stomach-twisting speed and soared on stubby wings, zooming over the facility, arcing toward a wide, flat space of cleared ground at the edge of the fence.

At the edge of, but still *inside*, the fence. Looking down, Dekka saw SUVs racing to the preprogrammed landing spot, and ahead armed men spilled from a small guardhouse, automatic weapons at the ready.

She was sure the skin of the escape pod was not bulletproof and they would blow her to straight to hell before the slowing escape pod could land at its preprogrammed target.

Time to change.

Dekka shredded the windshield of the pod, cleared it away, and then tore up the ground between her and the guards, showering them with a hailstorm of dirt and debris.

The escape pod landed gently, its only gentle move so far, and Dekka was out, leaping with the sure-footed agility of a cat. The fence was ahead and beyond it the woods, but she was not fast enough or strong enough to run for long, certainly not fast enough to outrun the fit guards, let alone the SUVs racing to cut her off.

And then she saw it at the edge of the parking lot: the dirty vinyl cover. She ran toward it like a burning woman running for water. She snatched off the cover and in a single fluid bound was astride her motorcycle.

"Chase this, assholes," Dekka said.

She kicked the engine to life, popped the gear, and rocketed ahead, swerving dangerously—this body balanced differently from her own—and went straight for the nearest section of fence. Gunfire erupted behind her, and she crouched low, flat across her gas tank, twisting the throttle all the way open.

She raised a hand and howled, and the double row of barbed-wire-topped chain-link became a shower of penny nails.

Into the woods, between tall pine trees, tires bouncing over roots and ruts, fishtailing as she turned. She hit a glancing blow at a tree but kept her balance, and there was tarmac ahead: the road!

Up onto the road she motored, loving the welcome smoothness, and the motorcycle passed seventy, eighty, ninety miles an hour, trees whipping past on both sides.

The SUVs wouldn't catch her. The SUV had not been built that could keep pace with her Kawasaki. But in her rearview mirror she spotted two drones closing the distance.

B-r-r-r-r-r-t!

Bullets pinged off the tarmac and ricocheted into the trees.

Faster!

At a hundred miles an hour the drones were no longer gaining. At 110 they fell back, machine guns sputtering futilely as she outdistanced them. Dekka racked her memory: How long was this road, where did it come out? If she reached populated areas, would Peaks still attack?

A hundred and twenty and Dekka was pressed low and flat on her gas tank, morphed paws gripping the handlebars, wanting to revert to her more easily balanced body but knowing that if she skidded out at this speed it would certainly kill her human form.

A new sound, like the bike, but in a different pitch. She risked a glance. Nothing. Risked a second glance, and spotted a helicopter gunship, dark, dangerously sleek, and bristling with missile pods.

There would be people in that helicopter, a pilot at least, maybe more, just government employees, not people deserving to die, but was there an alternative? Her bike was fast, but the gunship would have at least fifty miles an hour on her.

Then, appearing ahead, the gate and the guardhouse!

The helicopter fired; Dekka heard it, heard the explosive thrust of a rocket motor, hit the brakes while downshifting, and fought to control the bike as the missile overshot and exploded the ground before her. The bike rolled through a storm of smoke and debris, and Dekka was skidding on her side, the bike sliding away from her, skidding and then tumbling, and finally coming to a stop in a cloud of dust and pine needles.

She rose, her body screaming with pain, raised her hands, no time for regrets, no time for second thoughts, saw the helicopter coming in slow to blow the smoke away with its rotor wash and get a clear shot.

She had a glimpse of the pilot, a woman from what Dekka could see of the face below the helmet.

And then as Dekka wearily readied to destroy the helicopter, something white and shockingly quick tore from the woods. It leaped fifty feet, used a tall sapling as a sort of parkour launchpad, and flew through the air, claws—for it had claws—outstretched. The creature smashed into the side of the helicopter and seemed to lose its mind, ripping, tearing, bashing, as the helicopter went into a spin and the pilot leaped to what would surely be her death.

And then the helicopter, the creature, and anyone else aboard the doomed aircraft crashed to earth like a duck in hunting season.

Dekka hobbled to her bike, lifted it far more easily than she could ever have managed with her own body, prayed, kicked the starter, finished the prayer with a heartfelt *Amen* to the engineers at Kawasaki, and zoomed toward the gate, which she shredded and blasted through, off the facility grounds and through the trees, and then kept going at speed until she reached a town.

She stopped in the parking lot of an In-N-Out, panting for breath as she resumed her normal form.

She was shaking. Her whole body, like she had fever chills.

For what felt like an eternity, Dekka sat there on her bike, sat with the engine still throbbing, as she tried to put together the pieces of what she'd just seen.

Living heads. A boy named Lashawn Wilkins from who knew where. A monster named Carl Pullings from El Segundo. A vast underground chamber of horrors with God only knew what other atrocities.

And murder. Hers, of Carl. Hers, of the guards with the blanks. And others.

One thing was clear: Tom Peaks had not waited for his ASO Mother Rock to be recovered before preparing the Ranch and its chambers of horrors. The secret underground at the Ranch must have taken years to build.

In fact, four years, she guessed. DARPA had been preparing since the FAYZ. DARPA hadn't been waiting around; they'd been conducting ruthless, horrific experiments that testified to great fear, and great ambition.

Peaks was a criminal, a madman. A madman serving a

government that had lost all remnants of decency. A government that had simply torn up the Constitution and used fear to justify horrors that belonged in the darkest pages of history.

Dekka knew she needed to get off the grid. She needed to avoid her home, her friends, anything Peaks and company might be able to track easily.

Where should she go?

Where should she point her bike?

But of course deep down Dekka already knew where. She had made a promise to the man she killed. So, south. South to find Carl's mother.

What do I tell her? How do I lie to her?

Then she spotted the unusually tall blond boy wearing nothing but a pair of stretched and baggy underwear. He saw her, too, and with a laconic grin stuck out his thumb.

"Who the hell are you?" Dekka demanded.

"I'm the guy who took out that helicopter. And I'd really like to get the hell out of here."

"The pilot?" Dekka asked.

The white boy shrugged. "Last I saw, she was limping away."

Dekka closed her eyes in relief. "Look, I'll take you a few miles, after that you're on your own."

"Fair enough," said Armo.

He swung a long leg over the bike and settled on the seat behind her, more than doubling the passenger weight on the bike. He put his arms around her waist.

"Careful," Dekka snarled. "I'm not into guys, and I'm not in a great mood for bullshit."

"Thanks for telling me," Armo said. "Because sex was totally what I was thinking of right now."

"You got a name?"

"I go by Armo."

"Dekka."

"Where we going, Dekka?"

"Home," she said.

Dekka turned her bike south, south along the Pacific Coast Highway, which would eventually take her to Carl's mother in El Segundo.

But first it would take her to Perdido Beach.

PART TWO: HERO, VILLAIN, MONSTER

Interstice

I am person from Golden Gate and LaGuardia. Terribly
sorry for loss of life. I am unable to control creature
called #Knightmare. 1/2

Given alien substance by government. Not my fault!
#Knightmare is result. Trying to gain control of it. Pray for
me. Justin DeVeere. 2/2

Instagram:
My name is Justin DeVeere. I am an artist. I was given
a substance originally from the Perdido Beach Anomaly
by people with the US government. They lied to me and
used me. The result is the monster Knightmare. I have no
control over Knightmare, he is a creature who is easily
angered and very, very dangerous.
I am terribly sorry for the destruction and chaos and loss
of life Knightmare has caused.

I ask that people leave me and my friend Erin alone as I attempt to gain control over the beast. Attacks on us will only unleash Knightmare and more will die. Please, I beg the government that caused this to back off as we work tirelessly to control the danger. —Justin DeVeere, AKA Knightmare.

Tweet from @CalNewswire:
CHP issues BOLO for black female age 19 riding red motorcycle 101 south. Consider armed and extremely dangerous.

Tweet from @ConspiracyWATCH
Secret Monterey-area DARPA facility site AKA The Ranch is ID'd as experimental site, scene of multiple fatalities cause unknown. #ExposeDARPA

Tweet from @NewsUncensored
#Knightmare @JustinDeVeereArt part of USG conspiracy to exploit PBA alien technology?

Tweet from @GlennBeck
#Knightmare How many deaths before government admits truth that "powers" are loose in the world? #ExposeDARPA.

Tweet from @cnnbrk
White House denies rumor that alien mutagenic fragments are still reaching earth.

Tweet from @BBCBreaking
MoD rushing troops to Islay after reports of destruction
caused by monster. New Loch Ness monster hoax?

Tweet from @washingtonpost
NTSB unable to reach preliminary conclusion re causes
of LaGuardia plane crash. Cover-up alleged.

*NSA intercept of phone call between Shade Darby and
Professor Martin Darby:*
[Call begins]
SD: Hi, Dad, it's me.
MD: Oh, thank God. Where are you? Are you all right?
*SD: I'm okay, for now anyway. Dad, I am so sorry. I never
thought it would come back at you.*
*MD: Well, Shade, it was perfectly predictable, don't you
think?*
SD: (Silence)
*MD: I mean, if you're smart enough to have tricked us all
and smart enough to have taken the ASO, you're smart
enough to realize there'd be consequences.*
SD: Yeah.
MD: (Sigh. Silence.)
*SD: I don't have anything good to say, Dad, I'm just . . .
I was just looking for a way to [inaudible] not a victim.
I mean, the world is changing, nothing is going to stop
that, it'll be powers against powers. I . . . I don't want to
be helpless. Waiting.*
MD: You're not making sense, Shade. Surely you know

you're not making sense. You have to come back and give yourself up. You don't know the kind of people you're dealing with.

SD: If they're so bad, then giving myself up seems like a bad idea. Who's not making sense now?

MD: Fine, great debating point, Shade, give yourself a gold star. But what do you plan to actually do?

SD: I don't know yet. I have this power now. I mean, what's done is done, I am what I am now.

MD: Sweetheart, they will catch you. If they catch you, it will be worse than if you surrender peaceably.

SD: I hear you.

MD: You hear me. And you ignore me. Same as ever.

SD: Dad?

MD: Yes?

SD: I miss Mom.

MD: Yeah. Me too, kid. Me too. I try to do her job, too, but I'm not her, I'm just me.

SD: You've been a great father.

MD: Don't make that past tense, sweetheart. I am still your father. I will always be your father.

SD: And I'll always be your daughter. But . . . But things have changed now. Things have . . . Look, I have to go. They'll be tracking this call. I have to hang up.

MD: Shade, don't—

[Call ends]

CHAPTER 14
A Career Setback

THERE WAS OF course only one reason for Tom Peaks to be summoned to the Pentagon: he was to be fired.

Failure had a taste, at least for Tom Peaks: it was the flavor of scotch. He poured his third scotch, held the bottle up for inspection, and laughed mirthlessly: it was Lagavulin, from Islay, Scotland. He wondered if the distillery would survive what was being called, with a confusing lack of geographical accuracy, the Loch Ness Caterpillar.

"Best enjoy it," he told himself. "There may not be a next year for Islay scotch."

Peaks took a sip, set the glass aside, and resumed packing his carry-on bag.

"Do you know when you'll be back?" his wife asked, leaning out of the walk-in closet.

Peaks shook his head. "Nope. Probably just a quick overnight."

"Well, be sure and tell them you need some time off. The

kids feel like they've barely seen you lately."

Well, they'll see a lot more of me when I'm unemployed, Peaks thought. He was not overly worried about finding another job; he'd made lots of contacts during his time with HSTF-66—there was a man who ran a security company, and a woman who was vice president of a major pharmaceutical, who had both tried to recruit him at various times. But what kind of jobs would those be? Organizing security details for spoiled rock stars and self-important billionaires? Or running the in-house security for some big pharma outpost?

Maybe I'll just watch TV and stay drunk for a week. Or a month. Or whatever.

He grabbed his bag, kissed his wife on the cheek, stopped by each of his two daughters' rooms to tell them he was heading out of town, and then he was taken by staff car and helicopter to Travis Air Force Base. There he was ushered aboard one of HSTF-66's small fleet of passenger jets, popped an Ambien, and slept till Andrews Air Force Base, where he was picked up by a Pentagon staff car.

His appointment was for nine a.m., which was not a good sign since it was neither a breakfast nor a lunch meeting. Nine a.m., early, no doubt so that Undersecretary of Defense Letitia Pope could get the distasteful part of her day over with early.

Somewhat to Peaks's surprise, Pope did not keep him cooling his heels in her outer office. He was shown in promptly at nine.

The undersecretary had a pleasant office in the E-ring of

the Pentagon, the outer ring where VIPs got windows looking out over parking lots. Peaks glanced at her ego wall: pictures of Letitia Pope with the secretary of defense, the president, the ex-president, the king of Jordan, various NATO counterparts, and of course, her degree from Princeton.

Pope was middle-aged, with bottle-blond hair formed into a hair-sprayed helmet. She wore a tweed business suit that gave her a vaguely corporate air.

"Tom, how are you?" Pope asked, extending her hand. "How was your flight?"

"Fine, fine," he lied, and took the seat she indicated on the couch in a small sitting area. Coffee was carried in on a silver tray by an enlisted man.

"Well, Tom," Pope said, sounding regretful, "things are not going well."

"Ma'am, we've had some difficulties," he acknowledged.

Pope raised a skeptical eyebrow at his mild choice of words.

"But our core research is going well," Peaks added, "very well, despite—"

"Despite a destroyed airliner and a destroyed Golden Gate Bridge."

"As I said: difficulties."

"And nine dead at the Ranch."

Peaks nodded. He was not surprised by the negativity. He had excuses, reasons, explanations, but the Pentagon had never been a big fan of explanations for failure.

Pope looked at him searchingly, as if making up her mind about him. "Give me the short overview on the research."

Peaks nodded again. "Yes, ma'am. Well, as you know, we are working on several solutions concurrently. Broadly there are three avenues: robots, cyborgs, and biologicals. The robot technology is performing nominally in tests. The cyborgs show great promise, though we are having technical issues with the head-to-computer interface. And we have proof of concept with the biological approach, though we did lose Carl and—"

"—And your most hopeful biological test subject refused to cooperate and escaped, doing, what, ten million dollars in damage? And at least one other escaped at the same time. Have you located them?"

"Not yet," Peaks said stiffly. "We, um, can't really use law enforcement assets to their fullest, since of necessity this would be a shoot-on-sight situation. Cops don't do shoot-on-sight. But California Highway Patrol has a BOLO out for her, and once they or one of our surveillance assets locates her, we have a go-team in a high state of readiness."

The door opened behind Peaks, and Pope stood for the secretary of defense herself, Janet Oberlin. Oberlin lacked Pope's minimal approachability. She was gray, hatchet-faced, chilly, and, in Peaks's view, not up to the job, like most people in this government.

"Madam Secretary," he said, and offered her his hand. She looked at him, then at the hand, which she considered for a long moment before shaking.

"Go ahead, Ms. Pope," SecDef Oberlin said. "Don't let me interrupt." She sat equidistant from Peaks and Pope in the larger of the two armchairs.

"I was just saying that we have a rapid-response go-team ready to deploy as soon as we locate Dekka Talent and Aristotle Adamo."

"And what about ASO-Three? The Iowa rock?"

Peaks shrugged. "We know who had it, and we have a BOLO out for that girl as well—Shade Darby, her name is. And we are preparing to move her father, Professor Martin Darby, to the Ranch."

"You're grabbing a Northwestern University professor?" Oberlin demanded, and too late Peaks recalled that she was a graduate of that college.

"For use if we can't . . . can't *reason* . . . with his daughter."

Oberlin rose to her feet. "Do you have any idea how that looks if it ever gets out?"

"Why should it get out?" Peaks asked, and he allowed just the hint of a threat in his tone. Not enough to get him arrested right then and there, just enough to remind them that he, Tom Peaks, had all the secrets, and people with dangerous secrets needed to be treated fairly. Carefully. Respectfully.

Neither Pope nor Oberlin answered, but rather than feeling vindicated, Peaks could see by their hard looks that he was finished.

Still, he was employed at the moment, and he would continue to do his best.

"There again," Peaks explained, "there's the problem that law enforcement can only take things so far. We could ask them to arrest this Shade Darby person, but to what end? The young woman in question has powers that would make it all but impossible for her to be arrested."

"And do we have any notion of where *that* person is now?"

Peaks met her eye and tried to conceal his impatience. Why were they making him jump through hoops? If he was to be fired, he'd rather get it over with. "We have some sense that they are moving west. We think they're stealing cars, switching plates, stealing smartphones as well."

"No one's catching them stealing cars?"

"The girl's power involves speed. She can move faster than the human eye can see."

Oberlin shook her head and looked disgusted. "Jesus, what a cock-up. We've lost control of ASO-Two and -Three and -Four—"

"We have the Mother Rock," Peaks interrupted. "Or will as soon as the ship docks in LA."

"Swell," Pope said dryly. "But we've also got this Knightmare person killing citizens left and right; we've got your experiment, the Dookie person, whatever her name is, silly name, the girl from the PBA. And this speed-freak girl. And the kid who went berserk. That's four supers running around loose, here in the homeland."

"Yes," Peaks said tightly.

"And none of your countermeasures is ready."

"We are ready to begin testing additional cyborgs."

"That's where you stick a human head on a robot body?" Oberlin asked.

Peaks winced. "In effect, yes, though it's more complicated than—"

Oberlin waved that off. "What you have ready right now, today, is bubkes, am I right?"

"There are the rapid-response teams . . ."

"No, no, no," the SecDef said. "I remember the briefings, Mr. Peaks, I remember being in a conference room three, no, almost four years ago, watching your PowerPoint and you telling us that conventional means would be useless against people with enhanced abilities."

"Not useless," Peaks said. "Just . . . limited. Justin DeVeere, the one who calls himself Knightmare, is not fast; he moves at normal speeds, and we are confident that we can take him down. Dekka Talent as well, and the Adamo kid."

"But not the Chicago girl."

"As you know, we've studied powers. Super-speed presents a very tough challenge. The girl in the PBA who called herself the Breeze moved at just under the speed of sound in short bursts, or could travel distances at something like two hundred miles an hour. We think Shade Darby is faster, maybe quite a bit faster. And she appears to form some kind of protective armor over a streamlined shape. It's a physical impossibility to aim a gun at her—she's effectively invisible when she's moving."

"So how do you stop her?"

"We have to trap her," Peaks said. "We have to trick her into a trap." He almost added, *Problem is, we don't know how to do that,* but stifled the outburst of honesty.

Pope lifted some papers from the coffee table between them and peered sidelong at one. "This wasn't strictly your problem, but we have fresh confirmation that the Haqqanis have ASO-Four."

"As you said, that was not my operation, that was run by CIA. And the Adamo person was Colonel DiMarco's project, undertaken without—"

"That's General DiMarco now," Oberlin said. The last flicker of hope in Peaks's head was drowned.

"Do you have any idea how dangerous it is to have terrorists with enhanced powers?" Oberlin said, sounding as if she were giving a speech. "We are tasked with the job of keeping the American people safe, and so long as I hold this position, we *will* keep them safe."

"I believe I do understand the dangers," Peaks snapped. She was playing with him, like a cat with a mouse.

Silence fell. Peaks could feel rather than see the looks being exchanged between Pope and Oberlin. A decision had been reached and he could do nothing but wait.

Oberlin rose abruptly, motioning for Peaks to keep his seat. "I have a meeting with POTUS. I leave it to you, Ms. Pope. Good day."

Her assistant leaped to open the door and she was gone. Peaks turned back to Undersecretary Pope, assuming that he was about to hear the final words of dismissal. And yet, despite everything, every expectation, he was still stunned when it came.

"Tom, we've asked you to do an impossible job," Pope said

with a sigh. "You've done tremendous work. But we feel it's time to make some changes in the leadership of HSTF-Sixty-Six, and of the Ranch."

Peaks felt as if his whole body was tingling, like a mild electric current was going through him. He'd never been fired before; he didn't know the proper etiquette, he didn't know what to do with his hands or what expression to plaster on his face.

"We want you to take the next week, Tom, and ease the path for General DiMarco. She'll be taking over as overall director, which will free you up to focus on some aspects of your continuing research."

So that was it. They wanted to keep him on as a glorified project manager, a bureaucrat running the research program at the Ranch, but reporting to his former subordinate, the former colonel and now brigadier general Gwendolyn DiMarco. DiMarco was what was known as a "comer," an officer with a great future marked out for her. She was the first woman general with substantial combat experience, she had a double PhD in anthropology and engineering, and was a star of the war college, third in her West Point class. Absolutely no one would be surprised if General DiMarco ended up as Army chief of staff, perhaps even chairman of the Joint Chiefs, someday.

She'll march in and take credit for all my work.

"This is a mistake," Peaks blurted. "This is a big mistake pulling me out at this critical time. DiMarco has already screwed up, she tried to control the morphing process and—"

"*General* DiMarco," Pope said acidly.

"She's not going to know what's going on, it will take her weeks to get up to speed and her judgment . . ." His rush of words petered out when he saw the set expression on Pope's face. "Time will be lost," he finished lamely. "Time we don't have."

"The general will be at the Ranch to assume command tomorrow at fourteen hundred hours. I'd like you to fly back immediately and begin preparing staff for the transition."

Time stopped for Tom Peaks. It had happened: he had been fired, or at least demoted, which was the same thing really. This supercilious pencil pusher and her icy bitch of a boss had conspired to destroy his career and advance the career of, surprise, surprise, another *woman*. Peaks had never thought of himself as any sort of sexist, but it was becoming clear to him now that there was a good-old-girls' network working against him.

In fact, when he thought of it, most of his problems were because of women: Dekka Talent, Shade Darby, even that silly little social climber Erin O'Day with Knightmare. Now Pope and Oberlin and DiMarco.

Peaks could barely master his emotions as he left the office, turned the wrong way in the corridor, corrected himself, and walked as fast as he could toward the distant exit.

On the private jet back to California, he ordered a scotch from the cabin attendant—not an Islay product—drank it too quickly, and ordered a second to savor as he read yet again through the psychological profiles.

Justin DeVeere, a talented young artist, utterly amoral, a complete narcissist.

Dekka Talent, a seemingly average, underperforming young woman suffering from, but coping surprisingly well with, posttraumatic stress disorder and bouts of depression.

And Shade Darby, the one with the thinnest record, the sketchiest profile. Good grades, great test scores, impressive IQ. A young woman sufficiently determined—and sufficiently bold—to manipulate her father's data and pull off a heist under the noses of the entire security apparatus of the United States.

She was the one responsible: Shade Darby. It was her theft of the rock that caused him to rush Dekka's . . . introduction . . . to the role he had planned for her. It was her theft of the rock that first got the wind up Pope's skirts. A former secretary of defense had once talked about how there were known knowns—the things we know that we know, like the sky is blue and the sun rises in the east. Then there were known unknowns, like what is the cure for cancer? But there were also unknown unknowns, and these were the most dangerous: things we don't know we don't know. The things that came out of the blue. The things you didn't even know you had to prepare for.

Like a teenaged girl stealing some of the rock.

And using it.

And developing one of the most useful, dangerous, and hard-to-defend-against superpowers.

One little bitch of a high school girl.

He ordered a third drink. What did it matter, he wasn't the one flying the plane, and there'd be a car and driver waiting for his ignominious ride back to the Ranch. How should he make the announcement? How could he possibly frame it so it didn't look like a public humiliation?

He still needed the paycheck, and if he was a good little boy, if he knuckled under properly to the great generalissimo and the mighty bitch goddess of the Pentagon, they might let him stay on as chief of research. He should be able to stomach it, he told himself. It shouldn't matter, he told himself. Who cared if people snickered behind his back? he told himself.

Or . . . or he could quit. Just quit. He'd made plenty of friends in private industry, people who would love to have him and the knowledge he possessed, and who would pay twice, no three times, no ten times what he was making working for DARPA.

Nondisclosure agreements, and noncompete agreements, and, he reminded himself, the unfortunate fact that almost every single thing he knew was classified "Top Secret" and "Top Secret: Sensitive Compartmented Information." He had nothing to sell, really, nothing that wouldn't get him arrested and thrown into some supermax prison.

The cabin attendant, smiling, leaned over him. "Would you like another, sir? Or can I get you something to eat?"

"Another," Peaks said. "Nothing to eat." But then, as the attendant walked away, he said, "Wait a sec. What do you have to eat?"

"We have a cheese and fruit platter, sandwiches, and pastry

for dessert. In fact, we have chocolate éclairs, which look delicious."

"The scotch. Then bring me an éclair and have one yourself."

He downed the drink in two gulps, knowing it was a drink, or possibly two drinks, too far. Well, to hell with it. Desperate times. The most desperate ever, probably. The very nature of reality was changing, the underlying rules of the universe were being hacked. And those silly bitches thought they could deal with it? Without Tom Peaks?

Desperate times.

"Desperate times call for desperate measures," Peaks muttered.

He used his Swiss Army knife to slice the éclair open, exposing the creamy center. From his pocket he drew out a steel screw-top tube partly filled with gray dust.

They'd given Dekka Talent an ounce.

The éclair held three ounces.

CHAPTER 15
A Nice Talk

THEY WERE IN their third stolen car.

Felony, felony, felony.

They were using money taken from bank tellers who saw nothing but a vague blur and felt a gust of breeze.

Felony. Federal felony, at that.

And they were in possession of approximately ten pounds of alien rock taken by virtue of hacking.

Felony and felony, both federal.

Malik was keeping track.

And now, as they sat amid fast-food trash and empty water bottles in a stolen Lexus SUV in a Target parking lot in Silverthorne, Colorado, they were engaging in yet another felony: conspiracy.

"Attention will be mostly on this Knightmare person," Malik said, idly twirling a fry like a tiny baton in his nimble fingers. "But the FBI will have plenty of time to spare for us."

Cruz was in the backseat, experimenting with her power.

She had become adept at disappearing; now she was trying something very different: reappearing, but as someone else, altering her visible self. In the rearview mirror, Malik glanced up from time to time to see a partly transparent Cruz, looking sometimes like a badly lit version of herself, and other times like other people, often celebrities. She needed photos to picture the faces she mirrored.

At the moment it was pictures of beautiful women that held Cruz's interest. Malik saw her flicking through them on her stolen phone, her expression almost giddy with the possibilities.

Great, Malik thought. *And I was hoping Cruz would be the sensible one.*

"We need a goal, an objective," Malik insisted. "A plan!"

Shade flashed an irritated look at him, which softened quickly. Malik could all but read Shade's mind: Malik had rescued them. Malik had thrown in with them. Malik was in the same danger she and Cruz were in. Shade had heard his half of a stormy, painful call with his parents. Malik's life was coming apart. And Shade knew it was her fault.

Malik thought, *Yeah, you'd damn well better be nice to me.*

"According to Twitter, the center of all this is in California," Shade said. "So that's where we're heading."

"And why exactly would we be heading to the center of all the problems?" Malik demanded.

"This is all connected to the PBA. Most of the survivors are in California," Shade said.

"Which is not an answer, Shade."

Shade shrugged. "You're right. So, you have a better idea?"

"We need to disappear for a while," Malik said.

"Or . . . ," Shade said, glancing back at Cruz. "Oh, my God, Cruz!"

In the rearview mirror was what looked an awful lot like a translucent Taylor Swift.

"I know!" Cruz cried. "I've been trying to . . . and it kinda works! I can disappear," Cruz said, her voice heavy with awe and amazement, "and then reappear looking, well, however I want."

"And you went with Taylor Swift?" Shade demanded.

Cruz turned her newly stolen iPhone around and showed them both a photo of Swift. It was almost entirely identical to Cruz, aside from the translucence.

"I need a photo and, look, this is real creepy . . ." She turned her head sideways and the entire back half of her head was invisible. It was like she was wearing a Taylor Swift mask over an invisible head. Like the face was floating in air.

"Ahhh!" Malik yelped.

"Okay, *that* is amazing," Shade said. She reached to touch Cruz's face. "Amazing! It feels completely real." The skin dimpled where Shade touched it. She could feel Cruz's body heat. She could feel her agitated breath.

Shade touched the invisible back of Cruz's head, and it, too, felt real.

"You know you just poked me in the ear, right?" Cruz said.

"This is insane," Malik said. "This is . . . this is . . ." And then he started to laugh his strange barking-seal laugh, the laugh that had embarrassed him all his life, but that seldom failed to elicit a grin from Shade.

Shade's eyes narrowed and just a hint of her teeth showed through a tight grimace of a smile. "This gives us a whole new power."

"I know!"

"Are you, um," Malik began. Then he reformulated his question. "I mean, do you think it changed, um . . . uhhh . . . you know. Other things? Down-there things?"

Cruz-with-the-Swift-face patted her chest, her still-male chest. "No," she said, a bit deflated. "I'm still a boy . . . down there. I would need a visual, a picture. And la Swift does not pose naked."

Malik threw up his hands. "I don't even know how to start thinking about all this. We are way off the weirdness scale here."

"My God, Malik Tenerife just admitted he doesn't understand something. I want to record that," Shade snarked. "Hero, villain, monster, right? So help me figure out how to play hero. It's our only way through all this. I realize in your comics there's constantly some big crisis where the cops just sort of stand around helplessly waiting for a superhero to fly in, but that isn't real life."

"Is now," Malik said glumly.

Shade rolled her eyes. "Okay, you know I'm going to ask you why you think that, so why not just tell me rather than dragging it out."

"Knightmare," Malik said smugly—deliberately smug, to

annoy Shade. "He's the monster, although I strongly suspect he's really a villain."

"Not according to him," Cruz said from the backseat. "You saw his Tweets."

Malik waved that off impatiently. "Doesn't matter. He can play the monster role all he wants, but he's left a trail of death behind him, so we can treat him as a villain."

"Under the official rules of comics?" Shade drawled.

"He destroyed the Golden Gate Bridge," Malik said, and made a face that said, *What, that's not enough?*

"Definitely villain behavior," Cruz chimed in, herself once more.

They fell silent, Malik and Cruz both knowing Shade well enough to know that in the end she'd be the one to decide.

"Could I beat him in a fight?" Shade asked. "Until the other night in the cemetery, I'd never even been in any kind of fight."

Malik cast a sidelong look at Shade. "The thing is, if you're playing the hero role, you don't actually have to beat him, you just have to *try*. And people have to see you trying." Then, to Cruz in the rearview mirror, "Speaking of typical tropes, you and I are either sidekicks or enablers. I guess you're the sidekick, since you have a power."

"Did you see the videos?" Shade demanded, ignoring the byplay. It was a purely rhetorical question—they'd all watched the YouTube videos repeatedly. "That's a big, scary thing, that Knightmare."

"With your speed?" Cruz asked. "He'd probably never touch you."

Shade now twisted to talk to Cruz. "When you morph, when you use your power . . . do you still always feel . . ."

Now it was Cruz's turn to look grave. "The dark things watching? Yes. That's why I don't change for long. I feel them, and each time it's like I can hear them a little better, not that there's an actual sound . . . just . . ." She shrugged. "What is it, they, whatever?"

Shade shook her head. "I don't know."

"Guess," Malik demanded.

Shade was quiet for so long, Malik was sure she'd say nothing. But then, "I think of them as the Dark Watchers. I think they are the same thing that was inside that girl. Gaia."

"Which tells you what?"

"I have to pee," Shade said.

"Cut the bullshit, babe."

Shade took a deep breath. "You want a theory? I've got a theory. Everyone always thought the ASOs were benign life-creating viruses, basically. But what do real viruses do? They turn healthy cells into breeders of more virus. And sometimes they turn a healthy cell into cancer. I think somehow a consciousness is in that ASO virus, in that rock." Eyes down, she added, "I think they're using us. I think maybe we're . . . an experiment. Unless . . ."

"Unless?" Malik prompted.

"Unless we're just entertainment."

"And yet you think this is all still a great idea?" Malik said, harsher than he intended. "It would help me to not think you're crazy, if you'd at least admit this is all a huge mistake."

"I'm going in to use the ladies'." Shade did not invite them to come with, nor did she offer to get anything while in the Target store.

"We're in trouble, aren't we?" Cruz asked when Shade was gone.

Malik didn't bother answering.

"I don't think I should have eaten the rock," Cruz said.

Malik, with great self-discipline, resisted the urge to say and to shout and perhaps even to sing at the top his voice that he had told her so, that he had warned them both that they were taking on a fight with all the might of the government.

"I don't know what I thought would happen," Cruz said. "I don't know, I just . . . Maybe it's all a mental illness, like my father and, like, half of people think. I just wanted to . . . Just trying to . . . But maybe I'm fooling myself. Maybe it really is just gender dysphoria, a mental illness, a—"

"—So what if it is, Cruz?" Malik cut in impatiently. He was coming to have great affection for Cruz, but her unwillingness to stand up to Shade irritated him. Half the time she was in what Malik considered the rational world, and half the time she was a bit of flotsam carried along on Shade's obsession. "Look, Cruz, what if your trans thing is just some mental problem? Dysphoria, or whatever. What does it matter what the diagnosis is if there's a cure, and the cure doesn't hurt anyone? How has anyone got a single damn reason to care how you look or what you call yourself? If you're crazy, the people hating on you are a hell of a lot crazier."

That brought a crooked smile to Cruz's lips.

"Your friend in the Target ladies' room is perfectly sane,"

Malik went on bitterly. "There is not a shrink on earth Shade couldn't convince she's all right. Smart as hell. Very good at rationalizing. And yet, look where we are, Cruz. She's sane and smart and here we are, and I wouldn't bet ten cents we'll be alive a week from now. So how smart does that make the two of us that we follow her? What the hell is the matter with *us*?"

"You follow her because you love her," Cruz said.

There followed a silence. Then, "Goddammit, Cruz." Malik lowered his forehead to the steering wheel and banged it softly.

"It's true," Cruz said.

"Of course it's true. Jesus, Cruz! You're not supposed to say it."

Cruz lay her hand on his shoulder. "I'm sorry you're in this mess, Malik, but I'm so glad you're here."

"Playing the part of the idiot ex-boyfriend," Malik grumbled. "The official enabler."

"Maybe," Cruz said softly. "But she needs you, and so do I. You can call yourself an idiot, but I would give . . ." Her voice choked and for a moment she couldn't go on, and when she did it was in an emotion-roughened tone. "I would give anything, anything in the world, to have just one person love me the way you love her."

Malik placed his hand over her hand on his shoulder. Then he jerked his chin in the direction of the restaurant. "The superhero cometh."

Cruz followed the direction of his gaze. "I think of her as

being half human, half shark."

"Yep. That'll do," Malik said.

"All right," Shade announced through the window. "California and the hero track it is. Right? Because none of us had a better idea."

"Fait accompli," Cruz said.

It took them two days and three more stolen cars to reach California.

En route they listened to the radio for news reports, and Cruz kept an eye on social media, but there were no new sightings of Knightmare. The Coast Guard stopped the ship Knightmare had snagged at the Golden Gate and found no sign of Knightmare or the woman with him. The ship's crew all agreed that the creature and the woman with him destroyed the ship's radio and forced them to launch a lifeboat just off the coast of the Monterey Peninsula.

Shade, Cruz, and Malik approached Monterey, but they turned back when they got word of roadblocks ahead. They spent the night in a motel that accepted cash and monitored both the TV and the web. But there was no news of Knightmare.

The next morning they drove twenty miles and found a second motel, and again spent a night watching TV and cursing the slow wi-fi.

At the motel Kim Kardashian made an appearance. A very *complete* appearance, since Cruz had full-body shots to work with. An appearance that, to Shade's undisguised disgust, managed to stop Malik in mid-sentence, despite the fact that he was prosing away about Eddie Van Halen's guitar work.

By the third day of this, the hero option was looking hopeless. They heard of a fire raging in San Luis Obispo, but it was too far away for Shade to pull a dramatic rescue. They considered whether Shade could fly to a war zone and save a bunch of lives, but concluded that the FBI was quite likely to spot them if they bought tickets to Afghanistan.

They heard of two surfers lost beneath a freak wave, their bodies presumably swept out to sea, but it was hard to see where super-speed would be of any help there.

They watched *The Incredibles* and speculated about whether Shade could run on water like the kid in the movie.

And then: a sighting. Knightmare had just emptied a bank vault in Salinas, and that was only six miles away. They raced to the scene, but stopped well away as the town was crawling with every variety of law enforcement officer.

"Knightmare's got the same problem we have," Shade said. "He can't use credit cards, which means he's either sleeping in the open or hiding out in no-tell motels he can pay for in cash."

"There are dozens of those within an hour's drive," Malik said. "And the police will have figured that out, too."

"Yes, of course they will. And they have the resources. Which means we need the same resources, we need to know what the cops know."

"What if we had a police scanner?" Cruz suggested.

"That's just the public frequency," Malik said. "We'd need a radio tuned to whatever private frequency they're using."

Then, to Shade, "How far can you run?"

"I don't know. But we could park a couple miles away, that's just a few seconds' run. I can go right into Salinas and snag a radio."

"Might be worth thinking about," Malik mused, but Shade had already transformed and a second later was out the door. "Yes," Malik called after her, "it was good to discuss all this and work it out in advance and not just go running off like a . . ." He sighed, sat back, closed his eyes, and said, "So, Cruz. Know any jokes?"

But before Cruz could think of any, Shade was back and holding a squawking police radio. "And I got these." She handed a pack of Smarties to Cruz.

"Excellent," Cruz said.

It took seven hours of listening to intermittent chatter between a CHP captain, an LAPD commander, an FBI special agent, and a person who was never identified by affiliation before they sat up suddenly.

"*Suspects spotted, southbound PCH, nine miles north of Piedras Blanca lighthouse.*"

"Map it!" Shade snapped to Cruz.

"We're not far," Cruz reported, and Malik pulled out into traffic.

"Left at the light," Cruz directed.

"*Suspect vehicle is a light blue Mini Cooper, license plate two-golf-able-tare-one-two-three.*"

"Okay, that's straight down PCH. South. You want to go south," Cruz said. "South! Not north, south!"

"Floor it," Shade said. "The cops are too busy to write traffic tickets."

"Yeah, and maybe the EMTs will be too busy to scrape our bodies up off the freeway." But Malik accelerated anyway.

"You could run on ahead," Cruz suggested.

Shade shook her head. "That run to pick up the radio? That about gutted me. And the Watchers were . . . The longer I'm morphed, the closer they feel."

The purloined radio squawked. The fugitives in the Mini Cooper had run off the road as they tried to veer from the highway and presumably find cover in the lighthouse.

A CHP helicopter passed low over their heads, rotors tilted, moving at top speed. Behind them came the sound of sirens.

"Just a mile!" Cruz said nervously.

"Have you thought about how to beat him?" Malik asked.

"Now it occurs to you to ask? I'm fast and I'm strong and I don't bruise easily, that's all I've got," Shade said, her voice pitching upward in excitement and fear.

Malik considered. Then, "You can use the car. This car!" He explained his idea in quick, terse sentences even as they spotted the lighthouse, a stubby cylinder atop low rocks against the gray-and-white Pacific. The land on both sides of the road was gently rolling, hay-colored grass on low hills to the left, hay-colored grass on flatter land to their right, the ocean side.

There was a sign warning of a curve and advising forty miles an hour. The CHP helicopter was circling, taking a wide turn from following the highway to following the access road leading out to the lighthouse. Two CHP cars were already tearing down that access road, with lights and sirens.

Shade figured the heavy guns were coming, the military-level response, but they weren't here yet, just a distant Mini Cooper, two CHP cars, and a helicopter.

And me, Shade thought: *the superhero.*

CHAPTER 16
Shade vs. Knightmare

SHADE WAS ALREADY morphing as Malik sent the stolen SUV barreling after the CHP. "Let me out here," she said in her eerie transformed voice.

Malik for once did not argue and hit the brakes. Shade was out and gone before the vehicle came to a stop, effortlessly leaping from a moving vehicle and feeling a rush of pure joy from that ability. It was a joy that lasted for a half second before the fear flooded back as the Dark Watchers made their presence known.

The access road was less than half a mile long, a heartbeat for Shade. Ahead was the lighthouse compound: a handful of one-story, red-roofed buildings, a network of trails, some windswept trees, an ancient water tower, and the tall, austere, white-painted lighthouse itself.

It was a savagely beautiful location, with waves crashing on rocks and the long sweep of the California coastline to the north and south. Three cars were parked neatly in front of the administrative buildings. The Mini was not so much parked as abandoned. Abandoned and then torn apart, like a steel egg from which a gigantic bird had hatched.

And there stood Knightmare.

A pretty blond woman cowered against the nearest wall and covered her head with pale, bruised arms.

The CHP cars advanced at what to Shade was a ludicrous crawl. The helicopter's rotors were beating so slowly that Shade could see the individual blades. The woman—Erin O'Day was her name, Shade recalled—was screaming, but the sound was an eerie warble. The creature—Knightmare—stood with claw and sword spread wide in a gesture of defiance. He was massive, not quite twice Shade's height, and wider still, measuring from sword tip to claw tip.

He tore apart the Golden Gate Bridge!

There was still time to turn around, run back to her friends. Save herself. She didn't really have to do this, did she?

Run away, run away, live to fight another day.

It was the Dark Watchers! They didn't want this fight. The malicious glee was gone, replaced by alarm. They feared what she might do.

They fear me!

This realization was like a bolt of steel added to her spine. Knightmare was a monster, a villain, a murderer. And the Watchers did not want him hurt.

I'm not your puppet!

Knightmare was even bigger up close and radiated power and violence. Shade vibrated to a stop, forcing herself to speak slowly.

"Hey. You. Should. Um . . ." She had not exactly thought about what to say to the monster. "Stop. Being. An. Asshole."

With slowness that tried Shade's patience, the creature turned malevolent pupil-less black eyes on her. "What the hell are you?"

"I'm. The. Hero."

Shade was pretty sure he would blink at this if he had eyelids. He did not appear to. His eyes were black balls, inhuman, soulless.

The CHP arrived. Their car doors opened. Two officers were slowly, slowly taking positions behind the cover of their doors, handguns drawn.

"Go ahead, shoot, you puny nothings!" Knightmare bellowed in his crack-of-doom voice.

Bam-bam-bam-bam-bam-bam-bam!

The highway patrolmen emptied their clips at point-blank range. Shade saw the bullets flying. She saw the slugs strike their target. She saw them spin away.

Guns don't bother him, so what am I supposed to do?

Cruz and Malik coasted up in the stolen vehicle, taking their sweet time. Malik and Cruz piled out. Slowly. Malik left the engine running, then reached back in and threw it into gear. The SUV crawled forward, just as they'd planned. Shade to distract so that Malik could get the vehicle closer.

Well done, Malik.

She returned to the SUV in a single bound as Malik was still slowly walking away. She opened the door and climbed in. Her morphed body was a very poor fit for the seat, but she was able to jam one foot down on the accelerator and watch the speedometer move from eight miles an hour to twenty to forty-five, at which point the SUV was just a few feet from impact. She leaped out, easily matching what to her was not even walking speed, and watched as the SUV advanced on Knightmare.

His dead eyes turned, spotting the SUV, and he began to move.

It was a surreal ballet, the SUV advancing at a seeming crawl, Knightmare swinging his sword at a slightly faster pace. SUV . . . sword. SUV . . . sword.

Shade shifted position to see better. The front bumper was inches from Knightmare's left leg as the sword arm completed an awkward arc.

The SUV crashed into Knightmare with a loud *crumpf!*

Knightmare's sword arm sliced into the SUV behind the driver's seat.

Knightmare's leg was slammed by the impact of the big SUV and he lost his balance. His sword arm had carried him around with its momentum and now he fell on his back atop the SUV.

Erin's unnatural warbling scream rose in pitch.

The CHP in the helicopter had their door open and fired down at him with a shotgun, the fat slugs clearly visible as they flew.

Shade looked around, searching for some tool, some weapon. By the main highway was a barbed-wire fence. She raced back and ripped lengths of wire free, coiling it, then ran back just as Knightmare climbed—apparently unhurt—off the crushed SUV. He glared up at the helicopter and then did something Shade would not have thought possible for a creature of his size and weight: he jumped.

Knightmare jumped twice his own height, and at the top of his rise he swung the sword arm.

"No!" Shade cried in a millisecond buzz.

But Knightmare was too high and the helicopter was too low and the sword arm smashed into the whirling blades, which shattered and came apart, hurling jagged steel in every direction.

Then the sword's arc cut into the top of the helicopter and down through the passenger space. Shade watched in horror as the blade sliced down through the body of a patrolman, down through his shoulder, down through his chest, out through his hip.

The helicopter crashed into one of the administrative buildings, bashing in the red-tile roof. Shade saw it all in slow motion with exquisite detail: the tiles flying, the stucco crumbling, the rotors shattering, the pilot struggling with the stick, mouth open, starting to scream . . .

Am I fast enough?

Shade ran straight at the disaster. She ducked beneath a stumpy, turning rotor, leaped atop a crumbling wall, paused for a millisecond to aim, and threw herself through the air. She landed hard against the nearside door of the helicopter, hands scrabbling for purchase, one foot finding a skid, fingers finding the door handle.

She yanked the door open, swung into the helicopter's cockpit, started to grab the pilot, saw he was still buckled in, and unsnapped the seat belt as the glass bubble of the cockpit smashed into crumbling brick. Masonry was pushing its way through the glass. In a heartbeat the pilot would be dead.

"Hang on!" she yelled at morph-normal speed, which of course the pilot could not possibly understand.

Shade grabbed the pilot by his jacket with one hand, grabbed the doorjamb with the other, and shoved off blindly, backward. The pilot flew out of his seat even as Shade saw a wooden beam pierce the glass. The beam was driven so hard into the pilot's seat that it pushed all the way through, tearing stuffing and springs out of the back.

But the pilot, like Shade, was flying backward through the air.

The fall was at normal speed, so Shade had time to wrap her arms around the pilot and twist in midair to take all the impact on her back. She hoped she was strong enough to take it.

W-h-h-u-u-u-m-m-m-p-h-h-h!

The landing seemed to take forever, but that did not lessen its impact. She had fallen only twenty feet, perhaps, but still the wind exploded from her chest and she lay dazed for a long while—perhaps three seconds in real time—before she could suck in air. The pilot lay on his back atop her. She rolled him away. He was dazed but breathing.

Hell yes: superhero! Shade thought.

"Are. You. All right?" she asked, noticing that she had ripped his jacket to shreds.

The pilot was not in the mood for conversation. He was more in the mood for incoherent, babbling terror.

A pillar of dust and smoke rose from the crashing helicopter, and then something Shade almost did not recognize: the sound of an explosion, a single loud *Bam!*, and then a protracted roar as fuel ignited.

A piece of steel flew like a scythe toward the stunned pilot. Shade snatched it out of the air.

In the meantime one of the CHP had turned and run in pure animal panic. The other one was emptying his reloaded pistol at Knightmare, but the creature barely noticed him.

Shade glanced left and saw more CHP lights coming. But what were they going to do that these doomed patrolmen had not already tried?

For only the second time in her life, Shade was suddenly, and without training or preparation, on the verge of an actual, physical *fight*. And Knightmare was many times more dangerous than the vandals in the cemetery.

"I really wish I prayed, because now would be a good time," Shade buzzed.

Shade retrieved her castoff barbed wire and launched herself at Knightmare. She loosely tied one end of the barbed wire around one leg, then ran in a tight circle, looping the wire five times around Knightmare's legs before she bounded away to a safe distance.

Knightmare tried a step. She could actually watch the dull

emotion form on his face, the puzzlement, the worry, the frustration, the fear, as he fell, tripped by the wire.

He would break free in seconds, but for Shade a few seconds was a long time. Long enough for her to snatch the pistol from the patrolman's hand just as he'd slammed in a fresh clip. There was no time for her to register the fact that she had never held a gun in her life before this moment. She ran, bounding, and leaped atop the downed monster. She aimed the gun at his right eye and . . .

Blam!

This time it was her bullet she watched. It was her bullet that flew harmlessly past Knightmare's eye.

"Damn!"

She jumped closer to the eye, which was slowly focusing, dark circles within still-darker circles. From a distance of three feet she fired again. This time the copper-jacketed slug plowed into the eye. It dimpled the surface, like a marble dropped on Jell-O, but then the Jell-O exploded outward, the vitreous black goo displaced by the bullet entering the membrane.

It was like watching a water balloon filled with ink explode in slow motion.

Shade jumped clear and now the Dark Watchers seemed almost to be singing, but in discordant tones, as though disagreeing with themselves. The attention was intense, distracting. She panted hard, limbs all leaden, heart pounding like it was trying to break through concrete. The exhaustion was utter and it gutted her. For a moment she could only stand as her head swam and her stomach wanted urgently to be sick.

Knightmare snapped the barbed wire easily, just so much thread to him. He roared in pain, roared and clapped his claw hand over his face, roared and swung his sword around, trying to hit his nearly invisible foe.

Shade had hurt him, but not fatally, not by a long shot. One eye was a black stain, but the other one still worked.

Justin DeVeere might be a violent psychopath, but he was no fool. With a quickness of mind that worried Shade, Knightmare saw his best shot. He turned and bounded away, each stride carrying him two dozen feet, straight toward the lighthouse.

The lighthouse was on a small man-made hill. A set of stone steps led up to a surprisingly grand porticoed entryway and a narrow door through which Knightmare barely squeezed sideways.

By the time Shade had conquered her nausea, Knightmare was all the way inside. Furious at the loss of time, Shade leaped to the lighthouse. It was a leap unlike anything she had tried before. It was as if her thick, morphed thighs contained some kind of spring-loaded mechanism, and it quite simply hurled her through the air, hurled but also tumbled, for she had no way to control her flight. She cartwheeled, head over heels, had plenty of time to see the curved wall of the lighthouse but absolutely no way to avoid crashing into it.

The impact knocked the wind out of her but was not

painful. No, the painful part was when she fell to the ground, banging off the portico.

She was mad now. Mad at Knightmare, mad that she couldn't control her body, mad at what felt like some kind of psychic interruption from the Watchers.

With one powerful foot she kicked in the door. Inside, things were much as she expected. There was a small desk and a chair, but really the only important feature was the steel spiral staircase.

"Counterclockwise. Of course."

Somewhere Shade had acquired the knowledge that in ancient castles the spiral staircases always went counterclockwise, because in the old days of sword fighting you defended your castle from the top down. A spiral that went counterclockwise meant your sword hand—usually your right—was free, while those coming up the stairs had their sword hands cramped.

This was one of those pieces of data Shade had never imagined being useful. But as it happened, she was in a tower, and she was facing, in effect, a swordsman whose "sword" was on his right.

The stairs were narrow, too narrow for her to squeeze past the lumbering monster above her. He had used the lighthouse to minimize the advantage her speed gave her.

Knightmare stopped at a platform halfway up, turned, and aimed his sword arm downward, waving it side to side, daring her to try to get past.

"Who are you?" Knightmare cried.

Shade vibrated to a stop just beyond the slow sweep of his sword arm. "Shade. Darby. Pleased to. Meet you."

"Leave me alone!"

"Can't. You're. The. Villain. I'm. The. Hero." The silliness of her response would have made Shade laugh at herself if it were not for the rising nausea as ghostly tendrils tickled the boundaries of her mind, prodding, pushing, like blind burglars trying to find an open window.

"It's not my fault! I can't control this creature!"

"Yeah. We think. That's. Bullshit. You're talking. To me. So you are. In control."

Knightmare slowly took that on board. His remaining eye glared black hatred at Shade. "Leave me alone!" His bellow was so loud, Shade worried it could bring the old structure down around their ears.

"Can't. Hero. Villain. Monster. Long story."

On the one hand, dialoguing with Knightmare gave Shade a moment to rest. On the other hand: *They* watched. *They* probed.

"What do you want?" Shade raged at those dark and distant objects. "What do you want from me?" Just a loud buzz to Knightmare.

Standing there on the staircase, looking up at an armored freak, reminded Shade of a very important point: she had no natural weapons. She had tossed aside the gun, and now she had only her speed.

Leave him be.

The thought came unbidden, and it puzzled Shade. Leave

him be? Leave the monster who had killed a planeload of people and dozens more in the course of destroying the Golden Gate Bridge?

It made some sense: she likely could not stop Knightmare. It made sense to save her own life and those of her friends and get as far away from this terrible creature as she could.

And yet: *Where exactly did that thought come from?*

"Yeah, I don't think so," she said, defiant, speaking to creatures who might be nothing but figments of her imagination. Somehow addressing the Dark Watchers made her feel steadier. More herself. Stronger.

No, no, she was not about to just run away. She had the power she had sought; her own actions had brought her here. This was another Gaia, a superpowered villain, the very thing superheroes were meant to cope with.

Right?

Her thoughts went to weapons. The cops outside had guns, but they hadn't been very useful. The only vulnerability Knightmare seemed to have was his eyes. His eyes and maybe that ferocious mouth.

Run away, run away, live to fight another day. The bit of doggerel was playing on a loop in Shade's mind. Just leave him be. Just turn and go. Live to fight another day.

Why the hell should I care what this lunatic does? I'm only playing hero because of Malik!

No, that was not true. No, that was not her own thought, that was a thought that came from . . . *them.*

She closed her eyes and looked inward, looked without

eyes, with thought alone, at the seething, black, liquid image. She faced it cleanly, straight on.

"What do you want from me? What is this game about?"

Was that a ghostly laugh? Was it a sneer echoing across light-years?

Knightmare seized the moment as the transformed Shade stared into space, frowning with crinkling plasticine features. He did the unexpected, the awkward. He swept his claw toward her, stabbing it at her.

Shade shook off her reverie and sidestepped the blow, but this was what Knightmare expected and he had already begun the sharp, quick forward thrust of his sword arm.

The point came within millimeters of Shade's chest before she twisted and slipped the blow. The sword arm stabbed past her and right through the thick brick wall of the lighthouse. A narrow shaft of daylight entered through the hole.

It was through that small hole that Shade saw something puzzling: the CHP vehicles were pulling away. Men on foot were running. And from far away she heard voices yelling, "Shade! Run! Run!"

Not the Dark Watchers, not this time. That was Cruz and Malik.

Shade spun and bounded back down the stairs, racing out the door, shot a look over her shoulder, and saw the F-16, high out over the water.

She saw the plume of smoke and fire as the F-16's Hellfire missile launched, flew, then veered unstoppably toward the lighthouse.

Shade reached the flattened SUV and spotted Malik half in an abandoned CHP car. Cruz was in the backseat. Shade jumped into the passenger seat and began to de-morph as the Hellfire, with an enormous *crack-BOOM!*, annihilated the Piedras Blancas lighthouse, turning it into flying rubble.

For Shade, the world began to move very fast as she de-morphed and sighed with intense relief when the Dark Watchers disappeared from her mind.

Malik backed the CHP car up, executed an impressive skidding turn, and went tearing away.

"Okay," Cruz said, breathless as they bounced onto the 101. "That was some serious superhero stuff."

"And now we're stealing a cop car," Malik said. "Better and better."

CHAPTER 17
Battle of the Lighthouse

THIS IS WHAT Justin DeVeere—Knightmare—saw: the disturbing half plastic, half insect, half girl had suddenly run away.

She was gone. He'd seen her blur-quick glance outside and in a heartbeat she was gone, leaving nothing but a short, sharp blast of air.

Why?

He followed the direction she looked, out through the hole he'd made in the side of the lighthouse, and saw the police pulling back at top speed.

He had a very bad feeling.

Knightmare spun, stabbed his sword through the back side of the tower, ripped it up, ripped it sideways, and beat on the wall with his claw. The bricks clattered away and he was out through the hole and leaping for the ground when he saw the missile, a blur, and actually felt the wind of it inches above his massive shoulder. It hit the tower and the whole world exploded.

There followed a period of blackness. He was vaguely aware, vaguely conscious, but his thoughts were scrambled. He was on his face. There was something heavy on his back. He opened his one eye and saw jagged sections of brick wall piled around him.

Erin was there, yanking at him with her weak hands, yelling things he could not hear for the ringing in his ears. But he could watch her lips, her quite pretty lips, not the time for that, and anyway what was she saying?

Get up?

Thoughts and memories all snapped into place and Justin knew. He shrugged off the tons of debris and struggled to his feet.

Did the Dark Watchers just cheer?

On his feet, feeling the pain in his eye and the new pain in his back, but defiant and with a growing rage inside him, Justin spread his arms, threw back his head, and roared, "You cannot stop me! I. Am. *Knightmare!*"

Erin was there, yelling, and as the ringing in his ears quieted he began to hear, "It's the girl from Iowa! It's the girl from Iowa!" and the penny dropped as Justin realized what she was saying, and who he had just faced down in battle. The speed demon was the girl from the field in Iowa. The girl who now apparently had acquired super-speed and a desire to meddle in the affairs of Knightmare.

You're the villain. I'm the hero.

Justin pushed away the pain in his eye, or told himself to at least—the pain was terrible and absolutely impossible to ignore. Her name, that unusual name, came to him and he bellowed, "Come and get me, Shade Darby! Come and fight Knightmare!"

I'm not the villain, I'm the artist!

But the speed demon and her friends had hopped into a CHP car, slammed into reverse, and were racing at speed for the main road as more vehicles with flashing lights closed in from north and south. The F-16 circled to come around for another attack. And now, flying low over the water, came two Apache attack helicopters.

For a moment Justin wanted to cry.

It's not fair!

Erin was just beside him, pleading with him to run, run, run!

But he was weary. And though he was fast, he was not the girl from the Iowa cornfield, and he could not hope to outrun the missiles he saw already arcing with deadly grace toward him.

"Sorry," he said to Erin.

She seemed puzzled. Her eyes widened. And there were three massive explosions.

Justin regained consciousness as Justin, no longer Knightmare.

He could tell that he was in the back of a tractor trailer— the dimensions of the long rectangle were the dimensions of every trailer on the highway, and he felt the vibrations of wheels on tarmac, heard the diesel engine and the sound of wind.

He was on his back, naked, on a stainless-steel table.

Titanium bands two inches thick clasped his neck, elbows, waist, thighs, and ankles. And there were heavy cement blocks encasing his hands.

No!

Four people in Army uniforms and maroon berets had four automatic assault rifles aimed at him.

A middle-aged woman in an impeccable, razor-creased uniform stood watching with avid eyes. The uniform was adorned with small blue and gold rectangles framing a single brass star on the shoulders.

"You would be Justin DeVeere," the general said. "I am General DiMarco. Your girlfriend is vapor, thanks to you."

"Erin?" he moaned.

"Let's get this straight right from the start, you little psycho: each and every time you address me, you will do so as 'General' or 'Ma'am.'" She leaned down close, close enough for him to notice a twitch in her right eye.

"Is she . . . did . . . Is she dead?"

The general smiled, showing too many small white teeth. Then she grabbed his nose between thumb and forefinger and twisted it viciously. He cried out and she twisted again, wringing a louder cry of pain from him.

"What did I just tell you?"

"I just . . . Is she dead. General?"

"Deader 'n hell, private, deader 'n hell. You are all alone in the world, Private DeVeere, all alone in the great cruel world."

"Why do you keep calling me 'Private'? General Ma'am?"

DiMarco patted him on the side of his face. "Well, son, it's like this: although we don't use it, we do still have the draft on the books. So you, you sick piece of shit, are now a private in the US Army."

"What? I mean, what, General?"

"Very good: you learn. I like 'em bright, easier to train that way."

"But I'm not . . ." The memory of their plan, the one that involved pretending that he had no control over Knightmare, came back, like a life preserver tossed to a drowning man. "I'm not him, General, I can't control him! Ma'am."

DiMarco laughed. It was a surprisingly nice laugh, full of genuine warmth and perhaps even a touch of maternal concern. But her voice when she spoke carried no such warmth.

"Listen to me, Private, and listen good. You have two choices going forward. Choice number one is you work for me."

Justin was about to ask what choice number two was, but a glance at his own helplessness and the barrels of four expertly handled automatic weapons left no doubt about alternative number two.

He sagged, exhausted, depressed, beaten. Utterly beaten. Erin, dead! He was alone, all alone, with the whole world out to kill him.

"I guess I work for you," he muttered under his breath. Then quickly added, "General."

"Welcome to the war, Private," DiMarco said with obvious satisfaction. "Welcome to World War Three."

Aboard the *Okeanos Explorer*

THE COMBINATION WAS 8-4-9-6-6-1.

It was amazing what high-def video could capture.

Two days passed during which the *Okeanos*, escorted by elements of the US Navy and watched minutely by satellites belonging to most of the major nations on earth, carried its precious cargo toward the Port of Los Angeles.

They were just forty-eight hours out of Los Angeles when a storm came up from the south and lashed the ship with near-horizontal rain. Visibility was down to less than a mile and all hands were busy working the ship.

The box was guarded twenty-four hours a day by an armed member of the security detail, but when hiring the contractors, HSTF-66 had overlooked one small matter: three of them suffered terribly from seasickness. Especially with the ship moving like a roller coaster.

So the box was unguarded for three hours, and that was more than enough.

Vincent Vu punched in the combination and slipped inside. He had a flashlight, his camera, and a ball peen hammer he had swiped from the bosun. He spent some time taking pictures, but the rock was a massive gray lump inside a massive gray box and there wasn't much he could do with that. He could, however, use the cover provided by a howling wind to chip off a goodly sized chunk of rock, which he took back to the hammock that had been slung for him in one of the storerooms.

By this point Vincent—like everyone aboard except for the largely deaf cook—knew what the rock was. He had overheard nervous jokes from scientists talking about what the rock might do. Talk of mutations. Superpowers. A world on the brink of a revolution that might cause all of civilization to crumble.

All that sounded good to Vincent Vu. The voices in his head liked it, too.

He had no mortar and pestle, so he had to smash the rock as well as he could with the hammer, scooping up the flakes and crumbs with his student ID. Then, falling into a depressive state, he did nothing for the better part of a day. But when he woke in the middle of the night, feeling himself elevated into a manic state, feeling a sudden urgent need, he swallowed what he had, choking it down as the larger chunks scarred his throat.

In the end, five ounces of rock found its way to Vincent's stomach.

He went to sleep after a while and dreamed of a strange

sort of argument. The voices in his head were arguing with a new voice, but one that did not quite make sounds. No, this new voice did not speak, but it made itself felt, and that feeling was of vast emptiness, of impossible distances, but at the same time of intimacy so immediate it felt as if this new force had cowed his old voices. Those voices, the auditory hallucinations of his schizophrenia, faded. They did not go away, but they spoke now sotto voce, in hurried, frightened whispers.

The new voice—the voiceless voice—was less angry than his hallucinations. These dark things, these distant yet intimate things, did not touch his auditory centers but seemed to speak directly to his emotions.

Vincent felt that they liked him. He felt that they had high hopes for him. And he felt, somewhat to his surprise, since he had never quite bought into the hallucinations in which he appeared as Abaddon, that these Dark Watchers agreed, that they were . . . content . . . to have him truly become Abaddon.

When he woke from the dream, Vincent found reality stranger by far. For unless this was some new hallucination, he was changing in dramatic, extreme ways.

CHAPTER 18
Going Home

DEKKA WAS IN a hurry to get to the last place on earth she'd ever expected to visit again. She was on Highway 1, throttle almost all the way open, her Kawasaki throbbing steadily between her thighs . . . and a large white boy with one powerful arm around her waist. The speedometer read ninety miles an hour, and the road signs said it was another fifty miles to Perdido Beach.

She had no phone and no apps and thus nothing to warn her of police roadblocks or speed traps ahead. She hoped the BOLO for her had expired or that something more urgent was occupying the authorities. And she was being smart, spending the better part of two days crawling southward on back roads, some no more than dirt tracks, and sleeping one night in a winery shed that smelled of fruit and mold, and the other night in a tumbledown hunter's shack.

To her relief, Armo had been a decent traveling companion. He seldom spoke, he asked no questions, and he had managed to procure food for their overnight stay by raiding a nearby farm. He had also purloined a pair of denim overalls that were about six inches too short. Shoes remained a problem—he wore size 13E—but he'd found a pair of flipflops that were too small but slightly better than nothing. He was less conspicuous than he'd been in nothing but stretched-out boxers, but he was still something of a spectacle.

After much careful evasion, Dekka had rejoined Highway 1, the famous Pacific Coast Highway, planning to stay with it through the gloom of the Stefano Rey National Park and past the nuclear plant, and from there to Perdido Beach along the back roads that eventually become Ocean Boulevard.

A XYLØ song kept going through her head:

We're diving in the deep end
We can't turn back again.

She was between the devil, Tom Peaks, and the deep blue sea of painful memories and lingering terror that was Perdido Beach.

She had not yet found a convenient excuse to dump Armo, and truth be told, she did not entirely mind having him around. He had certainly been formidable in taking down the helicopter. The only problem was getting him to do anything that was not his idea. She had quickly learned that she could *suggest* to Armo—*Armo, would you be willing to fill the tank while I go take a pee?*—but could not *order* him to do anything. Even things he wanted to do.

While sneaking up on an isolated farm, she had had the following conversation:

"Armo, go left, I'll go right."

"You go left."

"Left is darker and you stand out more in the light."

"Yeah."

"So go left."

Long Armo silence and outthrust, pouting lip.

"Okay, which way do you think you should go?"

Shorter Armo silence. Followed by "I should go left. It's darker."

Brief Dekka silence. "All right then. Good idea."

But there was, despite this, something charming about Armo, who was not bright or even slightly cooperative, but was also not a jerk or a sexist or a racist, or any other form of "ist," unless it was "defiantist," which was probably not a word.

And really, Dekka had to admit, she was hardly the easiest person to get along with, either. She might not have Armo's extreme ODD, but instinctive defiance was definitely part of her makeup.

And the nice thing was that Armo extended the same extreme courtesy to her, never ordering, only suggesting or wondering aloud.

Suddenly, through her helmet and the thrum of the engine, she heard sirens, and they were coming closer. She looked left and right but the highway was flanked by low hills, all covered in scrub grass and squat bushes. There was no place to hide the bike or herself, no turnoffs, no businesses to slip into. Nothing.

"Maybe I should . . . ," Armo said, leaving it open.

In her rearview mirror Dekka saw two CHP vehicles practically levitating as they topped rises and bounced through dips.

Seconds away!

Could she outrun them? Maybe, but not for long. They would radio ahead for a roadblock or call for a helicopter. And on four wheels they were more stable than she was, especially with two hundred pounds of passenger—one pothole and she would go tumbling down the road.

The nearest CHP flashed its headlights and gave the siren a *whoop-whoop-whoop*, and Dekka realized with infinite relief that they were simply warning her to move aside. She slowed onto the shoulder and the cars flew past.

"Now I just need to get my stomach back down out of my throat," Dekka muttered.

"Hey, where are we headed?" Armo asked.

"I'm heading to Perdido Beach; would you like to come?"

"Sure."

She headed south again, going fast but not so fast she looked as if she was chasing the CHP, which, in any event, were soon out of sight around a curve.

Out of sight, but not for long.

She motored past an abandoned roadside motel, and a sign announcing a scenic lighthouse ahead. Seconds later she saw not a lighthouse but a pillar of smoke, and a military helicopter landing, and what must be every emergency or police vehicle within fifty miles.

It looked as if the CHP were starting to set up a roadblock on the PCH, but she was there ahead of them. She gave a saucy wave and passed by, unchallenged.

"What the hell was that?" Armo shouted above the engine.

"I don't think we should stop and ask," Dekka said. Then added, "What do you think?"

"I don't think we should stop and ask."

"At least we know every CHP in the area is busy."

They came at last to the edge of the Stefano Rey National Forest and passed a CHP car driven not by California Highway Patrol troopers, but by a young black man with two white-looking kids as passengers.

"There's a story there," Dekka said, before accelerating past them.

Into the forest, into deep shade with a watery autumn sun strobed by the trees. Dekka's stomach churned and her breath came short and too fast. It was near now. She was already within the diameter of what had been the FAYZ.

She slowed without really meaning to, her throttle a reflection of her state of mind. Still she missed the turnoff and had to come back around to find it. Now the SUV she'd passed earlier passed her, still heading south.

Then she was at the edge of town. She pulled over to the side of the road just to let the feelings wash through her. This place . . . the people . . . the horror . . . She felt as though if she went any farther, she would be trapped. She'd been within the FAYZ ever since she entered the forest. But for Dekka the

FAYZ meant, above all, the town of Perdido Beach.

This was where she had fought. This was where she had starved and had been thrilled to have a rat leg to eat. This was where she first met Sam Temple, Edilio, Lana . . .

This was where she had loved Brianna.

The Breeze.

She slowed to low gear like a motorcycle at a parade. She kept her helmet on less for safety than in the paranoid sense that someone might recognize her. This wasn't old home week for Dekka; this was a return visit to hell.

And yet, didn't you enjoy parts of it?

By the end of the FAYZ, the town had been largely burned down, hundreds of homes lost. The businesses had all been looted and gutted. Since then, much had been rebuilt—the traffic lights worked, the street signs had been put back up. The shattered storefront windows were all plate glass again.

There was light traffic, a strangely surreal sight to Dekka. During the FAYZ, gasoline had quickly become scarce, and any vehicle you saw either was Edilio and one of his militia or it signaled some kind of trouble.

"Hey, what exactly is this place?" Armo asked.

"The FAYZ," Dekka said. Then, with a sigh, "The Perdido Beach Anomaly. The PBA."

"Okay, cool," Armo said, apparently satisfied.

They came to the town square, site of so many bloody battles, site of so much horror and death. The town square had been the symbolic heart of the FAYZ.

A boy named Edilio, who had started his life in the FAYZ

as an undocumented kid with no friends and zero status, had become the single most trusted and relied-upon person in the FAYZ. If Dekka had been Sam Temple's strong right arm, Edilio had been his endlessly competent executive officer, his rock-solid support, and at times his conscience.

It was Edilio who had taken on himself the job of burying the dead. Edilio had dug the graves and fashioned the simple markers, and stood by those graves with bowed head asking God to watch over the souls of the dead.

To Dekka's amazement and gratification, those graves had not been removed. On the contrary, someone had arranged for stone grave markers to be erected in place of the wooden crosses and awkward stars of David and the one weak effort at a Muslim crescent that had marked those shallow graves.

She parked her bike. "This part I do alone," she said, then amending, "Unless you'd like to come."

Armo did not want to come. He climbed off the bike and headed toward the McDonald's.

Dekka walked on trembling legs to the graves. An informational marker had been set up. In raised bronze letters it read:

In respectful memory of both the wise and the foolish who struggled to survive unspeakable horror in this place.

And in smaller letters:

This space is maintained by the Albert Hillsborough Foundation.

That brought a rueful smile to Dekka's lips. Albert the capitalist, the businessman, the hustler. Lord, how she had hated him at times. But with later reflection she had come to realize that while Sam Temple might be the warrior hero, and Edilio the capable, brave, and moral day in, day out manager, it was Albert who had fed and watered the kids and kept them alive.

She raised a hand in a small salute. "Good for you, Albert. Good for you."

And then, with every fiber of her being suffused with a leaden resistance, she moved among the tombstones. Names she knew—Mary Terrafino, who had been a saint until mental illness had taken her over the edge; Duck Zhang, just a nice kid who'd been given a power he never wanted; poor Hunter.

And Charles Merriman, who had carried the nickname Orc. Orc the bully. Orc the drunk. Orc the murderer.

Orc the redeemed Christian who at the end had sacrificed his life to save others. There hadn't been much of a body left, and Dekka wondered just what Albert found to bury. But that was not really important, and Dekka laid a hand on Orc's tombstone. "Better late than never, Orc. You died well."

Caine had died just minutes before the end of the FAYZ, and there had been nothing but dust to bury. But Albert had nevertheless given him a stone that read:

Caine Soren
"King" of the FAYZ
Blaze of Glory

"Dammit." Dekka brushed tears away. "Really, Dekka, really? Shedding tears for Caine?" Half the bodies in the graveyard were there *because* of Caine Soren. Caine the bad boy. Caine the unloved son. Caine the abandoned brother of Sam. Caine the power-mad, the grandiose, the ruthless.

Caine, who so loved Diana Ladris that he gave his life for her, and for all of them.

And finally, there it was, what she was looking for, and what she dreaded finding.

Brianna Berenson
"The Breeze"
None More Bold

Dekka's entire body shook with emotion, her mouth an ugly grimace of pain and regret. And now the tears could not be brushed away, they came too fast, and she did not wish to brush them away. She wanted her tears to fall here, on this ground, a small offering.

Dekka fell to her knees, leaned against the cool stone, and sobbed.

"I'm so sorry, Breeze. I'm so sorry I haven't come earlier. I . . . I was too weak. I didn't want to . . . I keep your picture with me all the time, I haven't stopped . . . I still love you. I will always love you. It's okay that it was one-way, Breeze. All I ever needed was to love you."

After a long while, she stood up and dried her face on her sleeve.

"This goddamned place," Dekka said quietly. "This bloody, goddamned place."

She saw that the church had been partly rebuilt, but only partly, and the scaffolding looked old and unused, as though the project had been abandoned.

The town hall was in better shape, but there was only a single car parked in front, and it did not look like a place that had much going on.

The McDonald's that Albert had kept open for a while after the start of the FAYZ had been rebuilt to shiny new perfection. But even there she saw signs of neglect, litter on the sidewalks, a cracked window.

"Hello, Dekka."

Dekka knew the voice even before she turned. Diana Ladris was still beautiful, though she looked years older than her actual age. Her dark eyes were haunted, her voice quiet and respectful. But there, at the corners of those ever-alluring lips, was still a hint of the old Diana, wry and amused.

"Diana. I did not expect to find you here."

Diana jerked her chin toward a small hatchback parked a few spaces from the red Kawasaki where Armo lounged, shoving a Big Mac into his face. Flowers were visible inside the little car, and flowers were in Diana's hand. "I come once a week, whenever I can, to put flowers on the graves. I had just cleared away the faded ones when I saw you."

Diana laid the bouquet at the base of Brianna's tombstone, and now Dekka would have cried again had she any tears left.

"I should have . . . ," Dekka began.

"Nah," Diana said. "No should haves, okay? They taught me that in therapy. Don't waste time regretting, just find a way to undo whatever harm you've done, as well as you can. This is my thing. My little penance."

"How have you been, Diana?"

Diana shrugged. "I have a job. You are looking at a semi-competent Peet's barista. I have my own place, finally." The wry smile appeared. "I am seven months and three days sober. And I haven't tried to kill myself. Lately. You?"

Dekka hesitated before answering. The vacuous "fine" was on the tip of her tongue, but she owed Diana more than that. Diana was one of the very few people she could talk to about what was happening without being taken for a madwoman.

"Got a few minutes?" Dekka asked wearily.

"Help me place the flowers and we'll talk."

Dekka smiled at that, happy to help, happy to have a few minutes to collect her thoughts. When they were finished, the two of them walked the few blocks to the beach. Armo followed at a discreet distance, like a bodyguard. The beach was as long and beautiful as ever, curving away to the northwest. The debris of Albert's water-purification device was gone.

Dekka shaded her hand against the lowering sun and looked southeast. "Have they got Clifftop open?"

Diana said, "It's a Sheraton now."

"Huh."

"The bar there serves themed cocktails: the FAYZ, the PBA, the Sam Temple—that's something with vodka and limoncello, for some reason. The Lana is vodka and some nasty green tea drink, you know, for healing supposedly. You and I didn't rate."

Dekka shook her head slowly. "I guess the irony that FAYZers have a tendency to drink too much is lost on them."

"Big hotel chains don't do irony," Diana said. She led them to a bench, and the two old not-exactly-friends sat side by side and looked out at the ocean as the horizon rose to meet a reddening sun.

Without further preamble, Diana said, "You're in some kind of trouble."

"How do you figure?"

"Suddenly you're back here. And you're actually talking. Dekka Talent, who had never been known to speak more than a dozen words a day."

Dekka smiled. "Well, I'm all about action."

"And I guess you know there's a big white dude in sad overalls following us."

"Yeah, I . . . I sort of picked him up along the way." She sighed heavily. "He's all right, so long as you don't try to tell him what to do. The boy makes *me* seem easygoing."

Diana laughed. "Right. You. Easygoing."

"Diana," Dekka said, her grin disappearing, "it's all starting again. But this time it's not just a twenty-mile-across dome, it's the whole world."

She told Diana all she'd seen, all she knew. From time to time she glanced at Diana and saw the young woman's face grow red from the sunset, then dark from shadows and darker still from concern that deepened into worry.

"Well, that's all . . . bad news," Diana said at last. "You were good to keep Sam and Astrid out of it."

"Yeah, well, now that I've gone rogue, HSTF-Sixty-Six may take a run at him," Dekka said regretfully. "But I didn't have a choice, Diana. Peaks and his whole operation are an atrocity."

"So now you're right back in it," Diana said.

"Yeah, I noticed."

"In the old days I could have held your hand and told whether you were a three bar or a four or a five."

"Five," Dekka said flatly. "Maybe six if there is such a thing. This power is . . . it's incredible. But each time I use it, I have to change into this . . . thing, this creature. And when I'm morphed, I sense . . ." She shook her head. "It's something dark, Diana, very dark. It watches. Sometimes it's like it's laughing. Other times it's annoyed or impatient with me."

"You didn't just come here for old time's sake," Diana said. "You came to see if . . . if *it* is still alive."

Dekka nodded slowly.

"They've closed the mine shaft," Diana said. "At first they had crews down in there, but various bad things happened, so they blew up the shaft. They sealed it up like they meant it this time. Concrete."

Dekka said, "They took it. They dug it out. That's the only answer. HSTF-Sixty-Six has whatever is left of the gaiaphage.

I should have realized that's what they were using for their
god-awful experiments. Jesus, Diana, they put some of the
gaiaphage in me! Part of the thing that made Gaia, the thing
that killed . . ."

Dammit, will I ever be able to say it without choking up?

"Peaks tried to tell me there was still something dark and
sinister in Perdido Beach," Dekka said, back on less emotionally draining turf.

"There is," Diana said. "The town is still about half empty.
Drive through the neighborhoods and you see houses half
rebuilt, then abandoned. The school's running again, but
they're closing it next year for lack of students. No one even
tried to reopen Coates Academy. I guess when your private
school lists alumni that include Caine and Drake and me . . .
Anyway, no, it's not all gone. There's something still here, like
a sort of echo, a memory of what happened here. The whole
town is like a graveyard, not just the square. It creeps people
out. You know about the shoot-out?"

"Which one?"

"Bunch of bikers—gang type, not weekend riders—and
cops. Like, a year ago, before they sealed the mine. Bikers had
moved in, set up a kind of camp. They were actually conducting tours down to see the rock. Cops rousted them and
there was a gun battle. Bunch of the bikers were arrested. Two
died."

"That never made the news."

Diana formed her wry, seen-it-all smile. "Yes, news out
of Perdido Beach tends not to be widely covered. The whole

world wants to forget this place, Dekka."

"Don't we all. But I'm afraid the world is about to get a wake-up call."

"So, what do you do next?" Diana asked.

Dekka took her time considering her answer. "Peaks and HSTF-Sixty-Six want to keep the whole thing quiet so they can create their own army of superpowered warriors. Supposedly just to stop whoever might get their hands on the rock." She shook her head. "But that's bullshit. The government wants the power and doesn't want anyone else to have it, and that scares me. The Mother Rock is supposedly heading to LA. Once they have that . . ." Dekka shrugged.

"Are you sure it's a bad thing, the government having the rock? I mean, they are the government."

Dekka kicked at the sand with her toe. "What they're doing at the Ranch, that's way past anything a government is supposed to do. They're experimenting on people. Doing awful things. Nightmare stuff. No, that's not a government I need to obey."

They walked back to the town square in silence, both young women lost in thought and memory. Armo went ahead and now waited by the motorcycle.

"Diana, Armo," Dekka said.

They shook hands. Dekka offered no further introductions or explanations.

Then Dekka offered Diana her hand.

Diana took it solemnly and held it for a moment. "Take care of yourself, Dekka. There's one thing your Peaks person was not wrong about: if anyone can be trusted with this power, it's you."

If, Dekka added silently, recalling the dark and distant whispers.

If.

"Hey, I thought of something," Armo said as they crossed what had been the southern border of the dome. He was behind her on the bike, which put his mouth near her ear. She'd lost her helmet along the way and now her dreads streamed back, whipping at his face, so he hunched close to avoid being whipped. His powerful arms were around her waist, and his hard chest was against her back.

This is the most intimate I've ever been with a dude, Dekka thought. *Meh.*

"Like what?" asked Dekka. "I made a promise to see Carl's family . . . But first I wanted to, I don't know, I had to see Perdido Beach. I couldn't just drive on by."

"So, what are you up for?"

"Up for?" She had to yell to be heard over the engine and the wind and the steady rhythm of tires on concrete.

"I mean, are you *hiding*? Or are you *fighting*?"

Dekka breathed a small laugh. "You have a nice way of getting to the point, Armo." She rode on, silent, lost in thought. *Well*, she asked herself, *what are you doing, Dekka? Are you hiding or are you fighting?*

Part of her desperately wanted to find Sam and Astrid. She'd been Sam's sidekick; she'd never before been the one making all the decisions. She, like most of the kids of the

FAYZ, had left that burden on his shoulders.

No, she wasn't doing that to Sam.

Finally, Armo tired of waiting on her. "Wanna know what I've been thinking?"

"Yeah?"

"The Port of Los Angeles."

Dekka digested that for more than a minute, couldn't figure it out, and said, "Why?"

"Because people think they can drug a guy like me, but they can't. And I hear things people don't think I hear," Armo said smugly. "The big one, the big rock, the Mother Rock, DiMarco calls it. That's where it's going. LA."

A warning light went on in Dekka's head. *Something.* Something wrong about going to the Port of Los Angeles. No, not something wrong, exactly; more that it sounded familiar. Like she'd heard the suggestion before. Like it had been whispered to her in a dream.

"I mean," Armo added, "assuming you're going to choose fight over hide."

"Why assume that?"

Armo laughed. He had a nice laugh. "Well, hey, I don't know you, but I'm kind of thinking you don't seem much like a girl who hides."

Oh, but I have been hiding, she thought. *I've been hiding for four years.*

It came to her then that if she couldn't talk to Sam, she could still guess what his answer would be. His . . . and Brianna's.

"Neither of us has a phone," Dekka said. "We should pick up a map."

"A map to where?"

"A map to you know damn well where," Dekka said, and Armo laughed into her ear.

CHAPTER 19
Meet the Psychopath

PEAKS LAY ON his back, staring up at a darkening sky. He was shattered.

He picked himself up slowly, not bothering to brush away the dirt that clung to him.

He had done it. He had become . . . *something*. Something very much not human. Something huge and hugely strong, something brutal and indestructible.

He looked around at a scene of awesome destruction. Thank God he had the sense to find an isolated place, driving well out into the desert. Because everything within a hundred yards had been crushed, ripped apart, thrown, or burned.

The ubiquitous tumbleweeds? Scorched. The nearest Joshua tree? Kindling. The sand itself was gouged or dusted with ash or, in a few places, had been crystalized, turned to brown glass by extreme heat.

Very extreme heat.

Peaks had gone to the Ranch, told a few close associates

about the change in command while putting a happy face on it and fooling no one. Then Peaks had spent a couple of hours downloading the contents of the computer onto a hard drive—his insurance policy, if DiMarco and the rest of them ever tried to throw him under the bus for all the, well, questionable judgment calls he'd made.

And he purloined another pound of ground rock. He had left just in time, it seemed, since his successor (now his superior) had been diverted to a battle at the Piedras Blancas lighthouse and would be delaying her arrival at the Ranch, a battle Peaks suspected involved the art student calling himself Knightmare.

DiMarco's problem now, not mine.

Then Peaks had flown down to Palm Springs, rented a car, and driven out into the desert. He had followed highways and then roads and then dirt tracks out into the middle of nowhere, out to where there was nothing in view but the austere, scalloped hills, the desiccated scrub, and the occasional lizard.

There he had given full vent to his rage, his sense of betrayal, his thirst for what he saw as justice and another person might have called revenge.

And in his rage he had become a monster.

He had reveled in the extraordinary power.

He had tested these new gifts.

And he had felt the eyeless gaze of Dark Watchers.

Then he had returned to human form, shaken, overwhelmed, scared, and yet excited. He had become what he had been tasked to destroy. And now he would destroy those others, one by one: the Darby girl and those with her; the traitor Dekka; Justin Knightmare, if DiMarco had somehow failed to kill him.

And anyone else who opposed him.

His mission was vindication. He would prove that he and he alone was capable of addressing the threat to all of humanity and all of human civilization. He was far greater, far more powerful than any of the weapons—biological or mechanical—that he had overseen at the Ranch.

I am the most powerful single creature ever to walk the earth!

He was fascinated by the process. After all, Peaks was not just an administrator; he had degrees in the fields of nanotechnology and zoology. But one thing was clear: lacking the support of HSTF-66 (temporarily at least, he reassured himself), he needed an ally, at least one. No matter how powerful his own morph was, Peaks knew he could not see in every direction at once. He needed someone to watch his back. Someone to throw into battle at just the right time to tip the scales. Someone to launch diversions when necessary.

Someone with power.

Someone with nowhere else to turn.

Someone with absolutely no moral qualms who would happily follow orders to maim, torture, or kill as Peaks required.

And thus had he come here, to this particular stretch of desert.

Peaks returned to his parked rented car, now broiling hot under the desert sun. He pulled clothing from his bag and dressed quickly. He turned on the engine and the air-conditioning and opened his laptop. He stuck the stolen hard drive into the USB slot and opened a file he'd read many times before.

Then he opened the detailed analysis derived from news reports, police reports of strange deaths, and the reports of sadistic rapes. The clever geeks at the Ranch had cross-tabbed all the data they had, analyzed possible hiding places, and reached a tentative conclusion: Quail Mountain.

Peaks drove the few miles to Juniper Flats, nothing but a flat space between mountains, but an easy place to take the trail that led across a mile and a half of sun-blasted desert to Quail Mountain.

He had a large bottle of Fiji water weighing down one side of his light jacket, and granola bars stuffed into the other pocket. He carried a burner phone with a spare battery pack— not that there was any coverage out in the middle of nowhere. And because he was still far from sure of how exactly to use the monster that now lived within him, he carried a Colt .45 automatic pistol and a spare clip.

It was not so easy to search the mountain. Quail Mountain was almost six thousand feet high and cut with multitudes of gullies eroded by the infrequent rain and more frequent wind, each of which was an obstacle to movement. Other obstacles were prickly bushes and cacti, the blinding sun, the burning heat, and the ever-present possibility of poisonous reptiles. He soon wished he had more water and better boots. Hours of climbing yielded no clues, and by the time the sun touched the distant western horizon, he was feeling defeated.

He was torn between continuing his search and racing back to the car—now something like three miles away—and continuing the search the next day, or sticking it out, possibly through the night. In the end he could not bear the thought of slogging all the way back to his car and spending the night in a motel. So he gathered bits of brush and knocked the limbs off a dead Joshua tree and made a fire.

He made the fire the old-fashioned way, with a lighter. That fact made him grin.

Night came with a suddenness familiar to those who've stayed too long in the desert. The fire soon consumed the dry-as-dust kindling and he had little of anything larger to burn, so he sat hunched over in front of dying embers as the sky above blazed with stars and planets. He listened to the too-near yips of coyotes.

He had no warning.

Half asleep, he heard a sound like a bat flitting through the air, and then something was around his chest and he was yanked away from the fire and onto his back.

He yelled an inarticulate "Hey!" and the thing that had grabbed him now pulled away, only to come slicing forward to land on him with such force that it tore his jacket open at the shoulder, ripped through the shirt beneath, and bit into his flesh.

"Aaaahhh!" The pain was shocking and Peaks was mortally certain that he would be dead in a matter of minutes, if not seconds, but in his pain and panic he still cried out just the right word.

"Drake!"

No second blow fell. The pain was what branded cattle must feel, but he rose shakily to his feet, trying to peer into the darkness.

"You know me?" The voice was oily smooth, utterly confident, unafraid but curious.

"Yes. I know who you are. You're Drake Merwin. I've been looking for you."

Peaks heard someone move closer but stood his ground, and slowly Drake emerged from the pitch black into the weak orange light and sinister shadows cast by the embers of the fire.

Drake stood tall, relaxed, his ten-foot-long tentacle arm wrapped casually around his waist, the tip twitching eagerly. He was, Peaks thought, exactly as he'd pictured him: handsome but cruel, with a predatory, animal quality to his gaze.

The nightmare of the PBA.

The killer, the rapist, the torturer.

The brutal, psychopathic monster: Drake Merwin.

"Well, you found me," Drake said laconically.

"I have a proposition for you," Peaks said, tenderly touching the agonizing slash on his chest.

"You are not the first to claim he had some good reason why I shouldn't whip him to death. And the women, oh, they always have some sob story to tell." Drake laughed.

Peaks swallowed his revulsion at this, at the vicious scenes his imagination supplied. "Tell you what, Drake. I'll say what I have to say, and then you decide what to do with me."

"I decide regardless," Drake said with a sneer. "But tell me your story."

"Okay," Peaks said, shaking with fear, fighting the urgent pain. But Peaks was not overly worried: Drake could not defeat him, not if he morphed. That said, he knew he could not morph into the monster if Drake struck too quickly. "First, do you recall a certain Dekka Talent?"

Drake's hiss sounded like a rattlesnakes.

"One of the things I'd like you to do, Drake, is kill Dekka Talent."

There was a long silence. And then Drake unlimbered his whip arm and casually uprooted a bush, which he tossed onto the fire, causing it to flare brightly.

Drake sat down, cross-legged, his whip arm now draped over his shoulders, a slow, writhing python.

"I'm listening," Drake said.

"The world is changing. Changing in ways none of us can really imagine. ASO . . . the rock. The one that became the gaiaphage, that same rock, more of it is landing. It was my job to stop it getting out into the hands of, you know, civilians. Regular people."

Drake's eyes narrowed.

"But that effort has failed. The rock is out in the world, already in too many hands. And with it comes incredible, unpredictable powers."

"Just like the good old days," Drake said.

"Actually, much worse. You see, the rock is like an opportunistic virus. It affects, it interacts with, its entire environment, using whatever it finds at hand, to shape the change."

"The change?"

"The only two people to escape the PBA with powers intact

were the two people who were physically changed. Morphed. Taylor, and you, Drake."

Drake was perfectly still, listening, waiting, like a cobra watching a mouse. The end of his whip twitched.

"The rock, very much like a clever virus, has found a way to survive without the dome. It altered the physiognomy—sorry, the body—creating a sort of hybrid creature made out of the person's DNA, any other DNA that happened to be nearby, and in some cases seemed affected by need, by desire, as if it was reading synapses inside the brain, feeding on memory, on passion." Peaks shook his head ruefully, admiringly. "Oh, it is a very, very clever piece of work, this rock. Millennia ahead of human science."

He snapped out of a reverie and looked into Drake's soulless eyes.

"It . . . they . . . will win. The rock will have its way, you see. That's clear to me now. I don't know why, I don't know what it plans, but it is not a mere virus. No. It is being watched. Perhaps it is a sort of lens that allows connections through a bent and folded space-time, I don't know, but I know that some consciousness . . . is watching."

Drake nodded. "I know it. It never left me."

This got Peaks's attention. "Are you telling me it's in your head ever since . . ."

"Before and after," Drake said in a dreamy tone. "It never leaves me. Just like *she* never leaves me."

"She?"

Drake grinned. He tugged at the neckline of his filthy T-shirt and pulled it down to reveal the pale flesh beneath.

And there, like some mad 3-D tattoo, was a face, the face of a girl with twisted braces' wires sticking out from between cracked lips.

"The Brittany Pig," Drake said, enjoying the look of horror on Peaks's face. "We were melded long ago, me and Brittany Pig, but our relationship has changed, you know? We used to be two separate people, one replacing the other at times. But eventually she grew on me. Get it?" His laugh was a form of assault, a brutal challenge. "She grew on me."

Peaks managed to nod but did not trust his voice. The face on Drake's chest was not an illusion, not a tattoo. It was a living face mouthing silently, staring at him with eyes that were windows into madness.

"Sometimes she says *their* words," Drake said. "Sometimes the banshees wail and it comes out here." He tapped the face and the braces-filled mouth snapped at his finger.

"The banshees?" Peaks whispered.

"Them. The dark ones. The demons. The Dark Watchers."

"What do they say?" Peaks asked.

Drake made a mirthless chuckle. "Mostly it's *Kill*. Yes, they like that, killing. Pain. Terror. It entertains them. They like to be entertained."

Peaks had seen freaks. He had created freaks, nightmarish creatures like Carl. He had a very high threshold when it came to fear. But the thin, handsome, vicious boy with the living face on his chest and the lightning-quick whip hand? Well, this was a new level of malice. This was a creature in long-term, close contact with the Dark Watchers that Peaks had only glimpsed, or read about in the statements of experimental subjects. There was a force about Drake, a sort of invisible but unmistakable aura of malignancy.

I tried to recruit the stable one, Peaks reminded himself. *I tried to do the right thing.*

"Time to try the wrong thing," Peaks muttered under his breath. "Here's the thing, Drake. I just underwent my own change. I became . . . well, very powerful. Very powerful. I know half your mind is thinking of killing me, but you would not succeed, not with just your whip hand."

There was a tantalizing suggestion buried in there somewhere, and Drake sensed it.

"What do you want?" Drake asked.

Same question Dekka asked more than once. *Well, it's a fair question*, Peaks thought. *What do I want? I wanted once to save the world.*

That realization was bitter now. Save the world! Save the world from superpowered freaks like . . . well, like Peaks had now become. Like this sick piece of once-human garbage with the whip.

And now? What did Peaks want *now*? To survive in the world that was coming. To be the greatest of the powers. To dominate. To control. To prove himself and avenge his humiliation.

Yes, he still wanted to save the world. But the world he saved would be *his* world, a world where he received the recognition he deserved.

But first and foremost, he had to acquire as much of the precious rock as he could, keep it safe and under his control.

With the Mother Rock, Peaks could stop the government's plans and substitute his own. Their army would be his.

"The biggest of the rocks is on its way to the Port of Los Angeles. The Mother Rock," Peaks said.

"Ah," Drake said. "I've been meaning to head into the city."

"That one piece, well, you could transform an army with it. I . . . we . . . could control a force like nothing the world has ever seen. We could crush any other mutant force. We could even fight HSTF-Sixty-Six and the US government to a standstill."

"Then what?"

The question surprised Peaks. He blinked. He hadn't really thought in detail about what happened next; he'd been focused on fantasies of revenge and self-justification.

"Well, then I suppose you, Drake, if you've been a faithful lieutenant, could have whatever you like."

Drake leaned forward. He unlimbered his whip hand and poked at a stick in the fire, sending up a cloud of sparks amid the smoke. Then with his normal hand he pulled his shredded T-shirt up over his head so that the face, the disgusting wire-filled mouth, could be seen clearly in all its disturbing horror.

"Tell the nice man what we want, Brittany Pig," Drake said.

The eyes opened, black-on-black eyes that reflected no light but seemed to blaze with a dark fire within. The glittering mouth spoke just one word.

"Fun."

"Fun?" Peaks could not believe he was talking to a sort of three-dimensional, living tattoo with broken braces. But normal had left the building, and crazy was in charge now.

"My kind of fun," Drake said.

"You really are a psycho," Peaks said, shaking his head in amused disbelief.

To his surprise, Drake seemed to consider the idea seriously. He was silent for a while, long enough for Peaks to get nervous. At last Drake said, "I used to be this kid. Probably a little messed up, but still, this kid. Then Sam Temple burned me. Diana had to cut my arm off. Then the gaiaphage gave me this." He unwrapped his snake arm. He brought the tip close to Peaks's face, not quite touching, not quite threatening. "I am what the gaiaphage made me."

He laughed then. "And they like it. The Dark Watchers. They like pain, which is good, because so do I." Then his mood changed abruptly. "But don't call me a psycho or any other names you come up with. You can call me Drake, or you can call me Whip Hand. You call me anything else, old man, and I will make you scream my name till your throat is raw."

Well, Peaks thought, Dekka had not overstated just what a monster Drake was. No, not even a little. He might make a useful ally if he could be controlled.

Big if, he admitted silently. *Very big if.*

PART THREE: ROUGH BEASTS

CHAPTER 20
First on the Scene

THE PORT OF Los Angeles was a massive, sprawling complex of docks and jetties, huge cranes for off-loading containers, vast parking lots full of Japanese and Korean cars awaiting transportation to dealers, hundreds of container-hauling trucks, warehouses, great cylindrical fuel tanks, motor pools, and squat, unadorned office buildings that looked like overgrown backyard sheds.

All that was on the land, which had been shaped to form multiple bays and inlets and channels, but the land was mere servant to the sea and its ships and tugboats and pilot craft.

Malik drove onto the Vincent Thomas Bridge, a smaller, uglier version of the Golden Gate Bridge that soared over the main channel, just high enough to allow loaded container-ships to squeeze beneath. Traffic was sparse on the bridge and Malik pulled over halfway across.

Shade hopped out and went to the rail. To her left was the cruise ship terminal, where a sleek, massively top-heavy

Emerald Princess was just tying off. Beyond it, closer to the open sea, was the retired battleship *Iowa*, its great guns long silenced.

Two ships were in the channel, passing beneath the bridge: the Coast Guard cutter *Berthold*, and the *Okeanos Explorer*.

The *Berthold*, at 420 feet in length, was at once innocent and dangerous, blazingly white with the usual red chevron slanted down the side of the bow, but with a Bofors 57 mm gun in a turret ahead of the superstructure. That superstructure was topped by a mast festooned with sophisticated electronics.

The *Okeanos*, which the *Berthold* had escorted into port, was half as long, white but lacking the sort of perfectly maintained, obsessively clean, and painted look of the Coast Guard ship. It was topped by what looked very much like a giant golf ball, a shell surrounding sophisticated radar and other sensors.

Malik and Cruz joined Shade. She pointed and said, "They may not need a superhero; they have some kind of big cannon on that Coast Guard ship."

"Just be ready," Malik snapped. "Sorry. I haven't slept in, like, forever."

"That container must be for the Mother Rock," Cruz observed.

"I think they're pulling in," Malik said. "Across the channel."

They hopped back into a freshly purloined SUV—the CHP car had been left in a Costco parking lot—crossed the bridge, followed an off-ramp that led down past seemingly endless expanses of concrete topped by stacked containers, scruffy warehouses, and administrative buildings, crossed some railroad tracks, aimed right for the wharf where the *Okeanos* seemed to be heading, and ran into a number of signs, one stating that they were nearing Terminal Island, a Coast Guard base, and a second indicating that they were also approaching the Terminal Island correctional facility.

"Great," Malik said darkly. "It'll be a short walk to prison."

There was security in place, so they stopped again, considering their next move.

"We need to get in there," Malik said. He glanced in the mirror and saw a white van approaching.

"I got it," Shade said, and immediately began her transformation. She forced herself to look down at the monstrous, insectoid legs that gave her such speed. Her flesh crept and her mind rebelled, still unable to really process it, unable to quite believe that she was *physically* something other than she'd been her whole life. The liquid, sluicing sounds came through her bones as her body shifted and moved, as she quickly—down to mere seconds now—transformed into a creature that only a close friend would recognize as being Shade Darby.

She glanced at Malik and Cruz. They were staring, and blinking ever so slowly. The white van that had been tearing along at good speed was now barely moving. She ran to it and looked inside. There was only the driver, a burly, thirtysomething white man in overalls. He had an ID lanyard hanging around his neck.

Shade yanked open the van door and hauled out its driver

as carefully as she could—although she heard one of the bones in his arm snap—and deposited him beside the road. She couldn't have him conscious, but he was an innocent bystander, so she slowed her fist so that when it impacted the side of his head the blow wouldn't crush his skull.

It did, however, snap his head around and cause his eyes to flutter and roll up in his head. He began a slow-mo collapse.

Shade raced back to her friends and de-morphed, feeling clever for having changed back before the Dark Watchers could fully turn their attention on her.

"Come on," Shade said. "Cruz? I believe your power may come in handy."

The three of them went to the white van, and Shade handed the unconscious driver's lanyard to Cruz. "Can you pass as this guy?"

Cruz looped the lanyard over her neck and went to take a much closer look at the man, turning his head this way and that, adding it to what she had come to think of as her face file, the faces she had memorized well enough to mimic.

By the time she stood up, she *was* the unconscious driver, clothing and all.

"This good enough?" Cruz asked, a bit smug, knowing that of course it was perfect.

"Okay, listen, you have to drive, Cruz. Malik and I can hide in the back, but you have to drive."

"But—"

"No alternative," Malik chimed in. "It's just, what, five hundred feet to the security gate? You can do it, Cruz, you got this."

"Straight road," Shade said, making a chopping gesture.

"Oh, my God," the "driver" said, sounding entirely like Cruz. "I . . . I don't . . ."

There began a hurried, impromptu driving lesson from Malik as Shade shielded her eyes from the glare and squinted to see the cutter and the *Okeanos* closing with the crane-burdened dock.

As it happened, Cruz was perfectly able to drive slowly, with Malik behind her giving her instructions. At the gate Cruz flashed her lanyard, and then the guard said, "See the game last night?"

Of course Cruz had not, but she read the guard's doleful expression and said, "We were robbed."

The guard snorted. "We were robbed when they traded away Vasquez."

"Tell me about it," Cruz answered in her best approximation of a gruff and masculine voice.

And then they were in through the gate. The prison—not a huge facility—was on their left. The dock was to their right. Cruz scooted into the back as Malik clambered into the driver's seat, and they motored past low buildings to approach a parking lot with space for perhaps a hundred cars.

There was a whole new level of security in place in that parking lot: a dozen vehicles either marked LAPD or unmarked but clearly official. A big, black LAPD SWAT van the size of a UPS truck waited beside a small armored car with massive rubber wheels painted with the stencil. The vehicle was marked "RESCUE LAPD." A Los Angeles Port Police motorboat cut figure eights into the gray-green water of the channel. A police helicopter hovered overhead.

Their way forward was blocked by Port Police on motorcycles, with men and women in dark suits and dark glasses nearby. These did not look like folks who would be tricked by a lanyard; they would search the vehicle and demand to see specific permissions to enter the area. So again Malik pulled over, beside an improbable baseball diamond. A basketball court occupied the space between the baseball diamond and the parking lot. He made a point of leaning out of the window and staring, like any curious dockworker might upon seeing a very unusual sight. Even a boat suspected of bringing in drugs did not merit this kind of reception.

"I can't get any closer," Malik said. "I doubt even Cruz could get through."

Shade nodded. "Mmmm. I can. But I don't want to until it's necessary. The less time I spend with the Watchers, the better."

The *Okeanos* touched the dock. But it did not remain quite still; it seemed to be drifting. Then a strange figure covered by a poncho with hood pulled up despite the stunning Southern California weather rushed to the stern to throw a cable to waiting hands ashore. That same cloaked figure then ran forward to throw the second line.

"What, have they only got one crewman?" Malik wondered aloud.

And that was when a car pulled up just ahead of the parked van. Malik tensed. Shade watched, ready to morph at the first sign of trouble. She could see two heads silhouetted in the car.

The driver got out. He was a middle-aged white man with sandy hair. He had a passenger with long, dirty blond or light brown hair. The passenger turned in his seat and looked right at Malik, who instinctively shrank back.

To the amazement of everyone in Shade's group, the middle-aged man now began stripping off his clothing, carefully folding each item and laying them on the driver's seat, until he was down to a pair of boxer shorts.

"Crazy?" Malik mused.

But then the pale, skinny, unimpressive, and mostly naked man began to change.

"Worse than crazy," Shade said. "He's a child of the rock."

CHAPTER 21
Cooking Drake

PEAKS FOLDED HIS clothing with trembling hands. He saw a parked van, but there was just some kid at the wheel, and Peaks had bigger issues to deal with.

"You coming?" Peaks demanded.

Drake grinned. "When I'm ready. I want to see what you've got first."

Peaks shook his head slightly and under his breath said, "I wish I knew what I've got." Louder he added, "What I've got, my friend, is big, hot, and unhappy."

Peaks focused his mind on the thoughts most likely to enrage him. In fact, he replayed the scene of his firing, of his humiliation. And change came to Tom Peaks. He heard a sound like wet gears grinding through mud, a sound that vibrated through his bones. The ground began to recede, seeming to fall away from him as he shot up. He looked down and saw misshapen feet already so large that they extended beneath the car, and down through the sunroof he saw Drake watching him with wary blue eyes.

Peaks raised his hand to look at it, and it was no longer human in size, color, or shape. His hand looked like one of those Fourth of July "snakes," like magma vomiting from the mouth of a volcano, black crust over a glowing red beneath.

Peaks was perhaps the most experienced person on earth when it came to the ASO virus and its effects. At the Ranch he had run many experiments, first on test animals and later on humans. He had seen the gruesome, disturbing morphing process, like something out of a demented movie special effects computer.

He had seen it all. But in others, not himself. It was like being trapped in a nightmare, that same helpless feeling, that same dread. But against the astonishment and the fear was fascination.

My God: look at me!

He grew still larger and larger, broader and broader, until he was as big as an African elephant. He glanced down and now Drake was no longer smirking. There was an expression of something like awe on the creep's cruel face. That look calmed Peaks's fear. There was nothing as good for calming fear as seeing that you terrified someone else.

Then . . . *rage!*

It erupted inside Peaks like a muffled bomb of fury and hatred, a rage far out of proportion even to the indignities he'd suffered. He felt as if liquid fire was coursing in his veins, like a nuclear pile was burning in his gut. He felt exalted, transformed!

The power!

Peaks felt as well the presence of unseen eyes, a mocking, interested, malicious gaze, but that did not trouble him while he was in this state, not while he was rising ever upward on a geyser of mad fury.

A red veil fell over his sight and he felt himself, his mind, Tom Peaks himself, flickering like a candle about to go out. But that would not do, it would not do at all, he needed his wits about him, he needed to be able to see and react. And with all the determination at his command, he held on to his consciousness, retained awareness, moving fingers and feet to prove to himself that he controlled this beastly body. But with this accomplishment came the certainty that his control over this monster was tenuous at best. It was as if the creature had a simple, brutal mind of its own, a rage-fueled single-mindedness that competed with Peaks's own sophisticated consciousness for control. It was a bit like two drivers trying to steer the same vehicle. He could direct his morph, but could not entirely contain its fury.

He was far above the car now, towering over it so that Drake might as well have been a pedestrian passing on the sidewalk beneath a five-story building.

And that was when Peaks made a mistake he would not have made had he had more time to test out this morph. He glared down at Drake and the rage took control. Peaks roared down at Drake, roared in a voice that shattered the windshield and set off the car alarm. And as he opened his mouth and roared, a wave of liquid fire vomited forth.

It was napalm, some rational corner of Peaks's mind observed, like jellied gasoline, and it did not burn like a flame or even a blowtorch, it stuck and burned. Gallons of it sprayed across the vehicle, instantly peeling paint, dripping down into the car through the sunroof, melting seats and dashboard controls, wilting the steering wheel, sending up a cloud of stinking, oily black smoke.

And Drake, too, burned. He burned and his flesh melted from his face, so that Peaks saw a flame-wreathed skeleton with blue eyes sizzling like frying eggs in their bone sockets.

Drake calmly opened the door of the car, rolled out onto the grass of the baseball diamond, and kept rolling as the napalm clung to him, burning, peeling skin away, frying the meager fat, boiling his blood. Drake rolled, keeping his whip hand tightly coiled around him, then jumped up to run across the grassy field, dropping flaming gobbets of melting flesh as he ran. A long, narrow gap separated the land from the dock, a gap forming a sort of freshwater ditch between dock and land. Drake leaped and disappeared from sight.

For a terribly long time, Peaks stared in furious horror, dimly aware that he had gone to great trouble to recruit a henchman and had now killed him.

But then . . . a whip snapped up from the water and the end wrapped around a tall, lithe palm tree, and with a single, powerful yank, a dripping-wet Drake landed nimbly back on the grass.

He was more skeleton than flesh, white bone clearly visible, his skull, his ribs, one entire shoulder. What flesh remained was the color of a steak left to burn on a too-hot grill. And yet, from the upper part of Drake's chest, a tangle of chrome wires protruded. But perhaps most terrifying of all, Drake's whip hand was now a snake's skeleton, a long, flexible vertebral column and hundreds of circular ribs.

"You're alive?" Peaks roared, meaning to whisper.

"You'll have to give me a few minutes," Drake said, sauntering quite nonchalantly back across the grass from third base, not even seeming resentful. "It takes me a while to regrow."

CHAPTER 22
Fire, Water, and Shade Darby

"JESUS H. GODZILLA," Malik said through chattering teeth.

The creature that had once been an unremarkable, middle-aged man now towered over them, and unless Shade was hallucinating, he had just melted a boy with a long octopus-looking arm, and that boy had just climbed out of the car, jumped into the water, and emerged like some unkillable slasher movie villain.

Cruz screamed in sheer, out-of-control terror. Malik's face was a mask of horror, teeth bared, eyes wide. Shade's insides turned to water. She felt a desperate urge to find a bathroom, preferably one on another continent. But she did not scream, she had no right to scream, she was a monster, too, or would be in mere seconds.

"Malik!" She grabbed his shoulder. "You and Cruz get the hell out of here. Now! I have to—"

But what she had to do was not made clear, because the

magma creature had turned his attention back to the *Okeanos* nestling up to the dock.

He . . . it . . . began to run.

One step and he was twenty feet away. Another great bounding step on legs as long as telephone poles and as thick as ancient redwoods. The vibration of each planted foot was like a low-level earthquake.

"He's not exactly slow himself," Shade muttered as she pushed open the door and stood on legs not quite her own.

The police forces in the parking lot didn't need to be told to fire—they blazed away with handguns and shotguns, but if the bullets struck the magma creature, there was no sign that they were a problem for him. And then the monster threw wide his arms, a defiant *Is that all you got?* gesture.

Bang-bang-bangbangbangbang!

The police fired until their clips were empty, reloaded, and fired again, and all to no effect.

The monster bent to bring his hideous, burned-reptile head lower, mouth wide in a grin full of fire and smoke. He let go a sound that even from more than a hundred yards shook Shade down to her bones.

Ggggrrrahhhh-hah-hah-GARRRRR!

They had made a stop at a martial arts store and picked up various weapons for Shade: throwing stars, nunchakus, an actual sword, but they were pitiful stuff to use against this creature. Shade retrieved a pathetically small knife and an absurd set of nunchucks and realized looking at them that she had no chance, no chance at all.

Run, Shade, run away!

She could be in the next county in five minutes' run. She could be in Mexico in twenty minutes. This creature was orders of magnitude too strong, too dangerous for her to battle.

But you've got nunchakus! a savagely sarcastic inner voice reminded her.

I need a damn tank!

She glanced at Malik and Cruz, frozen in their slowness.

"Hero, villain, or monster," Shade said shakily. "And I'm supposed to be the hero."

In her imagination it had always been a battle against the blood-smeared girl, against Gaia. In her fantasies she'd had powers of her own, and though the battle had been hard, she had always prevailed. She had always triumphed. Her throat had never been cut. There had been no scar to serve as a constant reminder that she, Shade Darby, was responsible for her mother's death. That she, Shade Darby, had been helpless and weak.

But this was not fantasy. This creature was thirty or forty feet of very real fire and death.

I can't beat that!

If she turned away, if she ran like every ounce of her brain was screaming at her to, it would all be for nothing. She'd have condemned Cruz and Malik and herself to eventual prison. She'd have ruined her father's career. All for nothing.

Was this how real world heroes felt? Trapped? Too committed to run away? You didn't see that in the movies, Shade thought, you didn't see the bone-rattling fear that came with facing deadly battle. Hopeless battle.

He'll kill me. He'll kill me!

She had impetuously attacked Knightmare at the lighthouse, but she'd figured she could hold her own with him. Knightmare was big and dangerous, but this? This magma beast wasn't some art student playing the villain and waving his sword around; this was death made flesh.

What a fool she had been, what an arrogant, stupid fool. And now she could either run away and live with the knowledge of her cowardice or endure the pity of Malik and Cruz, and then their bitter resentment that their lives had been disrupted and perhaps shattered for nothing. For nothing.

For nothing but my fantasies.

Fight or flight? Basic human hardwired survival instincts. Fight or flight?

She had read somewhere that every battle at some point turns on the willingness of one person to run toward danger . . . or to turn and flee.

Fight or flight?

The answer when at last it came should have been a triumphant shout, but it came out as a shaky, doomed whisper.

"Fight."

Shade kicked off and zoomed after the creature as he kicked at police cars, crumpling them like empty beer cans. Shade saw a police officer, his uniform aflame, flying through the air like a football.

The monster was fast, able to move at more than human

speed, but Shade was moving at bullet speed and she easily caught him. She raced rings around him, dodging gobbets of fire that dribbled from his mouth, looking for vulnerabilities, for weaknesses, but he was to all intents and purposes a massive pile of walking magma. From twenty feet away it was like sticking your head into a pizza oven. The heat of his touch boiled the tarmac beneath his great reptilian feet.

And in Shade's head the Dark Watchers leaned forward, excited, like spectators at a football game.

Shade took a step back and then another. The magma creature had not yet seen her. She could still run. *Should* run!

But now she noticed something about the creature: the black crust of rock was no longer morphing, it had steadied, becoming what it was now: a sort of jigsaw puzzle of oddly shaped plate armor, like poorly made chain mail. Hard, cooled (though still blisteringly hot) volcanic rock over a core of fire.

An idea formed in the cold, clear core that in so many ways defined Shade Darby. Terrified, roasting hot, appalled, and overwhelmed, she nevertheless . . . *thought.*

Shade raced back to the SUV. Malik had made no effort to leave; on the contrary, he had one foot out the door and Cruz had begun to open her own door.

The fools are coming to help me? Against . . . that?

She vibrated to a slowness that was barely tolerable and said, "Get. Out! Run! Run!"

Then she popped the back door, shoved the gate upward so hard and fast that one hinge snapped and the whole rear door hung by a thread. There she found what she was looking for: the golf bag that had belonged to the owner of the SUV.

Balls and clubs. She grabbed some of the throwing stars as well, tossing them into a small runner's backpack, which she slung over her shoulder and then, cursing a blue streak to keep her courage up, zoomed back to the creature who now was nearly at the docked *Okeanos*.

She pulled out a club and beat it on the ground until the head twisted off, leaving a somewhat bent, high-tensile-strength shaft with a jagged end.

Deep breath.

Insane!

Deep breath.

Hero time!

Gripping the pointy club, she raced straight at the creature, sighted the gap between two hard plates that formed part of his right lower calf, just above where his Achilles tendon would be if he had such a thing, and with all her considerable might, with a power driven by shocking speed, Shade leaped and stabbed the shaft deep into the red marrow. She bounced off the creature and to her relief felt no pain—it was like quickly touching an iron to test its heat.

Sparks flew but they flew too slowly to reach her.

The monster was as hot as the center of a volcano, hot enough to melt lead and copper bullets, but it was not hot enough to melt the golf club's titanium shaft.

The monster's next step was a stumble, and while it was still plowing forward trying to catch its balance, Shade grabbed a second club and plunged it into a narrow gap on the top of its opposite foot.

And then the magma beast . . . *fell!*

It fell directly toward a policeman, who stared up, paralyzed with horror.

Shade ran, grabbed the policeman, and shoved him out of the way, snapping ribs like twigs, but better that than being crushed. Too late she saw a policewoman still in her patrol car, and the magma creature crashed down on her like a rock slide, sending up showers of sparks and smoke. Shade heard a desperate cry, quickly annihilated.

The monster was fast on his feet, but not so fast at standing up. He disentangled himself from the police car, crushed to half its normal height. A burning hand stuck out from the crumpled windshield. The beast stared quizzically at the two small shafts and pulled them out like they were splinters.

The beast stood, but even before he was fully erect he opened his mouth and, with a glottal roar that sounded like a hundred men vomiting at once, sprayed forth a gusher of liquid fire.

Shade backed away quickly as the napalm fell and a pillar of flame and smoke swirled like a tornado around the great monster.

The creature was fast, not fast enough to catch Shade, but too fast for her to manage as easily as she'd have liked. The fire that blew from that gaping jaw was faster still, forming an obstacle course of melting tarmac and tornadoes of smoke. If she wasn't careful, she could too easily run *into* the flame, and she was not at all sure it wouldn't burn her, however fast she was.

Worse than his quickness was the simple fact of his size. She wasn't going to stop him by stabbing at his ankles. She had to be able to inflict more damage than that. She had to be able to cripple or even kill the creature.

The shark Shade Darby supplied an answer: the eyes. She could try to blind it, just as she had destroyed one of Knightmare's eyes. Unfortunately, this thing's eyes were in a head that was now way, way up in the air.

A leap?

Could she make it? And could she land somewhere safe?

She backed up and took a run that quickly turned into great, bounding steps, like a high jumper approaching the bar, culminating in a leap.

It was like nothing she had done to this point. It was the next best thing to flying. But her first leap missed the head and instead landed her feet first against the massive chest, from which she could only rappel away, turning a neat somersault in the air before landing hard enough to knock the wind from her.

Shade lay stunned on the concrete, sucking for air that would not come. She glanced up just in time to see the devilish eyes focus on her, see her for the first time.

"You!" the monster roared. That single comprehensible syllable coming from the fire-breather was surprising. But then, in a voice that sounded huge and clotted and yet was understandable, he said, "I believe I have the pleasure of speaking to Shade Darby!"

Shade blinked. What? It knew who she was?

"How. Do you. Know. My name?"

"I thought you might be here," the monster said, dribbling fire like random punctuation. "Something my new friend Drake said. At first I didn't catch it, but then I knew: They *want* us here. They've been guiding us here!"

"What. The hell. Are you. Talking about?"

"We are their playthings," the monster said, sounding almost regretful. "Smile: you're on TV!"

"Go away," Shade said, suddenly acutely aware that she had no clever banter for this situation, no cocky Spider-Man bon mots to toss out. "I will. Stop you."

"Will you, Shade Darby? Will you? But of course, you have to try, don't you? Ah well, we must strut and fret our hour upon the stage, eh?"

He vomited fire at her. She backed away, still puzzling out how this creature could know her name. She backed away just quickly enough to avoid the edge of the fire as it crept toward her.

Fast enough . . . but too distracted to look behind her as a thick whip, bone and oozing flesh, wrapped itself with speed to match her own around her waist.

CHAPTER 23
Late to the Party

THERE WERE NO longer guards on the gate at the Port of Los Angeles by the time Dekka and Armo arrived. The gate was wide open and cars were racing out. People, too, dockworkers and folks in short-sleeve white shirts and ties, running in panic.

Dekka noticed a police officer running and shedding his gun belt, as if he was quitting the force right at that moment.

"Looks like things started without us," Dekka said.

A pillar of smoke like something from a tire fire rose from the dock, boiling into the blue sky, almost obscuring the *Okeanos* tying off to the dock. The Coast Guard held position in the channel, the cutter's deck lined with sailors pointing.

"What the hell is that?" Armo asked, his mouth near Dekka's ear. Dekka was creeping the Kawasaki forward against the tide of fleeing workers, coming around to a clearer view.

Dekka pulled off the scrunchie she'd used to keep her dreads from slapping Armo, shook them out, and said, "That is big trouble, that's what that is."

It was massive, a black jigsaw puzzle over a core of blazing orange fire. Its head was reptilian, like a Komodo dragon's, but no snakelike tongue tested the breeze. Instead, liquid fire dribbled from a cavernous mouth ringed with teeth like black diamonds.

"Damn," Armo said. "What the hell do we do with *that*?"

Dekka said nothing for a full minute. She had told Peaks she wouldn't be his soldier. She had said her war was over. And yet, when Armo had suggested coming here because here was where the Mother Rock would be, she had agreed.

Why?

Because life as Jean from Safeway is boring.

"I used to know someone," Dekka said. "A girl. She died in the FAYZ."

"Yeah?" Armo said, puzzled.

"She died because she went out to fight one too many times. I told her. Everyone told her. No, don't. You can't win, Breeze. You'll die . . ." Tears filled Dekka's eyes. "But she went. And she died."

"So . . . you're saying we do the smart thing and turn your bike around?" Armo asked.

"That would be the smart thing to do," Dekka said. "Look at that thing! That thing belongs in a movie!"

"Scariest thing I've ever seen, and I was at the Ranch," Armo said with a sigh.

"That was her grave I stopped at, you know, up in Perdido Beach. 'None so bold.' That's what's on her tombstone." Dekka's voice changed as she said, "You were bold, Breeze. Goddamn, you were bold and brave. And crazy." Then her tone changed again, hardening. "I loved that girl. I don't know if she's up in some kind of heaven watching, but if she is, well, she'd be pretty ashamed of me if I just walked away now."

Armo said, "I didn't know your Breeze person, but I know common sense. And common sense says that thing there cannot be beat by the two of us."

Dekka nodded. "I understand. You make your own choices, Armo. I've figured that much out about you."

Armo laughed. "You understand squat. I've never chickened out of anything yet, I'm not going to start now. But hell, look at that thing! It's like fighting a dragon!" He shook his head in amusement, as though this was all an entertaining joke. "My family goes all the way back to Björn Ironside, a very badass Viking. Tell you what, if old Björn had ever run into a dragon, he'd sure as hell have gone after it."

"You're gonna go die because you're descended from some crazy-ass Viking?"

"You're gonna go die for some girl named Breeze?"

"I am."

"Me too, then," Armo said.

Dekka shook her head and laughed. "Well then, white boy, should we get started?"

"You're the one driving," Armo said.

Dekka gunned the engine and the bike leaped eagerly. They were both morphing before they had cut the distance in half. Dekka glanced around for a safe place to park her motorcycle, realized there was no longer any such thing as "safe," and simply left it.

The magma creature spotted her walking steadily toward him, already morphed, and laughed. "Why, it's Dekka Talent!"

That caused Dekka to miss a step. How did the creature know her?

"Don't you recognize me, Dekka the righteous?" the monster sneered. "It's your old friend Tom Peaks! Although I think it's time for a name change. So call me . . . Napalm! Hah hah hah! Napalm! You like it?"

Of course, Dekka thought grimly. Of course: Peaks.

"And I have another friend of yours, too!" Napalm crowed. "You can call him . . . Whip Hand!"

Dekka stopped dead. Armo ran past her, roaring as he ran, but beyond him Dekka saw the one thing more terrifying than Peaks.

Drake Merwin was squeezing the life from someone who looked like a bizarre cross between a flea, a Power Ranger, and a teenaged girl.

Armo leaped, sailed through the air straight at Napalm, roaring as he flew, but the brave roar ended abruptly as Napalm simply swatted him aside like a mosquito.

Every fiber of Dekka's being wanted to go at Drake. She had hated him for a year in the FAYZ, hated him since, hated him when Peaks had shown her the video, and hated him now, hated his cruel eyes and his chiseled cheeks and hated, above all, the twisting, writhing python tightening relentlessly around the unknown super.

But Dekka was not new to combat. Dekka was a veteran of many, many fights, many, many battles. She was only nineteen, but she was old in war and she knew Drake was a distraction. Peaks was after the Mother Rock. And *that* was to be the point of this fight.

"Armo!" Dekka yelled. "Take out Whip Hand!"

Armo, lying winded on the ground, heard Dekka. And what he heard from her sounded a lot like an order. Instinctively he rejected it. No one told Armo what to do. No one. He was going after—

And then Dekka stopped, looked right at him, and said, "Please."

Orders? Armo did not take orders.

Requests? Well . . .

He threw Dekka a mock salute with his paw and charged straight at Drake.

"Now, let's talk, Tom Napalm Peaks, you liar, you criminal freak," Dekka said.

She raised her hands, palm out, opened her mouth, and shrieked.

Instantly Napalm's volcanic rock shell began to come apart, flakes of stone rained down like hail, and Napalm bellowed in outrage. He opened his mouth and ejected a mass of lava. Dekka's shredding lacerated the molten rock, sent drops in every direction, but too much got through. A glob of liquid fire attached to Dekka's forearm, another to her belly. She backed away, batting at the fire, but it stuck to her claws now, and even her higher pain threshold did little to lessen the excruciating, imperative, panic-inducing agony of burning alive.

Dekka dropped her hands and dodged sideways seconds ahead of a full load of fire that spilled across the ground she'd occupied, spread out in a puddle, and reached the tires of a parked car. The tires melted and burned. The heat of the fire was so intense that the fur on Dekka's arms singed and curled. Her snake dreads twisted away, sheltering behind her head.

Armo, looking like some deranged artist's conception of a polar bear mated with a human, ran straight at Drake, straight at Shade, an out-of-control berserker beast in a furious charge. Drake frowned and tried to jump aside, but in the process he lessened his grip on Shade for just a split second—a split second that was the equivalent of a leisurely ten seconds to Shade. She bent her knees back, dropped through his coiled arm, and then stumbled forward, landing on hands and knees in the liquid fire.

"Aaaahhhh!" came the mosquito buzz of pain.

Armo hit Drake like a ton of bricks and sent him skidding on his back. But Drake was quick and, like Dekka, was a veteran of many fights. He rolled to his feet and aimed his whip and . . . And Armo ran straight into him again, an irresistible force, a wild white-furred beast gone absolutely mad, slashing with its diamond-hard claws, biting with steel teeth,

pummeling with knees and elbows, a whirlwind of incoherent, insane animal violence.

"You brought a sidekick?" Dekka said to Napalm. "Me
too."

Once again she raised her hands, trying to ignore the pain
of burns, and again the stony shell began to come apart, to
disintegrate. It was like a time-lapse video of a mountain
eroding, but still small drops of fire burned Dekka. She was
hurting Napalm, but not fast enough, and this time the liquid
fire was a flood, a fire hose spreading smoking destruction,
Napalm turning his head from side to side. The magma
rolled into and over Dekka's feet and she screamed, an eerie
part-feline howl of pain and terror and rage.

The fire spread toward Drake as well, on his back beneath
Armo's berserker onslaught. Drake dug in his heels and
tried to scoot himself away, but like a tsunami the fire swept
around him, frying him like a piece of pork fat in a barbecue.
Drake felt no pain, but the fire did damage, eating into the
sinews of his newly regrown back, melting the meager flesh
of his buttocks.

The face on Drake's chest howled in shrill hysteria.

Armo's knees were in the flames, and if anything could
penetrate his berserker madness, that was it. He jumped
back, balanced atop Drake, and used him as a launchpad to
leap free.

Dekka was beyond pain. Her feet were melting. Flame
ran up the fur that covered her. She screamed in pure panic,
screamed, and ran as flame engulfed her, ran as flame rose to

blind her, straight for the water, straight toward the *Okeanos*.

Water! Water!

Napalm turned away with a derisive laugh and with long strides marched, unstoppable, after her, the *Okeanos* momentarily forgotten in his hunger to annihilate one of the two young women who had destroyed his career and life's work.

The Coast Guard cutter then opened up suddenly, spraying Napalm with machine-gun fire.

To no effect.

A military helicopter gunship arrived in a rush, tilted forward, a deadly, matte-black insect. It launched a missile that hit Napalm squarely in the shoulder, exploded, and blew smoking chunks of volcanic rock from him, baring a patch of fire like some inflamed scab. Napalm bellowed incoherently, wordlessly, at the helicopter, but did not slow his progress.

Now the Coast Guard opened up with the Bofors gun. Its 57 mm shells carried less punch than the missile, but it could fire two hundred rounds a minute, three rounds a second, and its aim was accurate. The shells exploded against Napalm's chest like a jackhammer: *Bam! Bam! Bam! Bam! Bam!*

Napalm took a step back, took another, and dodged to his left, which placed the *Okeanos*'s superstructure between himself and the Bofors gun. The shelling stopped.

Dekka hit the water and was already de-morphing by the time the oily liquid closed over her head. As she changed, the clinging liquid fire was drowned by the water and fell away. She stayed under as long as her wind lasted, then pushed back into the air and began clambering up over sharp rocks. To her intense relief, the burning pain was gone.

She raised a foot from the water and saw that it was still there, and human once again. But now the memory of the flames consuming her weighed her down, made her hesitate. The Dark Watchers did not like that, not at all, and with urgent silence they cheered her on.

A burning Armo suddenly splashed into the water beside her. He thrashed and roared until he, too, resumed his normal human shape.

The two of them, beaten, terrified, and with searingly recent memories of unimaginable pain, bobbed in the oily water, trembling from cold and fear.

And Napalm faced the *Okeanos*, ready to claim his prize.

CHAPTER 24
There's Always Something Worse

SHADE DARBY DE-MORPHED to escape the pain. It was unlike anything she had ever endured before. Her morphed hands and knees were burned deep, burned to the bones, and it was agony that all but obliterated thought.

But as she resumed her normal form, she felt the pain disappear and sighed in momentary relief. It was an important fact: she could change shapes, and each time the shape—herself or the morphed herself—was renewed, fresh and unmarked.

She ran at human-normal speed back to Cruz and Malik. Malik put his arms around her and she shook as if she was freezing.

Cruz hugged her from behind, and to her amazement Cruz felt Shade sobbing.

In the near distance Drake could be seen staggering around almost comically. His entire back, the backs of his calves, his buttocks, were all melted. He looked as if he was made of

Play-Doh. His burned muscles could not walk properly. But he did not seem to be in pain, just unable to move very well as he lurched after Napalm like a poorly made robot.

Moving was not a problem for the creature calling itself Napalm. It was at the *Okeanos*.

Shade freed herself from Malik, but gently, and wiped her eyes. "That was bad," she said. She needed no embellishments—they had seen. Napalm was unstoppable. Shade had tried and nearly died. Two others with morphs and powers had joined the fight and been similarly brushed aside.

"Let's get out of here," Malik said. "We're not winning this fight."

Shade's eyes were bleak, like nothing Cruz had ever seen. She seemed empty. She did not argue with Malik, but she didn't get in the car, either, instead stood staring hollow-eyed after the mighty monster.

"If we all worked together . . ." Cruz hadn't even meant to say it out loud.

"Together against *that*?" Malik pointed, incredulous. "That girl with the dreads is badass, but her partner is basically just a big, pissed-off bear." And Shade had done enough, more than enough. He put a protective arm around Shade, and again she let him.

"There's me," Cruz said.

Malik stared at her. Shade raised her eyes.

"No," Shade said. "No, no, no. You'll die. You'll die, Cruz, and it will be my fault. Again."

"Don't, Shade," Malik said tenderly, leaning his forehead against hers, looking her in the eyes. "It was not your fault then—it never was."

Not Shade's fault then, Cruz thought, but Malik wasn't denying that what was happening here and now was Shade's fault. And wasn't it? It wasn't Malik—or for that matter Cruz—who had become twisted by guilt and obsessed with finding a way to reverse her earlier weakness. It wasn't Malik or Cruz who had laid plans to steal the rock. It was Shade's fault. It was.

But whose fault will it be if more people die while I do nothing? Cruz asked herself.

Cruz felt herself moving without meaning to move, walking without quite intending to. It was as if her body had made a decision her brain was not yet ready to endorse. But she did not stop. Not even when Malik yelled, "Get back here, you idiot!"

The stocky black girl with ripped and burned clothing stood now beside a very tall white boy, both with their backs to her, both staring at the scene unfolding.

"Hey. I'm Cruz. My speedy friend back there is Shade Darby. I think maybe we're all on the same side."

Dekka and Armo spun toward her, tensed for a fight. But on seeing Cruz with her hands up as if surrendering, they relaxed.

"Do you have powers?" Dekka snapped.

"A little. I can . . . um . . . I can look like other people." Cruz demonstrated by turning briefly into Katy Perry, then back. She half expected this formidable pair to laugh. But they exchanged a look, Dekka and Armo.

"Have to stay behind him," Armo said to Dekka. "That's his only weak spot, and it isn't real weak. But head-to-head he just spews, and everything burns."

"How's your friend?" Dekka asked.

"Not great," Cruz admitted.

Dekka nodded. "Yeah. Been there."

"You know what you do with a fire?" Armo said. "You put it out, right?"

"Knock him into the water?" Dekka asked skeptically.

"He's close," Armo said. "Ship is kind of in the way."

Dekka sighed. "Okay. You, Cruz, your job is to distract him. We'll hit him from behind—if Armo agrees. We'll try to knock him over, down by the water." Dekka peered closely at Cruz. "You think you can do this?"

Cruz didn't trust her voice. She didn't trust her body, either, but it was apparently making all the decisions, so she turned and started walking fast, breaking into a run and veering left, winding through crushed and burning vehicles, aiming to get to the left of Napalm.

It wasn't far, just a quarter of a mile perhaps, and as she ran she heard Napalm's voice shout, "Ahoy there, *Okeanos*! I am Napalm! Give me the rock! Give me the rock or burn!"

If any of the ship's crew was answering, Cruz did not hear them. Nor could she see any of them, at least not at first. Then she saw a hooded figure walk calmly up to the side of the ship and look up at Napalm.

The hooded figure must have said something, because Napalm roared, "Give me the rock or die!"

More inaudible conversation, and then Napalm began counting down.

"Ten . . . nine . . ."

Cruz had reached the edge of the pier, up near the *Okeanos*'s stubby bow.

What would distract Napalm?

Then she knew. The idea came fully formed. But was it possible? She searched her memory for shapes she had assumed. Some had been larger than her true self. She had looked the part, but when Shade or Malik touched her they sometimes found they were touching air. She, Cruz, continued to exist, the changes were an illusion, basically a hologram.

So it *should* be possible.

Cruz began to change. It was easier with a living model right in front of her. It was an exceedingly bizarre thing, unlike any of her previous efforts, for always before she had become humans, humans whose eyes would be at least close to her own eyes in height. But now her altered appearance, her holographic self, was so huge that she, Cruz, was like a tourist standing on the bottom tread of the stairs that led up inside the Statue of Liberty. She could see her version of Napalm from the inside, as if she were standing behind a movie screen, seeing things from behind, except that she was within.

Napalm's eyes were forty feet up and Cruz's eyes were only a little over five feet off the ground. She saw through the hologram, seeing her own illusory volcanic rock skin and orange fire, but as a translucent filter.

But when she moved her hands, the holographic hands moved.

"Hey! You!" Cruz yelled.

Napalm turned and froze in place. He was staring at himself, a perfect mirror image.

"What?" Napalm said in a surprisingly puzzled, unmonsterish voice.

Two identical, nearly fifty-foot-tall, living volcanoes stared at each other down the length of the dock. Cruz was all too aware that his fiery spew could reach her, drench her, burn her to death. Fear choked Cruz, and most of her brain was yammering, *Run, run, run!*

And now, the unwelcome guests, the Dark Watchers. They were curious. Surprised. Cruz almost felt an "Aaahh" of pleased expectation from them, as if they were watching a movie and were surprised by a sudden plot twist.

"Who are you?" Napalm demanded.

And that was when Dekka morphed once more, came running up behind Napalm, raised her hands, and screeched.

Napalm twisted frantically, but Dekka moved with him, staying behind him, out of sight, peeling layers of stone from him. Napalm batted helplessly at his back with stubby arms and roared in pain and frustration.

Armo had morphed and dived into the water by the stern of the *Okeanos*. He came up now through the gap between the pier and the ship, white fur soaking wet. He dug claws into pilings and climbed the tarry wood like a squirrel going up a tree.

Then with one tremendous effort he leaped into Napalm, bounced off, hit the side of the ship and propelled himself off, bounced again against Napalm, and leaped higher still until he was atop the upper deck of the *Okeanos*, from where he clambered madly up the mast beneath the golf ball. Then, almost eye level with Napalm, he kicked off with a mad roar, landed on Napalm's head, and gripped him. Steam rose from Napalm's head and the pain seared Armo, but he did not jump away, holding on grimly for as long as he could while Dekka shredded the monster's back and Napalm staggered blindly and in pain, slammed against the side of the ship, all the while batting at Armo and twisting to get at Dekka.

And for a while hope flared in Cruz's breast. They were winning!

Then the big loading crane on the dock came to life with a whir of electric motors. The sturdy steel arm, an arm capable of lifting entire containers as if they were no heavier than a Lego, swung in an arc toward Napalm.

At the last second, a steaming, charred Armo jumped free.

The crane arm struck Napalm in the shoulder and knocked him hard against the ship. Fire spilled onto the decks. Dekka never ceased in her attack, while Armo slunk away to change back to pain-free human form.

Cruz stared at the crane, at the glass-enclosed cabin, and saw the strange, plasticine version of Shade.

The crane backed away, then swung its ponderous weight

again and hit Napalm in the chest. The crane rose, straight-
ening its articulated arm, and slammed down on Napalm's
head.

Sparks flew from Napalm, and liquid fire gushed through
the cracks and ran down like blood.

Napalm fell to his knees. His back was a tornado of stone
and magma, as he was slowly, relentlessly, ripped apart.

And then, all at once, it no longer mattered.

CHAPTER 25
Something Worse

THE MOTHER ROCK had sunk deep, deep under the Pacific. It had not stayed long, but in the time it was there it had encountered many amazing life-forms. And when it was raised from the ocean floor it had retained DNA in its little cracks and pits and holes. A cornucopia. A giant buffet of some of Earth's strangest DNA.

The Mother Rock, itself a tiny fragment of the original planetoid, was suffused with an alien-engineered virus of incredible sophistication, programmed with a sort of instinct that could give an impression of conscious will. It absorbed DNA and used it to play with other life-forms, mixing and remixing like a malicious DJ.

So when Vincent Vu ate some of the Mother Rock, he ingested not only the alien mutagenic virus it carried, but also the DNA of two of nature's stranger creatures: *Leptasterias aequalis*, a starfish, and the more boringly named sea star associated densovirus.

The *Leptasterias aequalis* had five arms, each coated with spiny armor. Beneath each of the five arms were dozens of tiny tube feet that moved the starfish. Most of its vital organs were in the central disk, the nexus of the five arms. It was one of nature's more harmless creations—in its natural state, for in its natural state it was so small it could rest comfortably on the pad of a man's thumb.

But matters of scale were no problem for the Mother Rock's own virus.

The Mother Rock's virus was fascinated—in a purely mechanical way—by a very, very distant relation, the densovirus (as were a number of human scientists), for the densovirus had a very strange and gruesome effect: it caused sea stars to tear themselves apart. It caused starfish to amputate their own arms.

One arm of an affected starfish would simply start to walk away from its body. It would motor its tube feet and pull and pull until it began to tear, until the skin ripped and white meat appeared. It would pull away, marching on its hundreds of tube feet, each a tiny white cylinder ending in a sucker, and it would keep pulling as viscera separated and strings of gut were stretched to breaking.

The alien mutagenic virus found that the densovirus fit its profile for something . . . useful.

Vincent Vu had first morphed thirty-six hours earlier. Then he had filled his mother's cabin so quickly that he'd had to squeeze out into the corridor, which itself was too confined, so he had simply started pushing down bulkheads and then bursting through decks, spreading his growing bulk through the ship.

The captain kept a pistol aboard for emergencies, but he died before reaching it. The six security people came at the morphed Vincent with disciplined but harmless fire, and he had killed them as well.

His mother had pleaded with Vincent, begged him, told him he needed help . . . and he had crushed her beneath one massive arm, tube legs tearing her dying body apart.

Vincent Vu had felt bad about that, but he'd had no choice. She was trying to stop him! And the new voices in his head, the ones that spoke without words, had seized on his delusion and encouraged him to believe that yes, he was Abaddon, yes, he really was Satan's angel, yes, he was being sent to purge the earth of verminous humans. Vincent had never been the most stable of humans. He'd already listened to the mad voices in his head, the voices of the most dreaded of all mental illnesses, schizophrenia. But now he had acquired shocking power and a whole new set of voices. And he had murdered his mother. The unstable, deteriorating Vincent was now beyond mere instability; he was, in short, stark raving mad.

Stark raving mad, and terrifyingly dangerous.

Vincent Vu morphed was a creature of five massive, thick, crusty, bright red arms. He filled the *Okeanos*. At the center of this starfish body, rising like a flower's stamen, was Vincent . . . or at least Vincent from the waist up. He appeared almost to be riding the great starfish.

Where Vincent's human body melded into the starfish

was a sort of girdle of tentacles, another gift of aquatic DNA, very much like Drake's whip hand but thinner and twice as long, and each—as he had discovered to his delight—carried a corrosive, acidic tip.

During the long trip to the Port of Los Angeles, Vincent's starfish body had torn itself apart, arms walking off on their own. But as the densovirus caused him to tear himself apart, new legs grew quickly to replace the departed sections.

And the runaway arms, driven to tear themselves free, were still mostly under the command of Vincent Vu. Those runaway arms had become his servants, his henchmen. They slithered and crawled throughout the ship, smothering crewmen to death—and those were the lucky ones. The less fortunate ones were disassembled, piece by piece, square inch by square inch. Some had taken hours to die.

Even less lucky crew members were . . . absorbed. The arm sections crawled over the backs of screaming men and women, penetrated their bodies with their tubular legs, grew inside the helpless victims, and made puppets of them— twisted, scarred, disfigured puppets. One such puppet had concealed his disfigurement with a hood and had been the one to tie off the ship.

But the need for concealment was past. The ship was under attack by a powerful monster who was after the Mother Rock. Vincent could not allow that.

He was too big to simply emerge from belowdecks. His red arms extended down corridors into engineering, into the labs, into the sleeping quarters, into the holds. From the tip of one leg to the other, Vincent Vu now stretched 140 feet. For the last six hours, with land in sight, and the Navy handing escort duty over to the Coast Guard, Vincent had been in complete control of the ship. His puppets had said all the right things over the radio, had done all the right things bringing the ship into port.

Vincent hated the idea of leaving the ship, but Napalm was leaving him no choice. So he squeezed himself and pushed his human form up through the hold the better to see the situation. He was, at first sight, a thin, bare-chested boy.

And then, having seen Napalm, Vincent simply pushed upward with all parts of his great, extended body. The upward pressure buckled the decks. The few remaining bulkheads broke free from decks with a series of crunches and snaps. The superstructure tilted. The sides of the ship bulged outward.

Finally, with the earsplitting noise of steel being torn like so much canvas, he began to truly emerge. A red arm rose from the foredeck, an elongated triangle, tube feet waving. Another erupted through the side of the ship. A third swelled within the superstructure, bursting portholes and hatches. The big golf ball that sheltered the radar crumpled, the legs of the mast snapped or bent, and the golf ball smashed down onto the pier.

A fourth leg rose behind the container that held the Mother Rock and wrapped itself around the prize.

Napalm took a step back and stared in blank astonishment. But Peaks recovered quickly and recognized the threat:

this new beast was after the rock, too. And Peaks meant to have that rock for himself.

"Fascinating," Peaks said with his monster's voice. "I'd love to study you. But sadly, I have to destroy you."

Vincent's answer was a soft but defiant "Try."

Napalm sprayed fire at the crusted leg cradling the container. The leg drew back, dropping the heavy container onto the deck with two loud bangs—the noise of the container hitting the deck, and a split second behind it the deeper thump of the Mother Rock slamming around inside the container.

Napalm bounded over the side, crashing down in fire and smoke on the deck of the *Okeanos*. But that deck was being torn apart, with great jagged rips opening, as if the entire ship was exploding in slow motion.

Napalm rained fire down into the gaps and was rewarded with a very human-sounding scream. Then, from the direction of the bow, an arm no longer attached to Vincent's main body came at Napalm, trailing its ruptured viscera, running on tubular legs like a red torpedo.

Napalm turned and blew flame at the arm, but it did not stop. It burned, but it did not stop, and Napalm felt rather than saw a second detached arm slithering toward him from the starboard side, crawling up and over the rail like a sea monster rising from the water.

"Burn!" Peaks roared, and he spread his liquid fire everywhere. It rolled across the deck, blistering the paint, seeping down into the holds, lighting up anything flammable, food supplies, scientific gear, specimens, bodies, the ship's cat . . . and Vincent.

But Vincent's detached arms continued their advance on Napalm, their tubular legs burning and regrowing, burning and regrowing. They marched like fearless warriors through walls of flame, over blistering magma. They burned and smelled of fish. They burned and sent up an oily smoke. They writhed and twisted and were consumed, and yet kept growing.

Impossible!

The scientist in Peaks, the rational mind that still worked feverishly beneath the animal rage of Napalm, could not believe what it was seeing. Could not imagine that anything biological could so ignore its own destruction. It wasn't courage; the sections were mindless automata, indifferent to their own survival, driven by the will of the thin boy with the glittering eyes.

The ship was sinking. One of Vincent's legs had pushed through the wrong part of the ship and water was gushing in through a five-foot hole below the waterline. The deck, already a crazy quilt of twisted metal and fire, tilted as the bow began to settle.

Vincent did not feel the agonies of his detached sections, but he felt a dull pain from those parts of his core that burned, dull pain being all his starfish nervous system could convey. The pain was tolerable. What was not tolerable was the fact that he had been forced to let go of the box and its precious contents.

Furious and afraid, Vincent now began willfully ripping the *Okeanos* apart, tearing off great slabs of steel and hurling them at Napalm with shocking force.

A two-ton segment of deck hit Napalm like a sharp-edged Frisbee, cutting deep into him, spilling a gusher of magma, and causing Napalm to howl in pain and fury.

On the wharf Dekka and Armo, Shade and a de-morphed Cruz, stood watching in confusion.

"Which one do we fight?" Dekka asked.

Off to their right, Drake seemed equally nonplussed. He stood there, whip arm twisting in agitation, as his body regrew melted flesh.

The Coast Guard was less indecisive. They were getting frantic, screamed orders from DiMarco on the radio: *Sink the ship! Sink it now!*

The Bofors opened up at point-blank range, firing into the port side of the already-sinking *Okeanos*.

Cruz covered her ears with her hands. The noise was staggering: ripping steel, the furious sound of a fire running out of control, the *BamBamBamBam!* of the Bofors gun, the *thwack-thwack* of the helicopter, all punctuated by Vincent's shrill screams and the rumbling roar of Napalm.

The *Okeanos*, or what was left of it, settled into the mud. Its main deck was now well below the level of the dock, its superstructure looking like a tin can after someone had dropped in a cherry bomb, shreds and tatters hanging.

And now, no longer hidden by hoods, nightmare creatures leaped onto the land. They looked like humans being hugged from behind by giant red centipedes. And as they advanced, they sprouted tendrils like worms, tendrils that grew from human stomachs and chests, whipped furiously like electrocuted spaghetti.

"You're. Dekka," Shade Darby said, slowing her speech.

Dekka shot her a surprised look. "Do I know you?"

"Shade. Darby," Shade said. She pointed at the advancing meat puppets and said, "I've. Got. Them."

Vincent's human meat puppets were quick, but not to Shade. The whipping tendrils were bewilderingly fast to a normal human, but not to Shade.

She unwound the thick rope that had been used to tie the *Okeanos* off to the dock. The end of the rope was burning. She whipped the rope around over her head, not at her maximum speed—the rope would have come apart—but far faster than a human could. Then she smacked the rope end into the nearest meat puppet. The impact slammed the creature so hard, it careened off the edge of the dock and fell into fire.

She went after the second of the puppets and this time whipped the rope around its human legs, dropping the creature to the ground. She ran up on it, twisted the rest of the rope around its waist, cinched a knot, held on tight, and gave it a burst of speed. The meat puppet split apart, two pieces falling with wet sandbag sounds.

Two more of the meat puppets closed on her, recognizing that she was the immediate danger. One Shade dispatched by hurling a section of steel mast like a javelin. It skewered the foul creature, but then something struck Shade's neck.

She jerked away with speed that saved her life, but barely. The place where the tendril had touched felt like someone had jabbed a cattle prod deep into her neck.

Shade bolted, ran, then . . . slowed. Her limbs had gone heavy. Her insectoid legs had lost their spring. The world around her sped up as she slowed.

Poison!

She began to de-morph, but instinct warned her not to, and she stopped, fearing that the poison within her would not be eliminated by resuming her human form. Suspecting that out of morph, the poison would kill her.

She folded her legs beneath her and sat hard on the dock. Breathing was coming hard. Her vision blurred and her head swam, as the dock turned beneath her. Nausea rose in a wave.

A meat puppet advanced, and it was all Shade could do to keep it in sight as the whole world went sideways and slanted and prismatic.

Tendrils whipped the air and in seconds would stab her again and again, filling her body with enough poison to kill any living thing.

Water. She had to reach the water. Get away.

Her legs were as awkward as stilts badly attached to her body. Her hands were better and she clawed at the dock, hauling herself inch by inch . . . but there, just before her, a pool of liquid fire.

Too weary. Stop right here.

The meat puppet advanced, as all around Shade Darby raged a battle like nothing the world had ever seen.

So much for being a superhero, Shade thought as the meat puppet and its flails loomed closer.

CHAPTER 26
Innocent Bystander

ONE PERSON ON that dock had ever been in many a fight to the death. Only one had come near to death so many times that she and death were practically on friendly terms. Shade had fought, but only Dekka was a true combat veteran.

Her eyes surveyed the scene. Armo, morphed again, stood wet at her side. The Shade Darby person had knocked out two of the meat puppets, then fallen.

The shape-shifter or whatever she was, Cruz, was human once more, crouching in fear.

The simple fact was that they did not have the power to beat Napalm, and they certainly did not have the power to beat the incredible beast tearing itself free of the ship like a man fighting his way out of a paper bag.

"Armo," Dekka said, "I suggest retreat."

The white-furred berserker glared at her through slitted eyes and made an animal roar. But then, in a more human voice, he said, "Let them fight it out?"

"Shade!" Cruz cried, pointing.

Dekka trotted down the dock, aimed, howled, and fired. The meat puppet flew apart as if it had swallowed a bomb. Cruz ran to Shade, and Dekka rejoined Armo.

"Where were we?" Dekka wondered aloud.

"Thinking about running away," Armo said.

Dekka nodded. "Let them fight it out and we take on the winner."

Yes, that was the logical thing. It was the unemotional thing. Two vastly powerful enemies were fighting each other. She had a vague memory of a quote, something about not interfering with your enemy when he's making a mistake.

But logic was not everything. There was also . . . *hate*.

Dekka turned toward Drake, who seemed transfixed by the great red beast now grappling with Napalm, and shouted, "You! You and me, Drake. You and me!"

Drake's eyes glittered. He smiled. "My pleasure, you fat black dyke bitch!" Drake ran at her, fearless as ever, stumbling slightly with his limbs not entirely regrown, whip hand already sailing through the air.

They had fought before, back in the FAYZ. But Drake had never faced *this* Dekka.

She raised her hands, screamed in his face, and Drake disintegrated, reduced to a squall of bloody bits flying through the air.

In two seconds, he was gone aside from a stain on the dock.

Dekka nodded, satisfied, but not so naive as to believe he'd been truly destroyed. It would, however, take him a while to put himself back together.

And damn, it felt good.

Now Dekka and Armo started backing away, but Dekka found it hard to disengage. Partly her veins were drenched in adrenaline, and that adrenaline was urging her to take one more shot at either Napalm or the creature on the ship.

But there was more to her reluctance to retreat, for the Dark Watchers were not happy with her prudence. Shushed but urgent whispers in her brain egged her on, demanding she fight, fight, *fight!* It was all she could do to force herself to step back, to take another step . . . and now there was a black kid, face wild, rushing past her to where Cruz knelt beside a stunned Shade Darby.

Then, with a herculean spasm and a crashing, splintering noise, Vincent surged all the way up and out of the wrecked ship, heaved his bulk onto land, once more holding the container aloft like a prize with one red arm, and surged straight at Napalm, who backed away on the dock, leaving flaming footprints behind him.

"Get her out of here!" Dekka yelled to Malik.

Napalm vomited a gusher of magma at Vincent and the red flesh sizzled and smoked, but Vincent did not stop. His flesh burned as he grappled with Napalm, wrapping his massive thick arms around the writhing fire creature. Steam billowed and Vincent's shrill and very human voice was a long, drawn-out howl of rage, but he did not let go of the living volcano. Slowly, inexorably, screaming incoherent gibberish words, mad Vincent dragged Napalm toward the water by the *Okeanos*'s bow.

For a heart-stopping moment, the two great monsters

wrestled for control, Napalm spraying fire and roaring, Vincent screeching and pulling.

Dekka felt like a mere human watching the gods battle. They smashed and battered each other: Napalm belched fire, Vincent's poisonous flails stung him again and again, and with each passing second Vincent dragged Napalm another foot closer to the channel.

Now Vincent's remaining meat puppets rushed at Napalm, slammed into his legs even as they burned, slapped him with their own tendrils, which curled like leaves in a fire.

Then, with the majestic slowness of a falling redwood, both Vincent and Napalm fell backward, banged against the prow of the *Okeanos*, and tumbled into the water.

Steam erupted in a geyser, searing Dekka and Armo, even as they backed hurriedly away.

Malik was between Dekka and the ship. He had his back to Napalm and Vincent, was huddled protectively over Shade. He was talking to her.

"It'll be okay, babe, I'm getting you out of here."

The boiling cloud of steam rolled over him.

Malik did not have a morph. He had no special power protecting him. He was an innocent bystander, a civilian wandering onto a brutal battlefield to protect the girl he loved.

The steam rolled across his back. Blisters rose over the back of his thighs, his buttocks, his shoulders, his neck, the back of his head. Dekka saw his eyes widen in sudden realization.

"Aaaaarrrrgh!"

Malik screamed, an eerie, spine-tingling scream of unbearable agony.

His mouth opened to scream again, but before a sound could come he collapsed onto the dock. He thrust his left hand out to stop his fall and his palm landed in liquid fire. His knees struck right at the edge of the creeping magma and he tried to pull away, but he had lost the use of his left hand.

Malik had taken the blast that would have cooked Cruz and maybe Shade as well.

He shrieked again, an eerie, animal howl, inhuman, like nothing Dekka had ever heard before, the sound of a person in more agony than the human mind could accept.

Cruz jumped up and body-slammed Malik, knocking him clear of the fire, but too late, too late, because a slab of Malik's skin sloughed and hung like a limp flag from the back of his neck.

Shade had seen it all. She had been looking into Malik's eyes when the steam hit him. She forced herself to stand, feeling the effects of the poison weakening. She limped after Cruz, crying and de-morphing.

In Cruz's strong arms Malik bellowed in pain, writhed and heaved. Cruz touched still-burning flesh and dropped Malik, and Shade tried to help her, tried to lift Malik, tried to ignore his terrified eyes, tried to gather him up, to hold him close and somehow put out the flame that still chewed at his flesh, but her arms were too weak, too leaden.

"Malik," Shade croaked. "Malik!"

Cruz, summoning courage she did not imagine she possessed, lifted Malik into a fireman's carry, draping his arms over her shoulders, lifting his weight with her legs, ignoring the drops of burning human fat that fell onto her shoulders and neck.

"Malik," Shade cried. "Malik!"

A morphed Armo came then and took Malik from the struggling Cruz, lifting Malik's weight as if he was a small child.

"To that van!" Cruz panted, nodding exhaustedly toward the damaged van. She ran ahead and opened the back door, and Armo slid Malik in.

"Good luck," Armo said, and ran back to Dekka.

Shade, feeling like a drunk, arms and legs working but not well, slid into the driver's seat. "Map, Cruz. Hospital."

Before Cruz could respond, Shade floored the accelerator and turned so sharply the van was momentarily on just two wheels.

Get him there alive, Shade told herself grimly, *just get him there alive!*

But driving was hard with numbed limbs and blurry vision and the howls of unspeakable agony behind her.

"Saint Mary Medical Center," Cruz said. "Right at the Forty-Seven. It's seven miles. Malik, hold on, hold on, we're going to the hospital!"

The van went tearing erratically through the port, weaving almost miraculously through a stream of LAPD cars all rushing the other way.

The battle had drawn the curious, and traffic was dense as drivers slowed to gape at the pillar of smoke and the circling helicopters of the LAPD and three separate news stations. But now Shade was morphing again, head clearer, awkward limbs stamping hard on the accelerator, and the world around her slowed. With complete indifference to the damage, she pushed through every gap, tearing off side mirrors, leaving great gouges in paintwork.

I've killed Malik!

Perdido Beach, all over again. Her mother and now Malik. If he somehow survived, he would never be the same, he would never be the beautiful boy she'd once loved.

Still loved.

Seven miles took them just six minutes. Shade pulled the van to the emergency entrance, leaped out, grabbed Malik's shoulders as Cruz grabbed his legs. They ran him inside, yelling, "Help him, help him!" The triage nurse stared in confusion. Shade pushed past, kicked open a swinging door, and found herself in the midst of chaos. Wounded police officers and dockworkers, some horribly burned, some with blood-soaked bandages, and doctors and nurses with heads down rushing from patient to patient.

There were no empty beds, so Shade and Cruz set Malik down on the counter of the nurse's station.

An ER nurse yelled, "What the hell are . . ." before she saw Malik's condition, and then, as if someone had thrown a switch, she was rapping out orders and demands. A young doctor rushed up and began yelling his own instructions.

Shade stood back, panting, human again.

"Is he going to die?" Cruz asked, sobbing.

"I don't know," Shade said. "I don't know."

Now Malik was concealed by half a dozen doctors, nurses, and technicians. Needles plunged into veins, a tube was pushed down Malik's throat, status reports came in rapid succession. Pulse, oxygen level, blood pressure.

"Is he allergic to anything?" a nurse demanded.

"No," Shade said. "Can you—"

"We're trying," the nurse snapped.

"You've killed him, Shade."

Cruz's flat statement was a knife in Shade's heart. Time froze as the awful reality became a new and insidious poison in her veins.

The medical team lifted Malik onto a gurney and, still surrounded by white coats, he was wheeled away.

And Shade was left with Cruz. They stood side by side looking stupidly at the swinging door through which Malik had disappeared.

"Pray," Shade said to Cruz. It was somewhere between an order and a plea. "You believe in all that, so pray. Okay? Pray."

"I am praying," Cruz said. And silently added, *For him, for you . . . for the whole human race.*

CHAPTER 27
Heroes, Villains, Monsters

DEKKA AND ARMO stood side by side watching the huge mutant starfish struggle in the water, watching steam billow up, watching the surge of water splash up and over the dock.

A new helicopter, much larger, was hovering, looking for a place to land that wasn't aflame. The Coast Guard cutter pumped futile cannon and machine-gun rounds into the water.

"What do we do, bet on the outcome?" Armo asked.

"If I had my old power, I could move that rock somewhere, well, I was going to say 'safe,' but what the hell does that even mean?" Dekka wondered.

One of the meat puppets seemed to notice her, and the creepy human-starfish hybrid creature came at a run. Dekka shredded it with barely a glance.

But then, one of Vincent's legs slapped the dock and with its tubules began slowly, wearily, it seemed to Dekka, pulling itself all the way onto the dock.

The Coast Guard ceased firing because a miss now might kill innocent civilians.

Dekka and Armo backed away, retreating faster and faster, as the creature filled most of the parking lot, not quite as big as it had been since it had lost arms to both the densovirus and Napalm's fury, and the regrowing sections were shorter. But it was still enormous, and the belt of poisonous tentacles still writhed and lashed, reaching out almost as far as the creature's red legs. And, like a model riding atop a nightmare vision of a parade float, Vincent Vu still emerged from the central circle at the nexus of the arms.

"We have a winner," Armo said bleakly.

"Yeah." Dekka raised her hands and howled and . . . nothing. "Too far away. Damn. I was sure hoping this worked from a distance."

Vincent wrapped one thick leg around the Mother Rock and seemed almost to cuddle it.

Behind them the big new helicopter hovered a few feet above burning wreckage. The helicopter's door slid open, and Dekka saw its main passenger.

"It's that Knightmare guy!" Dekka said. "Great, now the freak show is complete."

Knightmare jumped down from the chopper, indifferent to the fact that one talon foot landed on a charcoal corpse, crushing it to powder.

"Whose side is he on?" Armo wondered.

"Ours. For now," Dekka said, pointing out that Knightmare stood facing Vincent, the long sword arm at the ready.

"You want to help him?" Armo asked.

"Do you?"

Justin DeVeere, aka Knightmare, had fought Shade Darby. He had murdered airline passengers in cold blood. He had torn the Golden Gate Bridge apart. None of that his fault, all of it simply . . . necessary and thus forgivable.

DiMarco had tortured and twisted him, had stuck her vile control devices in him and used electric shocks to force him to morph for her. But in his own mind, Justin was still an artist. His eyes still sought out the unique, the extreme, the shocking.

Nothing in his experience had prepared him for what he now faced. It was, in its own way, a demented masterpiece. Something small and perhaps creepy but not in any way frightening had been turned into this creature that somehow combined absolute terror with an element of the comic. The thin brown kid was like something out of a cartoon, a weird, impossible blend of incompatible life-forms conjured by alien artists working on a huge canvas.

Justin swallowed in a dry throat. His mind yammered a running commentary mostly consisting of places he could run away to, and curses directed at DiMarco. That and the phrase *It's too big!*

The hated female voice came from a loudspeaker in the air, from the Sikorsky, which had risen to a safe two hundred feet and now beat the air over their heads. "Attack! Attack!" the voice ordered.

Justin sighed shakily. Attack, or DiMarco would send intolerable pain exploding through his body. Attack, or let DiMarco reduce him to helpless immobility to be destroyed by the creature.

But still, part of Justin's mind noted the color of the creature, admired the uncanny valley effect of a boy half riding, half absorbed into a creature that had never, could never, exist in the dull and predictable universe where Justin had lived his life.

He had a vision of a painting, an abstract using that fantastic, unique red, and the oily black of the smoke, and . . .

The creature moved forward with surprising speed, mincing on delicate tubules like a centipede.

"Attack, Private! Attack!"

Justin spared a moment for self-pity. How had it come to this? Erin, dead, and now that she was gone he missed her. She had never loved him, he'd known that, but at times she had been kind. She had been all he had. Now here he was, drafted into a fight he did not want. But the threat of pain was too compelling. He had no choice.

Anyway, Justin told himself in a weak attempt at buttressing his ego: *I am Knightmare! And Knightmare fears no one!*
Right?

With a cry that was meant to be a roar but came out as a frightened whimper, Justin ran straight at the nearest arm, swung his sword, and sliced effortlessly most of the way through where the arm was as thick as a sewer pipe.

He grabbed the injured leg with his claw, pulling the deep

gash wider, and swung his sword again. This time the blade went all the way through to the concrete beneath and a chunk as big as an elephant came away.

Came away but did not die. Rather, the detached leg instantly crawled at Justin and he swung again, cutting a third of it away.

This third, too, did not die.

"Hydra," Justin whispered. He had paid very little attention to any part of school, but he had done a paper that referenced the Moreau painting *Hercules and the Lernaean Hydra*. In Greek mythology, the Hydra was a beast with many heads, but if you chopped one off, another grew in its place.

"Go for the boy!" DiMarco's voice, distorted by the loud-speaker and even more by the incessant *whap-whap-whap* of the helicopter.

The boy was at the far end of a fifty-foot arm and sitting easily twenty-five feet up.

"Sure, no problem," Justin said, gritting his teeth. It would take speed, and once he started he wouldn't be able to stop. All or nothing.

He gathered his courage and broke into a run, straight at the beast. He jumped atop the nearest uncut leg and ran its length even as it curled up behind him like a trailing wave.

Easy! In two seconds he would cut the creepy kid in half.

But as he swung his sword the tentacles whipped at him, smearing his armor with caustic poison and, worse in the short term, entangling his legs, so that Knightmare went sprawling. His outstretched sword arm stabbed right for

Vincent, but three tendrils snatched at the blade, were cut through, but managed nevertheless to steer the blade harmlessly away.

Knightmare jumped up, looked down, and saw smoking holes in his chitin armor, but the pain was distant and the poison would never reach his bloodstream. He charged again, yelling, "Die! Die!" and swinging his blade like a scythe through the whipping worms, which sprayed poison like severed arteries pumping blood.

At last he was face-to-face with Vincent; only a few stubby tendrils whipped frantically between them.

"Who the hell *are* you?" Knightmare roared.

The boy had a surprisingly sweet smile and a musical voice. "I am Abaddon. I am the destroyer anointed by the god Satan! I am . . . the star!"

"You're batshit is what you are," Knightmare said, and prepared to slice the boy off the monster like a wart.

"You haven't even figured it out, have you?" Vincent said, and it was his taunting voice that stayed Knightmare's sword. "You don't even know what this is, do you, Knightmare? I guess you're stupid."

Justin gaped. This kid was taunting him, insulting him. He sounded like a not very bright high school bully.

"Stupid old Knightmare," Vincent said, voice dripping sarcasm. "You know nothing. You want me to tell you? Do you?"

Knightmare's great armored head nodded.

Vincent held his frail human arms out, palms up, tilted his head back, and with a laugh in his voice said, "It's all TV. It's all entertainment!"

Knightmare did not move as the human brain of Justin DeVeere digested this statement.

"It's a show, you dumbass," Vincent said. "And you're just an actor."

Suddenly the leg the bemused Knightmare stood on heaved so violently that it crumpled Knightmare's knees. He rose a dozen feet into the air, and like a baseball bat, a thick arm smashed into him sideways. Knightmare went flying, tumbling through the air, and skidded to a halt within a few feet of where Dekka and Armo stood.

He raised his head and, in a shadow of his usual ground-pounding rumble, said, "A little help?"

"You're garbage," Dekka snapped. "But I guess he's worse." She glanced at Armo. "On three? Or some other number?"

Armo nodded. "Three works."

"Sword boy, you go around the back and start hacking. I'll try to get close to the center of the star and do my thing. And Armo?"

Armo nodded. "Berserk time."

Knightmare picked himself up, and Vincent, supremely confident now that he had either killed or disabled Napalm, glided serenely past, rolling over crushed vehicles and dead bodies.

"One," Armo said.

"Where's that Shade Darby person?" Dekka demanded angrily. "We could use her help!"

"Two."

"But whatever," Dekka said.

"Three."

They were three, and on three, all three kicked off simultaneously. Dekka ran for the gap between the two nearest arms, howling and shredding as she went.

Armo leaped atop a leg and launched himself, snarling, toward Vincent's fragile form.

Knightmare attacked from the back, swinging his sword arm with vicious strength, hacking and plunging and scything through arm and tendrils.

Once again, Vincent merely jerked his muscles and knocked Knightmare to the ground. He swung two legs together, pinning Dekka, and now she was between two closing walls of flesh, shredding and sending up a tornado of fleshy bits.

Armo was inches from burying his teeth in the smugly smiling boy. And then, a shadow behind him, a panicked glance, and the Mother Rock, wielded like a hammer, smashed down on Armo's back.

In less than sixty seconds the attack had failed, and a winded, battered, shaky threesome watched helplessly as the monster plowed toward the city and the Dark Watchers writhed in glee.

Vincent was on a manic high. He had battled the great fire-breathing Napalm and left him broken in the mud of the channel. He had tossed Knightmare around like a toy. He'd had more trouble with Dekka; she had hurt him, and he suspected that the day would come when she would be a problem, but that day was not today. He could see her defeat in the weary droop of her shoulders. Armo, too, had been casually shrugged aside.

Now what Vincent wanted was rest. The mania was softening, ebbing, and melancholy now tainted his great victories.

The Dark Watchers loved him, he could feel it. He was the star! And wasn't that a nice pun? A starfish star. Ha!

Five separated sections crawled beside him, a small but dangerous meat puppet army. He was unstoppable! He was the greatest power on earth! And *they* loved him for it.

He slithered across the parking lot and with a negligent swipe of one leg smashed the side of the main prison building. Crumbling masonry revealed shocked prisoners in khaki uniforms, some of whom promptly bolted.

It gave Vincent an idea, though. He could create havoc by breaking open jails and prisons, like in that Batman movie. On the other hand, if you wanted to mess up Los Angeles, all you really had to do was create traffic jams, right?

Did he want to mess up LA? Vincent hadn't really thought about the next step. In fact, he had no clear goal in mind, other than providing the Dark Watchers a delightful entertainment. He'd done that in spades, but what was next?

Vincent understood his place in the emerging new world: he was a super-villain. *The* super-villain! Clearly. Okay, so what did super-villains do, exactly? Take over the world? What would he do with the world if he did take it over? That sounded like a complicated job, and he wasn't at all sure it was a job he wanted to do. It felt as if there would be math involved.

The old voices were whispering to him. They no longer yelled, as if they were cowed by the new force that had taken root in Vincent's scrambled brain. They reminded him that he was Abaddon, a dark angel, a destroyer of worlds. He could begin the work. He could kill and kill and kill!

Vincent sat atop and at the center of the star, riding high. He had a clear, unobstructed view of the port around him, and he considered taking some time to annihilate the dozens of great cranes, smash the containers, sink the ships—all things he was sure he *could* do. But why? It was all much clearer when he was manic. When the mania passed, what followed was a passive, abstracted state that normally sent him to his bed to read or watch videos and eat snack food products.

But now he was this, this great and powerful monster, Abaddon! And he was his puppets as well, seeing through their dim eyes when he chose, controlling them if he needed something from them, otherwise letting them follow like ducklings after their mother.

He kept moving, then looked left and spotted the battleship *Iowa*, long decommissioned and now just a tourist destination. He slid into the water of the channel and found that he could sink or swim as he chose, walk across the muddy submerged bottom, or float over the flat water.

Destroying the battleship would be fun at least, the Watchers would enjoy that, even if he took no joy in it himself.

But then, coming up the channel was the Coast Guard cutter. The Bofors rounds had bruised him but not done serious damage, exploding against the surprisingly tough outer skin. So he wasn't terribly worried to see the white ship.

But the Coast Guard had learned. They had only a few armor-piercing shells on board, mostly to sink derelict ships that could not be salvaged. The first armor-piercing shell penetrated Vincent's skin before exploding. It was sharply painful and left a crater. Chunks of Vincent's body flew through the air, but even before they landed he felt their separate, dull, subservient intelligences awaken. His puppets! Each shell would make more.

On the other hand, Vincent was not at all sure what would happen if he, himself, the still-human part of him, was hit. He submerged, cool water flowing over him as if he was a submarine diving. His human form was the last part to go under. He'd already discovered that he did not need to breathe underwater, but something about it still made him nervous.

The gray steel of the *Iowa*'s hull was a wall ahead of him, the keel just a few feet out of the mud. Vincent slid two legs beneath the hull and pulled sharply. The *Iowa* tilted crazily, sending the stupidly brave folks who'd stayed around to watch tumbling across the deck.

But when Vincent tried to break the ship, he found the hull still too strong. All he could really do was rock the great ship back and forth, which was not very exciting to see. Not really . . . entertaining. Not at all what one expected of Abaddon.

Besides, after a week on the *Okeanos* he was tired of ships and the sea. So he slithered up onto the far side of the

channel, keeping the *Iowa* between himself and that sting-
ing Bofors gun. Leaving the port, he rolled into and over a
neighborhood of inexpensive, two-story apartment blocks,
smashing cars, knocking down stucco walls, and collapsing
tile roofs, and that at least was entertaining because people
came running out into the street, hopped into cars or fled on
foot, sometimes only half dressed.

He broke power lines and gas lines with predictable results:
fires blossomed in his wake.

He felt weary, though. Hollowed out. The voices whispered
and the Watchers silently urged him on, but every movement
was an effort now and he came at last to a stop, planted in the
midst of a residential neighborhood. People fled before him,
and that was nice, but his energy was all gone.

He wanted a rest. He wanted everyone out of his head. He
needed to sleep.

A brave homeowner fired at him with a handgun. Vincent
barely noticed. The homeowner, out of bullets, dropped the
gun and fled.

Three big Sikorsky helicopters were veering to get in front
of him, looking for a place to fight him again.

No more. Not now.

And Vincent Vu began to change.

The great red arms shriveled and shrank. The flails lay
limp and curled up like doodlebugs. He was surprised when
his feet—his own, human feet—touched pavement.

Sirens rose and fell. Red lights came rushing down the
street. But when they came screeching up and leaped out

with guns drawn . . . they found nothing but a frightened-looking kid.

"Hey!" a cop shouted. "Get the hell out of here!"

"Where should I go?" Vincent asked plaintively.

"Go home, you damn fool! Don't you know it's the end of the world?"

So Vincent did just that. He walked away, joined a crowd of rushing people, passed many more emergency vehicles, and finally found his way to the home his mother would never see again.

His father greeted him with a hug. "Thank God, you're okay! Do you have any idea what's happening down by the port?"

CHAPTER 28
Consequences

"ARE YOU FAMILY?" the doctor asked Shade and Cruz.

"No, but—" Cruz began.

"We're all the family he has here." Shade talked over her. "Everyone else is back in Chicago."

"You need to contact them," the doctor said, and his expression was grim. "We may be able to keep him alive for twenty-four hours."

Shade fell into a molded plastic chair. They were in a hectic corridor, weeping family members, gurneys preceded by shouts of "Clear a path, clear a path," doctors and nurses and people carrying iPads to take down health insurance information.

Twenty-four hours!

The enormity of it threatened to overwhelm her.

Cruz said, "Shade, I didn't mean what I said about it being your fault . . ."

"Yes you did," Shade snapped. "You meant it because

it's true. He's here because of me! He's burned because of me!" She slapped her chest with a clenched fist. "He's dying because of me!"

She covered her face with her hands, wishing tears would come because that at least would be some kind of release. The doctor was still talking, explaining that they had given Malik painkillers, but that they were going to put him in a medically induced coma because not even the strongest fruits of the opium flower could hold this pain at bay.

"Can we see him?" Cruz asked.

The doctor, already heading away to his next emergency, waved a hand over his shoulder and said, "You won't like what you see."

"I can't see him," Shade said.

"You need to say good-bye to him," Cruz said. It came out harder, more accusatory than she intended.

Shade shook her head. "I saw her, I saw my mom in the body bag, and every night before I fall asleep . . . I don't want to be haunted by Malik, too."

Cruz knelt before her and took her hands, prying them away from Shade's face. "Honey, if you don't you'll be sorry later."

"How the hell could I be more sorry than I already am?" Shade raged.

"Well, I'm going," Cruz said. She stood, feeling the after-effects of adrenaline wearying her muscles.

Malik was alone in a bed, his head slightly elevated. He was entwined in electronic leads and plastic tubes, one of which was down his throat. He was swathed like a mummy with only a strangely undamaged left hand free.

He trembled, every muscle in his body seeming to vibrate like a tuning fork. Pumped full of morphine, he was still conscious, with one eye open, staring through a gap in the white gauze. That eye looked at Cruz, stared at her from the bowels of hell.

"Hey, Malik," Cruz said softly. And then, with nothing useful to say, she asked a stupid question. "How are you?"

Malik blinked. Stared with feverish intensity. And with his free hand he made the universal sign for writing.

"You want paper?"

Blink. And a choked moan that might be a yes.

The machine that breathed for him made a shushing sound. The digital readout over his head drew electric green lines, reducing his beating heart and his still-firing neurons to abstractions.

Cruz found a pad on the table and after a fruitless search ducked into the hallway to borrow a pen from a nurse. She placed the pen tenderly in Malik's hand and held the pad as firmly as she could.

He was right-handed and writing with his left. The penmanship was never going to be good, and it was a barely legible scrawl.

Cruz frowned at the paper.

"It says 'rock,'" Shade said. She had entered silently and now stood looking at Malik, her chest heaving. Tears ran down her cheeks.

"What?" Cruz asked, turning the pad to see more clearly. Then, with a slow realization, she saw that the single word was indeed . . . "rock." It was as if Shade had read his mind.

"It's the only way," Shade said dully. "He figured it out, same time I did." She managed a bleak smile. "Of course he figured it out. Of course."

Shade moved closer to Malik. She laid her hand on the only exposed part of him and whispered, "I'm so sorry, Bunny. I'm so sorry."

Cruz had never heard Shade use a term of endearment for Malik.

"Do you think you can swallow?" Shade asked him.

Blink.

A water bottle stood on the table, half drunk. Shade twisted the top off and pulled a baggie of gray powder from her pocket. She funneled the powder into the water and shook the bottle. The powder swirled.

Shade put the bottle to Malik's mouth, pushing the main tube aside just enough. She spilled a gulp of the laced water into his mouth and watched as his throat convulsed in a gulp.

"You can't go into a coma," Shade said.

Blink.

"I can stop them, but it will mean you'll be in pain." Another gulp of the rock water.

Blink.

A nurse burst in. "What are you doing? He can't drink!" She snatched the bottle away and set it back on the table. "There'll be another nurse by in a few minutes. I have to go,

I'm sorry, but the news says that . . . that *thing* . . . is headed right for my home. My son is at home!"

She left as quickly as she had come. And a minute later, that same nurse was standing beside Shade again.

"I've got this," Cruz said. "I'll give him the rest and I'll stay with him." She gripped Shade's arm. "You're not needed here."

Shade nodded, numb with grief and roiled by self-loathing.

"Go, Shade. Go and do what you can. This is sidekick work; you're the superhero."

The Dark Watchers seemed sullen, or perhaps exhausted, and they watched Shade's mind with only distant interest as she raced the van back to the port until she hit impassable traffic. She ran the rest of the way and found Dekka swinging her leg over her miraculously undamaged Kawasaki. Armo was waiting his turn.

"Where is it?" Shade buzzed, then slowed down to say, "Where. Is. *It?*"

Dekka shook her head. "Cops say it just disappeared. Crawled into a neighborhood, shriveled and . . . poof."

"He. De-morphed!"

"Yeah, most likely."

Shade de-morphed as well, resuming her normal shape.

"How's your friend?" Dekka asked.

Shade was panting, unable to slow her breathing or the pounding of her heart. No. No way that monster just walked away. No way it still lived!

"Hey," Dekka prodded. "Your friend."

"He'll live," Shade said, the words feeling like a lie, a betrayal. He might live. But he would never again be Malik.

And she would never be free of guilt for what she had done.

Dekka knew that look. She had seen it on Sam's face after bloody battles. And she knew that he had seen it on her face as well.

"You have to let it go," Dekka said, knowing there was no way, no way at all, for the girl standing before her to do that.

"I'm going to kill it." The words grated. Shade's mouth twisted down and tears filled her eyes again. "I'm going to kill it!"

Dekka nodded wearily. "Well, maybe so."

"You're Dekka Talent," Shade said, eyes blazing. "I know you. I know all about you. I need your help. I need you to help me, help me, help me *kill that fucking thing*!"

Dekka waited patiently while Shade Darby, the girl who held her emotions under iron control, stopped screaming.

"Listen to me," Dekka said. "I know. I know exactly how you feel. Exactly. But honey, it's not one battle, it's a war." She picked around in her saddlebags and came up with a piece of paper bag. "Damn, I don't have anything to write with."

Shade stared at her through burning eyes. Then she raked one fingernail down the inside of her arm, gouging the flesh. Blood seeped. She held her bloody arm out for Dekka.

And Dekka touched her arm and used the blood to write on the paper bag. "Email."

Shade nodded dully.

"There will be more," Dekka said. "It's all going to hell

now. There will be a lot more. When it comes, reach out to me."

"Yeah," Armo said. "Me too." He swung his leg over the back of the bike and settled in behind Dekka.

Shade's face, which she had managed to form into a stiff mask, now collapsed. Her jaw quivered. In a strangled voice she said, "How do you do this? How do you live with this?"

Dekka started her engine, leaned toward Shade, put a hand on her trembling shoulder, and said, "Welcome to the FAYZ, Shade Darby. Welcome to the FAYZ."

She drove away, and Shade folded the blood-smeared paper.

The White House
Office of the Press Secretary
For Immediate Release
Remarks by the President on Events in Los Angeles

The Oval Office
1:59 p.m. EDT

THE PRESIDENT:
Good evening. My fellow Americans, five years ago we were confronted with a great mystery in the area around Perdido Beach, California. The existence of the Perdido Beach Anomaly, the dome, and the effects on the unfortunate children trapped inside that dome were events far outside our understanding. These were disturbing events.

Yesterday we saw events that are more disturbing still.

I want to tell you what we know at this time. Fragments of the same meteorite that initiated the events at Perdido Beach are falling to Earth. Those fragments contain an alien virus, probably a deliberately engineered virus, which has the effect of causing extreme mutations in some of those who are exposed to it, or who consume it.

We all saw the video from Los Angeles. We mourn the terrible loss of life. At this time we have fifty-two confirmed deaths, including the crew of the Okeanos Explorer. *Many of the fallen were first responders, police, federal agents, and emergency medical personnel. These brave men and women went into harm's way to perform their duties, and paid the ultimate price. We honor their sacrifice.*

This is a great and unprecedented challenge. But I want you to know that your government is responding. We are redoubling our ongoing efforts to understand this phenomenon. We have already appropriated hundreds of millions of dollars to explore countermeasures. But we will need more to cope with this unprecedented threat to our way of life. In light of yesterday's events, I am asking Congress for an immediate appropriation of thirty billion dollars to study the causes and begin to find solutions.

Let me be clear: that will not be the end of our efforts, but the beginning. At the start of World War Two, the US government launched the Manhattan Project to develop the atomic bomb. The threat we face now demands a similar level of commitment. Therefore I am, by executive order, establishing a crash military program to give us the knowledge and the tools to fight back against this threat.

And I call upon the world—not only our allies, our friends, but all nations, even those with which we have had differences—to work together.

We stand on the brink. The threat we face is serious. The challenges we face are daunting. But we have no choice but to face up to our problems, to come together not only as a people, but as the human race, to work together, to face the danger squarely, and not to give in to fear.

Thank you, and God bless America.

Federal Bureau of Investigation
The Hoover Building, Washington, D.C.
For Immediate Release

FBI Ten Most Wanted

Vincent Vu
Thomas Peaks
Shade Darby
Dekka Talent
Aristotle Adamo (aka "Armo")
Justin DeVeere (aka "Knightmare")
Malik Tenerife
Hugo Rojas (aka "Cruz")
Drake Merwin
Francis Specter

CHAPTER 29

Aftermath

SHADE DARBY DID not immediately return to the hospital. Instead, she drove aimlessly along the cracked and decaying freeways of Southern California. The car she drove was stolen. The money she spent for gas was stolen.

The things she could not do formed a damning list that churned endlessly in her head.

She could not bring back the dead.

She could not go home.

She could not undo what she had done to herself, or to Cruz.

Or to Malik.

She pulled off to the side of the road in . . . she wasn't sure where . . . and cried. The last time she had cried was four years earlier, and she had vowed then . . . well, she had vowed a revenge she had now failed to perform, an impossible revenge. In fact, she had screwed up everything. The proof was lying in a hospital gritting his teeth against pain Shade could hardly imagine. Didn't want to imagine.

Her friend Cruz was staying with Malik, having to watch him, to listen to his cries. She was staying in morph, playing the part of nurse, and withstanding the insinuating attentions of the Dark Watchers for hour after hour.

Sorry, Cruz.

Sorry, Dad.

Sorry, Malik.

Sorry, Mom.

Such a terrible long list of people to apologize to. If she spent the rest of her life groveling and crying, she would never be able to find . . .

Find what, Shade Darby? Find what? Forgiveness. Redemption?

No. Only one goal was attainable now. Only one.

Revenge.

As her tears dried, the other part of Shade, the cool observer, the analyst, what Cruz called "the shark," slowly reemerged.

What had happened had happened. What was done was done.

The world was changing. The old order was dead or dying. The center, to quote the poem, was not holding; it was coming apart. And rough beasts, their hour come round at last, were already slouching toward Bethlehem to be born.

Hero, villain, monster.

She, Shade Darby, had power. It didn't matter anymore how it had happened, only that it was true. She had power, and the villains and monsters would have to be stopped. There was no other way forward for her, no escape from her fate.

"I'm a hero, whether I like it or not," Shade said to no one but the steering wheel. "Just thought it would be less . . . terrible."

She wiped away her tears. She punched the address of the hospital into the GPS—she still had no idea where she was—and, dry-eyed, went to face Malik and Cruz and the consequences of playing superhero.

Vincent Vu had been unable to stay home—it was quickly surrounded by the FBI. So he used two of his meat puppets to clear a home a few blocks away of its inhabitants.

Now he sat on a couch that was not his, watching a much nicer television than he owned. He was watching video of himself, replaying his battle with Napalm, going frame by frame to try to see the speed demon, and the one with snake hair, and the big white beast.

Like a football player, watching tapes after the game.

Abaddon was within him. The beautiful, powerful, devastating beast . . . was him, Vincent. Sooner or later, the voices in his head warned him, Abaddon must be released again.

Vincent figured the voices were right. But for now he was content to watch TV and eat the snack foods belonging to the three dead people lying at his feet.

Tom Peaks had barely survived by de-morphing at the last possible moment as his fire was extinguished and his strength faded under the brutal assault of Abaddon.

He felt the disappointment, even scorn, of the Dark Watchers, but once he was himself again, they were gone, replaced by his own demons.

He had always been a decent swimmer, even made it onto his high school team for a while. He swam underwater as much as he could, surfacing to grab a lungful of air as the battle raged behind him.

He made it to the far side of the channel and barely avoided Abaddon as the monster slunk by. But Abaddon had not seen him, or if he had he'd ignored the wet, naked man panting on the dock.

Peaks was less conspicuous than he would have been under normal circumstances—the area was full of panicky civilians—and a kind, if scandalized, woman offered him some of her husband's clothing.

He took that gratefully and then beat the woman unconscious with a lamp and cleaned out her purse.

What should he do next? He wasn't at all sure. But in the back of his mind, a list was taking shape. A kill list. General DiMarco topped that list, followed by Dekka Talent and Shade Darby.

Napalm still lived within him, and Napalm would be unleashed again when the time was right. Of that he had no doubt.

The keys he'd found in the woman's purse belonged to the Toyota Corolla in her driveway. Peaks saw that the tank was three-quarters full. More than enough to get the hell out of the area, find a peaceful place to hide, and plot what he was sure would be his ultimate revenge.

The Royal Navy frigate *Argyll* raced south along the eastern coast of Islay. The very hungry caterpillar, now over two hundred feet long, having fed on dozens of sheep, two horses, the contents of various homes and markets and taverns, as well as nineteen humans, including his sister, had been spotted on the coast just north of the Ardmore distillery.

The entire crew lined the rail, watching with mute awe at the great beast contracting and releasing, contracting and releasing as it moved along the top of a cliff.

"Action stations" was called, and the crew rushed to their weapons.

Ten minutes later the *Argyll* opened up with everything it had. And the caterpillar—once a cranky, teething toddler named Sean—was blown apart.

Flaming fragments fell down the cliff and into the water.

In Islamabad, Pakistan, a creature who could turn men inside out was engaged by Pakistani military. Twenty-three Pakistani soldiers died, and the creature escaped.

Just outside Moscow at the Federal Biomedical Agency, three fragments of ASO-2, which had been recovered on Islay by a hastily detailed Russian FSB agent posing as a tourist, led to frowns of concern at the CIA, where analysts studied satellite imagery of the FSB's Biomedical Agency campus aflame.

In Evanston, Illinois, Professor Martin Darby—cleared

of complicity in his daughter's actions—tracked the last two ASOs from a newly secure computer and passed along to General DiMarco the grim news that one rock would land in China and the other in northern Brazil.

In the bowels of the Ranch, work proceeded apace.

The FBI were at the door.

"We're looking for Dekka Talent," Special Agent Carlson said.

"Well, she's not here."

That exchange was repeated in various forms several times more before Agent Carlson—and the other agents behind him and out in the street—grudgingly walked away.

Once they were gone and their cars had pulled away, Dekka emerged from the closet where she and Armo had hidden.

Dekka sighed. "I'm so sorry to bring this down on you. I didn't have anywhere else to go."

"Well, Dekka, maybe it's time that I was *your* strong right arm instead of the other way around," Sam Temple said.

Acknowledgments

Monster, like all my books, profits enormously from a crew of talented professionals. These include above all Katherine Tegen, my pal and publisher. On Katherine's team are Mabel Hsu, Kelsey Horton, Kathryn Silsand, and Mark Rifkin. Credit for the gorgeous cover and equally lovely interior goes to Matthew Griffin, David E. Curtis, and Joel Tippie. Keeping the production train running on time are Oriana Siska and Kristen Eckhardt. And the reason anyone knows about the book is the hard work of Rosanne Romanello, Bess Braswell, and Audrey Diestelkamp. I would also like to thank my UK team, especially Stella Paskins and all her talented folks.

Read on for a sneak peek at

the next book in the
***New York Times* bestselling Gone series**

CHAPTER 1
It Rhymes with Villain

"HEY, FREAK? WHAT are you looking at?"

The drunk tank, the catch-all common room used as a first stop for drunks and druggies, was a large space lined with a wall-mounted steel bench. The floor was bare cement, sloped down to a drain in the center of the room. There was a single window with both bars and thick wire over filthy glass, allowing neither sunlight nor cheer, but a grim, gray reminder that there was an outside world.

The walls of the drunk tank were painted a sickly yellow, the color of baby puke, which went perfectly with the reek of vomit.

There were maybe fifteen adult men in the room, and the barely eighteen-year-old Dillon Poe, and Dillon felt very, very bad. Bad to a degree he had never felt before.

Is this what a hangover is? Oh, my God!

Dillon being Dillon, part of his mind was already looking for the potential humor in the situation. And it wasn't hard to find. He'd gotten very drunk the night before, after walking into a bar and asking for whiskey like some cowboy in an old movie. Having no choice or will of his own at that moment, the bartender had poured, and Dillon had gagged down the first fiery shot, then another, and . . . and the next thing he knew was right now, waking up with throbbing eyes and aching head and a mouth that tasted like he'd spent the night eating roadkill.

No, not roadkill, that was generic. It was funnier to be specific. Like a dead beaver? Like a dead opossum? Rats were overdone. Like a dead raccoon?

Yeah, dead raccoon. His mouth tasted like he'd spent the night chewing on dead raccoon.

It was an absurd situation: an eighteen-year-old walks into a bar. Like the start of a joke where a priest, a rabbi, and an imam walk into a bar. . . . And, yeah, he admitted wearily, his brain was not quite up for writing jokes.

"I'm nah lookin' chew," Dillon managed to say to the belligerent man, a sandpaper tongue thick in a cotton mouth. Dillon sat up, rubbed sleep from his eyes, and instantly vomited on the concrete.

"Hey, asshole!" This from the same man who'd challenged him. He was a big, very hairy white man, though it was hard to comment on his complexion given that he was almost entirely covered in tattoos. Including the tattooed tear at the corner of one eye that testified to a murder committed. Chest hair that included some gray sprigs spouted from a lurid chest tattoo of an American flag where the stars had been replaced by swastikas. "What's the matter with you, boy?"

Dillon stood up, wobbly, weak, and deeply unhappy.

"Nasty little punk, stinking up the place!" Tattoo said.

This, Dillon thought, was really not fair: the place already reeked of puke and piss and worse. There was a man passed out facedown on the bench, a brown stain in his trousers.

Tattoo swaggered over, grabbed Dillon's T-shirt, and kicked him in the knee. Dillon dropped to the floor, landing painfully on the concrete. "Clean that up, boy!"

What? *What?* How had this happened? How was he here, on his knees? Part of him counseled quiet submission: the man was bigger and had friends. But part of him, despite the alcohol-fueled misery in his brain, simply could not shut up.

"Can I use that mop on your head?"

First rule of stand-up comedy: never let a heckler get the upper hand.

Tattoo, whose limp salt-and-pepper hair did, arguably, resemble a mop, gaped in astonishment. Then he grinned, showing a row of overly bright, cheap false teeth. "Well, I guess I get to hand out my first ass-kicking of the day!"

Dillon closed his eyes and focused and almost immediately the brutal hangover faded, and subtle but utterly impossible changes began to transform Dillon's body and face. He said, "Ass-kicking, or ass-kissing?"

This earned him a hard kick meant for his stomach, but which deflected off his arm, knocking his hand into his own puddle of puke. Bad. But on the other hand, his hangover pain was fast receding.

A relief, but not the point, really. The point was that Dillon Poe was changing. Physically. The change was subtle at first and mostly visible in his eyes, which had shifted from brown to a sort of tarnished gold color. His pupils narrowed and formed vertical, thin, elongated diamond-shaped slits. His hair seemed to suck into his head, which now bulged at the back and tapered to a version of his own face rendered in the green of a new spring leaf.

Dillon knew about the physical change, or at least thought he did. He'd caught a terrifying glimpse of himself in a barroom mirror, seeing a reptilian version of his face visible past the bottles of booze.

But he had also begun to guess that there was something about this snakelike version of himself that caused more fascination than revulsion. If anything, the few people whose reactions he'd been able to gauge seemed to find him attractive, even mesmerizing. They stared, but not in horror. Even his fellow denizens of the drunk tank did not recoil in fear or disgust, but turned fascinated, enthralled faces to him.

Dillon was not in a happy or generous frame of mind. He had clearly screwed up the night before, outing himself as a mutant. And now he was in a cage with men, every single one of whom looked meaner and bigger and tougher than he—well, aside from the weeping tourist in the chinos and canary-yellow polo shirt. But it didn't matter, because Dillon Poe—this hypnotic, serpentine version of Dillon Poe—was more than capable of dealing with Tattoo.

Dillon looked up from the floor at the man and said, "You

clean it up, tough guy. In fact, *lick* it up. Start with my hand."

Without hesitation Tattoo stuck out his tongue and began licking Dillon's scaly green hand, as avidly as a dog welcoming his master. It was fascinating watching Tattoo's rheumy eyes, the expression of brute incomprehension, the alarm, the anger, the . . . impotence. The panic he was helpless to express.

"Now lick up that mess on the floor," Dillon said. Instantly Tattoo dropped to his hands and knees. He said, "I don't want to do this!" but without hesitation lowered his head, his long, grizzled hair trailing in the mess, and began lapping it up like a dog going after a dropped table scrap.

The entire room stood or sat frozen in stark disbelief. It was like they were an oil painting, all open mouths and wide eyes and expressions of disbelief. One man moaned, "Is this a hallucination? Is this real? Am I really seeing this?"

Dillon stood—his morph came with a lithely muscular body several inches taller than his own, an athlete's body—facing Tattoo's two buddies, who advanced, belligerent but nervous.

One said, "Hey, Spence, come on, man, stop that! Get up off your knees! Get away from that thing!" He tugged at his partner's shirt, but Tattoo—aka Spence, apparently—would not stop licking the puke. In fact, *could* not stop. He tried to speak but only incomprehensible grunts emerged—it's hard to talk with a mouth full of another person's vomit.

The other thug snarled at Dillon. "What did you do to him, freak?"

"I am really not in the mood to be picked on," Dillon said.

His voice, too, was subtly different now. His normal voice was a bit too high-pitched to ever be authoritative, and he had a slight lisp on "s" sounds. But this voice? This voice was like a musical instrument in the hands of a master. This voice persuaded, cajoled, and seduced.

The man frowned and stopped, then shook his head in confusion before finding his anger again. "I don't give a damn what you're up for, freak!"

Dillon turned to this fellow, younger than Spence, with a tweaker's emaciated body and rotting teeth. He would have tolerated any number of insults, but that particular one, "freak," was something he'd heard too many times in his young life, both at school and at home.

Freak for having no friends.

Freak for his physical awkwardness.

Freak for the way he looked at girls who would have nothing to do with him.

Freak for being the only one of five siblings who rejected walks and hikes and camping and biking and all the other physically tiring wastes of time his family loved.

Freak for sitting in his room for days on end watching stand-up comics like Louis, Maron, Frankie Boyle, Seinfeld, Chris Rock, Jeselnik, Jimmy Carr, and the few surviving videos of the godfather of stand-up, Richard Pryor.

And of course, *freak* for being a survivor of what people called the Perdido Beach Anomaly, but which Dillon, like all the survivors, called the FAYZ.

"Dude," Dillon said, "don't ever call me a freak again."

"Okay," the tweaker said.

"Say that you promise?"

The tweaker frowned and grimaced, but said, "I promise."

And Dillon almost stopped there. Almost. But Dillon's life was filled with times when he almost did the sensible thing or the smart thing or the right thing. A whole lot of almosts, and an equal number of "what the hells." Of the two, "what the hell" was always funnier.

The truth was he was rather enjoying the fear in the eyes all around him. Fear and confusion and mystification, expressed in frowns and mutterings and the sorts of threats not meant to be heard by the person being threatened—coward's threats.

Yeah, Dillon thought, *you losers should fear me. Every breath you take is because I allow it.* A nasty smirk formed on his lips.

"I'm not sure I trust you," Dillon said. "Let's make sure, huh? Let's make sure you never call me or anyone else names again. Bite your tongue in half."

A spasm went through the room. They leaned forward, disbelieving but enthralled. After all, a tough guy was licking the floor, like a dog determined to get every last chunk of Iams.

"You can't make me . . . uchhh ggghrr can't ma . . . ," the tweaker said.

"Sorry, having a hard time understanding you," Dillon said savagely.

The tweaker concentrated hard; you could see it on his

face. He was trying to fight, but putting far more energy into obeying. His jaw muscles clenched until the veins in his neck stood out. Blood dribbled from his mouth.

"Jesus Christ!" someone yelled. Then, "Guards! Guards!"

"Grind your teeth back and forth and bite down hard," Dillon said. The sound of dull teeth grinding on gristle was sickening, and Dillon might have relented had he not caught sight of the swastika tattoo on the tweaker's arm.

No pity for Nazi tweakers.

"Hey, can you say *sieg heil*?" Dillon asked.

Blood now gushed from the man's mouth. Tears streamed from his eyes and mucus from his nose. His eyes were trapped, desperate, terrified.

"Come on, mister tough guy, gimme a *sieg heil*."

"Ssnk thth stnch ccchuch . . ."

More prisoners were shouting, agitated, some wide-eyed and fascinated, others appalled, even sickened. And Dillon was sickened in a way that had nothing to do with his hangover. There was something electric about the feeling, but in both senses of the word. The power was shocking, and it shocked him in return. It seemed impossible, just absolutely, batshit impossible, and yet he could hear teeth on gristle. . . . *Life shouldn't be like that,* he told himself. *That could not be it. Could it?*

"Guards! Guards!" The cries went up with mounting hysteria, and men banged on the bars, all of which was fine with Dillon. He wanted guards to come, because he was more than ready to leave.

A portly guard came sauntering along, her face a mask of weary indifference. Then she took a look through the barred door and immediately keyed her radio. "Backup to the tank! Hats and bats! We have a situation!"

"Open the gate, guard," Dillon said in his calm, mellifluous voice.

The guard fumbled for keys, found the right one, and turned the lock just as two other guards came rushing down the corridor, helmets on heads, truncheons and Tasers in hand.

"Open all the gates, all the doors. Do it now," Dillon said, and heard the clanks and the buzzes, all the noises of unlocking doors. He stood in the open doorway and glanced at the denizens of the tank, shrinking back from him.

It was a strange moment, and Dillon recognized that it was the end of one life and the start of another. It was as if some giant, animated meat cleaver—shades of Terry Gilliam—had come down out of the sky and announced with an authoritative *thunk!* that life was now divided into "before the drunk tank" and "after the drunk tank."

The only way now was forward.

That could be a tagline. I could build a bit around that.

He had only realized he had this power two days ago. He'd tried it out—gently—on one of his brothers. Then on his father, a bit less gently, but all the while in ways that revealed nothing and raised no suspicions. He had intended to approach the matter after thinking it through, deciding on just how to use the power, if at all. His first thought had been to use it to get stage time at the LA Comedy Club, which despite the name was here in Vegas, and not just on an open-mike night. But that seemed a bit small for such a huge power.

There was not much point in having power if you didn't use it, and no point in using it if it didn't give you an edge. Right? That was the point of life, after all, wasn't it? To do the best you could for yourself, and perhaps for those loyal to you? And to deal with doubters and haters and enemies?

But then he'd been dumped by his girlfriend, Kalisha, which was not a heartbreak—he could barely tolerate her; the girl's sense of humor went no further than slapstick—but it was a humiliation. They'd only been going out for two weeks, and she was his first girlfriend. In the context of the senior class at Palo Verde High School, he would be reduced once again to the status of total loser. The unloved *freak*.

Dillon didn't do well with humiliation; he found it intolerable, in fact, as he had found it intolerable in the FAYZ. There, he had been just another thirteen-year-old kid without powers. He'd been forced to work in the fields, braving the carnivorous worms they called zekes, picking cabbages for hours in the broiling sun, at least if he wanted to eat. The kids with powers—Sam Temple and his group, Caine Soren and his—had never treated Dillon as anything more than a nuisance, another mouth to be fed, another random, powerless nobody to be ordered around by Albert and Edilio and Dekka, the big shots. Another nobody who might be crippled or killed if he happened to get between Sam and Caine in the ongoing factional war.

And then, after the end of the FAYZ, his parents had moved to Las Vegas. He had coincidentally enjoyed a big improvement in his internet speed, and he had learned of the dark web: the sites that sold illegal drugs and guns and even arranged meetings with hit men. And there he had come across someone supposedly selling pieces of the "Perdido Beach Magic Stone." That's what the ad had said. A hundred dollars an ounce, to be paid in Bitcoin. He had assumed it was fake, but he gave it a try anyway, and sure enough, a chip of rock had arrived in the mail. He had slept with it under his pillow for a full month before concluding that it wasn't working, and he'd been on the verge of throwing it out when something told him to try one last thing.

He had practically destroyed the blender. And he'd had to finish the job with a mortar and pestle that left the rock tasting like the basil that had been the previous thing crushed in the mortar. He had gagged it down.

And the next day he had made his brother do things, and his sister go change sweaters three times, and he had made his father go online and order a new and expensive VR headset.

But later that same day he'd gotten into a loud argument with his mother, and he had stormed out of the house and ordered a passing motorist to drive him to the TGI Fridays, where, using his new serpent's voice, he told the bartender to pour. That was a mistake, clearly, because passed out he had no power at all, obviously, and the result was this drunk tank and this very public revelation of his power. There would be video from the cell, video revealing him as a mutant, one of the so-called "Rockborn," he was certain, which meant police and who-knew-what government agencies would have his name, address, picture—both of his faces—fingerprints, credit report, and, worst of all, his most recent psych evaluation, which had labeled him a borderline personality—psych-speak for *freak*. The FBI would be interviewing his "known associates" before the day was out, and they would, to a boy or girl, roll their eyes and retell all the old stories of Dillon the loser, Dillon the freak, Dillon the virgin.

Terrible timing, terrible planning. He had not previously used the power for a violent end, and now that he had, he could expect to be treated no more kindly than the creature who had torn up the Golden Gate Bridge, or the monsters who had blown up the Port of Los Angeles.

The tweaker's rotting teeth finally came together, and he spit a hunk of bloody pulp from his mouth onto the floor, where it looked like a piece of calf's liver. Tattoo, still on hands and knees, looked quizzically at Dillon as if to ask whether he should lap the meat up as well.

Yes, life going forward would not be the life he'd led to this point.

Oh, well.

"I'm out of here, ladies and gentlemen," he said. "You've been a great audience, but . . ." He grinned as the old Marx Brothers ditty came back to him, and he sang, *"Hello, I must be going. I cannot stay, I came to say I must be going . . ."*

There was no applause. He could have made them laugh and applaud, but no, some things were sacred, and he would earn his laughs the hard way, the right way. All the people he admired had been freaks in high school, and they had all become admired and beloved and rich.

Louis C.K.: $25 million net worth

David Letterman: $400 million

Jerry Seinfeld: $800 million

"Ta-ta!" he said with a jaunty wave. Then an afterthought: "Oh, you can stop licking the floor now."

And with that, Dillon Poe—six foot two inches tall and decidedly green Dillon Poe—walked out through the cell gate, down the hall to the open security door, past guards he silenced with a word, past the jail's grim waiting room, out into the lobby of the county building, and out into brilliant Las Vegas sunlight.

A pretty young woman passing by gave him a definite once-over that was certainly not the way she should have looked at a green, scaly creature with yellow eyes, and he smiled at her in gracious acknowledgment.

Could I work the whole snake thing into my act?

It was mid-morning in Las Vegas. The air was only hot, not blistering, but the sun was blinding, a sharp contrast with what Dillon felt inside. Because in his head he was having visions again, like he had last time he had changed . . . well, maybe not visions, more like voices. Only the voices never spoke.

No, not quite visions or voices, he realized, more like the neck-tingling sense of being *watched*. It was more than just the faint apprehension you might get when you thought someone on the street was eyeballing you; this was both more real and insistent, and yet impossible to make sense of. It was as if somewhere inside his head was an audience, sitting in complete darkness and absolute silence, watching him act on his own personal stage.

Dillon was an empirical guy, not someone given to mysticism or even religion. He tested things. He sought truth, because all the best comics traded in truth. His suspicion was that the dark and silent audience had something to do with the changes—the morphing, as he had heard it called. So now he tested the hypothesis by de-morphing: by resuming his unimpressive human physique. And sure enough, the invisible audience disappeared.

"Huh," Dillon said, which a passing homeless person took as an invitation and held out a dirty styrofoam cup.

"Sorry, I don't have any money," the now-normal-looking Dillon said.

No money, just power. But Dillon was cynical enough to understand that in much the way that matter and energy are really the same thing, so are money and power. He could make anyone do anything. *Anything.* Which meant he could have anything he wanted.

He, Dillon Poe, ignored FAYZ survivor, was quite possibly the most powerful person in the world. In light of that, he asked himself: *Now what?*

And the answer was: *Whatever you want, Dillon; whatever you want.* The only way now was forward.

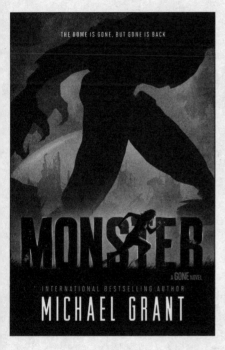
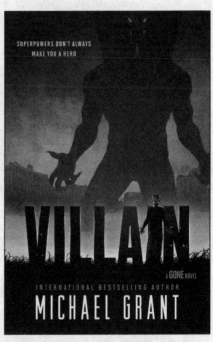